PIPELINE

Enemies Within the Gates

— Book Two —

A
NOVEL
BY

STEVE ELAM

1-13-14

*To Tammy & Jim,
Hope you enjoy the book.
Thanks for your support!!*

Steve Elam

Copyright

Book design and cover artwork by Robert Elam and Dylan Glover.

Special thanks to the Michigan rock band, The Outer Vibe, for the use of their song "Hoka Hey."

Quote used on page 14 comes from the 2004 "Water" episode of Battlestar Galactica, said by Commander William Adama:

> "There's a reason you separate military and the police. One fights the enemies of the state, the other serves and protects the people. When the military becomes both, then the enemies of the state tend to become the people."

FIRST EDITION

ISBN-13: 978-1480277847
ISBN-10: 1480277843

By Steve Elam

~

PIPELINE

BACKSLIDE

Coming Soon

DOWNRIVER

PEOPLE'S GOLD

ACKNOWLEDGEMENTS

My parents and grandparents had the motto: Always Say Please and Thank You. So it is with great joy that I offer thanks to the many people whom "please" was all it took for them to help me craft Pipeline.

The love of my life, Dona Louisa, gets a Thank You from the bottom of my heart for making it possible for me to write feature novels. And Thanks to all of my children and their spouses for their love and prayers!

A big Thank You to Rick Kacos for spot-on advice and editing another of my books. His eagle eye catches teensy bugs hiding in the pages.

I wish to thank my awesome son Jed and daughter-in-law Candy who opened their home and hearts during my time writing in Friedens, PA. They burned the midnight oil dozens of time helping me craft the story!

A big *hoora!* Colonel Bill Deetz, who inspected every page ensuring technology, weapons, tactics, and lingo passed muster. Go Army!

Thank You Mitch Nyberg for advising me on the USS Silversides and WW-II underwater warfare, as well as adapting the book to a screenplay.

To my life-long friend, Dean Ulrich, for keeping a constant presence during the writing of this book, offering encouragement, and letting me storyboard endlessly over the phone. Thank You for not hanging up, ever!

A big Thanks goes to my favorite pirate, cousin Jim Snoap for providing engineering and technical background!

Thank You to my sister Tami Elam for helping me develop characters and plots, as well as letting me be a novel-writing troll in her basement!

Huge Thank You's go to my nephews Bob Elam and Dylan Glover for their incredible work on the cover designs.

A giant Thank You to my daughter Novella and son-in-law Bhubanjyoti for technical support and helping with my author website!

John Ter Meer gets a Thank You for joining the crew in the final weeks of writing to act as a proofreader, and a double-agent in the book!

Thank You to my parents Pat and Keith Talsma for their love and support and a place to write during my time in Grand Haven, Michigan!

Several friends and relatives deserve Thanks for lending their support and personas to the book—though I may have scrambled their body parts and personalities just a tad. Here they are in alphabetical order:

*Actor Jed Allan, Lyle & Skip Berry, Toni Camp, Beckie Olin-Chilla,
Cathy Collins, Don Colon, Mark Dood, Lynda Edsall, Mark Egolf,
Lyn & Teresa Elam, Eli Gibson, Steve & Pat Hailey,
Craig & Mary Meade, Mike Rinard, John Sattgast,
Scott Terrill, Brenda Lee Weeks, Bruce West.*

THANK YOU ONE AND ALL!

IN MEMORY OF STEVE HAILEY

QUOTES

"Iran's Islamic Revolutionary Guard and Quds forces are partnering with major Mexican drug cartels. They're learning Mexican culture, as well as Spanish, and are starting to blend in with native-born Mexicans."

"Los Zetas and Hezbollah, a Deadly Alliance of Terror and Vice"
Terence Rosenthal — Center for Security Policy — July 10, 2013

~

THE RIGHT OF THE PEOPLE ... to be secure in their persons, houses, papers, and effects, against unreasonable searches and seizures, shall not be violated, and no Warrants shall issue, but upon probable cause, supported by Oath or affirmation, and particularly describing the place to be searched, and the persons or things to be seized.

4th Amendment – United States Constitution

~

"I am persuaded myself that the good sense of the people will always be found to be the best army. They may be led astray for a moment, but will soon correct themselves."

Thomas Jefferson

PIPELINE

PROLOGUE

A towering purple thunderhead rapidly devoured the full moon above Lake Michigan. Then spidery veins of lightning burst across coal-black skies, turning the stormy night into day and back again.

With each fearsome strobe, a lone motor yacht blinked into view on the tortured waters below, exposing a silver-haired foreigner belted into the captain's chair of the pitching craft, gripping the helm with strong brown hands.

After making ten nautical miles west of Muskegon, he cut the engines and shouted orders to his crew in Arabic. "Bashir, Tariq, get those whores off this boat. Hurry, before the Americans discover our presence!"

The men mumbled at leaving the yacht's cozy interior.

"Rasul," the foreigner called out again. "Go stand watch! Now!"

"Yes, Qasem," Rasul replied then closed the door to the luxurious salon, muting the cries of its owners bound and gagged inside.

Rasul pulled a rain hood around his youthful face and climbed above the pilothouse to search the darkness.

Nobody would be on the lake in these conditions, Rasul thought, but gave it his best effort anyway. After all, Qasem threatened to kill them, too, for endangering their holy mission. But it was Bashir and Tariq who'd insisted on sexual delights before their approaching day of glory with Allah, and stole away the Spanish maidens to enjoy their last earthly pleasures. Then upon discovering the cell's transgressions, Qasem cut the women's lovely throats.

Rasul hadn't shared in his brothers' wickedness. He was content to await his arrival in paradise to enjoy such pleasures. Yet, he'd truly liked his partner, Mariposa, a 15-year-old virgin from a small mining town in Mexico, and two years his junior. They'd held hands and spoke in Spanish of better days ahead. She'd even let him touch the strange mark on her shoulder.

Nevertheless, Qasem killed her too. They'd been Gallina's women, slaves actually, smuggled across the Mexican border with the drugs, guns and human traffic the same way he and the other jihadis entered the United States—*through the pipeline.*

From his perch atop the yacht, Rasul caught the rattle of heavy iron chains over the howling wind and booming thunder. And then there were three distinct splashes, as Bashir and Tariq dumped the weighted bodies overboard, sending the only witnesses to al-Qaeda in America into the depths of Lake Michigan forever.

Qasem engaged the engines and motored deeper into the darkness.

1

PART ONE
Let It Burn

1

Billy Ray Jenkins had been walking for miles since leaving Texas, hundreds of miles actually, going to her, to Rebecca Payne. The road had been long and lonely. Motorists occasionally stopped, easing his fatigue. Kindly folks in small towns dotting the way brightened his journey. And there were dangers, too. Yet, he didn't mind being on foot.

Feeling the earth beneath him was better than being buried in it.

Now that road led upward, climbing high into the evergreen forests of Washington State. Only the peaks and valleys of the rugged Cascade Mountains stood between him and the woman he loved.

Billy Ray heard a familiar whistle overhead. He paused to watch a lone hawk circling in the blue skies above. The call of the stately bird echoed through the dark valleys of his soul, tempting him to stay in the mountains and never come down.

And why not? Rebecca would probably turn him away anyhow. She'd made it clear that it couldn't work between them.

So what good was love if it hurt?

"About like breathing," he said to the hawk. "Worth the try."

A vehicle approached from behind, it was large, judging by its engine and snorting air brakes. Then a motor coach rolled to a stop beside Billy Ray. Gold lettering on the side read Jackpot Tours.

The pneumatic door opened with a hiss and a man called out, "Hey, mister, twenty bucks gets you aboard!"

Only then was Billy Ray's focus interrupted. Visions of Rebecca's auburn hair, full lips, and shapely body, vanished. He turned to see a black man in a Jackpot Tours uniform standing on the coach steps.

"How 'bout it?" The driver flashed a warm smile and a big gold tooth.

Billy Ray looked skyward. The hawk was gone. Also, the angle of the sun indicated mid-afternoon. If he was to play Jeremiah Johnson in the high country, he'd best set up camp.

On the other hand, there was Rebecca.

The driver thumbed over his shoulder. "Long way to town, mister, and these lucky folks want to make the bank before closing."

Silver heads of men and women stared at him through smoked glass windows, their faces like so many others on his travels—innocent.

Billy Ray made his decision.

Mountain man life would have to wait.

He shucked off his pack, fished a twenty-dollar bill from a pocket, and handed both to the driver.

"I'll take that as a Yes," the driver said, pocketing the cash and then stuffing his pack under bus.

Without a word, Billy Ray climbed aboard.

There were a couple of seats available in the front. Billy Ray chose the back instead.

As he moved down the aisle, women blushed at his rugged looks: muscular chest and arms stretching a gray T-shirt, faded jeans, dusty brown hair, and hazel eyes. The men just stared suspiciously.

After making a short call on his cell phone, the bus driver boarded and resumed the trip.

The tour group reanimated. They chatted excitedly about hitting it big at the casino. The gamblers among them told how they couldn't miss, and how they were escaping with the tribe's money for once.

Billy Ray was soon forgotten—anonymous.

His thoughts quickly returned to Rebecca, picturing her still body lying in a hospital bed, recovering from a near-fatal bullet wound. It'd been a year since seeing her last in Texas. Sadly, their chance at happiness ended that day with a long kiss goodbye—except it didn't.

Because he couldn't get her off of his mind!

They'd barely survived a bloody battle at the Texas Waterland Family Park against an enemy hell-bent on murdering millions of gullible Americans with a ghastly new form of methamphetamine, called Rapture. Ironically, the bullet that nearly killed Rebecca that night hadn't actually come from the terrorists, but from the gun of her father, Sheriff Roy Payne—it was a bullet meant for him.

The ex-sheriff, Billy Ray reminded himself. Roy Payne now rotted in the same prison cell in Houston where he'd wasted ten years of his life for a crime he didn't commit, sent there by Payne for the death of Rebecca's older sister.

Miraculously, the copper jacketed hollow point slug missed Rebecca's heart. Then after recovering, she'd packed up everything she owned and left Texas for a new life in Seattle...alone.

Billy Ray could still feel the sting of Payne's hatred and how it caused damage no speeding bullet could ever match—it killed love.

Or had it?

He was eight years a Navy SEAL before his trouble with Payne. To complete such extreme training, and survive the rigors of war, required that a man never give up, no matter what. He hadn't rung the bell in surrender then, nor could he bring himself to quit on Rebecca now.

Then he realized a hard truth: warfighting was one thing, battles of the heart quite another.

No training on Earth could prepare lovers for hard times—only living.

Additionally, there was the matter of him having been engaged to Rebecca's sister, until the awful day when Brenda Payne killed herself.

So there it was, two sisters—one alive, one dead—and a hate-filled father who'd stop at nothing until Billy Ray was buried deep downriver.

Perhaps Rebecca was right, no good could come from their love.

A voice cut through the fog, "Excuse me, mister . . ."

Billy Ray turned away from ghosts in the window to see one of the tour passengers taking a seat across the aisle. The man had on a *Viet Nam Vet* ball cap. His face was weatherworn, but firm, and sporting a bristly mustache. Other than his piercing eyes, the most striking feature about the old warrior, however, was the empty sleeve pinned to his side.

The sight of it made Billy Ray sit up straighter. "Sir . . .?"

"I watched you come aboard," the veteran said. "You've had training."

"Training...?"

"Military . . . I saw you staring out the window as if the world was gone. I've seen the thousand-yard stare before."

Billy Ray breathed out. "Just tired, sir. Too many unwinnable battles."

"I thought maybe we could talk," the veteran said awkwardly. "I'm not big on this casino stuff. Hell, I don't even gamble, my wife does."

Billy Ray had that in common with the man. Beyond an occasional game of Liar's Poker, using the serial numbers on dollar bills, he wasn't big on betting his money either.

No, just your life! shouted the ever-present voice in his head.

The man pointed at a silver head up front. "That good lady wagered all her chips on me fifty years ago. So that makes me the big winner."

Billy Ray felt respect. He'd known some of the toughest hombres on the planet. None were big on speeches—real heroes whose humility was kryptonite to the arrogant—*men who could die and could cry.*

"Then I'll take a chance on you too, sir."

The man thrust out his hand. "Steve Hailey."

After introductions, Billy Ray added, "And yes, Mr. Hailey, trained by the U.S. Navy, and a bunch of hellcats who shall remain unidentified."

They talked easily, men connected by a special bond. Although they were from different eras, both had operated deep in enemy territory—dark places where no one would hear you scream.

Moreover, Hailey owned the kind of maturity that only came with having seen the elephant and heard the owl. He'd been a helicopter pilot in Viet Nam, ferrying Special Ops and CIA spooks with the 195th Assault

<=== PIPELINE ===>

Helicopter Company, until being shot down. Luckily, friendly villagers rescued him, patched him up, then risked their own lives hiding him from the Viet Cong and NVA.

So yeah, Hailey had made the ultimate gamble and it cost him an arm. But in the end he'd won at life. Furthermore, he was ready to do it all again, saying he still owned one good arm for working the collective on a helicopter, should he ever get the chance.

Billy Ray didn't doubt the veteran pilot's capabilities one bit. After all, he'd witnessed an elderly Marine in East Texas save an untold number of lives a year earlier.

Lesson learned—don't doubt a man with the fire in his belly.

The two veterans were enjoying their talk when they noticed the coach slowing, and not to negotiate another sharp turn on Chinook Pass, nor for its passengers to view the majestic summit of Mount Rainier or the dizzying cliffs along the roadway. Rather, three Caucasian men stood in the road flagging down the bus.

The first thing Billy Ray noticed about the men was they carried no backpacking equipment. Instead, they were dressed in business attire.

The bus door hissed open and the group's spokesman mounted the steps. He explained about having car trouble, and could they get a lift to the next town. The bus driver looked around at his curious passengers then pointed to the empty seats in front.

The trio boarded and made themselves comfortable.

To Billy Ray, the men looked innocent enough: professional attire, average height and build, mid-thirties—entirely nondescript.

But one item bothered him. Each of their sport coats showed the outline of a concealed weapon.

Off-duty cops?

Billy Ray resumed his talk with Hailey, but still kept a wary eye on the strangers.

A mile or so later, the bus drove past a viewing turnout. A slick new red Camaro was parked in the lot, its hood raised and a cloud of steam drifting skyward.

He managed to catch part of the car's license plate...MAX.

Hailey lowered his voice. "My wife hit it big at the casino today, so did some others on the bus. Pat and I can finally pay off the ranch."

"That's big indeed. Congratulations," Billy Ray said quietly.

Some minutes later, the bus entered another turn.

Billy Ray caught a flash of red outside the window. It was a new Camaro.

His instincts went on full alert!

5

Hailey noticed the distraction. "What is it, Jenkins?"

"I'm not sure. Would you mind moving to the far window and get a plate number on the red car tailing us?"

"Sure, no problem."

"And Hailey—"

"Ya . . .?"

"Keep this between us."

Hailey moved to the window. The bus slowed through the next turn, giving him a clear view of the suspect vehicle. Then he scooched back across the seat.

"MAX–616," Hailey whispered.

Billy Ray smelled a rat, three rats actually! Men with guns, a busload of seniors flush with cash from the casino, and a speedy chase car...?

He leaned close to Hailey. "Keep your cool with what I'm about to say. I think this bus is about to get robbed."

Hailey didn't offer comment, only stared forward at his wife.

"We can't phone for help, there's no signal." Billy Ray thought for a moment. "Go back to Pat while I head this off. But Hailey—"

"Ya . . .?"

"If I fail, stay calm. I'm guessing these guys only want your money."

"How do you know they intend to rob us, where's the proof?"

Billy Ray nodded at the new arrivals. "They're armed. And now their broken-down car is tailing us. As for proof, that'll be a gun in your face."

Hailey studied Billy Ray. "How do I know *you* aren't part of this?"

"You don't, so trust your gut."

Hailey showed nerves of steel staring into the eyes of a possible villain. Then he two-finger saluted and went forward.

Billy Ray scanned his surroundings—the battlefield—assessing height, length, and width. He made a quick study of the passengers, many still chattering on about blackjack, loose slot machines, and all the free stuff lavished on them at the casino.

And now these people were about to lose it all!

The heist team made their move. The group's spokesman rose and looked all around. Then he spotted the toilet in the back of the bus and started down the aisle. His actions would appear innocent to a casual observer, but not to Billy Ray. Toiletman's move was purely tactical—the heist team intended to cage the tourists fore and aft.

As the bandit went by, Billy Ray stared out the window at the passing scenery. He caught the man's reflection checking him out, probably wondering what a stocky dude half the age of the other passengers was doing on this bus.

<==== PIPELINE ====>

Billy Ray considered their dilemma. Here were men with guns, while he carried only a multi-tool on his belt and the trusty MPK dive knife strapped to his calf. The rest of his gear was stowed under the bus.

As had been the case so many times in his life, he found himself outmanned, outgunned, and all alone.

Three armed men needed to become two. He would begin by isolating the leader in the lavatory, then he could move forward to disarm the others. Afterward, he could return to settle Toiletman's problems.

That was the plan anyway.

The restroom door closed.

Billy Ray moved to the aisle and saw Hailey peeking back at him.

Hailey nodded at the commode and made hand gestures, to which Billy Ray signaled affirmative, and for Hailey to create a distraction at the front of the bus.

He hated involving Hailey. However, if these seniors were to be spared a terrible fate, he saw no other choice. Assurances from evil men were as worthless as a bucket of warm spit.

Hailey approached the bus driver playing the role of a carsick senior. He asked how soon they'd be off the mountain. The driver replied saying they'd only just cleared the summit, that it would be some time yet, and to please return to his seat.

Hailey made a show of getting agitated, which prompted alleged robber number one to react loudly. "Hey old-timer, you heard the man!"

Hailey spun around. "Who you callin' old!"

"Shut up and sit down!"

Bingo! A stranger manhandling a passenger was proof enough. These guys weren't cops.

Just where on Chinook Pass the thieves intended to perform their evil deed, Billy Ray could only guess, probably after they cleared the current stretch of SR-410 trapping the bus between volcanic cliffs on one side of the road and a thousand-foot drop-off on the other.

Billy Ray used the distraction. He unsheathed the dive knife and jammed it hard into the floor next to the restroom door. The razor-sharp titanium point sank an inch deep in the deck. Then he went forward, bidding the ladies hello, and zeroing in on targets and priorities.

Hailey saw him approach and returned to his seat next to Pat.

Billy Ray stopped next to the couple seated directly behind the driver and struck up a conversation. As he spoke, he calculated the distance and angles to the two crooks seated behind him.

Loudmouth told him to sit down, the driver too. Billy Ray ignored them.

Again Loudmouth yelled. "Are you deaf, dude? Go sit down!"

Billy Ray pretended not to hear, knowing the reaction it'd cause.

Loudmouth stood up. "Hey, mister!"

Billy Ray gauged the target rising behind him.

Three . . . Two . . . One.

He leaned forward as if to ask the couple another question, then pivoted counter-clockwise and snap-kicked the man in the head, sending him over the safety barrier into the stairwell, out cold.

A woman screamed!

Billy Ray came down facing thief number two. The man went for his gun, thus forfeiting all rules of engagement and earning two fast knuckles to the throat. The crook suddenly lost all interest in firearms and grabbed for his crushed windpipe, gasping for breath and not getting any.

Billy Ray ended Gaspy's struggle with an iron fist to the temple.

One bad guy who'll never rob again, he judged.

Shots rang out from the back of the bus!

Billy Ray saw three holes form in the bathroom door.

He retrieved the guns from the immobilized crooks and started down the aisle to ruin Toiletman's day.

But an icy voice behind him said, "Don't move or you're dead meat!"

Billy Ray froze.

So the driver was in on the heist, too!

A black driver and three stranded white businessmen? He hadn't seen that one coming. And the reason for the driver stopping his tour bus to offer a lone hiker a ride, actually made better sense now.

It was all a ruse.

The driver knew exactly where on Chinook Pass cellular service would be lost. But a lone hiker just happened to be at that exact spot talking to a hawk.

"Now put those guns on the floor and turn around. Slowly!"

Billy Ray put down the guns and turned around. The gangster he hadn't accounted for was gripping a pistol in one hand and the steering wheel with the other.

"If you're wonderin', I got me no problem drivin' and pluggin' yo' punk ass at the same time." The driver smiled and the gold tooth twinkled.

Just then the bathroom door flew open with a mighty crash.

Everyone turned toward the commotion except Billy Ray. He focused attention on the bus' large overhead mirror. While placing the guns on the floor, he positioned them for a quick retrieval.

Hailey seemed to read Billy Ray's mind.

Seeing that the driver had taken his attention off the road, Hailey pointed and shouted, "Look out!"

<=== PIPELINE ===>

The ploy worked.

The driver spun around, providing the split-second Billy Ray needed. He bent down, grabbed the guns, located Toiletman rushing up the aisle, and fired Annie Oakley-style between his legs.

Hot gunpowder burned his pants.

Toiletman got off a single shot before three holes stitched across his middle. Then he dropped his gun and fell to the deck clutching his gut.

Wasting no time, Billy Ray attacked the bus driver by swinging both pistols at the man's outstretched arm. The gun lifted a split second before discharging into the ceiling and then clattered onto the deck.

Billy Ray lost a pistol in the collision too. So he wrapped the free arm around the driver's neck and squeezed.

But the chokehold caused the driver to pull hard on the wheel and send the bus rocketing across the road to scrape along the cliff face.

An ear-piercing screech filled the cabin.

Sparks flew across the windows.

Again women screamed, men joining them this time.

Seat belts clicked.

While attempting to break Billy Ray's grip, the driver yanked the wheel hard the other way. The bus shot back across the road toward bright blue skies and a wide green valley thousands of feet below.

Their fate filled the windshield!

Billy Ray reacted instantly by releasing the driver's neck and then wrestling the wheel hard to port.

The action saved everyone's lives. It also allowed the driver to rapid-punch him in the stomach. The man was strong. If not for ten years of sit-ups in a Texas prison, the blows would've doubled Billy Ray in half. Furthermore, holding the second gun while trying to stabilize the bus was putting him at a terrible disadvantage.

Billy Ray let go of the weapon, grabbed the wheel with both hands, and righted the vehicle. Then he cocked an elbow and rammed it into the driver's face.

The big gold tooth popped onto the floor.

"Arrg!" the driver bellowed. "Let go or you'll kill us all!"

Billy Ray had no intention of letting go, and proved it by elbowing the guy in the nose this time. The whole bus heard the sickening crack of nose cartilage. Toothless went berserk, punching, twisting, then attempting to stand and dislodge Billy Ray's body. But in doing so, he inadvertently pressed the accelerator to the floor.

The bus shot forward with a burst of speed, kicking up a cloud of dust and gravel, and inching ever closer to toppling into the deep canyon.

Now everyone was screaming and bouncing in their seats!

Billy Ray struggled to guide the bus away from land's end.

The driver cuffed at his face, missed, and struck the door actuator. The coach door *hissed* open and ninety-mile-an-hour wind tore through the coach, creating a blizzard of paper and personal effects.

Loudmouth's unconscious body rolled out the door and onto the highway. Billy Ray felt the wheels go *thump-thump* rolling over the guy.

The struggle for the steering wheel reached a stalemate, and the bus inched closer to the canyon.

Billy Ray got a clear view of what lay beyond the steps—nothing—a thousand feet of nothing!

If he didn't end this now, surely they'd all die.

But how? If he let go of the wheel, there was no guarantee the driver would steer the bus to safety and give himself up.

Billy Ray got an idea. "Hailey."

No answer.

"HAILEY!"

"YA!"

"Get ready to fly again," Billy Ray ordered.

He couldn't see it, nor did he need to. He'd known men like Hailey, and had no doubt the old chopper pilot was ready to rock and roll.

"Now!"

Two things happened immediately—Billy Ray let go of the wheel, grabbed the driver, and log-rolled to the door. Balance and leverage worked their magic as the driver's body had no alternative but to follow. Then Hailey vaulted into the driver's seat, righted himself, and grabbed the wheel with a strong arm a half-second before the bus and all its passengers exited the roadway, permanently.

The driver was Billy Ray's same length, but huskier, very strong, and ten years younger. The worst of it though was that Toothless ended up on top, had already struck Billy Ray with a massive fist, and was rearing back for the killing blow.

Their bodies slid further down the steps as they grappled. A few inches more and they'd both go flying into empty space.

Billy Ray hadn't been fitted for wings yet so he needed a plan fast.

Top position was normally the dominant one in a fight, but not always. While battling for his life in Texas against the madman Joseph Wiggins, the enemy had top position.

However, the end result was Billy Ray still walked among the living, while Wiggins swam with the fishes. The same maneuver that saved his life then was about to do so again.

<== PIPELINE ==>

The driver pinned Billy Ray's head down with a powerful arm and drew back for the crushing blow, he feigned defeat and relaxed.

Sensing victory, Toothless let go his punch, but failed to notice how their weight had shifted and the angle of balance now pointed some distance beyond the door.

Billy Ray timed the ham hock-sized fist perfectly. At nearly the point of impact, he bucked upward and sent the crook flipping out the door into empty space.

Peace in the valley was spoiled by a long, hideous scream, until a sudden change in direction ended the crook's ordeal.

Billy Ray somersaulted, too, but managed to catch the bottom step with the toes of his hiking boots and the doorframe with his fingertips. His body formed a cross in the doorway.

And he was slipping.

Seeing Billy Ray's dilemma, Hailey steered the bus away from danger and called out to one of the passenger, "Craig, help Jenkins. Quick!"

A tall senior ran up and pulled Billy Ray aboard.

The coach door hissed shut.

Billy Ray grabbed his knees to catch his breath and whisper a short prayer. Then he straightened and went to check on Toiletman.

The thief lay curled in a ball, gutshot and bleeding out, Billy Ray saw.

Just what predators like him deserve.

Next he checked Toiletman for weapons but found only the one, some extra ammo, and a cell phone. He pocketed the items and returned to the front of the bus.

All eyes were on him. He could've heard a pin drop.

He broke the spell. "Thanks for saving our bacon, Hailey."

"Told you I could fly, Jenkins. But it was you who did the hard work."

Billy Ray searched the two dozen anxious faces. Thankfully, no one was hurt beyond bruises and frayed nerves.

"This may not be over with," he warned. "Those guys had a chase car."

Hailey spoke up, "If you mean that red Camaro, it's gone. Blew past us after seeing our driver make like a bird."

"Still, we can't know for sure. With all the money I've heard talk of, they could try again. How soon to a town?"

"Sorry, partner," Hailey said. "Pat and I are just cowpokes from Mesa looking for a little excitement. You'll have to ask Craig, the guy who saved your butt from a serious case of road rash."

Hailey signaled for Craig to join them.

"We need to get you all to safety," Billy Ray announced. "The quicker you're in the hands of law enforcement the better."

"What about you?" asked Craig. "Won't the police want to question you, too?"

"I'll get off as soon as possible."

One of the women said, "But you killed three men, for God's sake."

"Actually, it was for your sake," Billy Ray replied even-toned.

A voice in back called out, "Make that four dead. This guy just expired."

Seeing Toiletman lying in a pool of blood reminded Billy Ray of the Bible warning that whoever lived by the sword would die by the sword.

Unfortunately, that include him.

Billy Ray shook off the cold finger of death.

"So where to?"

Craig's wife Mary spoke up, "We don't trust anyone else, not even the police. Please take us home."

Voices agreed in unison. Heads nodded.

"That could land me in jail," Billy Ray said.

Hailey stated the obvious. "You're probably heading there anyway. But we'll back you. If you hadn't stopped those men, we could all be dead."

Billy Ray looked into Hailey's eyes, then those of Craig and Mary, and finally Pat and all of the others. Innocence cried out. Vulnerable souls beckoned.

Then he noticed the bus approaching a viewing area—likely the very turnout where the robbery would've occurred.

At last, Billy Ray made his choice.

"Pull over, Mr. Hailey. I'll take it from here."

And the devil be damned.

<=== PIPELINE ===>

2

Johnny Lam was the Special Agent in Charge of the Federal Bureau of Investigation's Dallas Division.

But he kept getting asked the same question, "Why Michigan?"

Even had the President and the ultra-secret K-KEY Group authorized him to provide the answer, Michiganders would've been shocked and frightened; shocked to learn a hallucinogenic form of methamphetamine, called Rapture, was in their fair state; and frightened to know the drug had been converted to a lethal poison in a secret lab in Texas by the ex-KGB assassin, Joseph Wiggins—a madman bent on destroying America and all she stood for.

The 2012 case of a naked man in Miami violently attacking and eating his live victim was believed to have been the appalling result of a single dose of the new designer drug.

Fortunately, the source of the Rapture was discovered in a small town in East Texas and destroyed before it could be dispersed to targeted cities across the United States.

But not all of the Rapture was obliterated. One tanker truck managed to slip through the federal government's robust nation-wide dragnet and remained unaccounted for. Cellular phone signals captured by the NSA revealed the rogue cargo was diverted to the Wolverine State by Angel Gallina, the same prick who once headed the notorious Gallina cartel.

Regrettably though, the dragnet had been cast so widely that the Fed's mass collection of electronic data ended up overwhelming analysts and muddying the signal intelligence stream.

By the time the NSA processed the SIGINT, analyzed all of its content, and released an intel report to Homeland Security, ten thousand gallons of the deadliest drug the world had ever known simply disappeared, Angel Gallina was dead, and the trail had gone cold.

It was believed by the K-KEY Group that no one outside their tightly controlled organization knew of the drug's poisonous nature.

Regardless, the President had made it abundantly clear upon promoting Lam as SAC in Dallas that the gloves were off in war on terror. He was to seek and destroy the Rapture, 'No matter where, No matter what, No matter how.'

So where in Michigan? A year had elapsed since being told to find the Rapture. And still Lam had no inkling where the drugs could be. Furthermore, it was puzzling why the missing shipment hadn't been released into the market yet. Once crystallized and broken into individual doses, Rapture would be worth hundreds of millions of dollars.

Maybe the cartel chemists hadn't figured that out yet, or maybe Gallina didn't get the chance to inform them before getting blown into little drug kingpin bits.

It could also be that Gallina was duped by Wiggins, and that the power-hungry drug lord never knew the Rapture no longer promised incredible riches, only death.

After all, Wiggins had screwed over Kim Jong-il, so why not Gallina?

It was too bad Joseph Wiggins met his end before the FBI could interrogate him—or Lam could get his hands around the sick bastard's neck for kidnapping his daughter Katie.

Since Wiggins' body was never found, Lam's only consolation was that his daughter was safe and an evil shithead was brown scum on the bottom of the Loma Reservoir by now.

Lam cursed. So many questions, so few answers. It seemed time was against him and the case got colder every day.

But he was sure about one thing—the Rapture was coming.

Unless he located the missing tanker soon, Michiganders could find themselves vexed by a nightmare of demonic proportions from thousands of drugged-up Miami-like zombies gnashing and clawing their way through unsuspecting towns and neighborhoods.

No one would be safe.

It was true he was in Michigan on a search-and-destroy mission. That was the *where* of his assignment. And locating the dangerous Rapture drug was the *what.* But troubling him to his core was POTUS' third and final directive, "No matter how."

Lam felt conflicted—safeguard the public from villains and lone-wolf terrorists seeking to rape and raze America, but doing so while stretching the nation's Constitution like a cheap rubber band.

Simply put, the *HOW* of his mission could tear a free society apart.

Safety within America's borders was considered the purview of civilian police forces, from the Justice Department, Homeland Security, and the FBI on down to the local patrol cop.

While keeping the nation secure from foreign actors was the charge of the United States military and spy agencies.

Lam had always believed there's a reason you separate military and the police. One fights the enemies of the state, the other serves and protects the people. When the military becomes both, then the enemies of the state tend to become the people.

As a federal law enforcement agent, he'd always held sacred the notion that he served the public . . . not the other way around.

But for some, that belief had changed.

<====== PIPELINE ======>

During the desperate hours after the terrorist attacks on New York's Twin Towers, a select group of scientists, businessmen, politicians, and military leaders assembled at the nation's capital.

They were the elite of the elite, the best and the brightest, patriots one and all. Their sole concern was for the survival of the United States America—*No matter how.*

They were called the K-KEY Group: men and women authorized by their Commander-in-Chief to form an invincible force to defend the country against all enemies foreign and domestic, and to prosecute bad actors irrespective of common law or the nation's Bill of Rights.

Lam now doubled as a K-KEY Group operative and carried two forms of identification, the first being his FBI badge for police work.

But the other leather case, to be used whenever necessary, branded him as a K-KEY agent. Ghosting across the front of this second ID were the words AUTHORITY OVER ALL while a peculiar trident pointed straight down at a photo of the President. He found the symbol and phrase terribly disturbing.

Who could be higher than POTUS?

It was this ID permitting him to act without warrant, conduct enhanced interrogations, and sanction belligerents with extreme prejudice.

Having been an Army Green Beret before joining the FBI, he knew how to conduct hybrid warfare. His Special Forces unit had been decorated for performing those very functions as specialized warfare jungle fighters.

But he was a cop now. Tracking dangerous drugs and chasing down criminals shouldn't require the suspension of the nation's Constitution.

Could he even bring himself to fire against his fellow citizens?

Lam's internal discord was interrupted by the loud buzzing of his Blackberry phone. It wasn't the Rapture.

The call was police work, actual crime-fighting. The text read *187* followed by the letters *H* and *T*.

One-eight-seven was the police designation for homicide, HT was his own shorthand for human traffic. It was the third victim in five days.

Local authorities suspected a serial killer at-large, due to a repeating M.O. of predominately Latin women stripped naked, signs of sexual abuse, torture, and no forms of identification beyond tattoos, scars, and dental work. Lam disagreed with that assessment, believing instead the women were unwitting victims of human trafficking rather than females chosen at random and murdered by a psychopath.

He stared at the text. Doing so reminded him of one immutable fact: he was a cop first and always, not a secret extra-constitutional operative.

Furthermore, battling the shameful crime of human slavery had become his own personal war on the very day Wiggins ordered his daughter Katie's abduction at the hands of the dearly departed Angel Gallina—made forever *departed* by a well-placed rocket propelled grenade fired by his friend Billy Ray Jenkins.

If not for the assault on his family, he would've told the K-KEY Group to take a hike. But now he could tap into their vast assets and bring the trafficking scum to justice . . . as a cop.

Lam keyed the GPS coordinates into his phone. A map appeared.

Port Sheldon . . . Pigeon Lake.

He put the rented Crown Victoria in gear and drove away from the FBI resident agency headquarters on Ionia Avenue in Grand Rapids. While departing the downtown area, he was struck by how different the city looked from his first visit years earlier.

The world had changed. And so too had Grand Rapids, converting from reliance on heavy industry to that of medical research and higher education. Impressive new buildings ringed the once-renowned Furniture City like glistening jewels, including an arena and downtown plaza. Century-old factories had been converted to modern uses. Even downtown culture showed new life, transforming from dingy limelight districts typical of dying factory towns to art museums, restaurants, microbreweries, and blues music venues.

His favorite kinds of fun!

Lam accessed the Gerald R. Ford Freeway and headed west toward the coast of Lake Michigan. An hour later, he arrived at the Port Sheldon public boat launch on Pigeon Lake, a body of water formed where Pigeon Creek widened before emptying into Lake Michigan through a channel lined by quarter-mile-long jetties. Waiting at the water's edge in a 25-foot Boston Whaler was an Ottawa County Sheriff detective in a stiff business suit and windbreaker, and accompanied by a uniformed marine officer.

Lam boarded the boat. "I'm getting tired of us meeting like this."

"So are the victims, Agent Lam," Lieutenant Keith Talsma replied.

"Good point, Tals."

It'd taken Lam no time at all to gain respect for the tough Sheriff Lieutenant. In sharp contrast to his own dark features and flashy clothes, Talsma was pure Dutch, all business, and owned a thick mane of blond hair to go with his probing blue eyes.

"What do we have today, Lieutenant?"

"Same as the others—naked Latina, throat cut, water immersion."

"Chains?" asked Lam.

Talsma looked down and then slowly nodded.

<==== PIPELINE ====>

Lam shuddered . . . *the devil's baptism!*

"But there's a difference with this Jane Doe," Talsma added. "There were no signs of sexual abuse prior to her throat being cut."

Lam thought a moment. "Conclusions?"

Talsma stated, "Too early. But I can offer you a theory—"

Before Talsma could respond, the boat banked hard right to avoid a speeding Jet Ski driven by a lobster-red cowboy chugging a beer. The marine officer toggled the siren, instantly changing Bronco Bob's day from rapt pleasure to dread, then slowing his toy in the no-wake zone.

"Dumbass," Talsma said under his breath.

The marine officer righted the Whaler and motored along the calm waters of Pigeon Lake. The sky was blue, the sun hot, and the crystal waters inviting—the very pleasantness that lured so many beach lovers to the sandy shores of Michigan.

They rounded a bend and all that changed.

A collection of large boulders and concrete slabs lined the north side of Pigeon Lake forming a breakwater. A massive steel discharge pipe from the nearby coal-fired power plant traversed atop the bank for a half-mile before submerging into the depths of Lake Michigan. Nestled in a tiny cove, formed where the breakwater bent toward open water, a group of police boats idled while investigators and CSI staff in white Tyvek suits gathered on the rocks.

Lam spotted the object of everyone's attention, a set of swollen brown legs with sun-blistered feet poking out of a clump of sea grass.

He turned to Talsma. "I'll hear that theory now."

Tami Tafoya snuck another peek under the table at her cell phone.

She should've been paying more attention to her date, a handsome butcher named David or Donald or . . . well, whatever.

She didn't get many dates. Not that she wasn't shapely and pretty, or lacked interest in men. Hell, she owned those attributes in spades.

Rather, it was her reputation—she was a full bore workaholic.

But so what!

She loved being an investigative reporter for the Channel 13 News. And she was damn good at it, too. She ate, drank, and slept crime reporting. Though sadly, that also meant she ate alone, drank alone, and slept alone—*talk of murder had a way of punking intimacy.*

"Are you listening to me?" asked Whatshisname.

Tafoya looked up from her phone. "Sure, veal cutlets—"

"No. I asked what kind of drink you'd like."

"Oh, sorry. A hurricane."

Dale . . . or Dan's eyebrows lifted in hopeful anticipation of the evening going to new heights. Hurricanes were strong drinks!

He flagged the waitress and placed the order, his voice brimming with hope that the rumors about the foxy Cuban reporter babe weren't true.

The drinks arrived, interrupting Tafoya cycling through text messages.

The rum felt really, really good going down.

It warmed her body.

Her date drained his beer and said, "Shall we have another?"

Tafoya looked up from her phone to her empty glass. "Sure . . . Darin. It's five o'clock somewhere."

"The name's Douglas and it's five o'clock here."

Tafoya gazed out the window of Captain Jim's Bar and Grill at the clear waters of Lake Michigan. The evening promised another glorious sunset. She felt a tickle deep down. Maybe this would be her lucky night.

It was obvious by her date's expression that he felt the same.

She checked her watch . . . five o'clock on the dot. "Well so it is, Douglas. Perhaps one more before the drum sounds."

Douglas grinned real big.

Tafoya gathered up her purse. "If you'll excuse me a moment, I need to go powder my nose."

Just as she reached the ladies' room, her cellphone chimed.

It was a text message that read, 187 - Port Sheldon - Pigeon Lake.

The police code for murder!

She looked back at her happy date, now placing an order with the waitress. Then she looked out the front door of the restaurant and spotted a taxi cab idling near the entrance.

Without a second thought, Tami Tafoya headed for the door.

So much for the drums sounding tonight, she thought.

"You can draw your own conclusions, Lam." Talsma pointed to the macabre scene. "The Medical Examiner is about to remove the body."

The marine officer slowed the police boat for mooring to a stationary pontoon. Suddenly, another boat sped past, beating them to the landing, and sending the Whaler rocking with the incoming boat's wake..

Without any hesitation, a thirty-something woman with long dark hair and shapely hips leapt onto the pontoon and jumped to the rocks.

Lam could hardly believe his eyes. "Who the hell invited J.Lo?"

Talsma said, "That's Tami Tafoya. She's a news reporter."

"What's she doing here? This is an active crime scene."

"She's an *investigative* reporter."

"So tell her to go investigate at the library. I don't want unauthorized persons mucking around our crime scene!"

Talsma grinned. "Can't do that, Lam, my hands are tied. That woman is hooked up with everyone from the Governor on down. But I do share your sentiment."

Lam was PO'd about a reporter tramping around inside the cordon, but decided not to press Talsma any further on the matter.

He transferred to the breakwater keeping mindful of his footing. The last thing he needed was to break a leg.

It only took a few minutes scouting among the rocks to determine he wasn't looking at the actual crime scene, merely where Jane Doe's body washed ashore after the recent storm.

He was well aware that weather on the five Great Lakes could be as dangerous as the world's oceans. They were actually freshwater inland seas, with waves rising as tall as a three-story building then reaching down to churn the depths. The Lake was beautiful beyond compare on a calm day, then within hours could rain down death and destruction, as many of the sunken wrecks could testify to.

As with the previous bodies, Jane Doe had been wrapped in chains and dumped in the lake until getting wrenched from her liquid purgatory to return from the dead.

There was little hope of finding evidence at the Pigeon Lake site. But Lam squatted low and searched among the stones anyway, hoping against hope that some clue, some stroke of luck, might reveal Jane Doe's identity or that of her killer.

Police work was like that—it took a large measure of hope and a big dose of luck.

As Lam searched, thoughts of his daughter came to mind, and how fortunate Katie had been to be rescued from her abductors. In reality, so few victims of human trafficking were rescued or ever heard from again.

It was as if the ground opened up and swallowed them whole.

Lam heard footfalls approach then a silky voice. "Hello, Johnny Lam."

He stood and faced the woman who'd raced past him.

She continued, "I'm told you're an FBI agent."

"Yeah? And I'm told you're not a cop," he replied coldly. "That makes you unauthorized to be here."

The woman didn't flinch. "Well, that depends."

"Depends on what?" Lam asked.

"On who's authorizing." She held out a business card. "Tami Tafoya."

Lam ignored her and hopped to another rock to resume the search.

Despite raw hands and sore knees, the area failed to produce any trace or actual evidence. A dead body remained the only proof that a terrible crime had taken place. Soon the yellow crime tape would come down, the area beneath the giant pipe would return to its former serenity, and another precious soul would vanish into obscurity.

Great care was shown handling Jane Doe. After photos, the body was placed into a bag, and the Medical Examiner began zipping it shut when something caught Lam's attention.

There was a wine-colored mark on the victim's shoulder about the size of a child's fist. It resembled a butterfly.

Lam pointed. "Is that a tattoo?"

"*Nevus Flammeus* . . . a birthmark," the Medical Examiner replied.

Lam lifted his Blackberry to snap a photo of Jane Doe's shoulder, but just then another flash lit the area and spoiled his shot.

He looked behind him and saw the reporter holding a camera.

"You can't do that!"

"Can't do what?" Tafoya asked innocently.

"You can't post that picture without authorization."

"Oh...? Not a big believer in the First Amendment, I see." Tafoya spun around, hop-scotched across the rocks, and boarded her awaiting boat.

Lam watched her leave, not happy with the exchange or its outcome.

The Medical Examiner slowly zipped the bag shut.

The sun was dipping low in the west by the time the Boston Whaler returned Lam to the Pigeon Lake public launch. He thanked the marine officer and then turned to Talsma for a final word.

"Call me with anything new, I want to crush these trafficking scum!"

"Preaching to the choir, Agent Lam. But I'll call you."

Lam bid Talsma farewell and trudged up to the parking lot already dreading the depressing drive back to town. But as he approached the Crown Vic, he was shocked to see the reporter leaning against the passenger door.

"It's about time," she said.

"Time for what?"

Tafoya softened her stance. "My taxi abandoned me."

"A wise choice. If I was your dog I'd abandon you."

"I don't need a dog, I just need a ride back to Captain Jim's."

Lam said nothing, just got in the car and locked the doors.

Tafoya pressed her hands and face against the window. Her muffled voice came through the glass, "*Pleeeasse?*"

Lam stuck the key in the ignition. He could turn it, start the motor, and drive away. Easy. After all he was a Federal official not an Uber driver.

<=== PIPELINE ===>

No, not easy.

He pressed the door locks. The passenger door opened and Tafoya slid inside.

"Where to, lady?" He didn't bother hiding his annoyance.

"Captain Jim's Bar & Grill. It's not far."

"What's at Captain Jim's?"

"My date. I got the 187 call on my way to the ladies room. Then I sort of skipped out on him for a minute."

Lam shot Tafoya a hard look. "It's been more than a minute. He'll think you fell in. By the way, how'd you know which car was mine?"

"Oh *puh-lease*. I traced all the cars until I got a hit. This isn't my first rodeo, you know.""

Lam shook his head. Talsma was right, the woman was definitely hooked up. He'd met plenty of reporters in his day—one major slimeball in Texas came to mind—but he'd never met anyone like Tami Tafoya.

"Just drive, Agent Lam, I'll show you the way."

It turned out Captain Jim's wasn't anywhere near Pigeon Lake.

The restaurant was located thirty miles to the north on a wide sandy beach in Muskegon. The place was popular with boaters who could drop anchor in the shallow waters on the lee side of the jetty and then wade ashore for burgers and beers . . . *no shirt, no shoes, no problem.*

Tafoya said, "I just don't understand it. How could he just leave me like that?"

Lam nearly plowed into a row of Harley Davidson motorbikes in front of the restaurant at hearing that.

"What! You get a man all juiced up, head off to the little girls' room for two hours, then wonder why he ditched you?"

Tafoya's dark eyebrows lifted as if to say, *Yeah . . . so?*

Lam just shook his head. "So now what?"

"I'm hungry."

Lam was hungry too. But he wasn't so sure eating with Tafoya wouldn't cause a major case of heartburn that no antacid could cure.

"And I'm thirsty," she added.

"Listen up, lady. We're not here to get wasted."

Tafoya acted hurt. "Is that how you talk to a gal on a first date?"

Lam parked, rounded the car, and opened Tafoya's door. "This is no date. We eat, we drink, we leave. Got it?"

Tafoya smiled and walked off.

Lam locked the car and caught up.

But being so distracted by Tafoya, he failed to notice a camo-painted pickup truck turn in at Captain Jim's and park at the back of the lot.

The two men inside of the menacing vehicle made no attempt to exit, nor were they dressed for volleyball on the beach.

The waitress seated them facing Lake Michigan, then brought their drinks: tomato juice for Lam, a hurricane for Tafoya.

The tomato juice went down slow. The hurricane disappeared.

"Hey, take it easy," Lam warned.

"I think I liked my other date better. At least he didn't act like a cop."

"I am a cop. And this is no date." But Lam began to see a change in the newshound, a softening of sorts.

Maybe it was the rum. But there seemed to be something else, too. *Loneliness?*

Not one to pile on, he loosened his shirt and dialed it down a notch.

The food came. It looked decent and was priced right. Plus it had those big Michigan portions. Lam lifted a bite to his mouth. But before he could shovel it in, Tafoya said, "Put your fork down!"

"Huh—?"

"I said put your fork down!"

Lam did so.

A moment later, Tafoya said, "Okay. You can pick it up now."

After a bite, Lam asked, "What was that all about?"

"Tradition," Tafoya said proudly. "When my family gathers for dinner, *mi abuelo* slaps the table and yells at everyone to put their forks down. Then he thanks God for America."

Lam eased his tone. "Your grandfather's a wise man."

They finished the meal and Tafoya ordered another hurricane.

Lam didn't say a word this time. He just sipped his tomato juice and watched a group of musicians setting up for the night's show. The band's signboard read *The Outer Vibe*. Tafoya waved at the lone female band member, a sexy gal in leather pants and sequined motorcycle jacket.

Lam wondered if Tafoya listed "biker chick" on her resume to go with pain-in-the-ass reporter.

She noticed his look and said, "Her name's Lisa. I did a TV special about the band's Teen Rock Camps."

Lam continued his bored expression.

"You're not an artsy guy, are you?" Lam ignored her question. "Well, mister, art begins with beauty." She stood. "Follow me."

After the fork thing Lam was suspicious. "Show me what . . .?"

She led him outside and pointed at the setting sun. "Behold, G-man."

Lam watched the massive yellow orb of the sun dissolve into the clear, fresh waters of Lake Michigan. Puffy clouds turned red and hung like rubies in the azure sky.

<== PIPELINE ==>

Then it happened. Just as the last rays of the sun passed through the prism of water, a green light streaked across the sky.

He'd never seen the green flash before.

Tafoya stared at him a moment, then went back into the restaurant.

Lam remained on the deck enjoying the view across the broad sugar sand beaches and endless surface of one of America's greatest lakes.

When Lam returned indoors, the waitress was asking if they cared for desert. He declined and readied to leave, but Tafoya ordered a coffee nudge. Again a drink with alcohol, though one with caffeine at least.

The Outer Vibe began their show with a Jimmy Buffett cover. It was a perfect match for the warm summer night at Captain Jim's. Had there been palm trees, Lam could've sworn they were at Margaritaville.

Next, the band switched to an original song that got the whole place clapping and hopping around. Tafoya came out of her chair, too.

"Hoka Hey! I love this song." She rounded the table and stood beside Lam. "Dance with me!"

"I don't dance."

"What? A tall, *dark,* and handsome man like you?"

Lam caught the racial reference. "Half dark, my mother was French."

"Well then, the best of both worlds." Tafoya slid backward towards the dance floor beckoning Lam with her finger. "Come on!"

He checked his watch. It was getting late. He should be going—

Hell, he should never have come!

"Oh well, when in Rome . . ." He rose from the table. "I've always dreamed of dancing with Jennifer Lopez. But I guess you'll do."

Closing time finally came to Captain Jim's.

They joined the crowd filing out to the parking lot.

The night air was balmy. Lam smelled the warm scent of fresh water blowing in from the Lake. He shed his teal sport coat and slung it over his shoulder. He wouldn't object to a permanent assignment in Michigan.

"Thank you for dancing with me, Agent Lam," Tafoya said politely.

Lam felt guilty, maybe he'd misjudged her. She actually wasn't so annoying once she got going. As they reached the car, he extended a hand. "How about we go to first names. Call me Johnny."

Tafoya ignored Lam's hand and stepped into his arms instead.

Her body was hot and moist from dancing. Her hair smelled of sweet shampoo. The rise and fall of her chest . . . her hot breath, it made Lam want to—— He pushed her away. For a long, awkward moment, Tafoya stared into his eyes, then slid into the car and pulled the door shut.

Lam cursed as he pulled away from Captain Jims!

Did he always have to be so professional, so hard—*so damn cold?*

Moments later, the camo-painted truck departed Captain Jim's, too.

Lam peeked at Tafoya. She ignored him and stared straight ahead.

He knew what she was thinking. "I'm sorry for pushing you away."

She looked at him a fleeting moment then back at the road ahead.

"With my job . . ." Lam began to explain then gave up. He'd never been good with excuses. "Let's just say I don't get out much."

Tafoya still didn't respond.

"I enjoyed our dance," he offered sincerely. "It felt good."

While staring forward, Tafoya said, "I feel so awkward sometimes. It's like I don't know how to act with men. I end up scaring them away."

Lam said, "You could start by cutting your time in the ladies' room."

Tafoya cracked up laughing, its sound honest and delightful.

Lam liked that.

"You're right, Johnny. I'm sure we'll be running into each other from time to time. Please call me Tami."

Before Lam could respond, he noticed a set of headlights in the far distance enter their lane. The road leading to the interstate was straight and flat, and bordered by farms. Car lights could be seen a long way off.

He turned back to Tafoya. "Let's hope our next meeting isn't so rocky." He thought of the breakwater at Pigeon Lake.

"Then you'll need to let me do my job at the crime scenes."

"But you're just a reporter—"

Bad choice of words.

Tafoya turned. "I beg your pardon. I'm more than *just* a reporter!"

"Tami, I didn't mean it that way."

"How did you mean it then?"

Lam didn't get a chance to answer. From straight ahead, headlights reappeared in their lane, and hurtling toward them.

Then without warning, a large truck sped up from behind and doused the interior of the Crown Victoria with powerful flood lights.

Two vehicles, front and back . . . they were trapped!

The glare made it impossible to see!

Lam estimated the next farm road and then pulled hard on the steering wheel. As he did so, a dark shadow appeared before them.

Tami Screamed!

Lam jammed on the brakes and cranked the wheel with all his might.

The last thing he saw before the world went black was a massive corn combine, its cutting heads pointed at them like a line of deadly missiles!

The noise of crashing steel filled the night air.

<====== PIPELINE ======>

3

The Jackpot Tours coach handled much better than Billy Ray would've expected, considering two blown tires and the awful pounding against the cliff on Chinook Pass, to say nothing of bullet holes and pools of blood.

The bus was attracting a lot of attention. Then again, how could it not, surrounded by a score of police cruisers and motorcycle units clearing traffic along the interstate with their flashing lights and shrieking sirens.

It'd been an incoming call to one of the passengers, a daughter checking on her parents, wishing to know how their luck had gone. The mother let it slip there'd been trouble, but couldn't say more, and abruptly disconnected. The daughter called back, got no answer, panicked, and phoned the Washington State Patrol.

Again Hailey proved his salt by dialing 9-1-1 and getting routed to the WSP District Two Field Operations Captain, a man named Eppenstein. Hailey smartly provided the Bud Light version of their ordeal, then convinced Eppenstein not to force the bus to a halt, assuring the good captain that the entire group of senior citizens would have far better memories to aid his investigators if allowed to cross home plate.

Eppenstein got the hint and ordered the escort.

Billy Ray learned from Hailey that their driver had been a last-minute replacement. That meant a rotten apple festered at Jackpot Tours.

He had no idea what would happen to him for killing the criminals, maybe jail time, or worse, back to a prison cell. His previous criminal record had been expunged on orders from the President of the United States, but people still had memories to draw from.

Nothing a person did in their lives was ever truly struck from history, especially a crime involving a member of the law enforcement community, whose memories were long, their bonds robust and far-reaching. Though surely not everyone in East Texas believed Roy Payne deserved to be behind bars.

At last, Billy Ray turned the coach into the lot of a busy bus barn. Coaches filled with tourists were coming and going, ferrying vacationers to all points on the map.

State troopers assisted by waiving him over to a secure area. The brakes of the battered vehicle squealed as it came to a stop. Then Billy Ray hit the door actuator.

It opened with the familiar hiss.

Immediately, three state troopers boarded with guns drawn.

The first officer headed straight to Toiletman's still form while the second trooper canvassed the passengers.

The last trooper checked on Wheezy, failed to get a pulse, and then turned his weapon on Billy Ray.

"Clear!" the third officer shouted.

At the signal, a man wearing the gold bars of a Washington State Patrol Captain boarded. "Which one of you is Steve Hailey?"

Hailey raised his hand. "I am, Captain Eppenstein."

With a commanding voice, Captain Eppenstein said "Mr. Hailey, all of you, I understand a terrible incident has occurred aboard this bus. I must request that you remain calm. You will all be removed from the bus in groups of two and escorted into the tour company headquarters for questioning. Please understand we have a very serious situation that mandates everyone's full cooperation."

A lady five rows back raised her hand for a question.

"Sorry, ma'am, no Q&A at this time. You'll have ample opportunity once attorneys are present and recording equipment is activated."

The woman lowered her hand.

Eppenstein turned to Billy Ray and motioned to the dead villains. "Your cooperation will also be most appreciated."

"You'll have no trouble from me, sir," Billy Ray assured the captain.

"Good. If you'll please stand and place your hands behind your—"

Mary yelled out, "But he saved our lives!"

Billy Ray knew the drill. He rose, calmly turned, and positioned his hands for cuffs. Cold steel clicked tightly around his wrists.

The passengers all stared at Billy Ray with shocked looks, minus one. Hailey smiled and gave him a thumbs-up. Then the troopers escorted him off the bus and to a conference room for processing.

He was ordered to sit, then a trooper remained to guard the suspect until Captain Eppenstein's arrival.

Twenty minutes later, Eppenstein and a plainclothes detective entered the room carrying Billy Ray's belongings, including his dive knife inside of an evidence bag. They placed everything on the conference room table and began questioning Billy Ray at length.

"Tell me again," the detective said.

"There were four of them," Billy Ray replied calmly.

"Including the driver," Eppenstein added.

"Correct, sir."

"But only two of the alleged criminals were found on the bus, both dead. Where are the others?"

<== PIPELINE ==>

It was Billy Ray's third time answering the question. "One is somewhere up on the mountain, and the driver didn't grow wings fast enough and is at the bottom of it. Other than that, I was a little too busy at the time to spot mile markers."

The detective interrupted Eppenstein's turn at the suspect. "Very interesting," he said staring at a computer screen.

Eppenstein pulled the detective's laptop in front him and studied it for a few moments. Then he looked up at Billy Ray.

"Now what?" Billy Ray wondered aloud.

"You don't exist, Mr. Jenkins."

"Dolittle——" Billy Ray uttered angrily.

"Who's Dolittle?" The plainclothes detective asked.

"I didn't agree to that," Billy Ray continued.

"Agree to what, Mr. Jenkins?"

Billy Ray waved off the cop. "Never mind."

Eppenstein took charge. "Agree to what, Jenkins? Must I remind you you're under arrest for murder?"

Before Billy Ray could answer, the conference room phone rang.

Eppenstein scowled. "I said no interruptions."

The trooper guarding the door stepped forward and answered the phone. "It's for you, Captain."

"Huh? Who could be calling me on that phone?"

"The Governor," the trooper said unsteadily.

Eppenstein took the receiver. "Yes, Governor——"

After a half minute of Eppenstein nodding like a bobblehead doll, he handed the phone back to the trooper and then said to Billy Ray, "If you'd please stand so I can remove your cuffs, Mr. Jenkins."

The detective registered shock. "What the——"

Eppenstein nodded at the detective's computer. "It seems Mr. Jenkins doesn't exist." Then he dismissed the trooper and the detective.

Without a word, the detective secured his laptop and exited, clearly not a happy camper.

Once alone, Eppenstein said, "In all my years of police work, I never met a person who *didn't exist.*"

Billy Ray couldn't wait to strangle his old friend John Dodd, aka, Dolittle. He'd turned Dodd down flat when asked to join the K-KEY Group in their covert war against the enemies within America's boarders.

He wanted to be done with fighting, to put death behind him——

To live at peace.

"I'm sorry for your trouble, Captain," Billy Ray offered apologetically.

Eppenstein switched off the recording equipment and faced Billy Ray. "Were they guilty, Mr. Jenkins? Did those men really deserve to die?"

"God only knows," Billy Ray said. "But they made their choices."

Eppenstein moved to the door. "Be that as it may, I have a job to do, Jenkins . . . or whoever you are. Therefore, I'm obliged to request your temporary residence in my fair city until this matter is completed."

Eppenstein walked out, leaving Billy Ray to himself.

Billy Ray savored the silence of the empty room. But he felt empty too. *Like maybe the devil wasn't the only one damned.*

Tami Tafoya awoke in a hospital room. Tubes ran to her arms. A monitor made an annoying beeping sound. And her body hurt all over.

She focused her eyes—even *that* hurt!

A nurse stood at the wall writing on a whiteboard. "Where am I?"

The nurse turned. "Hello, Ms. Tafoya. You're at Spectrum Health."

"How did I get here?" Tafoya forced her mind to remember.

"You and Mr. Lam were in a car accident and airlifted here last night."

"Lam?"

"He was the driver of the car and you the passenger."

Then it all came flooding back to Tafoya . . . vehicle lights coming straight at them from ahead. A truck or something coming up from behind with its bright lights. And then Lam turning hard to avoid a collision.

"Where's Lam?" Tafoya asked the nurse.

"I'm afraid I can't comment on matters involving patients."

Damn HIPAA rules, Tafoya cursed. *A reporter's worst enemy!*

"I'm not asking for medical information. I want to know where he is."

The nurse said, "I'm sorry, Ms. Tafoya. Unfortunately, I'm not at liberty to say where Mr. Lam is." She wrote a number on the whiteboard and gave a wink. Then erased the board and walked out.

Tafoya memorized the number, 3-1-7.

A doctor entered and began flipping through her medical chart. The man was tall and very handsome. Silver hair streaked his temples and a white doctor smock added to his perfect glow. Then another man entered the room and stood next to Dr. Wonderful, though lacking most of the qualities she preferred in a man.

He was Special Agent Ed Tompkins of the FBI: balding, bug-eyed, and pasty faced. There paths had crossed on several occasions when her investigative reporting required it.

The doctor finished the chart notes. "How do you feel, Ms. Tafoya?"

<== PIPELINE ==>

"Just peachy. And you?"

Then the doctor smiled and it rocked her world.

His teeth were perfect. His curly hair was perfect. Everything about him was perfect. He could be a cast member on Days of Our Lives or something.

Was he married?

Agent Tompkins broke the spell. "I need to ask you some questions."

Tafoya's eyes shifted from the movie star to the gumshoe.

What a difference.

"Unhook these tubes and I'll answer your questions."

Tompkins asked, "Would that be all right, Dr. Allan?"

"Of course. Except for an elevated heartrate, her vitals show normal."

The doctor leaned down to remove the tubes from Tafoya's arms. He smelled fresh . . . alluring. She wished there was more wrong with her.

Dr. Allan stepped back and said, "I wouldn't go hopping out of bed anytime soon, Ms. Tafoya."

Then you'd better leave now, she wanted to say.

"You're bound to be uncomfortable for a while," Dr. Allan continued. "I saw pictures of the car. You're lucky to be alive, and so is Agent Lam. But I'll let Agent Tompkins take it from here." Then Dr. Allan smiled that perfect smile and left her sad and alone with Tompkins.

"Tell me what you remember of the accident," Tompkins began.

She thought hard.

The pain in her head returned.

"I remember headlights coming at us. Then a truck, or something, shined bright lights into our car from behind. The glare made it impossible to see."

"What kind of truck?"

"I don't know, it all happened so fast. Lam spotted a farm road and made a hard turn. But there was a huge farm machine, and we . . . I guess we smashed into it. After that, I don't remember a thing."

Tompkins made notes on a writing pad.

Tafoya looked hard at Tompkins. "Where's Lam, is he all right?" The agent didn't answer. She struggled to a sitting position. "Where is he?" she almost screamed.

"He's alive. Sore ribs, most likely. But—"

"But what!"

"He's unconscious."

"So tell me which room he's in."

"Sorry, Ms. Tafoya, I'm not authorized to do that."

She rolled her eyes in frustration. *That hurt also.*

Tompkins continued, "Can you tell me any more details, anything at all that might help answer what happened to you last night?"

"I'll have to think about it and get back to you. Say, I'm not feeling so well. Would you be a dear and call for the nurse . . . on your way out?"

Tompkins bristled at the off-putting.

"As you wish." He placed a business card on the phone table. "Call if you remember more details."

A nurse walked in with a pill cup and glass of water. As soon as she was gone, Tafoya forced herself out of bed.

The room spun, slowed, and finally stopped. Then she went to the closet and found her cell phone. The battery was dead.

She gave up on the phone, slipped into a stiff hospital robe and went to find Lam.

A sign on room 317 read Authorized Personnel Only. She tried it anyway. It was unlocked.

Tafoya looked both ways. No one was paying attention to her, so she let herself into the room. There was only one patient inside, unconscious and hooked to monitors, like a car getting a diagnostic tune up.

It was Johnny Lam.

Tafoya turned and locked the door.

A security guard stood on the loading dock of the Norman Webster Power Plant and Paper Mill in Muskegon. He crossed his arms and smiled at the hideous camo-painted pickup truck pulling up.

Two burly men exited the truck and the guard's smile widened. "Duke, Tito, you queers are late." The arms unfolded. "Señor Gallina won't tolerate your sloppy shit much longer."

Duke responded, "We laid low in case there were any witnesses."

"Where's the butterfly girl?" the guard asked.

Duke jabbed his thumb over his shoulder.

The private guard looked past the two hitmen to a blue tarp covering an oblong object in the bed of the truck. "So were there any?"

Tito took the question, his voice surprisingly high-pitched for a man so large. "Any what?"

"Witnesses, you dumbass!"

Tito hated being called dumb and stupid. He balled his big fists and stepped toward the guard. Duke blocked the way with a muscular arm.

The guard smirked mockingly.

<==== PIPELINE ====>

Duke answered the question, "One witness. But Tito took care of that."

The guard looked at Tito's huge frame, his thoughts evident. Not much could survive a mauling by such a brute.

Duke continued, "We did both jobs. We put that nosey FBI agent out of commission and got the body from the morgue. So why are we here?"

"You can ask the boss, he's waiting for you, impatiently, I might add. Follow me, faggots. And try not to hold hands."

The guard led the way into the building.

Billy Ray packed his belongings and exited the Jackpot Tours building. He felt dirty, his soul heavy with the weight of yet more death.

He stood in the bus lot wondering what to do next.

Should he go to Rebecca? How would she take him showing up uninvited? And what if she turned him away?

Billy Ray hushed the voice of doubt.

He couldn't stay away any longer. He'd nearly married another woman, a good and lovely woman. But after a while they'd both agreed to end the engagement since their relationship would be forever haunted by the ghost of another woman. So he left Texas to go find his true love.

Billy Ray adjusted his pack and then began the final leg of the journey.

He didn't get far. His phone vibrated in his pocket. He fished it out and checked the number. It wasn't a number at all, but a single word—*Spartan!*

Spartan was the code word for trouble that he and Lam had conceived during the battle at the Texas Waterland Family Park. They'd agreed to use the signal only if either one were about to board the long black train and go spit in the devil's eye.

This was the first time he'd heard from Lam since then.

Billy Ray answered using his callsign. "Wolverine."

A woman's voice said, "Oh. I must have the wrong number."

"Wait. Don't hang up! Where's Lam, and why do you have his phone?"

There was a long pause. Finally, the woman said, "Agent Lam is here."

"Where's here?"

"Michigan . . . Johnny's in Michigan."

Lam was the Dallas SAC. *So why Michigan?* And how did the woman get Lam's phone, and know to dial that specific number?

"I'm a friend of Agent Lam. Who am I speaking with?"

Tafoya was tempted to hang up. She shouldn't have been snooping through Lam's belongings. She'd only wanted to help. But after finding his identification wallets—both of them—she was stunned!

She was familiar with FBI badges. It was the second ID that chilled her blood. Boldly displayed on the ID was the phrase AUTHORITY OVER ALL. Furthermore, some pitchfork-looking symbol hung above the President's handsome mug. It was a symbol she'd never seen before.

Then curiosity killed the cat. Tafoya found Lam's phone and began cycling through it for answers. It was password protected, except for three entries on his speed dial. One option read HQ-DAL, obviously referring to his office in Texas. Another read Katie, who she assumed to be a lover. It was the third name that piqued her interest—*Spartan!*

Billy Ray wondered if the line had gone dead. "Hello?"

"Tami," the woman said at last.

With a calming voice, Billy Ray thanked her then asked, "May I talk with Agent Lam?"

"You can't . . . I mean, he's unconscious."

"Can you please tell me what happened?"

The woman seemed to be deciding whether to answer or hang up. Then she said, "A car accident. We were run off the road, I'm sure of it!"

"Where exactly is Lam?" Billy Ray tread carefully. He didn't want to spook the woman.

The man sounded nice, and he was Lam's friend.

But how could she be sure? She asked a test question, "Who's Katie?"

"Pardon?" The man sounded confused.

"Katie—who is she? I found the name in Lam's phone."

"Katie is Lam's eleven-year-old daughter," the man said. "She was kidnapped last year and I helped get her back."

Tafoya made her decision. "Spectrum Health. Grand Rapids. Room 317. You need to hurry, I think we're in danger!"

The line went dead. Billy Ray called back but got a message saying the call couldn't be completed as dialed.

He tried again. Same result.

Lam was in trouble!

Billy Ray looked around the parking lot. Crime scene tape surrounded the wrecked coach. So did a score of cops and a television news crew.

<===== PIPELINE =====>

On the far side of the lot a bus was preparing to leave. He could get on it, but a bus would be too slow or even heading in the wrong direction. Also, he preferred not to fly in airplanes if he didn't have to.

What to do . . .?

He dug Toiletman's phone from his pocket and dialed the last number.

A gruff voice answered, "Yeah?"

"I got the money from the old folks."

"This ain't Frank. Who da' hell is this?"

"Frank hired me as backup."

The voice cracked a little. "What do you mean, backup?"

"Frank didn't trust the bus driver, and he was right. The greedy bastard shot Frank and the others and robbed the passengers. So I threw his ass off the bus. He's probably bear shit by now."

There was silence. He'd struck a chord.

It was time to drop the hammer.

"Frank shouldn't have trusted you either. What good's a fast car if its driver abandons the team? I got a mind to cut your balls off for that!"

Billy Ray heard nervous breathing through the phone. "But I'll give you another chance to get your split."

The gruff act was over. "What do I have to do for it?"

Billy Ray scanned the area. There was a Starbucks on the corner. "Meet me for coffee outside the Jackpot Tours depot."

"Are you crazy? The place is crawling with cops. I saw them!"

"That's why it's the safest place in town."

"You have stone cojones, dude. How will I recognize you?"

"I'll be wearing a backpack."

"Like, you're the hiker that got picked up!"

"That's right." Billy Ray hung up. No use giving the moron time to think.

Twenty minutes later, a red Camaro pulled into the Starbucks across from the Jackpot Tours depot. The license plate read MAX–616.

Billy Ray held two steaming cups of coffee, just to make it obvious.

The car pulled up and a teenager with purple hair and a nose ring popped his head out of the window.

"Are you the hiker?"

"No. I always use backpacks as a disguise," Billy Ray said with a deep sarcastic tone.

"Ok. So what now?" the kid asked.

"Now you get out and open the trunk so I can put the pack in it."

"Is the money in the pack?"

"What do you think?" Billy Ray stared hard at the junior criminal.

If the punk had any street smarts, he'd pull a gun and demand the cash. But then he would've earned a face full of scalding coffee.

The kid got out of the car and opened the trunk.

Billy Ray held out the coffees. "Mind holding these while I shuck this damn thing off my back? I never knew cash could be so heavy."

The kid took the drinks and Billy Ray set the backpack next to the car.

Purple hair said, "Dude, like, aren't you going to put that in the trunk?"

"No."

Billy Ray punched the wannabe crook in the forehead, managing to save one of the coffees as the moron toppled to the deck.

Then he dumped the kid in the trunk and drove to Michigan.

<== PIPELINE ==>

4

Patient charts . . . a never-ending chore.

Rebecca Payne managed to reduce the pile of charts by half. But like a living, breathing creature, the stack would be back on the morrow. As a clinical psychologist, her work could go on forever.

But it was late, and her head swam with a thousand horror stories from her clients, plus one particular tragedy of her own. She touched a jagged scar on her breast.

Yet it was more than that.

She felt restless—agitated for some reason. She hadn't felt this way since that awful night in Texas, in the pouring rain, wrapped in Billy Ray's arms . . . dying.

It was time to shut down the computer for the night, and her brain too. So she went to the kitchen and poured some brandy, then returned and switched on the television. She hoped for a movie or an episode of her favorite Cold Case Files show, anything to provide a healthy distraction.

The first thing to appear on T.V. was the KIRO News at 11:00. An anchor lady's face filled the screen and announced a developing story. Then the camera cut to a male reporter standing in front of a severely damaged tour bus, while in the background, State Police escorted senior couples into a nearby building.

The reporter pointed to the vehicle and launched his report. He spoke of a deadly crime occurring aboard the bus as it crossed over the Cascade Mountains. According to scant details, the group had fallen victim to an attempted armed robbery while returning from a successful trip to a casino in Yakima.

What little information there was had come from the daughter of a passenger who'd phoned the news desk to report her mother's bus picking up a lone hiker near the summit of Chinook Pass. Then moments later, the bus stopped once again for three supposed stranded motorists who attempted to rob everyone. Remarkably, the lone hiker managed to foil the robbery and kill the alleged villains, including the bus driver who was one of the armed robbers. The hiker proceed to deliver everyone to safety in the badly damaged bus.

In closing, the KIRO reporter aroused viewers' interest by firing off a string of questions. "Who is this mystery hiker? And what was he doing on Mt. Rainier? Is he a lone Samaritan caught in the wrong place at the right time? Or is the hiker a trained killer on the loose?"

With barely a pause, the reporter signed off saying his name really fast, "Jessie Jones."

As the scene on the T.V. faded and the camera panned wide, Rebecca felt the air sucked from her lungs. A familiar figure appeared in the background. It was Billy Ray Jenkins!

HE was the lone Samaritan—

And he'd come for her!

Billy Ray pushed hard on the muscular Camaro.

The getaway car had its advantages—modified engine for speed, equipment for avoiding traffic cops, and slim-to-none chance of ever being reported stolen.

He made the 2,300-mile trip from Seattle to Grand Rapids in twenty-five hours at speeds over a hundred miles per hour. He was bone tired, famished, and sore, having stopped only for gasoline. But there was no way he could be as miserable as the punk in the trunk, whose kicking and banging ended hours ago. Now the kid only sobbed occasionally and called out for his mommy.

Bad kids were the product of bad adults. Billy Ray would love to go slap the parents upside the head, then yank the bullring out of the boy's nose, shave his purple head, and have him in a Marine boot camp before it was too late. Hopefully, the kid would learn from his ordeal.

The lights of Grand Rapids appeared in the distance. Billy Ray decided to ditch the stolen car and call up a ride for the last few miles. He pulled into a Meijer super store on the outskirts of town, parked under a lamp, and switched off the big rumbling motor.

He listened for a few moments until hearing what sounded like a prayer coming from the trunk.

Good enough, he thought then grabbed his pack, tossed the keys on the seat, and walked to a payphone to hail a taxicab. An hour later, a scruffy road-weary Billy Ray Jenkins entered room 317 and scared the crap out of a night shift nurse.

The nurse stared at his crumpled clothes and backpack, then at his scruffy face. After re-hinging her jaw, she said, "Where'd you come from, Mt. Everest? This room is off-limits without authorization."

"Believe me, ma'am, I'm authorized," Billy Ray said testily.

"Show me some identification then."

"Don't have any."

The nurse reached for the bedside telephone. "I'm calling security."

<=== PIPELINE ===>

To her surprise, the phone rang and she jerked her hand back.

"Take the call," Billy Ray said. "I'm a federal agent. The man on the other end will confirm it."

The nurse did so. She listened for a moment then hung up.

"You're authorized," she said and hurried out of the room.

Billy Ray had guessed correctly. Admiral John Dodd was watching and listening. In fact, he was now convinced Dodd had been manipulating him from the start. He flipped open his phone and dialed a number that only a handful of people among humankind possessed.

"Wolverine, how are you?"

"Cut the crap, Dolittle. You shanghaied me!"

A rain squall moved across the waters of the Puget Sound.

Cold water droplets snaked down the glass of Rebecca's bedroom window, and gusting winds animated a cedar branch that scratched repeatedly against the siding.

She twisted and turned under the down comforter. Sleep didn't come easily. It had taken candles, a second glass of brandy, and music. But the alcohol warmed her stomach; the hypnotic flames soothed her restless spirit; and Adele crooned about fire and rain over the stereo.

Visions of Billy Ray filled her pre-dreams—their time alone in Texas, a few precious moments . . . then the tumult of war.

As she drifted further into sleep, dreamy images spiraled crazily, like a movie set on fast-forward.

Deeper she went. And deeper—

. . . *Ever deeper*

To a time when yesterdays and tomorrows become forever
  To a place where dreams and nightmares become one
    Where shadows dance, colors weep, and song becomes illusion
      To Billy Ray and the place of their love

        Then Billy Ray holding her in the rain . . . the cold rain
          Her staring up into the darkness . . . into the rain
            She was dying . . . their love was dying
              She set fire to the rain and let it—

A loud crash!

Rebecca bolted upright in bed. The brandy snifter lay in pieces on the floor. The stereo was off and the room silent, but for the wind and rain.

That dream again!

It'd been a year since Billy Ray kissed her one last time and then walked out of that hospital room. For a number of reasons, she'd ended their relationship. Those reasons no longer seemed to matter.

Not a day passed that she didn't think of him, or a night when she didn't dream of him, of holding him, feeling his strength—his passion.

She was in love with Billy Ray. Nothing in the world could change that. Not her father's loathing. Not her sister having been Billy Ray's first love. Not even a past filled with pain and torment.

And now he'd come for her—she was sure of it!

But where was he, it'd been two days since seeing him on the news. Why hadn't he made contact?

Rebecca went to the living room and switched on the TV, hoping to learn more about the tour bus incident, but only got useless infomercials.

She gave up and went to the kitchen for a cup of tea. A crumpled copy of the Seattle Times lay on the table. Then for the tenth time, she picked it up and read the front-page story about "The Lone Samaritan."

What to do?

Rebecca unplugged her cell phone from the charging unit and made a call. A groggy voice answered, "Hello?"

"Hey there, Shandi. It's Rebecca."

Shandi came more awake. "Is everything okay?"

Dear Shandi, Rebecca thought.

She'd put her college roommate through hell.

But it all worked out in the end as Shandi married Larry Bell, now the Sheriff of Upshur County in Texas, and Rebecca's best friend since childhood.

"All is well. May I speak with Larry?"

Bell came on the line. "Do you know what time it is?"

"Sorry to bother you, Larry. I need a favor."

Bell hesitated. "What is it this time?"

She told him about the incident in Washington State and Billy Ray's involvement. Bell said he'd check on the matter when he got to the office.

Rebecca felt hope rise in her chest. She thanked Bell and hung up.

Tafoya had stayed with Lam as long as she dared.

She hadn't wanted to be discovered in a place off-limits to the public, so she'd returned to her room.

But now what to do? That Wolverine guy said he was on his way, so where was he?

<== PIPELINE ==>

She was being discharged soon and didn't want to lose track of Lam.

His being handsome no longer mattered so much. Rather, she had a few questions for the federal agent, like what did *Authority Over All* mean?

She couldn't sleep, so decided to risk detection anyway and went to check on Lam. The halls were quiet. No one noticed her getting into the elevator, descending to the third floor, or entering his room.

She started toward Lam's unconscious body when a male voice said, "Not another step."

She spun around, mouth wide open, speechless. Standing behind the door was a man with tanned muscular arms, a five day beard, and absorbing hazel eyes. He looked like a homeless bodybuilder.

"What do you want?" the man asked.

"I'm checking on Agent Lam."

Billy Ray nodded at the robe and slippers. "You don't look like a nurse."

Tafoya put her hands on her hips. "Oh yeah, champ? And you don't look like a brain surgeon."

Billy Ray dialed down a notch. "Are you the woman who called me?"

"Is your name Wolverine?"

"No."

"Then I don't know you." She stepped toward the door. The man took a very quick step and blocked her way.

"Wolverine is my callsign. You can call me Billy Ray."

The lady seemed to debate fight or flight, then relaxed. "Tami Tafoya."

"How do you know Lam?"

"I don't—I mean we'd only just met at a crime scene before this happened." She pointed at the hospital bed.

"Are you a cop?" asked Billy Ray.

"No. I'm an investigative reporter."

"Uh oh."

Tafoya dropped her hands from her hips. "Uh oh, what?"

"Lam hates reporters." Then Billy Ray smiled.

She caught the tease. "I noticed. He's a dickhead, if you ask me."

"No need to ask, I already know."

Tafoya explained what had happened since meeting Lam, the women washing up on Lake Michigan beaches, the car accident, and her suspicion that the two could be related.

They moved to Lam's bedside. He was battered and bruised, but alive. Still, there could be no telling how long a coma might last.

Billy Ray said a silent prayer for his friend.

The nurse returned to take Lam's vitals and noticed Tafoya dressed as a patient. Billy Ray nodded. After the nurse's earlier experience, she readily accepted the authorizing gesture and left.

Tafoya noticed the wordless exchange. "Who are you?" She pointed at Lam. "And who is he? You two aren't federal agents . . . at least none I've ever heard of."

"What do you mean?"

Tafoya pulled Lam's special ID from her robe pocket.

Billy Ray studied the leather case then shot Tafoya a very serious look. "You aren't allowed to know this."

"Know what?"

Billy Ray didn't answer Tafoya's question. Instead, he phoned Dodd.

"Now what?" Dodd answered testily.

"You know what. She's seen your fancy identification. That secret crowd of yours can't stay secret forever."

Tafoya flashed Billy Ray a confused look.

"Listen, Dolittle. You'll not harm a single hair on Ms. Tafoya's head. Do I make myself clear?"

Tafoya's eyes got as round as saucers!

Dodd replied, "If I wanted her eliminated she'd already be gone."

"What's your deal, Dolittle? And as long as I got you on the line, why'd you make me disappear? I told you I didn't want to work for you."

"Lam said the same thing. But as you can see, he's come to the light."

"What light? Lam's in a damn coma!"

Dodd let out an audible breath. "Bad guys have entered the country. I can't tell you more than that unless you agree to work for us."

Billy Ray wanted to throw the phone through the window!

"There's no escaping us, Jenkins. We'll always know where you are."

"If you know so damn much, then find the bad guys yourself!"

"We don't know who they are."

"So you're not such badasses after all," Billy Ray said angrily. "You know *my* every move, yet the guys from the Dark Side have you running in circles chasing your own tails. Is that about the size of it?"

Dodd ignored the barb. "Whoever did this to Lam may not be done."

Billy Ray considered his former SEAL commander, remembering their friendship, even how he saved Dodd's life years ago. Dodd returned the favor in Texas, without whose help a number of hostages would be dead.

He looked from Tafoya to Lam's motionless body, and considered how Dodd had never led him astray.

"Okay, Dolittle. I'll agree to hear more. You'd best make it convincing."

Rebecca's phone rang. It was Bell calling back.

"There's no record of Billy Ray."

"What?" Rebecca was dumbfounded.

"I wouldn't worry your pretty head none. You know how that part of the government works, in the shadows."

"Then how will I find him?"

"He'll find you."

"He already did, Larry. And now he's gone. What am I going to do?"

"Maybe Agent Lam knows where he is."

Rebecca felt hope. "Do you have Lam's number?"

"No." Bell's reply lacked enthusiasm.

They were best friends, more like brother and sister. She'd always had a way of getting Bell to do what she wanted and they both knew it.

"Pretty please, Larry?"

"All right, Rebecca. I'll make some calls. But you'll owe me . . . again."

Dodd briefed Billy Ray on the nation's real and present danger.

The Department of Homeland Security and the FBI had received credible intelligence that an unknown number of al-Qaeda terror cells had illegally entered the country. Furthermore, it was believed those cells were operating under local command and control rather than guided from afar. And who that leader was hadn't been discovered yet. But their intentions were clear—*bring down the Great Satan.*

The collapse of America would throw open the gates to the waiting killers of all infidels. Whether Shia or Sunni was left holding the ultimate jihadi prize, would matter little in the end. Nothing would stop Islam's steady march toward world domination and religious conversation to the one true faith under Allah

"Impressed yet?" Dodd asked.

Billy Ray remembered a Bible story in the Book of Daniel about the hand writing on the wall warning a great nation at that time of its defeat by the Medes and Persians.

Remarkably, the descendants of those same conquerors were back. He hoped the *hand* wasn't back as well to stamp the same message on America's wall, that the great nation had been *weighed and measured and found wanting.*

"Sobering," Billy Ray admitted.

"Truly," Dodd said. "Now if you'll hand the phone to Ms. Tafoya."

Billy Ray did so. "Here. It's for you."

Tafoya looked confused. "Hello?"

"Ms. Tafoya, I'm well aware of who you are. And I watched you rifle through Agent Lam's belongings."

Tafoya looked around the room for hidden cameras.

"I'll say this just once, madam. You'll not reveal what you know to anyone. If you do, or even attempt to, you'll be spirited away and never heard from again. Do I make myself crystal clear?"

Tafoya's face went white!

"Your answer, please—"

"I promise. Who are you, anyway?"

"Do you really want to know?" asked Dodd.

"Yes!" she said defiantly.

"Good. That's why I chose you. Now hand me back to Jenkins."

Billy Ray took the phone.

"Your team is nearly complete, Wolverine."

"What team? Are you playing chess with people's lives again?"

Dodd ignored the question. "You're about to have a visitor."

The phone went dead.

Billy Ray faced Tafoya. "Go get dressed. We've been drafted."

Bell called back to report that Lam was in Grand Rapids.

Rebecca asked, "What's he doing there? Why Michigan?"

To which Bell replied that Lam wasn't doing anything on account of his being in a coma at Spectrum Health Hospital.

She was shocked by the news and immediately called the airlines.

She had to go to Lam. He had risked his own life to save her from a psychopathic killer in Texas.

The sales agent said her timing was perfect. A cancellation had occurred at that very moment for a flight to Grand Rapids.

Rebecca purchased the ticket then packed a carry-on bag and called a cab. She was in the air ninety minutes later.

With a mind so full of dread, reading was impossible during the flight. She thought of Billy Ray and why he hadn't called. Was he locked up because of the tour bus incident? But the State Patrol said they had no record of anyone named Billy Ray Jenkins.

Finding Billy Ray would have to wait. She owed her life to Lam, and needed to go help him.

The two *sicarios* were led by the smiling security guard to an empty office and told to wait.

Duke wasn't getting paid for his brains anymore, and Tito never was. Still, he couldn't help but marvel at the smuggling operation he'd helped to create, and right under the noses of the best intelligence services and law enforcement bodies in the world. Having the Gallinas get control of an American power plant and paper mill had proven ingenious.

The Webster Company provided a massive smuggling pipeline into the United States. Drugs, weapons, and human cargo could be secreted aboard incoming barges and coal trains used for fueling the hungry fires of the power plant's steam generators.

Meanwhile, outgoing freighters and long-haul trucks could deliver legitimate paper goods throughout the land. Hidden among the Webster Company's legal cargo, however, would be cartel contraband, never to draw the attention of law enforcement.

Hector was now the head of the Gallina cartel. The family's *patrón* had disappeared a year ago in Texas, and was presumed dead.

Details surrounding Angel Gallina's death were still a mystery, or so Duke had been told.

Then again, since he was no longer Hector's chief of security, he didn't get updates. He'd been demoted to the role of a hitman and replaced by the guard with the stupid smile.

Duke's thoughts were interrupted by the office door opening, then two stone-faced bodyguards armed with Uzi machine guns entering and positioning themselves behind him and Tito.

A moment later, an impeccably dressed man with a jagged scar running the length of his jaw strode past them and stood behind an ornate cherry wood desk.

Hector Gallina stared at Duke and Tito with eyes the color of death.

Failure to Hector was equal to sloppiness, and sloppiness in their trade brought the curtains down.

Duke felt a chill, like someone stepping on his grave, which may not be far off. No telling what the brute Tito felt, though, probably nothing.

But something Duke was sure about, the meeting would result in one of two outcomes—life or very sudden and painful death.

"You're late," Gallina said in a voice oddly effeminate for a murderer.

Tito began to speak. But Gallina raised a hand, and with it signaled the lifting of the Uzis. Tito shut his mouth.

Gallina continued to stare straight at Duke, the silence palpable.

Frost formed on the back of Duke's neck.

Finally, Gallina asked softly, "Why do they still live?"

Duke wasn't fooled. One wrong word could turn satin into steel.

"I haven't finished the job, Jefe."

"And why not?"

"I believed it was more important to recover the girl's body from the morgue first. If word ever got out who she really was, it could mean war between the cartels. As for that lucky cop and the reporter, I'll finish them off next."

Gallina stared at Duke as if remembering his *sicario* once possessed a brain. Duke hoped not too much of a brain, since showing up the boss could prove equally lethal to that of failing a mission.

"And when will you complete the job?"

Duke felt the frost melt, the question a reprieve. "Immediately, *Jefe.*"

"I should hope so, if you value your life. However, I have another job for you. I want those monsters that killed my women. Bring them to me. You of course remember the men monsters I speak of. It was you who let allowed them escape."

The chill returned. That was the event that had led to his demotion.

A shipment of human *pollos* had come north through the pipeline a year ago. Among the slaves were four men unlike the rest of the poor chickens from Mexico. They were computer experts wishing passage into the United States, claiming to have made a deal with Angel Gallina to work for the cartel. Hector had no knowledge of such an arrangement, but quickly saw the riches that could be made. Hector agreed to help the men on condition they earn their freedom by serving him for one year.

During their time, the men hacked into scores of banks and other businesses, gathered personal information on Hector's enemies, and orchestrated extremely lucrative internet scams.

Then one week shy of the year-long contract, the men disappeared before Hector could renegotiate the terms of their release. Worse yet, they'd taken three cartel women with them, including Hector's favorite, the beautiful young virgin, Mariposa.

Secretly, Mariposa was the unwitting daughter of a rival cartel boss. She'd been placed under the protection of Catholic nuns in a small mining town in Mexico after her birth.

Somehow, Angel Gallina learned of the girl and had her kidnapped from the convent to be presented as a gift to Hector. By his actions, the *patrón* had stabbed the heart of a hated rival while pleasing the heart of a beloved son.

<== PIPELINE ==>

As for the computer experts, Duke had suspected they only pretended to be Latinos. They were brown-skinned and spoke Spanish. However, Duke caught the men one day kneeling on rugs and praying in a strange language. He knew of no Hispanics that worshipped in such a manner.

He reported his suspicions to Hector. But the young *capó* saw only riches pouring in from the computer schemes and chose to ignore the warning. After all, what did it matter ow they prayed so long as the money kept flowing? And now, all three of the women had washed up on Michigan beaches with their throats cut.

Gallina had exploded at the news. Only Duke's warning to Hector had saved his life. But it hadn't kept him from getting demoted, replaced by that prick with the silly grin.

Duke filled with anger. "I'll find these men, *Señor* Gallina."

"I want them alive."

"*Si, Jefe.*"

Hector Gallina left the room. The Uzis followed.

Duke and Tito remained seated until the security guard came for them.

Neither man spoke during their escort to the truck. As Duke drove away, he saw the security guard, the man with his job, standing on the loading dock mocking them.

Tito pounded his palm with a massive fist. "When can I kill the agent and the reporter bitch?"

"You'll have your pleasures with them soon, my friend."

The taxi ride from the Gerald R. Ford International Airport to the hospital in downtown Grand Rapids seemed to take forever.

The short construction season in Michigan meant road crews were out in force. Plus there was the matter of not being allowed to make left turns on most streets, but rather drive past your destination then double back.

The cabbie smiled and explained to Rebecca that it was called a Michigan left. Regardless, the meter ticked away.

They arrived . . . finally. Rebecca paid the driver and got out. But before taking a step, her phone pinged, a text message, *Room 317.* There was no return phone number or other identifiers.

How creepy! Maybe Larry Bell was playing a joke on her.

Rebecca pulled up the handle to her suitcase and wheeled it inside the hospital. She was challenged inside the door by a nurse.

She was no stranger to hospitals. "My patient. Thank you for asking."

Act like you own the place, works every time.

The sign on door 317 prohibited entry to the public so Rebecca performed her own Michigan left by walking past her destination and looking for cameras and hospital staff before doubling back.

At last she tried the door. It was unlocked.

Billy Ray heard the sound of soft footfalls outside the door.
Tafoya had already returned, dressed and ready to leave.
The attending nurse had been told to buzz before entering.
And if it was a lost patient, why creep up to the door?
He motioned to Tafoya for quiet.
As the door inched open, he caught a familiar scent, vanilla and honey.
Then a woman entered the room pulling a suitcase.
"Rebecca?"
She turned around and Billy Ray's heart skipped a beat!
Rebecca dropped her luggage and rushed into Billy Ray's arms.
They hugged tightly . . . a lifeline to the past, a bridge to the future.
Fire for the present.
Billy Ray lifted Rebecca's face and looked into her green eyes. He saw his reflection and kissed her, softly at first, then harder.
Rebecca pressed her lips against his with similar force.

"*Ahem,*" came the sound of Tafoya clearing their throat. "You two should get a room."

Billy Ray and Rebecca lingered a moment longer, their passion once more delayed.

Then they turned and faced Lam's motionless.

<=== PIPELINE ===>

5

While the women talked at Lam's bedside, Billy Ray stepped into the hallway to telephone Dodd. It was time to have a serious conversation.

"You're one devious bastard, Dolittle. You played me!"

"Get used to it, Wolverine. You're becoming quite predictable to us."

Billy Ray felt his blood boil. "Maybe if your group didn't have eyes and ears in every bush and rock, normal people could go about their business in private!"

"Don't kid yourself, Jenkins. You're anything but normal. You're a highly trained and honed tool, and at this point in time, necessary."

Admiral John Dodd was the mastermind behind the K-KEY Group, which operated directly from the Whitehouse under the 100% control of the President. In a previous life, Dodd had been Billy Ray's commanding officer in the Navy SEALs, and his closest friend.

Then came Billy Ray's lost decade.

After his release from prison, Billy Ray returned to East Texas to redeem his life but was met with death instead, the murder of his little brother Ricky. He'd hunted Ricky's killers with a vengeance, and when he needed Dodd most, his Teammate answered the call to arms.

Together, along with Lam and Rebecca, they discovered Ricky's killer and so much more—they uncovered a madman bent on destroying America using a designer drug, called Rapture.

It was then Billy Ray learned of Dodd's secret life leading the K-KEY Group: their wealth, their reach, their possession of weaponry unknown even to battlefield commanders.

He'd witnessed those weapons lay waste to an evil enemy inside our nation's borders, with countless American lives saved, including Rebecca and Lam's daughter.

On the surface, Billy Ray had no problem with saving lives and putting down evil. The problem for him was the K-KEY Group did so irrespective of any formal restraints, operating solely at the pleasure of the President.

After the titanic battle in East Texas, Dodd had requested Billy Ray join the K-KEY Group, where his special skills could be put to good use. He'd flatly turned down the offer, wanting to live out his life in peace, wishing for no master but the One above.

But apparently, what Dodd wants Dodd gets.

"What's going on, Dolittle, and why all the spying?"

"'Spying' has such a bad ringtone. We prefer thinking of it as tracking."

"Tracking what and who?"

"Militant Islam . . . and the next wave in their holy war to kill infidels."

"Yeah, so what's new?" Billy Ray said.

Dodd dropped a bombshell. "POTUS suspended Posse Comitatus. All limits placed on federal armed forces acting in domestic affairs are lifted."

"He's unleased the dogs on our society?"

"Of course not. It's more surgical than that, drones and such. And it's just temporary."

Billy Ray was shocked, pissed, maybe both. By the stroke of a pen everyone's civil rights had been put in jeopardy.

"When?" Billy Ray asked angrily, assuming he was the "and such" part of the equation.

Dodd didn't hesitate. "Last year, the moment we learned what was happening in East Texas."

"But that was a whole year ago!" Billy Ray exclaimed. "That doesn't sound 'temporary' to me, sir. Plus Texas had nothing to do with Islamic terrorism, or public insurrection."

"No, but it provided the President with political cover he felt necessary to make the hard call. Besides, evil is evil, my friend. And there's a whole lot more of it coming down the pike."

"How odd," Billy Ray observed. "Why doesn't anyone seem to notice?"

Dodd let out a long breath. "I could say it's because the Presidential Directive was born classified and signed in secret so that it wouldn't appear in the Federal Register. Or I could point out that all military actions are being prosecuted by a very select few individuals. But let's be real about life in America, shall we. Even if regular channels were used in this case, we both know the country shows more interest in keeping up with the Kardashians than national security. Besides, who out there believes what they read in the press anymore?"

"If you're referring to people pursuing happiness, it's called freedom."

"Don't be a smartass, Wolverine."

Billy Ray cut to the chase. "Why is our government forcing us to choose between our liberty and our safety?"

Dodd was blunt. "We've uncovered an al-Qaeda plot to explode radiological bombs somewhere in the Midwest."

Dirty bombs? Billy Ray checked his hearing. Now the President's actions made more sense. "Where'd al-Qaeda get nuclear material?"

"We don't know . . ." Dodd's voice trailed off.

"Let me get this straight. You and your secret band of businessmen, lone rangers, patriots, and warfighters possess deep pockets, space-age weapons, and intelligence-gathering capabilities unparalleled in human history, not to mention having a willing President. Yet you can't find a few bad actors?"

<======= PIPELINE =======>

Dodd's silence was tantamount to an admission, or maybe Dodd was playing him, still dead-set on recruiting him to their secret war on terror in America.

Billy Ray felt incredulous and pressed the matter further, "And now your pals want me to find these terrorists because, despite the nationwide anal exam from a mass surveillance program, you haven't the foggiest idea where they are. Moreover, one of your agents is lying here in a coma and you don't know who's targeting him."

"Not bad for a knuckle dragger," Dodd replied.

"Oh yeah? I seem to remember dragging your half-dead knuckles out of that jungle in Panama. And now you're expecting me to work for a group that goes against something I hold most dear, my freedom!"

"No!" Dodd lost his cool for the first time Billy Ray could ever recall. "I expect you to work for your country! I expect you to button up your big boy pants and go save lives! I expect you to pretend, if that's what it takes. Just get the job done, sailor!"

The phone went quiet while heads cooled.

Dodd went first, "National security trumps liberty. What good is free expression and cultural fads if you're dead? You know better than most, Wolverine, that modern belligerents are conducting asymmetric warfare. Their happiness depends on blowing us 'infidels' all to hell. They're willing to sacrifice themselves so they can touch the face of Allah and get their 72 virgins. It's sad that no one told them the their virgins are all guys!"

Billy Ray couldn't disagree with that, except that a few women and children had joined the murdering ranks of 'virgins.' Such cult-of-death concepts were foreign to most freedom-loving Americans.

Dodd wasn't finished.

"Jihad isn't winding down, pal, it's just getting started. Even if we had time to mobilize the country's police forces, their standard of training would fail to adequately protect the public. So I believe POTUS made the right call by implementing military rule. Better still, he did it quietly . . . painlessly."

"Are you telling me freedom's just an illusion?"

"Face it, Jenkins, we're all pretenders one way or another."

The call ended.

Billy Ray noted how Dodd sounded genuinely scared. And that gave him a chill. History's pages were filled with frightened leaders during frightening times producing frightening results. And so were the cemeteries of those who followed those leaders.

He'd need to tread carefully while working for the K-KEY Group.

Rasul stood in front of a full-length mirror inspecting his naked form.

He'd just completed *wudu,* the ceremonial bathing process required in the Quran to ensure that his prayers to Allah would be valid, and his young body an acceptable sacrifice.

Rasul had cleansed himself vigorously and then shaved off all of his body hair.

There was still the small pimple on his nose, but that blemish would be gone by the day of his journey to paradise.

He'd been a vigilant student at his madrassa, eager to learn the strict ways of Islam and its holy struggle to cleanse the world by Jihad.

He was happy to be a sharp tool in Allah's Holy War against the enemies of perfection. To help in that effort, his faith allowed for living among human swine without fear of sin, even to deny Allah outwardly if necessary.

It was called *Taqiyya,* and it allowed him to lie, cheat, steal, or profane his bodily temple so long as his heart held the real truth.

Dispensation for those 'outward' sins would be granted at the moment of his martyrdom, when he became a witness to Allah's glory, a *shahid,* and entered his place in paradise.

The time approached when the whole world would be cleansed by Allah. But first must be the Americans.

He looked forward to the end of days. For dwelling among the infidel left him feeling stained—living as they lived, polluting himself as they polluted themselves—all necessary to rid the world of this heinous evil.

Insha'Allah.

Rasul always felt good again after cleansing. For the Quran instructed, "Allah . . . loves those who keep themselves pure and clean."

It was now time to offer the *Salah,* Islamic prayers.

Rasul gave a last look at his body.

Satisfied, he dressed, went to the bedroom, and spread his prayer rug on the floor in the direction of Mecca.

Then he prostrated himself and prayed to the One True God.

Nearly everyone turned their heads to see the intimidating truck. Camouflage paint, a double row of halogen lights mounted above the cab, a gun rack festooning the rear window, and two beefy passengers resembling Detroit Lions offensive linemen inside—how could they not notice it?

Duke cursed. The truck was nothing he would've chosen for the hits.

<====== PIPELINE ======>

Then again, he was no longer in charge. Yet, what was Gallina's new security chief thinking? Was the prick trying to get him killed, or worse, arrested? Death Duke could accept, life in a cage he could not.

Or maybe it was all just a joke to the guy, which would explain why the bastard was always grinning when he and Tito drove up.

Duke chose a parking spot near a line of dumpsters at the south end of the Spectrum Health Medical Center, beyond the line of sight of security cameras and away from curious pedestrians.

Now dressed in nursing assistant scrubs, Tito got out and went to rendezvous with their contact inside the hospital. It had been impossible to find scrubs to fit the giant, until the matter was solved by one of Gallina's women who made a uniform out of large bed sheets.

Tito now looked like a California king mattress with a brown ugly head popping out the top.

Duke had considered disguising himself as a doctor but rejected the idea since not many doctors looked like NFL linemen. But in the end, he chose a tailored suit, leather shoes, and a colorful bouquet of flowers, believing it best to hide in plain sight.

Duke exited the truck and headed for the main entrance.

The plan was for Tito to proceed to the FBI agent's room with orders to bathe the patient. Once alone with the target, he would break the fed's neck and escape.

And if plan 'A' failed, it would be Duke's job to put two slugs in the cop's head with a silenced .22 caliber pistol hidden in the flowers, and then escape before the nursing station could react to a flat-lining patient.

Billy Ray returned to the bedside next to Rebecca. Her eyes were full of worry for Lam.

Tafoya stood opposite them softly stroking Lam's arm. The monitors showed no change. Though Lam's vitals held steady, so did the coma.

Billy Ray announced, "Time to go. Dodd thinks another attempt will be made on Lam's life."

"You used that name last year in Texas," Rebecca said. "Who is Dodd, and what does he have to do with Johnny, or with you for that matter?"

"These guys are secret agents," Tafoya blurted. "And Dodd's the Wizard of Oz, only way worse. He's everywhere!" She looked all around the room.

Rebecca was more confused than ever.

"She's right, Dodd's the invisible man behind the curtain. He was my CO in the SEALs and now he's our new boss."

"Let's drop the drama. What's going on?" Rebecca demanded.

Billy Ray explained who Dodd was and his role in the group being run directly by the guy who sits in the big chair in the White House

Rebecca's eyes narrowed. "You mean like, THE President?"

"And he threatened me," Tafoya said. "He can't do that, I have rights."

A voice from the bed said, "No threat, Ms. Tafoya, it's a surety. Your rights have been temporarily suspended."

Both women looked down in shock.

The voice hadn't come from Lam. Rather, it issued from the intercom clipped to the pillow. It was Dodd.

Billy Ray rolled his eyes.

So much for dispensing with drama. Dodd was a genius who also owned a sick sense of humor.

The tinny voice continued out of the monitor, "Dr. Allan works for the K-KEY Group. He says it's okay to move Agent Lam. So all of you get out of there. I've arranged for a safe house on the coast, one I'm sure you'll all approve of."

Tafoya leaned toward the patient monitor. "What about transportation? Surely you don't expect us to load Lam's body on a city bus, do you?"

Dodd dropped all formality. "Don't push my buttons, Tafoya. I'm sure Wolverine can figure something out."

The monitor went silent and then Billy Ray's cell phone pinged. It was a text message with an address.

"What just happened?" asked Rebecca.

"I'll fill you in at the safe house," Billy Ray said. He turned to Tafoya. "It's time you put your special skills to work. We need transportation."

"Like what?"

"Hey, lady, Michigan's your sandbox. Rent us a car or something."

"That'd take too long. Besides, how do we get that," she pointed at Lam's hospital bed, "into a vehicle?"

An idea struck Billy Ray. "An ambulance—! We'll need disguises. Wait here, I'll go find what we need."

Tafoya stopped him.

"You're a mess, Jenkins. People will think you wandered in from the back alley."

"Gee, thanks—"

Tafoya turned on her heels and left the room.

Billy Ray returned to Rebecca's side. He wanted to talk. He wanted to hold her. He wanted to do so much more.

But these walls had ears. . . and eyes.

An equipment cart awaited Tito inside a rear maintenance door.

It contained bathing supplies, a clipboard with schedules, and a formal ID badge, all placed there by a hospital employee on Gallina's payroll.

Tito clipped the ID to his uniform then pushed the cart to the elevator.

As the elevator doors opened, several medical staff backed up against the wall, stunned by Tito's mass and his gruesome face.

He could never get used to people staring at him as if he was a freak. Or worst still, when people called him stupid.

He hated that!

To keep from ripping their tiny heads off, Tito made himself think of kittens and then gave everyone a happy smile.

The gawkers looked at his ID, then at the nursing cart, and his presence was accepted. It made Tito feel important.

And really, really smart, too.

"Poor Johnny," Rebecca said looking at Lam's serene face.

Billy Ray inspected his friend. Lam had taken a hard knock. But except for bruising along the side of the face, there was no visual damage. Blunt force trauma inside Lam's head was the culprit.

Dr. Allan's report provided good news. Monitor readouts of brain activity indicated Lam should recover fully. Regaining consciousness, however, would be entirely up to Mother Nature.

Billy Ray could see Lam's eyes moving beneath the lids.

Surely his friend would be all right. *Surely.*

Rebecca's arm came around him, it felt warm and reassuring.

Just then their peace was disturbed by the sound of something large and metallic thumping against the hospital room door.

Billy Ray moved behind the door a split second before it came open. He fully expected to see Tafoya returning from the scavenger hunt.

It wasn't her.

An equipment cart rolled into the room pushed by a mountain of a man dressed in white hospital clothing. Why hadn't the hospital staff warned them before entering as requested?

The door closed, exposing Billy Ray's position.

The giant orderly spun around, light on his feet for such a large man.

Then in a voice abnormally high-pitched said, "You surprised me!"

Steroids? Billy Ray wondered.

He stepped forward. "What do you want?"

"I'm here to bathe the patient."

Billy Ray read the man's badge. "Couldn't you do that later, Tito?"

Tito pushed the cart next to Lam's bed. "Sorry, orders are orders. This'll only take a few minutes. Please wait in the lobby."

Billy Ray didn't like it. Rebecca caught his look and then paused to read the nurse's instructions on the whiteboard before leaving the room.

"I wonder why they did that," she wondered aloud as she caught up with Billy Ray.

"Did what?" he asked.

"Lam's bath. It's not scheduled until this evening."

Billy Ray stiffened. Just then his phone rang. It was Dodd. He didn't need to take the call. He already knew what it was about.

"Hurry, find Tafoya. I'm going after that orderly."

Billy Ray rushed back to Lam's room. As he reached for the doorknob, there was the sound of a deadbolt locking into place.

He knocked. No answer.

And so he knocked harder. Again only silence.

He grabbed his phone.

Dodd was already talking as it flipped open. "He's going after Lam. Get in there, Wolverine!"

"The Door's locked. I'll find a key."

"No time!" Dodd shouted. "The window—I'll distract him!"

"His name's Tito!" Billy Ray yelled into the phone as he ran into the adjacent room to Lam's, thankful for it being empty.

He rushed to the window. Solid thermal pane . . . non-opening.

Damn!

Billy Ray yanked the dive knife from the ankle sheath, flipped it around, and banged the pommel hard against the glass.

Nothing, only a ding!

Dodd must've been watching through some device in the room, probably the TV, because his voice erupted through the patient monitor on the empty bed. "Score it first. Hurry, the killer's at Lam's bed!"

Billy Ray grabbed a bottle of lotion from the bedside table and smeared four lines in the shape of a rectangle. Then he pressed the sharp point of the hardened titanium against the glass and scored along the lubrication.

Next he grabbed a pillow from the bed and pushed against the glass.

Snap!

A square section of the window came loose. He slid the piece aside and repeated the process on the outer pane, which fell into the bushes below. Then he crawled through the hole onto a narrow ledge and cut Lam's window.

<====== PIPELINE ======>

As he worked at scoring the outer pane, he could hear Dodd's voice inside Lam's room trying to distract the killer and buy more time.

That was his chance.

He scored the interior pane and pushed with all his might. The glass gave way and he tumbled into Lam's room.

But before Billy Ray could stand, a massive bear paw smacked him on the head. At least he thought it was a bear, it was hard to tell through the fog and ringing in his ears.

Instinct forced his next move. He rolled under Lam's bed, both saving his life and allowing time to clear the cobwebs. Then he saw two colossal feet shift on the floor and a massive hand reach down and grab his ankle.

Billy Ray was ripped from under the bed like a ten cent rag doll. As his body slid helplessly along the cold tile floor, he spotted the dive knife, grabbed ahold of it, and speared Tito's wrist.

The big man let out a hideous cry!

With his free hand, Tito grabbed the hospital bed and flipped it over.

Billy Ray barely managed to avoid the avalanche. The noise of the crashing bed filled the room, followed by an object clattering on the tile and then a sickening *thud.*

Lam's body hitting the floor?

Dead or alive, Billy Ray had no way of knowing, or any chance to find out, because a huge boot came crashing down on his midsection. Only a last-second squirm prevented his ribs from being pulverized.

But now he was pinned against the wall with a human mountain about to come down on top of him.

Just then a woman yelled out, "Try picking on me, you stupid *puto!*"

It was Tafoya!

She was dressed in a doctor's smock with a stethoscope dangling around her neck. She was pointing at the killer with one hand while keeping the other one hidden in a pocket.

Surprisingly, the giant quit his Irish tap dance atop Billy Ray and turned to face Tafoya, blood oozing from his wrist.

"I've been looking for you, puta. Now I kill you and that cop."

Tafoya's eyes glowed. "Go ahead and try, *madre chingar.* I'll beat your stupid ass with just one hand!"

The killer roared. "No one calls me stupid!"

"I just did. Boy, you really are stupid." Tafoya slapped her hip like a downtown hooker. "You want some of this or what?"

Billy Ray could hardly believe his eyes—or ears! Tafoya was a she-cat, or maybe she was the biggest fool he'd ever met.

Either way, she'd just saved his life.

The beast charged, hands raised to choke the life out of Tafoya. Blood dripped across the floor from the knife wound in his wrist.

Billy Ray sprang to his feet and jumped on Tito's back. He tried getting an arm around the oak tree-sized neck but was tossed to the floor with barely a shrug of the big man's shoulders.

Lady Fortune blew Billy Ray a kiss by landing him next to the dive knife. He grabbed the blade, sprang back to his feet, and took the fight to the enemy.

He was too late.

The killer stepped toward Tafoya.

But that had been the moment she was waiting for and pulled her hidden hand from the pocket.

She held a Taser, and not the kind allowed for public use, but a police model. She pointed the device and pulled the trigger.

Nothing. Nada. Zip. The instrument hadn't been charged!

Tito snarled like a wild animal and struck Tafoya in the head, knocking her to the floor. Then he reached down, seized her by the neck with his bear-like paws, and prepared to finish his helpless prey.

Now it was Billy Ray's turn to save Tafoya. He stepped forward and thrust his knife three inches deep in the giant's butt-cheek!

The knife produced another screech from the killer, but did nothing to stop what came next. Tito spun around, dropping Tafoya. Then he grabbed Billy Ray around the middle with massive arms and began squeezing the life out of him.

The pressure mounted on Billy Ray's spine, with the pain becoming unbearable. He tried stabbing with the knife, but his hands were pinned too tightly at his side, and it dropped harmlessly to the floor.

He felt consciousness slipping.

He may have heard Rebecca shouting, and may have seen people in the hallway. He couldn't be sure.

Only seconds remained before he'd be made a cripple for life, if he lived at all. Then suddenly, three thunderous explosions filled the room, followed by the smell of sulfur!

The crushing sensation around Billy Ray's middle eased.

A fourth gunshot rang out!

Tito's arms dropped away and the brute toppled over, dead, much of his head now splattered on the far wall.

Billy Ray looked to where the gunshots had come from.

Lying prone on the floor, partly buried beneath an overturned hospital bed, Lam gripped his Bureau-issued Glock 21 in two steady hands. Smoke curled up from the gun barrel.

<====== PIPELINE ======>

The hallway crowd had hit the deck when the shooting began, except for a tall businessman holding a colorful bouquet. He tossed the flowers on the floor and ran off like a scared rabbit.

Rebecca rose off the floor and hurried to Billy Ray's side.

A nurse rushed in to aid Tafoya.

And finally, a uniformed guard arrived, gun drawn, to secure the room . . . the cavalry late as usual.

Billy Ray inspected the carnage in the room. The place was a wreck. And a dead assassin lay on the floor in a pool of blood and visceral matter.

He turned to Lam. "'Bout damn time you woke up!" he said and grinned from ear to ear.

He and Tafoya would nurse bruises, Lam, too. But they were alive.

Nonetheless, if Tito was any indication of what came next, they'd best not book any dream vacations just yet.

Billy Ray almost wished for the good ol' days of facing down diabolical geniuses with hard-ons for world domination.

Maybe Dodd was right—*he should learn to pretend.*

Duke hurried away from the Spectrum Health Hospital.

He cussed the entire time until reaching Interstate 196 toward Muskegon. He cussed Tito, he cussed the smiling guard, he cussed the cop, and he cussed Hector Gallina.

Tito had blown the operation, and there'd been nothing he could do to help, or eliminate the targets himself.

He'd been gathered in the hallway with a group of shocked hospital staff. So when the shooting began, and Tito's brains got spread on the wall by that damn FBI agent, he'd made a run for it.

Why hadn't they been warned about the others in Lam's room? And what of the agent being armed?

Gallina's mole had reported the cop was unguarded and in a coma.

And who was the stocky guy that cut his way through the hospital windows? The man showed extreme capabilities.

Duke had seen such skills before during his time in the Army, twenty years ago, prior to killing his commanding officer and ending up in Leavenworth prison. The bastard Army Captain had gotten greedy, demanding more cash to look away while Duke stole weapons for the Gallina family. So the man was paid a broken neck instead.

At his court-marshal, Duke claimed the death resulted from an altercation with his CO after catching the man stealing Army equipment.

He ended up being cleared of a capital crime. However, the Army still took a dim view toward enlisted soldiers turning on the officers, regardless the reason.

He still ended up getting a dozen hard years in a cage at the US Disciplinary Barracks in Fort Leavenworth.

But at least one good thing had come out of Kansas. Tito had been his cell mate.

After gaining his freedom, Hector gave him a chance to prove himself.

And he did, eventually rising to take charge of all security matters for the family. He'd even been allowed to bring Tito into the fold.

Duke owed his life to Hector. So how could he repay his benefactor with yet another failure?

Surely the Uzis would be waiting to zero their debt.

He needed a plan or he would end up just as dead as Tito.

Duke turned off the interstate. Why run headlong to his death by reporting empty-handed? He'd find those Arabs, or whatever they were, just as Gallina ordered. Only then did he stand a chance to save himself.

His only hope was results.

It was nightfall by the time Billy Ray parked the "borrowed" ambulance under the RV port of a magnificent mansion located on a private beach in Holland.

It was the kind of house only a billionaire could afford.

The K-KEY Group had deep pockets indeed.

The only greeting at the mansion's front door came from a tri-color Australian shepherd dog. Otherwise, the place was deserted.

The ladies assisted him getting the cumbersome hospital gurney inside the luxurious home, then into an elevator and to an upstairs bedroom. Together, they transferred Lam's dead weight onto a massive heart-shaped bed.

Dr. Allan had prescribed a sedative for Lam, who in turn argued that he'd been sleeping for three days and wasn't tired. The doctor countered by declaring it was Lam's brain that was tired. To which Billy Ray heartily agreed with a wry smile and got chewed out by the ladies.

But Lam did need rest, and now lay fast asleep.

They stood beside their friend's still body resting atop the unusual bed, thankful for knowing that he would be safe and sound.

Billy Ray had only seen a heart-shaped bed on TV. This one had red satin sheets and pink pillows, plus a set of silk pajamas set flat on either side of the mattress, needing only human occupants to animate them.

<===== PIPELINE =====>

He could hardly wait to bust Lam's chops over the sexy furniture and Liberace sleepwear.

Tafoya was impressed by the bed. "I've always wanted one of these! How about I stay with Lam while you round up some food. I'm starving."

Rebecca tugged on Billy Ray's hand. "I need to eat, too," she said.

They left Tafoya alone with Lam and scouted a trail to the kitchen.

The home was absolutely stunning. Each room was more spectacular than the last, including a grand ballroom lit by a massive Dale Chihuly glass chandelier. The exotic hand-blown glass radiated a kaleidoscope of color, which got Rebecca excited. While Billy Ray's big thrill came with seeing a custom dining table that sat twenty people, his thought being that a table so long could only mean lots of vittles in the kitchen.

No MRE's in this fridge, he bet himself and won the jackpot. There was a walk-in cooler with everything a starving man could want.

After running a plate of chow up to Tafoya, he hustled back to Rebecca and a heaping sandwich, and then dug in.

"I wonder who lives here," Rebecca said, finishing off a cob salad.

"Nobody," Billy Ray replied between bites. "Dodd told me it's a corporate house used only by special guests."

Rebecca set down her empty plate and stepped between Billy Ray and his dinner, a perilous maneuver had anyone else tried it.

She put her arms around him and said sweetly, "We're special."

Billy Ray lost all thought of food. He tossed away the half-eaten sandwich and wrapped his arms around Rebecca.

She nuzzled against his neck. Her hot breath flowed along his skin like lava, igniting a far-deeper craving inside of him.

Heat radiated through Rebecca's sheer blouse.

Billy Ray felt his own heat rising . . . swelling.

Rebecca looked into his eyes. "What now?"

Billy Ray's body felt ready to catch fire. They'd never made love. Death and hatred had blocked the way.

But not this time!

Billy Ray stared into Rebecca's lush green eyes, unable to get enough of her presence, powerless to suppress the primal hunger raging in his soul, and incapable of wanting anything else but her.

"'What next'?" he repeated her question. "A full moon. A billion stars. And just the two of us."

"Are we in danger?" She asked, referring to a time when worldly concerns had interrupted their passion.

"Not this night."

Billy Ray covered Rebecca's mouth with his.

He felt her firm breasts press against his muscular chest.

Then he ran his hands down her sides, guiding by her elegant curves, filling his hands with the gifts of her feminine form.

She returned the favor, lifting his shirt and pulling her warm hands across his flesh, then raking her fingernails down his muscular back.

Their breathing pulsed.

FASTER! . . . HEAVIER!

They tore at one another's clothing.

Each item dropped to the stone tiles.

Then their naked bodies pressed together.

Billy Ray ran his lips down Rebecca's neck until she purred with desire.

He wanted her so badly that he swiped aside the food and dishes, then lifted her onto the countertop . . . to take her . . . at long last—

He stopped.

Rebecca stared, cheeks flush, a look of wanting. Her body was ready, as was his.

He lifted her off the counter. "Not here like this. We deserve better."

Then he led Rebecca through the mansion and to a special place.

Their bodies shimmered as they passed under the Chihuly chandelier. They glowed beneath a full moon outdoors. And their feet swished across warm sugar sands, passing a cabana with a wide soft mattress. Finally, they arrived at the water's edge of the private beach. Then they waded into the water and wrapped up in each other's arms, pressing flesh together—molding, fitting. Becoming one body.

Billy Ray tilted back his head. Rebecca followed his gaze.

"I promised you the moon," he offered humbly.

"And a billion stars," she replied breathlessly.

The August moon cast silvery beams upon their bare skin. Countless stars sparkled in the heavens. All seemed magical, as if the world were a stage, and they the only actors upon it.

They returned their attention to one another and kissed . . . delicately.

The signal.

Billy Ray lifted Rebecca in his strong arms and carried her to the cabana. Then he set her down on soft linen and joined her.

She moved to accept his shape.

Billy Ray searched this beautiful woman's eyes. A message flash across her soul, brighter than the moon, more glorious than all the stars in the sky—she would be forever his, and he forever hers.

Then, at long last, the fire began.

And they let it burn!

PART TWO

Enemies Within The Gates

6

Tafoya awoke and immediately thought of Lam.

His butt was parked about three car lengths away on the monstrous bed where he hadn't moved an inch all night.

She wondered if that K-KEY Group doctor with the handsome mug had given him elephant tranquilizers.

She moved across the bed and studied Lam's serene face. He was definitely a handsome guy. His wavy black hair was soft, his face medium brown, a mixture of French and . . .? Lam hadn't said. She assumed African-American. His body was long and well-muscled, certainly athletic, and not a half-bad dancer either. Perhaps if he got out more.

She peeked under the thin sheet covering him and wondered what it would be like to lay close to him. Maybe it was just a school girl crush, but there'd been that electrifying moment, those fleeting few seconds in his arms after finishing at Captain Jim's—he'd felt like no other man ever had in her life.

Then again, who was she kidding, there hadn't been many others. In fact, there'd been a grand total of two!

She'd been a good Catholic girl in high school, so that was out.

Her first lover was that charming guy, Magic Hands Mike, in her senior year at Michigan State. But he'd gone on to practice dentistry somewhere in Pennsylvania.

Why couldn't ole Magic Hands have chosen some place tropical!

And then there was the producer at her first reporter job in Lansing.

What a joke!

But the joke was on her—never, ever, sleep with the boss.

And since then, no action. Not that she wanted action, or didn't want action, or . . . whatever.

She wasn't a virgin, though not far from it, if that even made sense, like someone being only a little pregnant. But in terms of romance, she was the nun's bloomers—stone cold untouched.

Tafoya stared at Lam. *Damn he was gorgeous!*

She could almost overlook how much of a dickhead he was.

Okay, maybe she'd also been a twit when they first met. Regardless, she hoped for another chance. Then she remembered Lam was working for *them,* and that she'd been 'shanghaied.' Whatever that meant.

All she knew was that a secret government agency, and *pinga numero dos,* Dodd . . . or whatever his name, wanted her to perform some kind of service to her country.

But wasn't she doing that already, as a crime scene reporter, digging dirt on criminals and chasing down murderers, kidnappers, and thieves? She may not possess the power to arrest people, like Lam, but she didn't need it, either. If her research showed a person had committed a crime, she could try the scumbag in the court of public opinion.

Oh sure, scumbags were supposed to be innocent until proven guilty in a court of law, by a jury of his peers . . . blah, blah, blah. However, if she thought a creep was guilty of a heinous act, she had no qualms about jamming a microphone in his face and a camera up his *culo.*

The public had a right to know!

A clock chimed somewhere in the mansion, bringing Tafoya's mind back on-camera. She switched focus to the new day then stopped—

What was she to do?

She'd been forbidden to call anyone: not family, not friends, not even her hairdresser. That one really pissed her off!

Above all, she wasn't to contact the media, including her employers at the Channel 13 Newsroom. That Dodd fellow had said she was "off the grid" so stay off the phone.

But some things were just unacceptable.

She tested her phone anyway. It refused to boot up, as if it had a mind of its own.

She finally gave up and decided to shower and do her nails instead.

Tafoya finished dressing. Before leaving the bedroom of her dreams, she cast a final look at Lam. Then she padded down the stairs to go find Jenkins and Payne.

She eventually found the kitchen—by way of Carnegie Hall and the Queen's dining room. What awaited her there nearly gave her a heart attack! Food and dishes were strewn about on the countertop and the floor. And there were clothes strewn on the floor as if discarded quickly.

Then it made picture-perfect sense. Unless Jenkins and Payne were abducted by aliens who liked naked people, it was evident they'd gone off to make rabbits.

Hell, they'd nearly went for it in Lam's hospital room!

There was just so much she didn't know about these people, or even why they had all ended up together in the first place.

More questions for dickhead #2, if she ever spoke to him again—

"Good morning, Ms. Tafoya."

Another heart attack! She spun around, but no one was in the room.

<== PIPELINE ==>

Laughter filled the air. "You still don't get it."

It was *him,* The Great And All Powerful Oz, Dodd . . . whatever!

She put hands on hips, pissed for being spied on . . . and whether that had included her private activities.

"What is this, the Robin's Nest?" she said derisively.

"Something like that, Ms. Tafoya. I know what you're thinking, and the answer is, *NO.* I was not watching you lying next to Agent Lam."

Tafoya blushed. "Then how do you know that much?"

"Just drop it. I don't spy on folks during their personal matters."

"But you could!"

"Yes, lady, I could. But I won't and don't. You'll just have to trust me."

"Ha!" Tafoya mocked. "You . . . the government . . . want trust? Then how about you start by answering a few of my questions."

"In due time my dear. Right now, I want you to gather your teammates for a teleconference that will begin in exactly one hour."

"Teammates?"

Dodd paused, likely rolling his eyes. "Jenkins and Payne, they're down at the beach cabana. And Tafoya—"

"Yeah?"

"The matter's most urgent. Take it seriously."

The house, or voice, went silent.

Tafoya gathered up the piles of clothing and headed for the beach.

They'd chosen a perfect time and place. Every element in nature had conspired to present the most perfect night of their lives—a full moon, soft sand, a gentle breeze, and quiet waves lapping on the shore.

They'd made love until exhaustion forced an end to their passion.

At dawn's first light, Billy Ray woke Rebecca with soft caresses and then carried her into the fresh blue-green waters of Lake Michigan. They held each other, partly for warmth, but mostly to absorb the wonder all around them.

After bathing, they returned to the cabana and folded up in each other's arms; the sound of their beating hearts communicating their joy, their love.

Time had no meaning.

Time . . .

Golden rays of sunshine streaked across the morning sky.

Seagulls circled in the blue heavens above or floated on the rolling surface of the lake. A sailboat drifted lazily past on the horizon.

Billy Ray wanted only this place, this time, and this woman to comprise his world. For out there, out in the world, hatred stalked each new day—probing, fouling, spoiling . . . rotting.

The Devil's due.

So much pain had come and gone in his life, so many battles. How many more awaited him, and now Rebecca too, out there, in the world?

Billy Ray's thoughts were interrupted—

"Yoo-hoo! Are you guys decent?"

"Hold on!" he shouted back to Tafoya.

Rebecca covered with the bed sheet, while Billy Ray managed to flip on his stomach a split second before Tafoya rounded the corner.

"Nice cheeks, Jenkins. The gym?"

"Prison—" Billy Ray caught the mistake and said, "What is it, Tafoya?"

She laid the pile of clothes on the corner of the bed and said, "Dodd wants us on a teleconference in one hour. He said it's urgent."

Rebecca made a sad groan, the meaning clear.

The world had found them.

The men who killed Hector's girls were imposters, Duke had no doubt.

But then who wasn't an imposter among the thousands of humanity smuggled into America through the Gallina pipeline? There was just too much profit to be made trafficking in warm bodies.

Most of the illegals were innocent working stiffs wishing a better life in America for themselves or their families.

But not all. There were also whores and thieves among the human traffic. Stranger still, had been a person in a full black burqa, like those worn by devout Muslim women, covering the entire body and a mesh screen over the eye slot.

It was impossible to tell if it was a man or woman, especially due to the person speaking through a trachea mic.

The person in black reminded Duke of a cast member from Phantom of the Opera but sounded like Darth Vader when they spoke.

The mystery only deepened when the masked person delivered a letter to Hector claiming to be written in Angel Gallina's own hand.

What the elder Gallina had said in the letter, Hector never revealed to Duke. Nor did Duke ever see the stranger again.

Worst among the human shipment were those planning to reduce the United States to a pile of smoldering ashes in the name of Allah. The fact that the four men were Middle Easterners, posing as Mexicans, hadn't bothered Hector. He figured their money was as good as anyone else's.

Only when the imposters stole Hector's property did everything change.

But by then it was too late for Duke, and Hector took away his job.

It was no secret that Hector's father had had grandiose plans for controlling the entire American drug market. But what role these imposters were to play in that scheme had disappeared with Angel Gallina.

The great man was dead, and so too his plan for America.

Or was it?

Duke attacked the question.

Why did these Middle Easterners choose to enter the U.S. using the Gallina pipeline? What did the Gallinas offer that the other cartels did not? And most importantly, what sorts of criminal endeavors interested these men?

Duke considered a link between the imposters and the tanker truck filled with Rapture, since both had arrived in Michigan at the same time.

He'd been at Hector's side the night Angel Gallina told his son to expect a shipment of a new drug that would be the key to controlling the American market. There'd been no mention of Muslim players before the elder Gallina's phone disconnected suddenly. And that was the last anyone heard from the *patrón*.

The shipment did arrive. But due to Hector being in the dark about the product, how to process and profit from it, he ordered the tanker hidden while his chemists worked to understand the mysterious new chemical.

A wise precaution, Duke thought at the time. Nevertheless, disposing of a ten-thousand-gallon tanker posed no small problem, particularly one filled with a substance so hotly pursued by the government. He happened on a solution while building a hunting cabin on his Meauwataka property near Cadillac, claiming on the building permit that the massive container was an environmentally-friendly septic tank. Bribe money made it true.

Duke rubbed his chin deep in thought. He'd watched the men for months. They hadn't been the least bit interested in the drug trade, rather focusing their attention hacking into various computer systems. Offhand, that suggested the imposters' arrival simultaneous with the Rapture was coincidental. And if so, what else could the men be interested in? And why the Gallinas instead of other cartels?

What was it about the Gallina pipeline?

He played a hunch and booted up his computer.

Then he accessed the private server through which the imposters had performed their work. It took the rest of the day, but he finally hit on the connection—power.

These men were professional hackers and much more. They'd ripped off more than bank accounts and credit card numbers while working for Hector. They hacked into American power plants and federal agencies.

The Webster Power Plant and Paper Mill had been the nexus!

But one power plant in particular tripled Duke's heartrate—the Paladin Nuclear Plant near South Haven. In fact, the more he learned the faster his heart beat. There were schedules of freighters moving natural gas, fuel oil, and coal. One manifest read ammonium nitrate bound for Ohio.

Duke suddenly understood the imposters' dastardly plan. These men weren't measly criminals, extorting the land of the free and the home of the brave, carving off a piece of the American pie. They were actual terrorists seeking to obliterate the pie!

Judging by their plan, they could very well accomplish their mission.

This was too big, Duke realized.

He had to report his findings to Hector, even if it meant arriving empty-handed. He only hoped it wasn't too late.

He also hoped Hector didn't stop his beating heart permanently.

They gathered in the theater room of the luxurious mansion where Dodd's face appeared on the ten-foot-wide flat screen with perfect clarity.

Billy Ray could swear his former CO had aged since Texas. Even his voice carried the sharp edge of a worried man.

The strain and drain of constant battle, he allowed.

"So that's Oz," Tafoya said. "I imagined someone more handsome."

"Can it, lady," Dodd ordered, displaying no mood for humor.

Billy Ray took the *conn.* "Let's get to it, Admiral."

Tafoya mumbled, "Oz is an admiral, too? Well that figures."

Dodd briefed them about an al-Qaeda terror cell rumored to be in the Midwest, and how they planned to detonate dirty bombs at high-value targets. It was yet unknown where and how terrorists acquired radioactive material, or how they managed to smuggle it into the country.

Friendly overseas sources had suggested several possible targets, but nothing actionable. Consequently, POTUS and the nation's intelligence services were buzzing at maximum velocity, chasing down every lead to prevent an attack to dwarf that of 9/11.

The Department of Homeland Security's National Terrorism Advisory System had been raised to *Elevated.* And unless something turned up soon, the NTAS would proceed to *Imminent.* At which point, the cat would be out of the bag and a media storm would follow.

"So we need to find these bastards ASAP," Dodd concluded.

"Any guesses, Admiral?" Billy Ray asked.

"Chicago tops the list with two possible targets. The Willis Tower, formerly the Sear's Tower, is especially concerning should it be brought crashing to the ground as with the World Trade Center buildings."

"And the second target, Admiral?" Tafoya asked respectfully.

"America's *other* twin towers, the Chicago Merc."

"Al-Qaeda sure enjoys evil satire," Billy Ray mused aloud.

"Merc?" asked Rebecca.

Tafoya provided the answer. "The Chicago Mercantile Exchange. It's the largest futures market of its kind in the world. Although the Merc also trades a number of financial instruments, think agricultural commodities."

"Like in pork bellies?" Rebecca said.

"Actually, pork bellies were delisted, but you're on track. Here's how it works. Take common staples like wheat, corn, soy bean, and meats, then bet on their prices at a distant point on the calendar, and there you have it, futures trading!"

"You're smarter than you look, Tafoya," Billy Ray teased.

She flashed him a peek at some hot pink nail polish on her middle finger, then turned to Dodd and said, "The belly of the giant."

"What's that, Tafoya?" asked Dodd.

"On 9/11, those scum punched the Great Satan in the wallet by targeting New York, the world's financial hub, and our military industrial complex at the Pentagon. Only because the brave passengers aboard Flight 93 stormed the terrorists and crashed the airplane into that Pennsylvania field, was the White House spared. Now imagine if they hit us in the *gut* next time by crashing the food market. Not everybody owned stocks then, but everyone damn sure has to eat. *VOILÀ*—food riots!"

"Excellent analysis, Ms. Tafoya," Dodd complimented.

"I still don't get it," Rebecca said.

Dodd gave a fuller explanation. "An attack on the Chicago Mercantile would shock the commodities market and trigger a meteoric spike in food prices. With a quarter of the nation's population on food assistance, tens of millions of Americans could discover that eating just became utterly unaffordable. Panic would erupt on a scale not seen since the Great Depression—if then. Hoarding and rioting would sweep the country.

"Moreover, food exports to the world would be cut by politicians responding to their angry constituents. Food shortages would span the globe, followed by famine. In the end, the Breadbasket of the World—the United States—would be blamed for starving a billion men, women, and children. And there would be war."

No wonder Dodd was a wreck, Billy Ray thought. *He knew too much!*

"That's insane," Rebecca sounded unconvinced. "It's not like terrorists will have salted our fields and bombed grain silos, or liberated chickens from those cramped facilities everyone's so upset about."

"Terrorists didn't bomb the banks on 9/11 either," Dodd countered. "But look what happened to the financial markets. The aim of all terrorists is to affect the mind. You should know that, Ms. Payne. You've had plenty of experience with insanity, as I recall."

Billy Ray shot up from his seat. "Hold it right there, Admiral!"

"Sit down, Jenkins. Rebecca is on the team. I chose her for exactly that reason. She understands the minds of psychopaths as well as any doctor in the land, and hard earned according to her file."

"What's gotten into you, Dolittle? You're acting desperate."

"Apparently you fail to see what's at stake here, sailor."

The tension in the room could be cut with a knife.

Just then, a shout came from the back. "What's going on?"

It was Johnny Lam. He was back.

After their cell entered the United States, Rasul enrolled in the local high school near their "home" in South Haven, the child of a single parent.

He possessed the necessary papers and ID to validate the backstory. The family name was Sanchez. The father, *Carlos*—Qasem—was an executive at the Webster company in Muskegon. His brothers *Terry* and *Bobby*—Tariq and Bashir—were college students, as would be expected by such a highly-educated father. The cover was textbook.

Randy—Rasul—had been accepted by his teachers and classmates. The aggressive American girls were paying attention, also, especially after he started an Ecology Club at the school. His Eco-Club gained instant popularity. Then again, with so much attention paid to environmental concerns in America, it was easy. He'd even lobbied the U.S. Department of Energy and received a financial grant for the Eco-Club—a thousand dollars—to begin a Going Green Program at the local community center.

He thanked Allah for such tolerance in America, where citizens were taught to accept one another's neighbor without judgment.

School authorities and neighbors assumed Qasem commuted to work. No one noticed his absence during the week. Being seen with his sons on the weekends at various South Haven events was convincing enough.

Each cell member was assigned a specific infiltration point. Rasul's was his high school, to cultivate unsophisticated American kids, and manipulate them into becoming unwitting accomplices to the mission.

<==== PIPELINE ====>

It was the same for Bashir and Tariq, with their mission easier still, as they trolled the shallows on college campuses to foment rebellion through anti-establishment organizations, anti-Semitic militants and other radical groups, like anarchists, environmentalists, and race-based activists.

Their efforts were aided greatly by college professors demonizing American exceptionalism and playing up the nation's sinful past.

Just like at his madrasa, Rasul thought.

The leader of the democratic world, the United States of America, was a perfect place to convert hearts and minds to Allah—or use its many freedoms to destroy the infidels forever!

The Western world stood no chance against the steady march of Islam. Its countries failed to recognize how Islam would supplant their evil Judeo-Christian laws, and then usher in the true way of life, and the one true path to Allah. Surely the ranks of new soldiers for jihad would grow as Sharia Law ended the West's secular dribble and liberal platitudes.

Rasul felt joy at the prospect of complete and devastating victory.

Insha'Allah.

All heads turned as Lam approached. He paused and looked down at Tafoya on his way to the television screen, but said nothing.

Lam took up a position in front of Dodd's electronically enlarged head. "I repeat, what's going on here?"

"Nice nap, I presume." Dodd said.

"Cut the crap, Admiral. I hurt like hell. I got bruises on top of bruises. And to make matters worse, somebody painted my toenails pink!"

Billy Ray remembered Tafoya's polished finger.

"I thought I was in Michigan to find Rapture. So what's all this about terrorists? What the hell happened during my *nap*?"

Dodd smiled and his eyes brightened.

For the first time since receiving contact from Dodd, Billy Ray saw his new boss act like the old boss. If they were to battle bloodthirsty terrorists, all of them would need clear heads—especially their leader.

After briefing Lam on the national security matter, Dodd told the group, "I'm granting you all one day for R&R. I suggest you enjoy it while you can. Beginning tomorrow, we hit the ground running." Dodd signed off.

Billy Ray studied the faces in the room, each one different, each person a mix of issues—a cop, a mental health provider, a news reporter, and a military guy—ordinary people needed to do extraordinary things.

They were his team—*and it was mission time.*

7

The TV screen winked out and the theater room lights came on.

Billy Ray suggested they gather in the kitchen for further discussion. Plus he was hungry. As if to answer in tandem, Lam's stomach growled.

They chatted over ham sandwiches and weight watcher salads—the guys porking out, the women mindful of their figures.

Lam ate so much food that Billy Ray thought the former Green Beret might actually turn *green*. Three days on feeding tubes must've been torture. It's hard to get a burrito down a feeding tube.

While they ate, Billy Ray caught Lam up on all that had happened in the past week, including the scenic bus ride in Washington State and how he'd gotten to Michigan.

The ladies filled in bits and pieces, too.

Billy Ray noticed Lam displaying some coldness toward Tafoya, but chalked it up to a pedicure gone bad.

As unlikely a match as each of them were, Billy Ray began to see Dodd's genius in bringing them together—two men and two women, each having different personalities, each possessing extraordinary qualities, and each with distinct ways of attacking problems.

He considered the group's makeup.

As for the women, Tafoya and Rebecca seemed to hit it off just fine. And for the men, he and Lam already had an established relationship.

Then cross-wise, he and Rebecca had faced mortal danger during the Texas affair where she'd shown great mettle, even holding her own in a violent combat environment. Now she was his lover. So like it or not, they were partners in *every* way.

That left the final two pairings: he and Tafoya, and Lam and Tafoya.

His opinion of Tafoya was solid. She'd saved his life at great risk to her own, which counted big in his book.

Furthermore, the feisty Cubana owned more brains and guts than she liked letting on.

What remained then was Lam and Tafoya.

And that's where Billy Ray had his suspicions.

He'd detected something between the cop and the newshound, something deep, and possibly troubling. He just couldn't determine which end of the rope it was—love or hate.

It didn't need to be love. But the team couldn't afford hate either. There could be no tug o' war with all of their lives hanging on the line.

He planned to discuss the matter with Rebecca. As the group's psychologist, maybe she could shed some light on the matter.

<=== PIPELINE ===>

Unit cohesion would be critical, especially when combatting an enemy whose ideology allowed for the wholesale slaughter of innocent women and children.

Against such a foe there could be no weak links.

Billy Ray hoped that Dodd was correct mixing the likes of Lam and Tafoya.

He let out a long breath.

Group dynamics could sure be a bitch!

Duke's left eye was swollen nearly shut.

Blood ran from his mouth and dripped onto his bare chest.

And he'd already spat out one tooth.

The security guard—the man who had his job—smiled incessantly during the beating, perhaps thinking himself a harsh interrogator. But the dumb bastard was junior varsity compared to his late father, who used to dispense worse punishment on Sunday mornings before church—always a light day of physical abuse for the young Duke.

Then he'd grown older and larger until, one day, he put an end to his father's beatings—exactly what he would do to the security guard when he snapped the man's neck and carved that asinine smile off his face.

However, Duke took the beating for what it was—Hector exacting a price for failure. Fortunately, that price hadn't included death.

But neither had Duke thought that it would . . . not yet anyway.

Not with the information he possessed.

Hector hated ever being wrong or seeing his personal weakness. And he'd been terribly mistaken about the imposters. Nonetheless, the head of the Gallina cartel didn't take punishment—he gave it.

Duke endured the beating, the questions, and the insults. He allowed Hector to extract the information about the Muslim terrorists in the manner that Hector preferred, bit by bit, taking immense pleasure in verifying truth through blood and pain.

There was a last punch and the ropes came off. Then Hector and the Uzis departed, leaving Duke alone with the grinning guard.

Damn he hated that stupid smile!

But it wasn't time to erase the man's face just yet.

Hector had granted him one last chance to make things right.

Lunch ended. The tension of the past days had been draining for everyone, especially Lam and Tafoya. Now it was time to relax.

The sun was hot, the sky blue, and the waters of Lake Michigan inviting. The beach beckoned to the women. A barber shop whistled to the men. Plus there was the little matter of returning a "borrowed" ambulance and then renting another vehicle.

Tafoya tried her cell phone. "Hey, I'm back on the home planet!"

"Dodd must figure you finally understand our mission," Billy Ray said.

Tafoya scowled. "Sure, I get it. But I'll be damned if I like it!"

"Nobody does," Billy Ray assured her. "Consider it the new reality."

"Whatever, Jenkins," Tafoya said and then dialed her hairdresser. "After you rednecks become GQ poster boys, how about you take Lam and go pop some tags. That teal sport coat of his is so grandpa's style."

Rebecca piled on. "Yeah, Billy Ray. Isn't that the same gray shirt you wore last summer?"

Tafoya jumped off the kitchen stool and took Rebecca's hand. "Wait 'til you see what I found in the upstairs closet!"

The women hustled off, leaving the men alone in the kitchen, Lam wondering what popping tags meant, Billy Ray staring down at his shirt.

After a moment, Billy Ray turned to Lam. "You had a close call, Army."

Lam rubbed the back of his skull. "Tell me about it."

"Good thing it wasn't a body part with any real value." He and Lam had some major ball-busting to catch up on, so might as well get started.

"At least I use my head, Jenkins!"

Billy Ray played dumb. "What do you mean?"

"There I was, waking up on a hospital floor with furniture piled on top of me, and what's the first thing I see?"

Billy Ray shrugged his shoulders. "I don't know, Sleeping Beauty?"

"No. Some Navy guy dry-humping the jolly green giant!"

Score one for the Army! Billy Ray thought. He was tempted to mention heart-shaped beds and pink toenails, but they had other concerns now.

"I noticed you didn't issue a warning before dropping the big guy. So what's changed you, Agent Lam?"

"Nice rules for nice people. That's what changed."

"Yesterday's world, my friend."

"Then stick me in the Wayback Machine, Sherman. Because this isn't what I agreed to when I joined law enforcement. I understand the point about pulling the trigger on vicious scum. But we're way beyond Miranda warnings." Lam tilted toward the ceiling. "You hear me, Admiral? I don't like it one bit!"

The overhead lights blinked twice.

<=== PIPELINE ===>

Billy Ray shook his head at Dodd's sense of drama. "Let's go. These spy games are starting to piss me off."

"Starting . . .?" Lam pressed.

"No, I'm already there," Billy Ray agreed. "You hear that, Dolittle?"

The kitchen lights went off and stayed off.

The ladies were elated with what they discovered.

Not only did the house have eyes and ears, *and* could talk, it knew what women want. The master closet held a beguiling array of expensive items to rival a Beverly Hills boutique. It was filled with clothing, shoes, perfume, jewelry and accessories.

There was even a box of dark chocolates.

Strangely, though, the contents of the closet offered only two choices of sizes and color schemes. Every item matched Rebecca and Tafoya distinctly, even down to swimsuits and underwear.

Tafoya lifted a tangerine-colored bikini from the rack and pressed it against her chest and hips. "Look, a perfect fit! Maybe getting spied on isn't so bad after all."

Rebecca didn't share the joy. In fact, it gave her the creeps.

Dodd's organization had her pegged down to her favorite brand of panties. It was as if Uncle Sam and Neiman Marcus had formed an unholy alliance.

"Pick one, Rebecca. We're wasting sunlight!" Tafoya said, slipping out of her clothes and into the hot citrus swimwear.

Rebecca plucked a lavender one-piece from the rack that perfectly complimented her longer frame.

It felt like she was picking the forbidden fruit.

Qasem closed the drapes and turned on the radio.

Then he carried a long aluminum tube into the dining room where Bashir, Tariq, and Rasul waited eagerly to discuss their mission.

Qasem removed a scroll from the tube and spread it across the table. It was a map of the Midwestern United States.

"Good news, my brothers. Our countdown to paradise begins now. Soon the whole world will bear witness to Allah's glory."

Bashir, Tariq, and Rasul stared in silence, awaiting an explanation.

"Your many months of gathering intelligence and infiltrating American society is about to pay off." Qasem tapped the map. "We will begin by making dry runs at these objectives."

Six targets were marked on the map—five circled in red ink, the sixth bordered by a green square. The red circles ranged from a major medical university in Minneapolis at the western edge of the map, to a massive automobile assembly plant near Detroit on the eastern edge. The northern-most circle designated the Mackinac Bridge for destruction. And the final two circles at the bottom of the map were both located in Chicago, one highlighting the T. J. O'Brien Lock and Dam on the Calumet River, the other marking the twin towers of the Chicago Mercantile Exchange.

Rasul studied the map. He was familiar with these five sites. Much to the pleasure of his teachers, he'd produced book reports on each location for his social studies class. He'd even traveled on school field trips to the mighty Mackinac Bridge and to both Chicago targets.

Unknown to his teachers, however, the research provided more than grades on a report card. It allowed him to use school computers and access state and federal agencies to collect intelligence critical to their mission without unduly alerting American counter-terrorism officials.

But the final location in the center of the map, the one marked by a green square, was only six miles from their home in South Haven.

Rasul tapped the map with a slender finger. "What is this one?"

Qasem rewarded Rasul with a paternal smile.

Just a boy, yet so intuitive. . . so beyond his years.

Of course, he was proud of all the young men for their extreme talents. Handsome Bashir was a talented actor, when not yelling and debating with others. With his glib tongue, Bashir could sell pork chops to rabbis. And with his dashing looks, he could entice most any women to join him under the covers. He'd even beguiled Gallina's women. Had he been an American politician, the thirty year old could win election by a landslide.

And then there was Tariq, who by virtue of his technical genius, was the dagger of their holy mission. Without Tariq's unmatched skill with computers and scientific knowledge, Qasem's plan would have no chance of success.

But Rasul . . . Rasul was *special*—pure, not given to material cares, nor yet having experienced the carnal knowledge of a woman's body.

The boy—*young man,* Qasem corrected himself, was a symbol of the purest of Islam: generous, a just soul, immune to lustful pleasures.

Qasem had known all along that Bashir and Tariq took cartel women.

Only Rasul passed the test.

HE was the one.

It was too bad that the butterfly girl had to be eliminated. She would have made a fine wife for Rasul.

He studied Rasul.

Allah's heart beat deeply inside the young man.

Like Mahdi, the Twelfth Imam.

He covered Rasul's soft hand atop the map with his own. "This marks your assignment, my young lion. It is the Paladin Nuclear Power Plant."

Rasul's chest swelled, pleasing Qasem by the reaction.

He continued, "Your ecology club will gather for a tour of the Paladin plant." Qasem removed a ballpoint pen from a lead-shielded case and handed it to Rasul. "You will take that with you. The inkwell contains a radioactive powder. Once inside the facility, you will sprinkle it on any item to be ingested by the tour group, including yourself."

Rasul handled the slender tube delicately. He felt his pulse quicken!

He'd read about the troubled facility, about its numerous safety violations, and the repeated releases of trace radioactive water into Lake Michigan.

He'd even participated in school debates on whether to close the plant.

And then there had been the protests at the entrance to the Paladin plant, spurred on by Bashir and Tariq. One of those protests had even turned violent and made the nightly national news on all the major networks.

Surely, he was born for just such a cause.

He would gladly swallow the poison.

And die for the glory of Allah.

Qasem noted the delight on Rasul's face. But unfortunately, the young man would not see paradise so soon. Rasul's life was to serve a far greater purpose for Allah than to die in martyrdom.

The boy had been handpicked from infancy by a Shia cleric sent to spy out the perfect vessel from among the opposing Sunni tribes.

Rasul's genuine worth would come in the future, *after* the fall of America. Whereas the plan for him now was to contaminate the school children with trace amounts of cobalt-60, a synthetic isotope produced inside the Paladin plant's own reactors then sold commercially to medical suppliers and research universities.

According to HUMINT reports from Qasem's agents, the Paladin plant employed standard airport security protocols upon entering the facility, entailing a magnetometer for weapons and metal objects, and a puffer machine for explosives and other chemical compounds. They also operated with several chemical sniffing canines at the main gate and throughout the facility.

It was only when exiting the nuclear facility that individuals would pass through a radiation portal monitor to detect the presence of radiological material, mainly as a deterrent against theft.

After all, who would bother smuggling radioactive material *into* a nuclear power plant.

Rasul's role would be to create a contamination event so repugnant to the media and the public—the poisoning of school children—that authorities could hardly act fast enough to shutter the offending plant and transfer all nuclear material to another facility.

Qasem had the men's attention. "We shall hijack that shipment."

Bashir bolted out of his chair. "A nuclear bomb!"

Tariq corrected Bashir. "No. A dirty bomb."

"A bomb nonetheless!" Bashir challenged excitedly.

Tariq stood and faced his fellow *mujahid*. "Such a bomb would be useless without an effective dispersal method inside the blast zone. Death would be minimal, and so too the contamination area."

Bashir pointed a finger at Tariq. "Not useless. It would create fear!"

Tariq pointed back. "Fear *and* panic, but not death!."

"I thought fear *was* our mission!" Bashir shouted.

Qasem slapped down hard on the table. "Our mission has changed. We are here to destroy the Great Satan not just hurt it!"

Qasem allowed his message to germinate in the fertile minds of the young martyrs. He knew what he was doing . . . having spent many years leading men, riling their spirits, and manipulating their minds.

He could get human beings to perform deeds to make the devil blush, like casting themselves on enemy bayonets for comrades to charge forward into victory; or showing nerves of steel boarding airplanes to be hijacked and rammed down the enemy's throats; or strapping explosives to their bodies and blowing themselves up in crowded malls, hospitals, or schoolyards.

Qasem's eyes blazed. "America is a house of cards, needing but a tiny puff to topple it. But we bring no small breeze, my brothers. We bring *sirocco,* the cleansing desert wind. We shall finish what Allah's brave martyrs began on 9/11 and blow this sinful country to the depths of hell!"

The three terrorists stared at Qasem with open mouths.

<===== PIPELINE =====>

Qasem switched to his paternal voice, like gentle rain after a storm. "My brothers, you are familiar with ANFO, the explosive made from ammonium nitrate and fuel oil. We shall construct such an explosive device."

Seeming impressed, Tariq said, "I suggest replacing the fuel oil component with nitromethane. The combination of ammonium nitrate and racing fuel is vastly more explosive than ANFO. Consider how a single Ryder truck containing ANNM destroyed the Alfred Murrah building in Oklahoma City and sixteen blocks of the downtown area."

"And it killed lots of people!" Bashir exclaimed.

Tariq dampened Bashir's zeal. "Actually, less than two hundred."

"What about injuries then?"

"Injuries heal. We must cause death."

"How then?" Bashir begged.

Tariq tapped the second of the Chicago targets on the map. "If we fill a truck with ANNM *and* radioactive material, then detonate the bomb near the twin towers of the Mercantile Exchange at rush hour, we could have both death *and* terror a full magnitude far, far greater than anything at Oklahoma City."

"Yes!" Bashir could hardly contain himself. "Plus radiation and chaos!"

Tariq continued trance-like, ". . . by targeting the MERC, food prices of all types would skyrocket. Famine would circle the globe causing suffering to untold millions. America would get the blame. The fall of the West wouldn't stop there, because futures market for other nations would plummet."

Bashir took it from there. "The world would turn against the West. Then Allah would have his legions!"

Qasem was thrilled by the passion of his men. They had even arrived at the same target as the planners in Tehran.

But they had failed in one respect.

They hadn't aimed high enough.

"Allah be praised, my lions, for adding tooth and claw to your intellect. But let us not sell genius short by using a tiny truck. Let us build the mother of all bombs. We will fill a cargo ship with ANNM and radioactive material. Then we shall not merely kill a few people or destroy a limited number of buildings, we will destroy them all!"

Bashir nearly shot through the ceiling. "Chicago will be no more!"

Qasem extracted another scroll from the tube and rolled it over the top of the first. It was a new map. He spread his arms wide as if saying, "behold."

All three al-Qaeda terrorists gasped!

The letterhead on the map was inscribed in Farsi, the language of Iran. Emblazoned across the top of the scroll was the emblem of Iran's most elite military unit, the Quds Force.

It was Rasul who stood this time. "Shia Islam—? But we're Sunni!"

For the first time, General Qasem Khatami, former commander of Iran's top-secret military forces, revealed his true identity. Then he glared at the men under his command—his *final* command.

There were others in the country awaiting orders, but these three men were the tip of Allah's spear to begin the destruction of the most powerful nation in the world—the Great Satan itself.

Five years earlier, Qasem had received word from the Grand Ayatollah of his imminent replacement as head of the Quds. There was a new generation of commanders pushing for advancement. He was promised a comfortable retirement by the country he had served so bravely, so brilliantly, and for so long.

But this he could never do, not in a thousand lifetimes—not while *Iblis* stalked the world.

So he begged the Supreme Leader to grant him one last assignment, one final mission against Iran's greatest enemy.

It was so ordered.

A great deal of planning had gone into the mission. Billions of dollars invested. A good amount of the money came from the Great Satan itself by way of oil purchases and quiet extortion. Then years of moving men and assets into position.

He had America's open society and porous southern borders to thank for that.

Qasem widened his arms, the inviting gesture of a patriarch.

"My dear brothers, I see your shock. But *Shia* and *Sunni* fight together now—under a new righteous caliphate."

The three Sunni terrorists were stone silent.

Qasem pointed at the new map. "After prayers, I shall explain how Allah will destroy America for all eternity."

<====== PIPELINE ======>

8

Billy Ray kept off of the major roads and highways.

The trick was to avoid the police, especially in a stolen ambulance driven by Texas dudes in sad need of haircuts, shaves, and new clothes.

Dodd helped suppress matters by pulling rank over state and local authorities, designating the battle at the hospital a national security concern and imposing a need-to-know protocol.

However, news of the deadly incident at the hospital spread fast. There was just no stopping the internet or cable news, and most people had cellphone cameras these days.

Dodd couldn't turn the lights off on everyone, at least not yet.

Furthermore, scrubbing their identities from the public record had only worsened matters, causing newshounds to smell raw meat and chase the story all the harder. The media was closing in on their target.

More sobering still was how people everywhere were growing wary of federal involvement in seemingly every aspect of their lives. Topics around water coolers, coffee shops, and family dinner tables increasingly turned to talk of government overreach, domestic spying, electronic surveillance, and secret police, topics normally professed by survivalists and conspiracy nuts.

Added to the hundreds of retailers and internet scammers monitoring everyone each and every day, citizens were fed up with the constant intrusion into their personal lives, regardless of where it originated.

As pressure on society mounted, behavior tanked, fractures would widen between races and ethnic groups crying for racial justice; the have-nots would look at the haves and demanded their fair share; and nihilists lit their torches; a single event could be all it took to spark revolt. Then Americans declaring they'd had enough and moving to outright rebellion.

Billy Ray hoped the breaking point didn't come from his actions. Then he wondered if he was becoming like Dodd—*a man who knew too much.*

He switched focus to the day ahead: haircuts first, then the hospital, and finally "popping tags." He hadn't heard the term before. After prison, he could've imagined saltier meanings than clothes shopping.

Tafoya's beauty parlor friends had agreed to "scrubbin' up" two scruffy dudes on the condition they deliver vanilla non-fat lattes. Whereby Tafoya was forced to explain, "they weren't those kinda' guys."

Though knowing of Lam's toenail secret and that heart-shaped bed, Billy Ray wasn't so sure . . . plus Lam's Army callsign was *Lover Boy.*

The Ultra Hair Salon was located in the Grand Rapids suburb of Grandville. Billy Ray pulled into the lot and parked the stolen rig.

In all the years Lynda had owned Ultra Hair, she never got a request like the one from Tami Tafoya.

But she'd agreed, and now finished cashing out her last client in preparation for two "emergency" customers. Her partner Cathy had done the same with her client five minutes earlier, and now sat in a salon chair worrying about canceling her regulars.

"Your friend owes us big time, Lynda. And no treats, either?"

Lynda shut the cash register. "Tami said we'd be well paid—"

She stopped midsentence and walked rapidly to the window.

"What's the matter?" asked Cathy.

Lynda looked back. "Did you call 9-1-1?"

"Huh?" Cathy joined her business partner at the window.

Together they watched two handsome men exit an ambulance and begin walking toward their salon. The dark guy on the left had style, be it from an earlier decade, sporting pressed slacks and a teal blazer. The man on the right looked to have just come down out of the hills, and simply wore a gray T-shirt, faded jeans, and hiking boots.

Regardless, both guys were in sore need of an Ultra Hair experience.

Cathy said, "Your friend was right, those aren't vanilla latte guys."

"Oh my, definitely not," Lynda said half under her breath.

Cathy turned from the window. "Since I'm better with wavy hair, I'll take the tall, dark, and handsome one."

"'Wavy hair?' Yeah right, Cathy!"

The door opened. Mountain man and the Miami Vice guy approached the counter. "Are you Lynda?" Mountain man asked.

"Are you my emergency—I mean, my one o'clock?"

Cathy laughed and then pointed at Lam. "Follow me, Tubbs."

Lynda and Cathy were a pleasant diversion.

Not only were the ladies expert hair stylists, they also had no difficulty tossing Billy Ray and Lam's teasing right back in their laps.

Billy Ray made apologies, saying there'd be no formal introductions. Being Michigan gals, Lynda and Cathy declared that unacceptable and assigned made-up names for the sake of conversation.

Lynda put Billy Ray in a chair, draped him with an apron, and then let professional hands take over. The same was true in the next seat where Cathy made Lover Boy's wavy hair look better than it ever had.

After transformation back to respectability, Billy Ray handed the ladies a thick wad of cash. Then he and Lam said their goodbyes and left.

"Where to next, Barney?" Lam asked as he shut the ambulance door.

Billy Ray said, "Well, Fred, I say we return this body barge."

"Don't try sounding hip, Barney, it'll never sell."

<══ PIPELINE ══>

"Gee thanks, pal. Can we stop with the Flintstones now?"

"Hey, Navy, you're the one who went all James Bond back there."

Billy Ray changed the subject. "How about using that FBI phone of yours and dial us up a rental car. I want to get back to hot women, cold beer, and a sandy beach."

"What is with you and modern gadgets, such as phones?" Lam jabbed.

"What is it with you and modern clothes?" Billy Ray countered.

Lam grumbled and made the call to a local car rental agency.

Billy Ray got the sense that Lam wasn't too enthused about the beach idea. Maybe it was that Tafoya thing.

Then again, the guy was a ground-pounder and probably hated water. *And man-eating piranha!*

After the beating by Gallina, Duke drove back to Grand Rapids, checked into a hotel, and rested his aching head.

He'd tipped the hotel maid fifty bucks to purchase him a bottle of rye whiskey and some ibuprofen.

After downing large amounts of both, he joined a soft pillow on the bed to catch some sleep.

He'd just closed his eyes when the cell phone rang.

Damn!

"Yeah?"

"Hey dumbass."

It was Gallina's security guard. His mocking grin came over the phone.

"What do you want?"

"Must be your lucky day, asshole."

Duke resisted the urge to drive straight to Muskegon and choke the son of a bitch to death. But instead—

"How so?"

"Our man inside Spectrum Health just spotted the guys who killed your retarded boyfriend."

"Tito wasn't my boyfriend. He was a *sicario*."

"And a shitty one at that."

"Just get to the point!" Duke shouted.

"The *point* is for you to get your lazy ass back to the hospital and pick up the security video, then get to doing your job!"

Duke squeezed the phone until it began to crack, imagining getting even with those pricks that killed Tito.

Then afterward he'd squash the sneering guard and get his job back.

They drove to the Amtrak station on Wealthy Street, where a barely used Crown Victoria awaited Lam in the rental lot.

Billy Ray watched Lam walk circles around the car like a pagan around a Maypole. Then he hung his head out of the ambulance window and said, "What is it with you and fancy cars?"

Lam ignored the question and got into the big Ford. After inhaling a noseful of rich leather smell, he drove off without waving goodbye.

Billy Ray remained idling at the Amtrak station. The plan was for Lam to arrive first at Spectrum Hospital and set up in the event all went to hell.

Five minutes later, Lam called to say he was in place.

Billy Ray should've parked the ambulance somewhere in town, hid the keys under the seat, and phoned in an anonymous tip to the Spectrum Health operator. But he'd taken the vehicle and felt duty-bound to return it, simple as that. Plus he had the added advantage of Dodd making him a non-existent person, though it irked him still.

The transfer could've gone much smoother, however, because just as he turned into the emergency lot, a medic van sped past, sirens wailing, and took his spot. Hospital staff rushed out to receive a new patient.

Billy Ray circled the block until the action settled, then parked the stolen ambulance behind the newly-arrived one.

He walked away and dialed Lam. "Is this the U.S. Army valet service?"

Pride goeth before a fall.

The old proverb entered Billy Ray's mind the same moment a medical tech rushed out of the hospital and yelled, "Hey! You're blocking my unit. Move it!"

Billy Ray didn't stop walking nor turn around. His fresh haircut may pass inspection, but the rest of him was a no-go.

Then he heard the EMT shout again, "That's our missing rig!"

Then more shouting, *"Stop! Security! It's him!"*

Lam had been forced to park at the rear of the lot, where he now stood beside his favorite kind of car wiping a smudge off of the hood with his coat sleeve.

His Blackberry rang. He put the phone to his ear and caught Jenkins' joke. Then suddenly, yelling filled the speaker.

Lam looked up from admiring the car and saw hospital staff spilling from the E-room, followed closely by security guards with guns.

Oh shit!

Lam jumped into the rental car and gunned it.

<===== PIPELINE =====>

Billy Ray ran!

Everyone at the hospital was on heightened alert after the previous day's mayhem. The E-room doors burst open. Hospital staff and armed guards poured from the building and gave chase.

The Crown Vic screeched to a halt and the passenger door flew open.

Billy Ray jumped in and yanked the door shut just as Lam floored the gas pedal and peeled away to a hail of bullets plinking into the trunk and rear bumper.

The sound of shouts and gun shots dissipated as they gained distance and finally tore off down the street.

Lam yelled, "*Returning* a stolen vehicle! Do you have to be so damn honest, Jenkins!"

"Don't you, Lam?"

There was silence, except for the revving engine. Billy Ray changed the subject. "Those hospital cops are phoning this in, and I'll bet the security cameras have us pegged for sure."

"Dodd?" asked Lam.

"He'll be too late scrubbing the tapes. We need to ditch this car, fast."

"But I just got it!" Lam griped.

"You sure have bad luck with cars, Lam."

"Who you kidding, Jenkins? Look what happens when you go off playing honest injun!"

Lam chose a spot beneath the US 131 viaduct and parked behind a concrete stanchion. From there, they hurried away, crossing the street to the grounds of the Gerald R. Ford Presidential Museum.

They slowed and fell in with the tour group gathered for a memorial service at the burial site of President Gerald Ford and First Lady, Betty.

"Never been here before," Billy Ray said scanning their surroundings.

"Just once for me," Lam said. "Some good folks rest here."

"Roger that, Army."

Lam scrutinized the crowd. "I think we're in the clear," he whispered.

Billy Ray took a last look at the grave of America's 38th President and his wife then just walked away.

Lam caught up. "So much for popping tags. We better pop us a ride."

"How about renting another one of those fancy cars?"

Lam blew a gasket. "You mean pause our escape, take time to make a phone call, be put on hold, finally reach a human asking to explain how the *first* Crown Vic got smashed to bits, and why the *second* one looks like Swiss cheese. Then ride a city bus to a rental lot, fill out reams of paperwork, empty my bank account for insurance, and still get you to the beach on time? Oh yeah . . . and somehow avoid every cop in Michigan!"

"Well, since you put it that way, what do *you* propose, Mr. Special Agent in Charge?"

"Follow me. I'll get us a ride." Lam hustled off.

They double-timed it across the Pearl Street Bridge into the heart of downtown Grand Rapids. As they jogged, Billy Ray pointed downriver at an enormous set of table and chairs placed atop a blue footbridge spanning the Grand River. "Where are we, Land of the Giants?"

"ArtPrize," Lam said huffing. "The city holds the event every year."

The luxurious Amway Grand Plaza Hotel sat on the eastern bank of the Grand River. A steady flow of Limos, Lincolns, and Cadillacs exited from the five-star hotel's motor lobby. Lam halted their forced march at the entrance to the hotel parking ramp.

Billy Ray whistled. "You Army guys sure have expensive tastes."

Lam slowed his breathing. "Would you prefer clunkers?"

"Maybe I would."

"Geez, Jenkins. Whose navy were you in, Cuba's?"

Another point scored for the Army.

Billy Ray knew just what Lam had in mind, and made a show of looking all around them.

"Now what are you doing, Jenkins?"

"Trying to spot Vin Diesel."

"We're not here to steal anything. Go stand over there." Lam directed Billy Ray to the opposite side of the ramp. "And Jenkins . . .?"

"Yeah?"

"Don't scratch your privates. It scares off the clientele."

"Are you sure this'll work?"

"Of course. I'll isolate a car and then flash my official identification."

"So you say, Lam."

"Then I'll order the driver to surrender the car in the name of the law."

"*The law* . . . why didn't I think of that?"

"'Cause you're Navy and I know thinking strains that organ between your ears," Lam stated quite succinctly. "Now get ready, I'll snatch the next vehicle."

"And to think you used to be an honest cop."

"Power corrupts, my friend."

"And absolute power corrupts absolutely," Billy Ray completed Lord Acton's quote.

"Just follow my lead, Navy."

Lam put his back to the wall next to the motor ramp and waited.

Billy Ray whispered, "You know this only works in the 'B' movies."

Lam ignored him.

<===== PIPELINE =====>

Perhaps it was the last of the lunch crowd they'd seen leaving the hotel, or maybe a political candidate fleeing with the donation bag. More likely, it was their bad timing. Not a single car had come down the ramp.

Billy Ray was about to suggest stealing bicycles when the sound of an approaching car echoed inside of the motor lobby.

"Psst!" Lam got Billy Ray's attention then stepped into the entryway.

Billy Ray hadn't yet peeked around the corner. But seeing Lam with his feet spread wide, badge held high, and the shocked look on his face was priceless. Whatever rolled down the ramp must've been unexpected.

Billy Ray rounded the corner then and came face to face with an angel on wheels.

It was a 2016 Corvette Stingray Convertible.

The rumbling engine vibrated his bones and made him forget about red Camaros.

A frightened hotel valet sat behind the wheel of the pricey auto.

Lam stepped close and showed the man his K-KEY Group ID. The valet's expression changed upon seeing the President's picture and the words *Authority Over All*.

"What's the problem officer?"

"An emergency," Lam said in his best authority-over-all voice. "I need to commandeer this veh—"

Lam didn't get to finish. The valet stomped on the gas, peeled into the street, righted the 'vette, and was gone in far less than sixty seconds. The air filled with the smell of burning rubber.

Lam dropped his arm down to his side, still gripping the strange ID.

Billy Ray joined his dejected federal friend and watched the Corvette turn the corner and disappear.

"Like I said, Lam, 'B' movies."

Lam wasn't amused. "Okay, smartass, show me how the Castro's navy would do it. I'll take a '58 Edsel Corsair . . . gold, white trim, please"

"Sorry, I'm a Chevy man."

At that moment, a white panel van turned onto Pearl Street. Billy Ray stepped into the road and waved his arms.

The vehicle stopped. It turned out to be a Rose Pest Solutions vehicle . . . and a Chevrolet to boot. *Perfect!*

Billy Ray made his pitch to the driver, a middle-aged man with an expanding forehead and Fu Manchu moustache. The name on the pocket patch of the man's blue uniform read *Deano*.

"What's up, man?" Deano said.

Billy Ray chose the plain truth. "My partner and I are in a bit of a jam and need a ride."

"What kind of jam?" Deano asked suspiciously.

Billy Ray said to Lam, "Show Deano your ID."

Deano's eyes narrowed. "Am I under arrest?"

"No. We're undercover agents and we lost our transportation. I can explain the rest later, if that's okay. We're kind of in a hurry."

"I just finished a bed bug job—"

Billy Ray and Lam looked over at the glorious Amway Grand Plaza.

"Not there . . . a competitor," Deano said. "But I'll 'explain later.' Hop in. You can tell me how undercover agents can lose their ride, and I'll tell you what a bug man does."

"Gladly!" Billy Ray said, earning the trophy seat up front for his superb efforts at scoring them a ride. Lam, however, was forced to sit in back on the top of rodent bait containers.

After an hour of vermin stories, and a heavily-edited version of how two federal agents managed to *lose* a rental car, they arrived in Holland.

Billy Ray requested that Deano drop them off at a corner party store. Then he thanked the professional bug killer and paid for his time and gas.

As the pest van drove off, Lam stared at Billy Ray.

"It got us here, didn't it?"

Lam scowled. "Next time, *you* sit on the rat poison!"

"Next time flash President Grant's picture at a Corvette, you might have better luck."

They left the party store busting each other's chops for the entire mile-long walk to Dodd's safe house.

Duke studied the security tape from the hospital.

The video showed the FBI agent and the mystery man who'd fought Tito the previous day. The tape showed the men fleeing, and then sparks from bullets striking their vehicle.

It was puzzling why anyone would return a stolen ambulance to the scene of the crime, or at all. Also, why had the agent felt it necessary to escape like a common bandit?

Regardless, he got what he needed, a clear plate number.

Most Americans were unaware that police used the Automatic License Plate Recognition system (ALPR) to capture photos of license plates, some even capable of getting snapshots of drivers. The tiny cameras could be mounted anywhere, and capture as many as 1,800 plates a minute on cars traveling at speeds of up to 150 mph. Every motorist passing a scanner had their license plate photographed as to time, date, and location, and the data went into state and national databases.

<====== PIPELINE =====>

The multiple entry of those plates served to establish a personal profile of the vehicle and, by extension, the motorist inside.

And although, the tracking system was hailed as a crime-fighting tool to nail tax cheats, traffic violators, and other criminals, civil liberty-types saw the potential for abuse.

Duke, however, cared nothing of civil liberties. Just the opposite, in fact. He loved the new technology because it made his job easier.

He called in a favor from a cop on the Gallina payroll and gave her Lam's license plate number.

The dirty cop returned in seconds with the information.

Indeed, the plate had already been captured, and an APB issued. Actually, the car belonged to a rental service. The customer's name didn't match with Duke's intel—likely an alias.

But no matter, it was Lam.

Next Duke considered all he knew of Lam, starting with him being so far off the reservation from Dallas.

So why Michigan?

It made no sense for the DOJ to dispatch the Dallas SAC to a northern state to investigate human trafficking or the murder of three female *pollos,* since those matters could've been handled by the local FBI.

It did make sense for another reason, however. Lam was digging into something much deeper.

Duke began connecting the dots, the dots formed a picture, and the picture made sense. Why hadn't he seen it before now? The real reason Agent Lam was in Michigan lay buried inside a stainless steel tanker under his hunting cabin in Meauwataka.

It was the Rapture!

But that was only one half of it.

How could the government even know about the Rapture?

After Angel Gallina ordered the shipment of super-meth sent north, he was never heard from again.

Duke's head was spinning from all the questions, as well as throbbing from Gallina's little head-bashing party.

He took another deep swallow of rye whiskey.

Maybe he was grasping at straws, but he was a dead man if he didn't produce results soon.

Then it hit him—the Feds *did* know about the Rapture but were keeping the matter top-secret. And Lam was the Department of Justice point man for an undercover task force.

And if that was true, could it be the feds killed Angel Gallina in Texas, or were holding him for interrogation?

One thing he'd learned from his sadistic father was that if something looked like a skunk and smelled like a skunk, it was a damn skunk!

So yeah, Lam knew the truth.

With that revelation, Duke's challenges intensified a thousandfold—

Nail Lam before the feds got to him, then nail down the Islamic terrorists before Hector punched his one-way ticket to hell.

Duke shook more ibuprofen into his palm and grabbed for the whiskey bottle.

His headache had just grown a thousandfold, too.

He was screwed both ways!

<=== PIPELINE ===>

9

Billy Ray and Lam walked up the long driveway to the beach mansion still engaged in rigorous ball-busting.

"Forget the Corvette, Lam. Had it been your sister's pink Schwinn the guy would've still kicked dirt in your face. He probably thought you were a kook after seeing that Presidential badge of yours."

"What if it'd been a garbage truck instead of Deano the rat assassin?"

"Then you would've ridden home on a pile of dirty diapers."

Seeing their approach, the same Australian shepherd dog that greeted them the previous day ran up carrying a Frisbee in its mouth.

The dog dropped the toy and to their astonishment said in a loud clear voice, "I want a treat! Come." The dog grabbed the Frisbee in its teeth and trotted back to the house.

Billy Ray and Lam said together, "Dolittle!"

Long before becoming an admiral, before commanding Billy Ray's SEAL Team, and prior to joining the Navy, Dodd had spent his youth and college years assisting his marine scientist father training dolphins, sea lions, and other cetaceans for the US Navy's Marine Mammal Program.

Tragically, Dodd's father was killed in a scuba diving accident off the coast of Oregon while researching volcanic hydrothermal vents. For a time, Dodd continued the family dream of developing communication methods between animals and man. Then the Navy closed down the lab in Hawaii, moved the animals to classified top secret locations, and converted the NMMP to a "black budget" operation. Finding himself out of a job, Dodd packed up his PhD and applied for a direct commission as a naval officer and enrollment into the Navy SEAL program. Upon graduating from Basic Underwater Demolition/SEAL training, Dodd was granted the right by his teammates to use his father's call sign, *Dolittle*.

"So now what?" Lam asked.

Billy Ray shrugged. "We get him a treat."

They followed the talking dog up to the talking house. It turned out the pooch's name was Augie. How Billy Ray learned that was that the dog told him. After providing water and a doggie treat, he joined Lam upstairs to recon the master closet.

They, too, found clothing specific to their sizes and tastes. Though compared to the women's wardrobe, their choices were slim pickings— outdated clothes and dime-store cologne for Lam, an austere collection of jeans and T-shirts for Billy Ray. There was even a bag of beef jerky and a jar of gummy bears.

Billy Ray was a jerky fan, so who were the gummy bears for?

They slipped into bathing suits.

Lam didn't seem to notice how skimpy his suit was, or worse, that times had changed. Billy Ray chose not to tell him, and wondered if the straight-laced cop still wore tube socks at the gym.

They grabbed beach towels and made their way out of the house.

Where was Lam? Duke wondered.

And who was the guy with him? Furthermore, what happened to the reporter babe? Phone calls to her television station only produced a voice recording saying she was out of the office and to call the help desk.

He got an idea.

If Lam did have a secret agenda, and was acting alone a thousand-plus miles north of his home turf, he would've been forced to ditch the shot-up rental car to avoid blowing his cover. So how far could he and the his stocky partner get in forty-five minutes, especially with the local police in close pursuit?

Not far, he concluded.

Duke spread a city map on the motel bed. Next he drew a mile-wide circle around the hospital to account for the first minutes of the escape. He repeated the process with a five-mile circle, and so on, until four time frames colored the map. Then he scrutinized his handiwork.

If it was him looking to ditch a shot-up vehicle, he would've done so immediately. That suggested the first circle. So to reduce the number of escape routes, he marked off topographical restrictions, like the Grand River, city buildings, neighborhoods, roads, and freeways.

Duke was left with two possibilities.

Time to move!

He grabbed the map and his belongings and checked out of the hotel.

It didn't take long to find Lam's bullet-riddled car hidden in the shadows under the US-131 viaduct at the end of the Pearl Street Bridge, opposite the Gerald R. Ford Presidential Museum.

He crept past Lam's vehicle, still painfully aware of his conspicuous truck and how he needed to do some vehicle-ditching of his own, before it was too late.

So now what? Did Lam have another vehicle waiting? Did somebody come to their rescue, a taxi even?

Or had they been forced to vacate the area on foot?

A hundred possibilities!

Duke again phoned his police contact in Detroit, and provided the credit card number Lam used to rent the car.

<=== PIPELINE ===>

Then he held while the cop searched the national database.

After a long minute, she was back with the word that there'd been no recent charges.

Duke considered all options. And then he bet himself that Lam was reentering the downtown area on foot, likely to acquire a new vehicle.

He decided to do the same and parked the truck on Pearl Street.

Then he began stalking his prey.

Tafoya caught a wave and bodysurfed toward shore.

She rose up out of the refreshing water, smoothed back her long dark hair, and plodded onto the beach.

"Michigan beaches, the best kept secret in the world!" she said as she plopped into an Adirondack chair.

"Mmmm," Rebecca purred from the next chair over, her eyes closed as she soaked in the warmth and sunshine.

Tafoya pulled a beer from the ice chest, twisted off the cap and jammed a slice of lime in the bottle. Then she reclined to let the sun do its magic on her skin. She wondered how the moment could be any more perfect. Well, maybe if Lam was lying next to her in a cute swimsuit.

She got her wish a few minutes later.

Seeing two men and a dog file along the beach, Tafoya slipped on her sunglasses to hide her wandering eyes.

Not many thirty-something men sported ripped bods like these guys!

Billy Ray stopped in front of the women and pointed at the line of chairs. "Excuse us, ladies. Are these reserved?"

"Yes, for a couple of hunks. But I guess you'll do," answered Tafoya.

Everyone laughed except Lam.

Billy Ray selected the seat next to Rebecca. Lam, however, chose the chair furthest from Tafoya. No one made mention of it, not even Tafoya.

Billy Ray enlightened the ladies about the Grand Rapids adventure, especially playing up the failed Corvette heist and the long ride home in a pest truck.

Tafoya said, "Nice haircuts, by the way. I hardly recognized you guys."

Rebecca smiled and reached for Billy Ray's hand. He took it.

If only time could stand still.

Rebecca motioned at the water. "How about a swim?"

Asking a Navy guy if he wanted to swim? Do dogs chase cats?

"Of course!"

"Catch me if you can!"

Rebecca bolted off into the water.

Her long legs galloped beautifully through the waves.

But Billy Ray caught her—or maybe she let him win. They wrestled and splashed and hugged.

Rebecca floated on her back while Billy Ray supported her from beneath. Lake swells lifted them up and down in sensual rhythm.

Billy Ray looked back at the beach and saw Lam and Tafoya seated at opposite ends of the row of chairs.

The span between them was a dozen feet, but it may as well been a dozen miles.

Even the talking dog lay some distance away.

It was time to get Rebecca's professional opinion on the matter.

He rotated her for a better view of the awkward scene. "Have you noticed something between Lam and Tafoya?"

"What do you mean?" she asked.

"Haven't you noticed how Lam avoids Tafoya like the plague, while she can't keep her eyes off of him?"

Sensing a longer conversation, Rebecca ended her float and wrapped her arms around Billy Ray. "She's smitten with him . . . like I am with you."

"Obsessed is more like it."

"Billy Ray, if you're asking for my professional opinion, *narcissistic* is the term. Some people see something or somebody they like and their personalities drive them straight after it. That would be Tami."

"You can say that again."

She added, "Her Type N personality serves her well, our team, too."

"What about Lam?" Billy Ray asked.

"Aggressive. Definitely Type A."

"*A* as in *Army?*"

"Not unless *N* means Navy," Rebecca countered.

"Good point. Every Special Forces guy I ever met was Type A."

"Including you, sweetheart, though more passive–aggressive."

"Is that a good thing?" he asked.

"Yes, if matched to the right occasion, like last night—"

Billy Ray felt last night returning, and his thoughts wandering there.

"Personality types are theoretical. The real human psychology story is that we're complicated beings subject to various internal and external influences."

No argument there, Billy Ray thought, seeing his life flash before him: childhood abuse, falling in love, good times in the Teams, his fiancé's death, wasted years in prison, Ricky's murder.

<== **PIPELINE** ==>

"Take your military training for example," she said. "It enables you to channel emotions during extreme challenges. Lam has some of that too, though toward upholding the rule of law. His personality presents with structure and rigidness, perfect qualities for a bulldog investigator."

"A hard-ass, in other words."

"Yes, Billy Ray, and thankfully so."

Rebecca was right. He appreciated Lam for what he was.

"Believe it or not, you and Tami have much in common, too."

"Oh?" Billy Ray's curiosity showed. "How so?"

"You both approach challenges asymmetrically. Your expertise is guerrilla *warfare*. While her talent is unconventional *thinking*." Rebecca nodded at Tafoya and the hot bikini. "The only *real* difference is you don't have her beauty."

"Or her plumbing," Billy Ray added.

Rebecca stated her opinion, "So assuming Lam is heterosexual, and there's no history influencing his discomfort with Tami's aggressiveness, then I'd conclude they're merely experiencing a personality clash."

"But we can't have clashes on the team," Billy Ray objected, turning deadly serious. "The mission's about to go red hot. Our lives depend on this unit's cohesion." He no longer spoke to Rebecca as a lover. Like it or not, they were fellow combatants now.

By the look in her eyes, she thought so too. "Don't you think Johnny understands the risks, too?"

Billy Ray studied Lam forcing himself to relax on the beach. While serving as a captain in the Green Berets, Lam had led a squad of Special Forces in the jungles of South America, chasing down some of the worst scum mankind ever produced, Columbian drug lords. And most recently, he saved all of their lives in East Texas.

So yeah, Johnny Lam knew the danger.

Groups of college kids milled along the Grand River walkway enjoying their summer break. Businessmen hurried to their appointments. Lovers strolled hand in hand absorbing the scenery.

Duke asked anyone who would listen if they'd seen two men fitting the description of Lam and the mystery man. No one had.

He approached a bag lady pushing a shopping cart filled with her ragtag possessions and asked the same question. She pointed to the Amway Grand Plaza's motor lobby.

Of course—transportation!

He shoved a wad of bills in the lady's shirt and hurried off.

As he approached the hotel, he heard a couple of valets talking about "two assholes" trying to steal a customer's Corvette.

Bullseye!

"Pardon me. I'm investigating an auto insurance claim."

One valet said, "You must mean the 'Vette those dudes tried jacking."

"Yes. How'd you know?"

"Hell, everybody knows. Security has it on tape, the crook flashed a phony badge at one of our employees and demanded the car."

"Phony?" asked Duke.

The other valet commented, "It had the President's picture on it. I mean how friggin' stupid!"

"What happened then?"

The first valet became suspicious. "Shouldn't you know that already, you being an insurance investigator?"

Duke plucked two Ben Franklins from his wallet and held them out. "I *am* investigating, but not for autos. Those two men attacked me." He removed his sunglasses. "I want some serious vengeance."

The valets looked at the bruises then the money. They took the cash.

Duke persisted, "Where'd they go, did they get a vehicle?"

The second valet laughed.

"What's so funny?" Duke asked.

"Nobody gets one of *our* cars. But those idiots did manage to dupe the driver of a Rose pest truck."

The valets pocketed their earnings and hurried off.

Duke was tempted to go after the hotel security tapes, but decided against it since his own picture would end up on a recording as well.

Then a simple solution came to mind, one that would get information and still allow him to remain anonymous. Just go to the pest company headquarters and ask.

It turned out the nice secretary at Rose Pest Solutions was happy to assist *Officer* Duke in his pursuit of two escaped convicts from Michigan's Carson City Correctional Facility.

But for safety's sake, though, she'd need to keep silent about assisting in the matter unless called on to testify. Nor did Officer Duke have any intention of charging Deano as an accessory in the men's escape, since the Rose employee was lied to and was only trying to be helpful.

Duke drove to the party store near the state park beach in Holland where Deano delivered the two men.

He parked and once again set off to find Lam. Though he soon discovered that most everyone he encountered was a beach-goer passing to the lake.

He needed to find a local resident.

It took an entire hour, but he finally got a positive response from a blue-haired elderly woman out walking her Chihuahua, ". . . for the fourth time that day," she explained. "Because poor Booboo ate something that upset her tummy, probably that Chinese product she'd gotten at the dollar store . . . there ought to be a law."

But alas, the old lady reported seeing the men during one of Booboo's earlier walkabouts. Then she pointed toward a very unusual residence, a property that made Duke wonder if the old gal had consumed some of Booboo's tainted chow. News of the home had been splashed all over the television several years back.

Actually, the word *home* was an understatement. It was a beachfront mansion owned by a billionaire whose company sold a popular line of home care products. Accessing *this* property would be tricky. A long driveway led to the house that would certainly be monitored by sensing equipment. Approaching from the beach posed the same issue regarding sensors, not to mention being a quarter-mile of open ground to cover.

Duke got back in the truck and relocated to a shady spot just beyond the mansion gates. He needed time to think.

He cursed his situation—stop the feds from discovering the Rapture *or* capture the killers of Gallina's women. And yet, the two matters weren't mutually exclusive since both concerned Hector—one business, the other personal. If the Feds found the Rapture, the Gallina cartel, the only *real* family Duke had ever known, could be brought down. On the other hand, if he failed to capture the Muslim imposters, Hector would kill him.

Worse still was the fact that both tasks had been rendered nearly impossible once Hector cut him off from cartel resources and forced him to operate solo . . . a trial by ordeal, perhaps?

Duke made a decision, business would trump vendetta.

Revenge for the dead women could wait.

Without proper surveillance equipment, he was left to assume Lam was inside the beach mansion. Without an armed crew, he had no alternative but to let the FBI agent come to him.

Sitting inside the obtrusive truck, parked on a street of million-dollar homes, Duke felt like a lion perched at the gate, waiting to devour its prey.

Lam eventually warmed to socializing.

Billy Ray guessed two things aided his friend's transition. One was the pleasure Lam got from tossing the Frisbee to the dog. The second item was Tafoya's blazing bikini and voluptuous tanned body.

Lam kept copping looks at the Cuban beauty whenever she left her chair to cool off in the lake.

So definitely heterosexual!

Billy Ray's thoughts were interrupted by a long dark shape cruising past a mile off shore.

He pointed. "Either I'm losing my mind or that's a submarine."

"I opt for the first choice," Lam stated unequivocally.

Billy Ray said, "No. Look closer."

Everyone leaned forward.

"A fully loaded freighter, perhaps?" Rebecca suggested.

"That's a conning tower," Billy Ray insisted.

Tafoya came to the rescue. "You're not totally insane, big guy. That's the Silversides, a World War II submarine."

"Here? I thought warships weren't allowed on the Great Lakes."

"The Silversides is a floating time capsule. It's the main exhibit at the Submarine Museum in Muskegon."

Lam said, "WW II? Now I've seen everything."

Tafoya explained, "A dedicated group of old submariners have spent years restoring the boat. It's conducting sea trials and will premiere at the Grand Haven Coast Guard Festival in August."

Billy Ray had heard of the festival. He had tons of respect for his Coast Guard brothers who kept America's waterways safe and commerce moving year-round. Plus they were the very best at search and rescue operations.

Lam said, "I've worked with the CG on drug interdiction and busting human trafficking. They're a professional bunch."

Tafoya provided more detail. "The festival is one of the most popular events in the country, drawing a million people to Grand Haven. The Silversides will be offering rides to raise funds for the museum.

"That's a lot of people for one small area," Billy Ray said.

Tafoya added, "We can beat the crowds, if you'd like. My friend Mitch was the marketing director at the museum and can get us a private tour."

Billy Ray reclined back in his chair. "Been there done that. Besides, I have a feeling our R&R is about over. Let's enjoy it while we can."

The dog roused from his nap, picked up the Frisbee, and approached Rebecca. "What a beautiful dog." She stroked its soft fur.

"His name's Augie," Billy Ray said.

Rebecca searched for a nametag but found only a flat device molded into the collar next to the dog's throat. "How do you know that?"

Lam and Billy Ray looked at each other with sly smirks.

"What . . .?" Rebecca pleaded.

<=== PIPELINE ===>

"The dog, *he* told me."

Had the ladies not already experienced some of Dodd's super-duper spy capabilities, they might've laughed. Instead, they stared at Augie.

As dogs do, Augie sensed the talk was about him.

He laid the Frisbee at Rebecca's feet and said in a human voice, "Throw it." His tail wagged. "Please—"

The women's jaws flopped open!

Rebecca picked up the toy and threw it a little ways.

Augie brought it back, dropped it at her feet, and said, "Farther!"

Astonished, she tossed the saucer repeatedly until Augie dropped the toy at her feet and said, "Thanks." Then he made a *normal* dog noise, laid down in the warm sand, and went fast asleep.

Billy Ray said, "What will he beg for if he rolls on his back."

"Same thing all males beg for," Rebecca said.

Just then, Augie jumped up, growled and said, "House!" Then he sprinted across the beach to the mansion.

"I guess I was wrong," Rebecca said.

All at once, everyone's cell phones began vibrating and ringing.

"Dodd," Lam noted.

"So much for R&R," Billy Ray said and took the call.

"Get back to the house, now!" Dodd commanded.

Billy Ray bolted out of his chair, cell phone tight against his ear. "Talk to me, Admiral!"

"The enemy . . . they're at the gates."

Ten minutes later, the group was dressed and gathered in the theater room. Even Augie joined them to lay on the floor at Rebecca's feet.

Dodd immediately informed them that their cover was blown, most likely due to Billy Ray and Lam's misadventures and van ride to the beach. "Which is why guys like you don't get vacations," Dodd ended sounding more than a little peeved.

The theater screen panned from Dodd's face to an expansive look-down view of the Midwestern United States supplied by one of the nation's spy satellites. The picture narrowed, focused on Lake Michigan, then Holland, and finally the mansion and its surrounding property.

Dodd's voice came through the speakers. "Our NGA analyst spotted *this* twenty minutes ago."

"NGA?" Rebecca asked.

"National Geospatial-Intelligence Agency," Dodd replied.

Whoever was controlling the satellite, whether Dodd from his secret lair in Arkansas or an NGA agent in Virginia, the picture zoomed in until settling on a hideous truck parked a half-block from the gate.

The real-time view showed the vehicle occupied, and a man's arm resting on the driver's window sill.

The arm moved, then moved again.

"He's displaying impatience," Rebecca stated.

"What about passengers, Admiral?" Lam asked.

"The trees are obscuring the bird's vision."

"Try infrared," Billy Ray requested. "Let's see what we're up against."

"Coming up now," Dodd reported.

The colors on the screen changed.

The truck had absorbed sunlight, which normally masked human heat signatures. But because the driver had chosen to park in the shade, the truck eventually cooled sufficiently to show the ghostly outline of a single body inside.

Dodd switched the satellite back to normal view.

"Please expand the picture a bit," Tafoya requested.

Dodd obliged. The view expanded to show the entire vehicle.

Tafoya gasped!

"What is it, Tami?" Lam addressed her by name.

She faced him. "Johnny, that's the truck!"

Lam stood up and studied the picture. Tafoya joined him.

She pointed. "That's the *puto* who caused our accident!"

Lam stared at the theater screen, forcing himself to remember details his brain tried to reject—lights ahead, blaring lights behind, the crash . . . then only darkness.

The lights!

He'd been checking the rearview mirror when a flood of light blinded him. There *had* been a truck, dark green or brown, no—camouflage.

The theater screen switched to a split view.

Dodd's face appeared beside a view of the menacing truck. "Here's what we know so far from the official databases . . ."

Dodd told them about the truck being registered to a paper mill in Muskegon, and that the vehicle had been reported stolen.

Then he explained how the K-KEY Group possessed very special tools for identifying humans, even many species of animals—

Whatever that meant, Billy Ray thought.

"Unfortunately, we don't have an adequate number of data points of the man's face to establish effective search parameters—"

Billy Ray quickly lost patience in yet another science lesson. "How about I just go ask the guy what he wants?"

Dodd was quick to pivot.

"Actually, Wolverine, I have a better idea."

Duke heard a noise.

He looked out of the truck window and saw a dog squatting beneath his window, wagging its stubby tail and holding a Frisbee in its mouth.

Because of the Chihuahua incident, he looked around for the owner.

There was no one else in sight, plus this dog seemed to be eating right.

"Hey there, boy," Duke said. "You lost?"

The dog dropped the toy, sat back, and lolled its tongue.

"I can't play now. Go home," Duke commanded.

Augie tapped the Frisbee with his paw. "Throw it!"

What the—!

"Throw my toy," Augie repeated.

It did talk! Was this some kind of a joke?

He shouted out the window, "Get out of here!"

The dog grabbed the Frisbee. Duke pointed. "Now git!"

The dog ran off.

Duke stuck his head out the window and followed the animal's path. It ran straight to the mansion. Then he got a real bad feeling.

"Are you getting this, Dolittle?" Billy Ray asked.

They watched in real-time as Augie approached the suspect, begged a game of toss, said some words, and was shooed away.

A moment later, the truck sped away, too.

Lam declared, "I think we spooked him."

"Ya' think?" Tafoya chided. "When's the last time *you* encountered a talking dog"

The screen changed back to Dodd's big melon. "No worries. I got a great voice sample, pictures of the man's tattoos, and most importantly, sufficient facial data to achieve biometric authentication."

Billy Ray said, "It would've been simpler to clobber the guy and drag his ass back here for a little interrogation."

"You would think that," declared Lam. "I say we track the bastard. He's got to land somewhere."

"Spoken like a true cop," Billy Ray countered.

"What's wrong with that?" asked Lam.

Tafoya chimed in, "I think Johnny's right."

"Me too," Rebecca cast a vote.

Dodd added his two cents. "Make that a majority."

Billy Ray played hurt. "Mutiny already? But I just got this job."

Dodd ended the reverie. "I'm getting feedback on our uninvited guest."

Tafoya said, "That was quick . . . faces, voices, personal preferences all the way down to my socks. What *don't* you people know about us?"

Dodd ignored Tafoya and provided the preliminaries on the suspect, "Caucasian: 6'3" . . . 250lbs . . . Duke . . . no last." Dodd looked up from his handheld device. "And he drinks rye whiskey."

Billy Ray turned up his palms. "That's it, a gun-totin', whiskey-chuggin' white dude with a pickup truck named Duke? That must be half the male population in Michigan!"

Dodd defended himself. "The algorithm is still processing. It takes official sources more time—"

Tafoya interrupted him, "Then use *unofficial* sources, the ones who know my bra size."

"Jenkins was right," Lam said. "We should've punched the guy out."

"Patience, folks, I have a bird tracking him. For the moment, *who* he is isn't as important as *where* he is—" Dodd stopped mid-sentence.

Billy Ray stepped closer to the video screen. "What is it, Dolittle? And leave off the drink ingredients this time."

Dodd looked up. "Belay my last. Duke *IS* important. He's the head enforcer for the Gallina cartel."

"I thought we killed Gallina last year in Texas," Lam said.

"Just the head. The body grew a new one—the son, Hector Gallina."

"A Mexican cartel inside America?" Tafoya thought out loud.

Lam joined Billy Ray in front of the theater screen. "You mind repeating all that, Admiral?" Lam shot Billy Ray a look. "And I'll take the whole recipe, if you don't mind."

Duke sped north on US 31, making haste to leave the Holland area.

He considered his choices. One was already made—getting the hell away from a government safe house and a talking dog.

Surely his identity was tits-up by now—*duped by a damn pooch!*

Duke pounded the dashboard. He hadn't drank that much whiskey, and he certainly wasn't nuts. So how had they done it? A two-way radio . . . a throat mic on the dog's collar?

A damn parlor trick had flushed him out!

And now he was on the run. Exactly what Lam, or whoever was behind the circus act, intended. And that led to his next decision—where to go.

Tito was dead and Hector cut him off. So the answer was nowhere.

He'd been exposed at last.

Life, karma, destiny—whatever its name—finally caught up with him.

<===== PIPELINE =====>

10

Admiral Dodd briefed the group about the man named Duke.

Several aliases surfaced for Duke's last name, though nothing definitive. The man had showed great discipline avoiding an electronic footprint—ducking cameras, ditching cell phones, using cutouts, and dealing just in cash.

The only hard fact was the truck, which had been reported stolen from the Norman Webster Power Plant and Paper Mill in Muskegon.

But the real mystery was why the head goon for a Mexican cartel would be parked outside of a government safe house presently occupied by the most top-secret organization in the entire federal government, and doing so in a pilfered pickup visible from the planet Mars.

Lam didn't like it. "So all that your vaunted K-KEY Group can come up with on our perp is the name Duke and he works for a crime syndicate? Boy, I'm really impressed!"

"Don't forget, he likes rye whiskey," Billy Ray piled on.

Dodd offered a terse defense. "We only have twelve years of metadata stored on American citizens. This guy predates that and has been mighty careful, only a few snippets of phone conversations and sightings on security cameras, just enough to ensure a sixty-two percent probability that Duke is the chief enforcer for Hector Gallina. But unfortunately, not enough to provide us actionable intel. Our analysts are still wading through antiquated data and old paper personnel files as we speak."

"What about metadata from retailers?" Rebecca asked, still feeling the creeps from her experience in the upstairs closet.

"That's how we learned his taste in whiskey," Dodd replied.

Tafoya shouted, "And my nylons!"

"It's hit and miss with retailer algorithms. We're negotiating with heads from several high-tech and social media companies. So far, though, they're resisting an allegiance in the war on terror."

Tafoya pressed, "Well, if you ask me, Admiral, this Duke guy sounds a lot like Jenkins, avoiding people and staying off the grid. Except for when he's knocking the crap out of people, of course."

"Gee thanks, Tafoya. I'll take that as a compliment," Billy Ray said.

"Tami has a point," Rebecca stressed. "This Duke person is obviously shrewd, just like Billy Ray."

Dodd's head nodded on the theater screen. "Precisely. Duke avoids big-box stores and only deals in cash, no plastic. He must be using anonymizing software to mask his presence on the worldwide web, too. There's just very little available on the guy."

Lam said, "How about some theories on why a guy like this, is trailing a group like us, in a truck like that, and doing so alone."

A picture flashed in Billy Ray's mind of a tall man in a tailored suit holding a bouquet of flowers at Spectrum Hospital—

"He *wasn't* alone."

"The businessman!" Rebecca exclaimed. "The one with the roses. He stood next to me in the hallway!"

Billy Ray said, "He and the Incredible Hulk were working together."

"Fine," Lam said. "But my question still stands. If Duke is the enforcer of a hugely powerful Mexican cartel, what's he doing slumming, and especially here in West Michigan?"

No one answered at first. Then the sound of snapping fingers broke the silence.

"I got it!"

Everyone turned to Tafoya. Even Augie popped his head up.

"Not the slumming part," she said. "But I know what connects Johnny, me, and a camo-painted truck."

"What?" Billy Ray asked.

"Dead women washing up on Michigan beaches!"

"Human trafficking! You're right, Tami." Lam stepped next to Tafoya. "Those girls must've belonged to Hector Gallina. And for whatever reason, the evil bastard had them murdered and is now coming after us."

"But why?" Tafoya asked. "Does the cartel know who you are?"

Lam said, "Who I am is public information, but not what I do. They may just be covering their tracks. Don't forget, you were also at the scene where the body was found and we left together."

Then Tafoya really upped the ante. "If the cartel is so brazen to attack an FBI SAC, what's going to happen with people like Lieutenant Talsma, the coroner, or the CSI folks?"

The room went silent as everyone processed the new revelations.

More mysteries, Billy Ray thought.

Then he faced Dodd. "You said a bird is tracking the truck, correct?"

"Yes, for the moment." Dodd gave a short answer.

"Good," Billy Ray said with a voice as cold as ice. "Here's what I want you to do next . . ."

Duke pulled into the parking lot of a Mel Trotter Ministries thrift store and cruised twice around the building looking for security cameras.

He spotted one mounted on the front of the building pointing at a row of used cars posted For Sale.

<===== PIPELINE =====>

Once indoors, he located a second camera. But as expected, both turned out to be relics, operating VHS technology instead of digital, if they worked at all.

Duke wasn't sure what he was up against or even who Lam worked for. Given that a talking dog with a Frisbee was used to flush him out, the FBI seemed unlikely. It'd been a clever trick, though, and the trick had worked.

He also had to assume an electronic dragnet was spreading far and wide to catch him. If the government wanted him bad enough, they'd deploy the right assets to do so, including ones in geosynchronous orbit around the planet or possibly a medium altitude drone.

It was time to change his looks and finally ditch the ludicrous truck.

Duke parked under a canopy of elm trees and went thrift shopping. Twenty minutes later, he paid cash for fresh clothes and an older model Chevy Tahoe from the lot.

Using his fake police ID, he questioned the store clerk about the security cameras. Sure enough, they were just for looks.

"Because God would protect them," the nice lady cashier said.

Duke wasn't so sure.

Billy Ray locked the doors to the luxurious beach house in Holland. As he did so, he wondered if he and Rebecca would ever experience another night like the one they just shared.

A boy could always hope.

It was time to break camp.

Little known to most common people was the length to which their government went to keep America safe.

Ever since the devastating terrorist attacks on 9/11, from border to border, sea to sea, urban and rural, the Department of Homeland Security, in collaboration with state and local police, operated a network of national fusion centers.

These centers were deemed absolutely critical to coordinating the various facets of responding to crises, such as intelligence gathering, analysis, and dissemination of threat-related information.

The intended result, beyond never allowing the homeland to be attacked again, was to prosecute with extreme prejudice enemies foreign and domestic, villains who of late were casting their lots together.

It was to one of those fusion centers that the team now headed.

Billy Ray had made several equipment requests of Dodd, beginning with providing the team with a new vehicle.

Lam had begged for a Crown Vic, to which Tafoya reminded Lam that the Ford Motor Company discontinued the model some year's back—rather like his clothing style.

Rebecca joined in on the tease by diagnosing Lam with a rare form of MAD, modernity aversion disorder.

But after seeing a tricked-out Ford Expedition roll up the driveway, Lam's sad expression changed and then so did his taste in automobiles. After boarding the big SUV and testing all of the intriguing gadgets, such as voice-activated navigation, hands-free communications equipment, and video screens mounted fore and aft, Lam smiled and lit the torch. The engine revved under the weight of his foot, which caused Dodd to plead for his agent to baby the pricey rig. Billy Ray piled on, by reminding everyone about Lam's terrible luck with anything having four wheels.

Lam mumbled a curse under his breath and pulled away.

Admiral Dodd's face flashed across the video screens mounted in the back of the headrests and on the front console. His voice issued clearly through the stereo speakers. The report wasn't a good one.

"We lost satellite view of the truck."

"I suspected that would happen, Dolittle," Billy Ray said.

"Give me the last verified position," Lam requested.

"Last seen cruising the parking lot of a thrift store one mile north of Holland on US 31."

"He's ditching the vehicle," Lam said immediately.

"And popping tags like you were supposed to do," Tafoya scolded.

The Expedition had a light bar and sirens mounted in the grille. Lam switched them on. "Time to light 'em up and rock 'n roll!"

After hearing Dodd's bad news, Billy Ray considered how machines were made for man, not man for machines. There was no denying the power of technology, advanced satellite capabilities, even the NSA's mass data collection. But nothing could replace boots on the ground and eyes on the target.

Trouble would come, it always did—the kind without arrest warrants and Miranda warnings. The only rule of engagement then would be to win. Then it would be *his* time—Wolverine time.

Presently, though, Billy Ray was content to let a damn good Special Agent take charge of the detective work. In fact, the bad guys better pray that Lam caught them first. Because what came after was the red horse of war—

No mercy, no quarter.

Billy Ray asked Dodd, "What about my *other* requests?" He'd provided Dodd with a list of weapons and special ops equipment.

<==== PIPELINE ====>

Chief among the gear was his preferred sidearm, a Heckler & Koch Mark 23 .45-caliber Special Operations Command pistol, or SOCOM for short. Long guns were preferred for keeping the enemy at a distance. But when battles turned up close and personal, fast and efficient, his trusted pals were his MPK dive knife and a suppressed SOCOM pistol.

"Done," declared Dodd. "I'm posting coordinates to the fusion center."

The video display switched from Dodd's mug to a 3-D navigation screen. A red dot marked the rendezvous point, which appeared looked to be located right smack dab in the middle of a corn field.

Tafoya touched the screen, changing from map to satellite mode. Sure enough, a real-time view showed two paths crisscrossing a large section of shoulder-high corn and a large unpainted old barn occupying the middle of the land.

"Good," Billy Ray said. "Now find Duke."

"We're searching," Dodd said and signed off.

Duke had been careful to avoid the police during the long drive to his hunting cabin. He'd stayed along the Lake Michigan coastline until reaching Ludington then cut east and north through a series of back roads and fire trails.

He'd made just two stops after leaving Holland. The first was at a small hardware store to purchase putty and paint for altering the license plate number. The other was to buy fuel and a bottle of rye whiskey at the Meauwataka General Store near his property. That was four hours ago.

Duke now sat at the dining table of his cabin, preparing for a battle that was sure to come. The long reach of the federal government was just too great. Sooner or later, they get you.

The feeling in his bones said sooner.

Duke took another pull of whiskey and swished it around in his mouth to cleanse the empty tooth socket left after Gallina's beating party. The alcohol burned going down, a reminder that he was still alive.

Next, he went to work on an array of weapons spread out on the table: breaking down, cleaning, re-assembling, cycling, and arming.

There were pistols and shotguns for close-in work, throwing knives and a crossbow for silent hunting, and night-vision optics for gaining an advantage on the enemy.

And there was his favorite handgun, a Colt M1911 .45 automatic. It had been his father's weapon in the jungles of Viet Nam. Tiny notches covered both sides of the pistol grip, carved by his father's hand. There was also a notch carved by Duke after he'd ended his father's abuse.

The M1911 wasn't a modern piece. And though it was limited on ammo capacity, it destroyed whatever it was pointed at. Plus the gun fit nicely in his large hand.

The workhorse of his cache also lay on the table, an M4A1 Carbine stolen from the Army.

The M4A1 was a high-tech, multiple-use assault rifle employed by most American Special Forces and SWAT Teams. It provided Duke with long range and accuracy, as well as full auto or controlled semi-automatic bursts. Furthermore, the weapon was a force multiplier, capable of transforming his presence from a guy with a gun into a deadly combatant.

He fitted a suppressor onto the weapon to quiet his presence in the woods. If he was to survive, one man against many, he had to be a ghost.

Lastly, he reached for an accessory capable of making a lone wolf seem like a platoon of killers, an M203 grenade launcher. He attached the launcher to the underside of the M4A1 and set the weapon down on the table.

Finished with his arsenal, he leaned back and rubbed his aching head. He still felt concussed. But who wouldn't be after nearly having their brains bashed in.

He was a big man, but not that big. So out came more pills for the headache and another chaser of rye. After a few minutes, both products took effect, and his mind felt free for what was to come.

Duke went to the window and looked out over the newly planted yard. This was his first home—something he'd never had in life. The sun was setting, and soon the floodlights would illuminate the cabin's perimeter, casting long shadows from the trees. The shadows had always reminded Duke of demons marching across the lawn . . . coming for him.

How quickly the hunter had become the hunted.

As far as he could determine, he'd managed to avoid the police and electronic surveillance.

But this felt like something different, something beyond typical law enforcement. Did *they* know the dark and deadly secret hidden beneath his cabin? Should he get Hector involved? The sophistication and breadth of the NSA's reach, and the capabilities of the nation's intelligence agencies, meant that whatever could be discovered about Duke Smith had probably occurred by now.

So, yeah, the feds *were* on their way. It was only a matter of time now.

Duke dialed Gallina's phone and left a short message. Then he went back to work hardening his fighting position.

He'd done his best to throw Lam off his trail. So if this was to be his last stand, he would not go quietly into the night.

Lam parked in front of a large steel building in the middle of the Michigan cornfield beside a line of unmarked federal vehicles.

"Looks like we're late for the barn dance, Johnny," Tafoya said.

Lam shut off the car. "Let's do-si-do on in there and find out."

"I think you mean, *promenade,*" Rebecca corrected him. "Your buddies in there might draw down on us if we enter back-to-back."

"I forgot you're a Texas gal," Lam told Rebecca.

Tafoya scrutinized her teammates. "One Michigander versus three Texans? I'll take those odds."

Three raucous *boos* filled the cab.

They stepped through the doors of the massive steel building and stopped to get their bearings.

Farm equipment ringed the outer walls.

A line of tables occupied the center of the barn that contained weapons and other tactical equipment.

And off to one side, a crowd of FBI agents dressed in tactical pants and blue windbreakers with yellow FBI letters on the back studied a wall map and got briefed on the latest intel.

As Billy Ray and the others approached, the agents stopped their discussion.

Then a bald man with sunken eyes stepped forward and extended a hand to Lam. "How's the head?"

Lam shook his colleague's hand. "Back to normal, Agent Tompkins."

After introductions, Tafoya said to Tompkins, "Good news, I found Lam's hospital room."

Tompkins ignored her deliberate dig and caught the team up on the briefing "And here's where we found the B.U.T."

"*BUT?*" asked Tafoya.

"Big Ugly Truck. Now if you don't mind, Ms. Tafoya . . .?"

Having scored her points, she gave the agent a wry smile. "Go on."

Tompkins continued, "The truck was found here," he tapped the map, "near the thrift store. A man named Duke Smith then purchased a twelve-year-old silver Chevy Tahoe and various articles of clothing."

"Popping tags," Lam said softly to Tafoya.

"What's that?" asked Tompkins.

"Never mind," Lam replied. "The Tahoe is a common model."

"And color," Tafoya added.

Upon Billy Ray's request, an agent set a laptop computer on a table next to the whiteboard and typed a command.

Dodd's face faded in.

"What do you have for us, Admiral?" Billy Ray asked.

Dodd got right to it. "Agent Lam presumes correctly. Chevy Tahoes *are* everywhere. We're still sorting chaff from the grain."

The gathering fell silent and waited on Dodd to provide further intel on the SUV and Duke's whereabouts.

Dodd returned a moment later.

"We've narrowed the possibilities."

"How many?" Billy Ray demanded.

"Eleven."

"Eleven! Can't you do better than that?" Billy Ray pressed.

"With time, yes."

"How much time?"

"Two days, minimum." Dodd said.

Everyone looked at Dodd's image then at Billy Ray.

He asked, "Can't you task more satellites to the area?"

"No. They're busy elsewhere."

"Then un-busy them!"

"Can't do that, Wolverine. Unless you wish to personally explain to the President of the United States why chasing a two-bit cartel thug somewhere in West Michigan is more important than monitoring Iran's march toward nuclear weapons, the ISIS threat in the Middle East, or Russia gobbling up former Soviet territory."

"I'd need only one word, *Rapture,*" Billy Ray argued.

Dodd shot back. "We don't know that for sure."

Tompkins cut in. "What's Rapture?"

Dodd quashed further inquiry on the subject. "Forget what you heard. It's need-to-know only."

Billy Ray and Lam eyeballed each other, obvious that they shared a common thought. Why would Dodd keep an extremely dangerous drug like Rapture a secret, especially from the FBI of all people?

Lam said, "How ironic that with all the capability of your group, and the impositions placed on the citizens of this country, that we're still left having to make a scientific wild-ass guess. I hope it's all been worth it to you, Admiral."

Dodd didn't bother to answer.

Billy Ray got them on track. "Then let's get busy narrowing the field."

Dodd provided relative GPS data for all eleven vehicles, most of them still in motion.

Tompkins marked the map for each Tahoe of interest.

For the next hour, reports filtered in from traffic cops, sheriff deputies, and state troopers until nearly all silver Tahoes were accounted for.

<==== PIPELINE ====>

Four of the vehicles were eliminated from the list after they'd arrived at residences that checked out clean.

Another four were pulled over along various interstates.

And of those, two were let go after an ID check; the third was ticketed for texting while driving and let go; and the last driver was arrested for operating a vehicle under the influence of an unknown intoxicant.

None of the eight vehicles were connected with Duke, however.

That left three silver Chevy Tahoes unaccounted for, and one of those had already dropped from the surveillance net.

"Maybe the driver ducked into a parking garage," Tompkins said.

"Maybe that's our guy," Lam said.

"Not many garages without video these days," Dodd countered.

Tafoya tapped the map where one of the two remaining vehicles had ended its trip. "I know this area. It's a rough part of Muskegon Heights."

"How so?" asked Billy Ray.

Tompkins fielded the question. "Abandoned factories, shabby homes, gangs, drugs, you name it—casualties of NAFTA."

Lam nodded at Tafoya. "Good catch, Tami."

Billy Ray was pleased to see the growing professionalism between Lam and Tafoya.

He tapped the list. "What about the last vehicle?"

"Probably a backwoodsman," Tompkins said, tracing a zigzag line with his finger that ran up the coast before veering easterly into the Manistee National Forest, then north toward Cadillac until finally disappearing off the search grid entirely.

The agent standing next to Tompkins said, "There's nothing up there but hunting cabins."

Lam checked his watch. "Time's wasting. It'll be sundown soon."

"I opt for Muskegon Heights," Tompkins said. "It makes sense to me for the horse to run back to the barn to join his fellow cartel goons."

"Are you sure we haven't missed anything?" Lam asked the group mustered around the table, including Dodd on the laptop connection. "I'm from Texas and this is y'all's backyard. So don't be shy, speak up."

Nobody did, not even Billy Ray, though his internal bells were sounding. Choosing Muskegon Heights just didn't feel right.

The meeting ended. Tompkins and several agents remained behind at the map making phone calls and planning the operation.

Also, a plainclothes Muskegon cop was dispatched to the address indicated by Dodd's spy satellite. Ten slow and agonizing minutes later, the officer confirmed the presence of the Tahoe parked in the lot of a condemned tool and die factory, along with ten additional cars and trucks.

Billy Ray and Lam excused themselves from the meeting and made their way to the equipment table.

They inspected the assortment—communications gear, tactical vests, boxes of ammunition, and weapons, such as the H&K Universal Machine Pistol, or UMP, chambered for the .45 ACP cartridge. The UMP was light and powerful, well-suited for a close-in environment.

Next Billy Ray lifted the SOCOM pistol. As requested, it was fixed with a suppressor, thus transforming the gun into a stealthy killing tool. He hefted the gun and checked the action.

It was a beauty! A testament to the fine art of weapons manufacturing.

Too bad there wasn't an opportunity to get in some range time.

Though Billy Ray was confident with center-mass targeting, headshots were another matter, requiring practice or proximity, neither of which he hoped would be necessary.

A part of him died with every pull of the trigger.

Hector Gallina summoned his new chief of security to his office.

The Uzi machine guns elevated as the smiling guard walked past and sat himself down in the lone chair in front of Hector.

Dried blood stained the armrests.

Hector pushed a button on his phone and Duke's message played. It was short and direct. "*They found the Rapture. If you want to save our family, come tonight.*"

A beep indicated the message had concluded.

Gallina stared into the security guard's eyes.

Finally, in his soft voice, he said, "Maybe I made a mistake replacing Duke with you."

The guard lost his smile and swallowed hard. His eyes grew as large as dinner plates. He knew—as everyone did—that Hector never paid for his own mistakes. He himself had disciplined others on Hector's behalf, including Duke.

"You will now prove your worth to our family. Take as many men as you need. But know this, you will win or you will die."

The guard's throat went dry.

"You are to secure the drugs. Then you will kill Duke." Hector stared at him with eyes vacant of warmth or life. . "Have I made myself sufficiently clear?"

"*Si, Jefe,*" the guard croaked. "I won't let you down like Duke did."

Gallina waved a hand and the guard was dismissed.

Night arrived and so had the time for the raid on the tool and die factory in Muskegon.

Agent Tompkins had received the proper warrants from a judge. All agents were in place. And the local police moved in to cordon off all streets and surround the area. Then the countdown began.

There would be no escape for the silver Tahoe or its driver.

Billy Ray, Lam, and the women were under orders to remain inside the Ford Expedition parked a block away from the action. This was cop time, and they weren't cops. Lam had argued differently. But in the end, they were forced to follow the action over a police radio.

Billy Ray still had a bad feeling about the target. In his gut, it felt like he'd missed something.

Lam was amped up. And why not? These were his guys, and this a police operation. Or maybe it was just a feeling that he was getting closer to finding the missing Rapture. At the very least, he hoped to crush a human trafficking ring and drug pipeline.

Billy Ray had traded seats with Tafoya and now sat quietly beside Lam. Rebecca remained stoic: observing, assessing, and diagnosing. Tafoya, even from the back seat, listened intently to the radio communications, acting every bit invested—no longer portraying the blindfolded *Lady Justice* and arbiter of everyone's civil rights.

Lam couldn't blame her for the transition, not after *two* attempts on her life and Dodd's chilling intelligence briefing. She'd had a come-to-Jesus conversion, swapping ink for lead, the power of the pen for that of a gun.

He felt sad for Tafoya's exchange.

Like innocence lost.

Lam lifted a set of binoculars and observed the operation.

All remained quiet at the condemned factory until a back door opened and a single candescent bulb cast its meager light on eight figures exiting to the parking lot. The suspects were led by a tall, heavyset person. But due to distance and darkness, faces were indistinguishable.

The leader could've been a kid or an old man.

Hell—it could've been a woman.

"This is frustrating!" Lam said through clenched teeth.

"True that, Army," Billy Ray agreed.

The radio speakers in the Ford suddenly erupted with shouts from Tompkins, "Now! Now! Now! Take them down!"

Gunfire erupted!

Blasting pistols and shotguns filled the night air. Then a lethal hail of lead from an AK-47 assault rifle made those sound like Childs play. The assault weapon was easily distinguishable from the others.

It was unclear who had fired first, the bad guys or the strike team. Lam couldn't take waiting any longer.

"Stay here, ladies. You too, Jenkins!"

He got out and sprinted off.

After several minutes of pitched battle, the AK-47 fell deathly silent, followed eventually by the other weapons.

"SITREP!" Tompkins commanded over the police channel.

Billy Ray listened as the voices of FBI agents and contractors called in their positions and conditions for the situation report.

Sounding satisfied, Tompkins ordered a ceasefire.

The night went abruptly quiet. Then all at once, neighborhood dogs began barking and howling. And finally, the shrill sound of police sirens joined the cacophony.

Billy Ray felt the same as Lam, hating being relegated to an observer. Though neither was he a fool, seeing no glory in dashing helter-skelter into a firefight . . . or any fight for that matter.

But still, observing an op through binoculars was definitely frustrating!

Shadows moved in the dark. The sound of a man's voice blared over a bull horn, demanding the suspects toss aside their weapons and lay face down on the ground, hands stretched far out to their sides palms facing up.

Then came more shouts, more sirens, and finally, bright spot lights.

The raid was over.

All agents reported in over the radio, minus one . . . Lam?

Billy Ray pulled his SOCOM pistol from the chest holster and left the Ford, hoping like hell that Lam was still alive.

He ran in a crouch toward the action then heard a familiar voice.

"Don't shoot! Jenkins is with us!"

It was Lam! Thank goodness he was alive!

But still, the good guys had lost a brave agent in the firefight.

By now, sirens and flashing lights surrounded the area, crime scene tape snaked throughout, and the dead lay covered with plastic tarps. Then two medic vans pulled up, followed a second later by a news van.

So much for a media blackout, Billy Ray thought.

It must've been the arrival of the news crew that got Tafoya to disobey orders. Because she came running up and joined the command team.

<=== PIPELINE ===>

Interestingly, Lam offered no objections. Maybe she could somewhat control the outflow of info to the media.

Billy Ray was pleased that these two members of his team had managed to establish a positive working relationship and an air of civility.

Of the eight assailants—gangbangers—five were dead: two male Latinos, two black males, and a young white female. Guns lay near each of them, including the AK-47 still on full auto with 2 loaded magazines taped together in opposite direction for quick load. Except for the girl, the dead bodies all looked to be in their mid-twenties.

Billy Ray shook his head. A pity they'd all chosen violence against their fellow man. Now those choices had ended their aging process.

The three living goons had sustained varying degrees of wounds, none mortal so far as Billy Ray could tell. Each one was being attended by an EMT and guarded by officers of the Muskegon Police Department.

After first inspecting the dead criminals, Billy Ray and Lam walked over to one of the lucky ones.

Lam dismissed the city cop. The wounded gangbanger sat on the ground, hands zip-tied behind his back. He looked older than the others, maybe approaching forty. An EMT was wrapping gauze and tape around a still oozing leg wound.

"What's the damage?" Lam nodded at the heavily-tattooed man.

The EMT reported, "Bullet missed main arteries, but it mangled his femur. I'm about to immobilize the leg and shoot him full of morphine."

Lam asked the wounded man, "What's your name?"

The guy didn't answer.

Lam said to the EMT, "You guys are spread pretty thin. Go ahead and shove off. My partner and I can handle this."

The EMT looked at Billy Ray then back at Lam. "You sure?"

"I'm sure," Lam said. "Leave the supplies. We'll take it from here."

Billy Ray stared at the wounded criminal. The guy's face twisted in pain from the broken leg. But there was nothing wrong with his voice box.

Lam said, "I'll ask you one more time. What's your name?"

The guy sneered. "Aren't you supposed to issue a warning or something, what about my rights?"

"I just did offer you a warning, didn't you hear it?" Lam said and then nodded at Billy Ray.

Billy Ray grabbed the roll of gauze, peeled off a handful, and pinched the back of the guy's neck near the base of the skull.

The man's jaws opened involuntarily and Billy Ray jammed the entire wad of cotton in his mouth.

The crook's eyes got big!

Lam got face to face with the criminal. "Here's my warning, you worthless prick. I'll ask you a question. You refuse to answer," Lam thumbed at Billy Ray, "my partner will test your leg. Like this—"

Billy Ray leaned on the crook's broken femur. The man's face turned beet red. The gauze muffled his scream.

Billy Ray grabbed the same pressure points behind the man's neck as before. The jaws came open and he plucked out the gauze.

Lam glared hard at the wounded criminal. "What's your name?"

"C—Carl. My name's Carl."

"Thank you, Carl. Now tell me where Duke is."

"Who?"

"Duke. The guy who owns the silver Tahoe."

"Please, my leg!"

Billy Ray squeezed the man's neck and jammed the gauze back in. Large beads of sweat began rolling down Carl's forehead. Then Billy Ray placed his hand on the broken leg again and pressed.

Carl acted as if a bolt of electricity shot up his back.

Lam continued, "If you haven't noticed by now, you do not have the right to remain silent. You do, however, have the right to a lot more pain should I choose to provide it, free of charge."

Carl nodded vigorously. Billy Ray removed the gauze.

The gangbanger huffed and puffed, nearly hyperventilating.

"Duke. D–U–K–E. Where is he?" Lam demanded.

"I don't know any Duke. The Tahoe belongs to the big kid over there." Carl twisted to point, further agitating the leg, and bellowed in pain.

Lam and Billy Ray turned to see one of plastic-covered bodies.

The owner of the Tahoe was dead.

Billy Ray jammed the gauze back in Carl's mouth, then he and Lam crossed over to the plastic sheet.

Lam pulled back the tarp and cursed. The lifeless brown eyes staring up at them belonged to one of the African-American males.

"We've been had," Billy Ray said. "Duke is the one who headed to the North Country."

Billy Ray realized what had bothered him about the Muskegon-bound Tahoe—it was too easy. The head enforcer of a vicious Mexican drug cartel would never act so bush-league as the dead guy at their feet.

In fact, the *real* Duke did exactly what Billy Ray would have done . . .

Head straight for the wilderness!

<═══ PIPELINE ═══>

11

As they drove north on US 31, they spoke to Dodd over the secure sat-link communications.

"We picked a blind alley, Admiral. I take full responsibility for the screw-up," Lam said.

Billy Ray countered, "Actually, it was my fault. I had a feeling but didn't act on it."

"Actually, I'm the one who suggested Muskegon," Tafoya argued.

Dodd looked straight at the camera and said, "And you, Ms. Payne? What would be your part in this SNAFU?"

"Sorry, Admiral. I should've come forward once I concluded you were all nuts. I just didn't want to hurt your feelings."

Rebecca's bit of humor broke the tension.

Billy Ray took over.

"I have a strong feeling we're heading into a shitstorm, Admiral. This Duke fellow just paid us back for tricking him. What's more, he bought himself extra time to go to ground and harden his defenses."

Dodd had been a Navy SEAL commander, and a darn good one. He saw it too. "You're right, Wolverine. This mission just went full-blown military."

"Sorry, Admiral," Lam said.

"Not your fault, Special Agent Lam. This matter has been military from the start. *We* just needed to prove it."

Dodd's phrasing sounded peculiar to Billy Ray "Prove what to who?"

"We have our own shit-storm in D.C. But I can't say any more, other than we must be prudent delineating law enforcement from military enforcement."

Lam chimed in, "What about my old boss, Chris Dreyfus? He's supposed to be navigating those waters for your K-KEY Group."

"Dreyfus is doing his best, but things may not work out this time."

Definitely odd, Billy Ray concluded.

Dodd may be one to pontificate like a science professor, but he'd never been one to beat around the bush. Whatever was spooking him inside the intelligence community had to be big.

"Replay that satellite intel," Billy Ray ordered.

The video monitors switched to the 3-D map. A blue line traced north on US 31 past Ludington, then east, and finally north into the woods.

Lam pointed at the console. "The line just ends. What's in that area?"

Tafoya worked the touchscreen. "State and national forest, small farms, hunting cabins. The nearest city is Cadillac."

Billy Ray gave it some thought. It'd been the mention of hunting cabins back at the barn that sparked his doubts about the Muskegon raid. Had it been him on the run, and with months, or even years, to anticipate the law catching up, he would've made a place in the middle of the woods, too—a place to escape to . . . and from.

"How are we going to find him now?" Lam asked. "There must be hundreds of similar SUVs. Going door to door is out of the question."

Billy Ray tapped Tafoya on the shoulder. "Switch to satellite view."

"What do you expect to find?" Rebecca asked, eyeing Billy Ray, not as a lover but as a clinician—searching, probing, analyzing.

"Myself," he replied. "And you're going to help me."

Duke finished rigging the explosives.

Now no one but a skilled jungle fighter stood a chance of defeating the booby traps on the dirt roads and foot trails leading to the cabin.

He thought back to when first planning his cabin and choosing a suitable building site. He'd had three tactical requirements. First was to acquire acreage bordering the national forest that could provide maximum privacy, as well as escapability by using an off-road motorcycle on all of the narrow hiking trails that crisscrossed near his property. The second was to have an ability to live off the land through hunting and fishing, and possess ample fresh water. The last requirement, was to gain tactical advantage against intruders. Meaning the cabin had to be situated on high, defensible ground.

He'd achieved all of his objectives. The cabin and surrounding property was now hardened as much as could be expected. He'd employed various types of trip wires: some providing forewarning, some offering nasty surprises, still others solely to aid his escape. But all would make for a terrible time in the woods for unwanted guests.

And now he waited.

Billy Ray poured over the satellite views of the vast forest.

Privately owned properties speckled the national park stretching across the state, as the Manistee National Forest joined the Huron National Forest.

He studied the elevation map next, what little elevation there was, and the numerous lakes, ponds, rivers, creeks, and swamps.

Finally, Billy Ray exhaled a long breath.

There were so many choices.

<===== PIPELINE =====>

Dodd had been checking the records of every home and every land owner in Wexford County. But there was slim chance of finding a guy named Duke on any deeds or government applications.

It was almost midnight, and everyone was tired and hungry. The day seemed to have lasted a week.

So Lam pulled into a McDonald's drive-thru for burgers and fries. Even the ladies shelved their careful eating habits for the moment.

Everyone got quiet when the food came, proof of hunger. So when Dodd's voice blared over the car speakers, it sounded like the blare of a semi's air horn.

"Got him!"

Everyone stopped in mid-bite.

"Duke?" Lam mumbled through half-eaten fries.

"We got lucky," Dodd said. "I just got off the phone with the owner of a small general store in Meauwataka. The owner's name is Bruce, and he recently installed a security camera to 'catch the pinhead' who'd been breaking into his business. Bruce's tiny net just caught a big fish."

Dodd kept talking while the grainy photo of a man's face appeared on the Ford's video screens.

The man wore a hat pulled low, casting shadows or perhaps they were bruises, it was hard to determine. Given the poor quality of the picture, positive ID was nearly impossible to the human eye. But not for a supercomputer employing facial recognition software.

Dodd continued, "Data points are sufficient to achieve a fifty-nine percent likelihood that the man in the picture is our suspect."

Billy Ray was skeptical. There were lots of Michiganders who shared features similar to Duke.

They'd lost so much time already and the trail was growing cold.

He tested Dodd. "Aren't you actually saying there's a forty-one percent chance the man in the picture is *not* Duke?"

"It's all we've got, Wolverine," Dodd admitted.

"I agree with the Admiral," Lam said. "Look at it tactically Navy. If you had a fifty-nine percent chance that an enemy was within your reach, would you go?"

"All right, then," Billy Ray said. "Let's establish a new search grid. Admiral, you check the county records for deeds, septic systems installs, building permits and building plans submitted to the townships. Lam can make calls to the local cops, Tafoya too. Meanwhile, Rebecca and I will study the maps and overheads. We need to get into this guy's head . . . discover how he thinks."

"It's a go, then," Dodd said. "SITREP in one hour."

"Hopefully sooner," Billy Ray said.

If the enemy was preparing for an assault, as Billy Ray fully suspected, an hour could be like an eternity.

A trained warrior could be waiting for them.

Gallina's new security chief wasn't finding much to grin about this day.

His life was already hanging in the balance after his visit with Hector.

And now things got a whole lot worse, he thought as he brought his car to a stop behind a Muskegon Police Department cruiser flashing its lights and blocking the road leading to his destination. Uniformed officers stood in the intersection turning away all traffic.

He switched on the radio and dialed up a local news station and caught a breaking story of a shootout between police and a violent gang of criminals.

That could only mean one thing—his crew was now dead or arrested. Somehow, the feds had learned of the crew and then raided the hideout. What he didn't know was that it was just dumb lady luck that the feds and locals had eradicated his team.

It had been arranged hours ago with his most trusted guy, a tall black kid with lots of brains, a thirst for money, and a real mean streak to match. The kid had reported over the phone that their *basketball game was a go,* and that they had two full teams.

But when the crew failed to arrive, the guard began sensing the worst.

There was no time left to pull together another hit squad. If he didn't get up to Meauwataka soon, he was a dead man for sure!

It was strange, the guard mulled as he approached the northbound lane of US 31, maybe this was how Duke felt . . .

Alone!

The dashboard clock showed four balls.

Admiral Dodd's face reappeared on the video screens in the Ford SUV. They'd each spent the hour leading to midnight working different angles in an attempt to find Duke.

Lam went first, "Sorry, Admiral, a dry hole. None of the local cops had information on the perp. The Wexford County Sheriff couldn't be reached on account of being home convalescing from a recent medical procedure."

Tafoya went next. "*Nada.* Zip. Zilch. I couldn't reach a soul at this late hour. Hope you had better luck."

<=== PIPELINE ===>

Dodd said, "I may have something, but let's hear from Wolverine first."

Billy Ray and Rebecca had taken an unconventional approach to discovering Duke's whereabouts. They paired military tactics with human psychology—his training teamed with her medical education. Rebecca had had a taste of asymmetric warfare during their battle in Texas against the former-KGB agent, Joseph Wiggins. Furthermore, she'd felt the sting of torture after being captured by the sadistic bastard.

Billy Ray reported, "We've identified seven target properties."

Rebecca took it from there. "Our theory is based on what Billy Ray would do if faced with the same circumstances as Duke."

Dodd said, "Please proceed, Ms. Payne. You've piqued my interest."

"We combined Billy Ray's psych profile with his tactical knowledge and created a template. We then used that to compare all we know about Duke, plus the information of all of the properties in Wexford County. We were able to narrow the choices to seven locations where a man like Duke might be. If we had more time—"

Dodd waved off the apology. "You did well, Ms. Payne. I'll run the data through our computers here. Sit tight, this will take approximately twenty-six minutes and thirty seconds." The video screen went black.

Billy Ray wondered where "here" was and why Dodd even bothered using words like *approximate*. He uploaded the GPS coordinates of all seven properties to Dodd.

And then they waited.

He and Lam closed their eyes for combat naps.

Nearly a half-hour later, they were roused by the women as Dodd reappeared on the screen.

"How can you guys do that?" Tafoya demanded.

"Do what?" Billy Ray asked innocently.

Rebecca piled on, "Begin snoring the instant you close your eyes!"

Lam objected, "I don't snore, Jenkins does."

Billy Ray argued, "Not the Navy. It's you ground-pounders that snore."

"You both do!" Tafoya and Rebecca shot back together.

Dodd ended the debate. "I think we have something."

Billy Ray came full awake, so did Lam.

Both felt refreshed after twenty-six minutes and *twenty-eight* seconds of beauty sleep.

Billy Ray went operational. "Talk to me, Dolittle."

"Five of the properties you identified checked out clean, two did not."

"Uh oh. Not another drug sting," Tafoya said.

"Potentially," Dodd answered. "We appear to have another coin toss."

"Maybe we can tilt the odds." Rebecca requested the property specs.

119

The first property suddenly appeared on the car monitors.

Billy Ray studied the view. The cabin was built in a clearing with no neighbors for several miles. Rather, the land abutted the National forest and access to hiking and ORV trails for stealthy movement. Logistically, the property had a spring-fed lake estimated at five acres to assure fish and fresh water. Lastly, the cabin was a stout log structure surrounded by outbuildings or huts situated every thirty yards in a crescent pattern beside the lake.

Duck blinds? Billy Ray wondered.

Overall, the first property was well situated, and could be defended easily, or abandoned quickly—which is why he'd chosen it.

"Okay, show me the other property," Billy Ray said.

The second property had some of the same features as the first: National forest, escape trails, adequate water, and a defensible main compound.

"What's the difference?" Tafoya asked.

"Nothing in a grand way," Billy Ray said, "just subtle things." He gave the short answer, wanting to hear what Dodd discovered before saying more. "What about deeds, dates of purchase, utilities bills, Dolittle?"

"Both deeds list corporate ownership. Property number one claims to be a private hunting club. Property two is owned by a plumbers union and used on the weekends by its members."

Billy Ray was busy absorbing the information when Dodd said, "That's strange. Both properties were purchased on the exact same day fourteen years ago. Although, the house on property number two was built only recently."

"How recent?" Billy Ray asked.

Dodd peeked down at his handheld device and said, "Four months ago." He looked into the camera. "And in case you're wondering, the building permits are legit. Even the septic system goes above and beyond using new green technology and an extra-large holding tank."

Billy Ray analyzed the differences between the properties. The hunt club was perfect for repelling an armed assault by utilizing strategic kill zones. An invading force would indeed be dead ducks.

Property number two shared some of the advantages to thwart attackers, and could prove equally problematic along the access roads and trails from tripwires and booby traps.

The real difference was the siting of the houses. The hunt club was cleared of trees and brush to provide line-of-sight targeting of advancing forces. Whereas, the plumbers' union house sat atop a hill and afforded views into meadows on three sides and down a treed slope in back.

Lam asked, "Which one do we choose?"

The two properties were miles apart, and would cost hours of precious time checking them out as a team. They could improve on that by splitting up. But Billy Ray wasn't in favor dividing his forces, meager as they were.

It had to be a choice of one or the other.

But which one?

Dodd said, "The hunt club looks ideal for cartel members to make a stand. Plus they would have escape options if the battle goes bad."

"Sounds logical to me," Lam said.

Billy Ray thought about *logic*. It'd been logic that led to the Muskegon debacle. They couldn't afford mistakes during a military assault. Mistakes cost lives.

Only Lam had had special weapons and tactics training. Rebecca was trained on small arms, a benefit to having a sheriff for a father. She could also claim one kill—*the one that saved his life in Texas.* Tafoya had said she passed a gun safety course as a kid and shot .22's at a church camp. As for Dodd, the best he could do was direct the battle from afar, but minus the full assets of the K-KEY Group, for reasons yet unexplained.

Even had the former SEAL been present, there'd be little Dodd could do from a wheelchair, his legs lost to an exploding mine years ago.

Furthermore, there was no way of knowing how many guns awaited them. Their own firepower and ammo stowed in the back of the Ford was adequate to battle a small number of combatants, nothing more.

Tactical advantages were definitely not in their favor.

Billy Ray tried telling himself that they were a team, but the word rang hollow. Facts were facts. They were a group of friends, each with unique abilities, none of which were bloodletting, except for himself, and Lam to a lesser degree.

His friends were common people, not Navy SEALs. The distraction of protecting them while battling a vicious enemy could end up getting them all killed.

Billy Ray felt the icy stab of doubt.

Qasem had a big surprise for the Americans. He was about to give up two of his sleeper agents. One was a woman chosen and groomed for a glorious death as a martyr for Allah. The other was a man in a motorized wheel chair who blamed the U.S. government for his disability.

Both would deliver similar packages into the heart of Chicago.

As Qasem left the woman's Hyde Park apartment near the University of Chicago.

He allowed himself a moment of blissful joy at his cunning plan—but only a moment.

Such levity could dull the mind.

The woman was eight months pregnant and showing considerably beneath her clothing. Neighbors often asked if she was expecting twins.

She was not. The pregnancy was a ruse.

Beneath her maternity wear was a silicone pregnancy belly that the woman had increased in size month to month to match the natural course of the *baby* forming in her womb. Each of the prosthetic devices had been convincing, garnering well-wishes from her neighbors, even gifts and offers to assist when her wonderful day arrived.

Unbeknownst to all of those kind folks, her glorious day had come.

The fake belly became a suicide vest containing plastic explosives, glass beads, and radioactive pellets of cobalt-60, stolen from a Tijuana cancer clinic then smuggled into the U.S. through the Gallina trafficking pipeline.

On the morrow, the *expecting* mother would board the "L" train and travel during the noontime rush-hour to the Willis Tower in downtown Chicago.

Formerly called the Sear's Tower, the building once stood as the tallest on the planet, reaching over a quarter-mile into the Midwestern sky. The disabled man would be delivered to the same address by a city bus that catered to citizens with special needs.

The plot called for the woman to position herself outside the beautiful glass entrance of the Willis Tower on Wacker Street, while the disabled man parked at the east entrance of the famous skyscraper.

At the prescribed time, the woman would trigger her device, followed one minute later by the man in the wheelchair. The resulting deaths would be gruesome and longer term than just the initial blast due to the latent radioactivity. Panic would sweep across the nation, if not the world.

The act would mark the first time that freedom fighters deployed radioactive bombs on American soil.

Furthermore, the glorious day would signal the birth of Allah's revenge on the Great Satan, or so the prerecorded martyrdom videos would claim.

Only it would not.

The entire operation was a red herring.

In addition to the two sleeper agents, he was about to expose the U.S. President and his administration for what they truly were.

And then the end would come.

There was much preparation before the *true* day of glory.

Midnight had come and gone.

Maybe the feds weren't really coming.

Or maybe his imagination was playing tricks on him, Duke thought as he sat at the computer monitoring the perimeter video feeds.

Fatigue was becoming a factor now. He wanted to lay his head down . . . his aching head.

An alarm on the computer activated.

Duke came fully alert. Fatigue was forgotten.

The camera at the road showed a car turning in.

He didn't have a gate at the road, only a sign posting *Private Property.* Cars sometimes used the drive as a turn-around.

This wasn't one of those occasions.

The car rolled to a stop and parked a hundred feet from the cabin. Then someone Duke never would've imagined stepped out. It was the guard from the power plant, Hector's new head of security.

For the first time Duke could remember, the man wasn't smiling.

Billy Ray felt perplexed. They needed to act. *But which property?*

"Dolittle, how about peeking inside both residences, I'd like to know how many bad guys we're up against."

"Sorry, Wolverine. No satellites. They're presently tasked elsewhere."

Billy Ray began wondering why Dodd had made such a stink of pulling the team together if they were just going to be used as benchwarmers or possibly just targets.

"What's going on here, Admiral? Why do I get the feeling we're the JV squad. Is there something you're not telling us?"

"We just need more proof before I can call in the big boys," Dodd said.

Dodd was Billy Ray's commander, then *and* now. They were brothers in arms. And in all that time, never once had Dodd lied to him.

Billy Ray was getting the feeling that something had changed. Why could he use a satellite to watch a beach house but not for checking out the hiding place of a drug cartel chief enforcer?

Lam checked his watch. "Make a decision, Jenkins."

Tafoya turned in her seat and faced Billy Ray. "Well?"

Rebecca was watching him, too, reading his face like a book. Her words revealed the plot. "You're worried about us, aren't you?"

All eyes were on him now.

"I don't want any of you to get dead," Billy Ray finally admitted.

"Too late, *amigo,*" Tafoya said.

Rebecca stared at him, anticipating his answer. She'd helped him to see beyond logic, past his training and military tactics, and into the core of his own soul. Together, they'd determined that the splotchy shadows on Duke's face were bruises, and the hideous truck an emblem of the man's disgrace. The once mighty enforcer of a vicious cartel, its tooth and claw and executioner, had become the old lion, an outcast.

Even as he'd once been in Texas, Billy Ray reflected. So beaten down that life seemed an undesirable choice.

He placed himself in Duke's skin, searching the soul of a hunted animal, an aging lion unwelcome by the pride, no longer capable of taking wild game—forced to make its meal on villagers.

But even old lions have teeth, Billy Ray reminded himself

Perhaps he and Duke were two sides of the same coin?

At last, Billy Ray said, "Admiral, please show that property again."

"The hunt club?" Dodd asked.

"No. The lonely house on a hill."

That's where they'd find Duke.

<===== PIPELINE =====>

12

It was arranged for the team to meet at the Meauwataka General Store to interview Bruce the owner.

Lam brought up a picture of Duke on his Blackberry and showed it to Bruce. "So do you know this man or have you seen him lately?"

Bruce adjusted his wire rimmed glasses for a closer look. "I only know him as a customer. He buys propane and a couple other items. We've talked about the weather or what's biting in the lake, nothing more."

"What kind of items?" Lam persisted.

"Rye whiskey and crackers." Bruce held up a packet of Savory brand crackers. "The hunters love these things."

Billy Ray motioned to the crackers. "Mind if I test the evidence?"

Bruce handed over the package. "And yes, I saw him earlier today."

Lam interrupted the infomercial, "You mind, Jenkins? I'm trying to conduct an investigation here."

"*Mmmm!*" Billy Ray crooned. "These *are* good. I'm naming this mission Operation Cracker Barrel."

He offered some *evidence* to the ladies. They declined.

Bruce agreed to let the team gear-up and assemble their weapons in the store. He even set out liquid refreshments, and more crackers.

Tafoya stepped to the next aisle for a modicum of privacy. Then the team stripped out of their clothing and snugged into jet-black formfitting jumpsuits.

Dodd claimed the skintight suits were made of graphene and secret nanopolymers capable of defeating both night-vision and infrared technology. But then cautioned that the one drawback to the hi-tech suits was their ineffectiveness in normal light conditions, or if caught in the glare of search lights or the glow of a full moon.

"But you should have no trouble, Wolverine. The moon has set and the clouds are blocking starlight."

"Thanks for the *weatherball* report, Admiral," Tafoya said, referring to the neon-lighted ball towering above her Channel 13 News station near downtown Grand Rapids.

Lam was familiar with the weatherball from his time in Grand Rapids, how it turned colors to indicate impending weather. He quoted a rhyme about the colors, "When red, warmer weather ahead. If blue, cooler weather in view. All green, no change foreseen. Blinking bright—"

"Kiss your ass goodnight?" Billy Ray interrupted.

"Funny one, oh fearless leader," Lam said stomping into his boots. "Actually, the rhyme goes, blinking bright—rain or snow in sight."

Tafoya zipped shut her suit and adjusted her breasts under the skin-tight material then rejoined the men.

"I could definitely use some rain in the forecast to cool me off," she said. "However, you missed the ending rhyme, Johnny."

"What's that?" Lam asked, checking the long fly on the suit a final time.

"Blinking black—nuclear attack."

"Well, that sums it up perfectly," Billy Ray said inspecting his black-clad teammates.

His message was plain—there'd be no pleasant weather.

People would die this night.

They joined at the front of the store under the round security mirror to darken their faces and hands with special light absorbing camouflage sticks. Then they pulled nanopolymer balaclava masks over their heads and inspected one another. Lam said Tafoya reminded him of his Army drill sergeant who all the recruits called D.I. Death. Tafoya came back at him saying Lam would look better if his hi-tech suit came in teal. Billy Ray just looked chunky.

Next came rigging all of the tactical gear, guns, and ammo. Then an initial weapons check. A final check would be done at the jumping off point to ensure everyone was locked and loaded and weapons were on safe, until needed.

"Okay, let's do this," Billy Ray said.

It was decided that Rebecca would remain at the store to coordinate communications and call in the Marines should the mission go to hell.

Predictably, she wasn't a happy camper for being left behind, but accepted her role. Nor did she send the team away with hugs and kisses or gloomy sentiment. Growing up with a Texas sheriff for a father, especially a man like Roy Payne, had tempered her mettle.

Lam led the way out to the Ford and they drove away.

Billy Ray sat in the front seat this time. He switched on the console navigation system and dialed in the GPS coordinates for the plumbers' property.

Meanwhile, Rebecca and Dodd tested the communications gear, the earbuds and collar mics, then both acknowledged the comms systems were good to go.

Tafoya asked Billy Ray, "Do you think Duke will be there?"

Billy Ray would've expected fear in Tafoya's voice. There was none.

It was then he truly appreciated Dodd's personnel choices. Certainly, he would prefer a SEAL team, Army Rangers, or a squad of leatherneck Marines to engage the enemy . . . anything to keep his friends as far away from the battlefield as possible.

But one often didn't choose a mission, the mission chose you.

Life could be like that, too.

"Yes," Billy Ray stated emphatically. "Duke will be there."

"How do you know that?" Tafoya asked.

"Because that's where I would be."

Duke didn't answer the door on the first knock, nor several knocks thereafter. He was too busy checking the surveillance feeds on his computer. Nothing moved on the property, not on the access roads, nor along the woodland trails.

The guard's knocking turned to pounding and then yelling.

What an idiot! Duke thought.

Finally satisfied that smiley was alone, he raised the Colt pistol and opened the door.

"Why didn't you make some more noise while you were banging away? What are *you* doing here?" Then he looked beyond the guard and said, "Where is everyone?"

"We're it, asshole." The guard pushed past Duke into the room.

Duke was stunned! Didn't Hector realize what was at stake? Why send only one guy, especially this incompetent Bozo?

The guard stopped in the middle of the room and looked around. Duke closed the door and latched the deadbolt.

Still pointing the gun at the guard, he said, "Start explaining."

The guard turned to find the dark hole of a gun barrel staring him in the face. "What ta Hell are you doing!"

"What does it look like, *asshole?* By the way, my father used to call me that so often I thought it was my real name."

"I don't blame him." The guard smiled mockingly.

Duke had had enough of this pompous ass. He flipped the thumb safety on the pistol. It made a loud click. "By the way, I killed him."

"Now hold up, Duke! I'm in charge here. You need to get that through your thick head."

Duke could hardly believe his ears. The guy either had brass balls or shit for brains. Maybe it was a lot of both. He was tempted to squeeze the trigger, but that would solve nothing. He needed answers.

"I'll ask one more time, *boss.* Answer my questions or you're fired."

The guard stopped smiling and nodded.

"Why have you come alone?"

The man looked nervous about answering, as if weighing his options. A bulky 45-caliber pistol pointing at his left eye offered an instant choice.

"They're all dead or busted," the guard said. "I don't know how, but the cops found my crew and wiped them all out."

Duke knew exactly how the cops had done it.

The man continued, "If what you told Hector is true then we're probably goners, too. Either way, it doesn't matter."

"What are you talking about?"

"You remember that skinny kid we used for recruiting gangbangers?"

Duke said, "Sure, the one who drives a silver Chevy Tahoe."

"Yeah . . ." the guard pointed out the window, "like the one sitting right there in your driveway. Say, what ever happened to Big Bertha?"

"You mean that stupid truck you had me parading about town? I traded it in." Actually, he'd chosen the Tahoe for the precise reason it was the same make, model, and year as the black kid's vehicle. He used putty and paint to mold a clone of the kid's license plate, and then he washed it clean after reaching the cabin.

Duke had one more question. Holding the gun steady, he said, "What'd you mean it doesn't matter?"

"Don't you see? Hector will blame me for the crew—he'll kill me!"

"What the hell does that have to do with me!" Duke roared.

The guard looked at him strangely.

"Hector ordered me to execute *you*."

Billy Ray wished for hard intel. The previous year, Dodd had had all sorts of Star Wars weapons. So where were they now?

Furthermore, Dodd was saying some strange things, as if indicating the K-KEY Group had been compromised, but he wasn't revealing the nature of the controversy, stating only that the team possessed adequate tools for the present assignment and assault.

Adequate? Billy Ray damned sure hoped so!

It was eight miles from the Meauwataka General Store to the entrance of the plumbers' union property. As they approached, Billy Ray instructed Lam to maintain a high rate of speed past the opening, and for Tafoya to record the pass using the special camcorder Dodd had provided.

If this really was Duke's property, and assuming Duke would do the very same as *he* would, the perimeter should be lined with surveillance equipment, plus a few nasty howdy-do's for unwanted guests.

Billy Ray had Lam make a return pass of the property, reasoning that a lost motorist would do the same. Then they stopped at the side of the road a half-mile from the target and uploaded the digital footage to be processed. After that they waited . . . and waited.

<===== PIPELINE =====>

Dodd opened the video link and came back with the results nine minutes and fourteen seconds later, or something like that. But again, Billy Ray felt miffed with the difference between this operation and the one in Texas.

"You nailed it, Wolverine," Dodd said. "Several devices are monitoring the driveway *and* the property line. But it's nothing out of the ordinary for paranoid absentee owners safeguarding their possessions—standard motion-activated video cameras, that sort of thing."

Billy Ray had learned that whenever Dodd began by downplaying a report to expect a bang at the end. He got one.

"Not standard, however, is the deployment of geophones for sensing ground vibrations. Plus there's the little matter of M18A1 Claymore remote activated anti-personnel mines and fragmentation grenades placed every twenty feet along the approach to the cabin."

Lam whistled. "These plumbers sure know how to unclog a drain."

Billy Ray was curious how Dodd came to know about the mines. "Where'd you get the hard intel?"

"I'd tell you, but then I'd have to let you walk near one of them."

"Not funny, Dolittle."

Dodd came back on track. "Those listening devices raised my hackles. Video is one thing, but listening stations quite another. They can be used to triangulate advancing combatants. I requested some look-down time from one of our special birds."

"I thought the satellites are all tasked elsewhere," Billy Ray said, still having a major trust dilemma.

"They are."

"Then one of your flying saucers?" Lam asked.

Dodd went silent.

Billy Ray imagined Dodd pulling his hair out at the mention of the nation's newest breed of aircraft.

But what the hell? Wasn't that why the government perpetuated the whole UFO conspiracy in the first place? A person would have to be nuts to believe in flying saucers . . .

Or nuts not to.

At last, Dodd said a single word, "Drones."

Betrayed!

Duke motioned with the pistol. "On the table. Empty your pockets—weapons, wallet, everything. Then take off your clothes."

The guard hesitated.

Duke raised the big pistol to eye level. "Do it or die right where you stand. I don't give a shit one way or the other!"

The man stripped out of his gray uniform down to socks and boxers. Then he placed everything on the table. "Satisfied now, you queer?"

To begin with, the man hadn't been wearing a wire. So working for the cops was out. That left the truth—or what the idiot claimed to be true.

Duke rifled through the assortment of tactical gear.

There were knives, a garrote, and a collapsible baton, plus a double shoulder holster housing two SIG Sauer pistols and extra magazines of ammo. There was also a 9mm Smith & Wesson secured in an ankle holster.

The armaments actually gave credence to Smiley's story that he'd been on his way to go to war .

Duke needed every bit of firepower he could get. His gut still told him it wouldn't be the local county mountie to come rolling up the driveway this time, or even the FBI.

Rather, it was a feeling of being stalked by a higher power.

So as insufferable as the idiot was, and foregoing the pleasure he'd get from beating smiley to death, Duke accepted the hard truth—he could use another gunslinger in the fight.

He holstered the big Colt pistol.

"Get dressed. We don't have much time."

Doubt was gone. They'd found Duke.

Fear was back. Land mines could do that.

Billy Ray considered the extreme danger awaiting them. Whoever designed the house had done so with advanced surveillance technology in mind, having employed countermeasures against radar penetration and laser microphones for eavesdropping.

Dodd's drone had only been capable of confirming the presence of munitions and surveillance equipment outside of the house. They had no way of establishing the number of combatants waiting on the inside.

Tafoya had an idea. "There's at least two."

"How can you tell?" asked Lam.

She raised two fingers. "That's how many cars are in the driveway."

"Brilliant deduction, Watson. But there could have been some passengers." Billy Ray said.

Tafoya lowered one finger, leaving the middle digit at full attention.

Dodd came back on line. "We have more SIGINT. The drone just completed its pass over the forest behind the property."

<====== PIPELINE ======>

"Let me guess," Billy Ray said. "The trails are also rigged."

"Give the guy a Kewpie doll," Dodd quipped.

"I'd rather have a K-KEY Group Star Wars machine."

Dodd ignored the complaint and reported, "I count four cameras near the cabin. Then along a hundred-yard section of trail at the back of the property, there's a run of geophones for detecting ground movement, and—"

"More explosives!" Billy Ray interrupted.

"Yes, a hundred acres of hell. Be thankful we know this much, Wolverine."

"I'll be thankful when I'm not dead."

Once again, tension rose between Billy Ray and Dodd. Lam was about to pitch a comment, too, when Rebecca's voice came over the comms.

"Roger up, boys. We survived Texas, we'll survive Michigan."

Tafoya hadn't been briefed on the Texas affair and shot Billy Ray and Lam a probing look.

But Rebecca's point hit center mark. The cavalry had been absent in the Texas battle, too, until the mop-up at the end. That conflict had come down to fight or die. So against all odds, far out-manned and out-gunned, they'd fought and they'd won—*Dodd's flying machines be damned!*

"Thank you, Rebecca," Billy Ray said.

"Ditto," Lam agreed.

"Me, too," Dodd ended the discussion.

Billy Ray took the lead. "Okay, team. Here's the plan . . ."

The guard's smile returned as Duke provided an overview of the deadly perimeter defenses for warding off an attack.

A SWAT team would get cut to pieces by AP mines and frag grenades, or killed with his bare hands, if it came down to it.

He wasn't going back to prison!

If the feds brought along the whole damn army, then all bets were off and he'd end up dead in a lethal game of capture the flag. And should he survive, there was still Hector's decree that he be eliminated. Plus there was the matter of pumping the Rapture from the fake septic tank and trucking it away before the feds could muster more troops.

The Feds—?

Duke still couldn't shake the feeling he was dealing with something entirely different this time . . . something special, and far more deadly.

Yes, it had been the FBI who took down the hit squad in Muskegon. Though *how* the raid had come about in the first place, plus the incidents leading to his flight to the North Country, suggested an elite unit with unbelievable assets, and talent equal to his own or better.

Regular law enforcement weren't known to employ talking dogs or magicians like the guy at the hospital who fought Tito. Neither could he explain the role of the female reporter. Were they a team from the CIA's Special Activities Division? But that couldn't be either, since the CIA didn't operate on domestic soil. It was true that Lam was FBI, or had been. So what was he now?

Those questions and others, like what to do about Hector's termination order, had led him to develop an escape plan. Which was the other reason why he hadn't killed the guard—

Smiley would take the fall.

Then he would get far away from America and start a new life . . . in Norway perhaps, on a mountain top where he could escape his past and never look back.

To hell with the Rapture.

And to hell with Hector Gallina!

Tafoya placed her hands on her hips. This time it was her *I'm highly skeptical* pose. "You want me to do what?"

Billy Ray repeated the plan, "Bend your legs at the knees, loop them over my shoulders, and hang upside down."

Her eyes narrowed. "Let me get this straight. You're expecting me to dangle like a ninja necklace while holding a gun in my hand for like a whole damn country mile. Meanwhile, Tonto here," she thrust a hip toward Lam, "gets to stand in stirrups."

Lam joined the debate. "Actually, it's only a hundred yards, Tami."

"It sounds like combat Kamasutra, if you ask me!"

Billy Ray countered, "I thought you were a cheerleader."

"Dude, that was in high school, not the circus!"

"Well then, baby, get ready to join the big top!"

"*Geez*, Jenkins! Who writes your stuff?"

As to Tafoya's main point, not the pornographic one, Billy Ray did steal the idea from a Vegas show featuring Chinese tumblers. The plan was to fool Duke into thinking that only one body was entering the gauntlet, not three people sneaking past the geophones.

Since there was no way to avoid announcing their presence, they may as well gain a tactical edge, and hopefully keep Duke from remotely firing the mines or triggering the frag grenades lining the trail. If not, three pseudo-acrobats were about to become Swiss cheese.

<=== PIPELINE ===>

Sustaining the weight of two people plus all the equipment for the length of a football field wasn't going to be easy. Moreover, football fields were flat. Whereas, the trail to Duke's cabin was not.

To support Lam, Billy Ray devised stirrups by looping pieces of rope and attaching them to his web belt. Whereas Tafoya would dangle upside down facing outward, legs bent across his shoulders, and shins tucked under Lam's armpits to relieve her weight and provide balance.

Lastly, they would all maintain hands-free firing with their pistols. Each could establish and maintain an adequate target sight picture in this configuration.

If it worked, and if they didn't die, maybe they really could take their act to Vegas, as The Tres Ninjas.

IF they didn't die.

Duke's computer monitor pinged.

"What is it?" The guard asked.

"We have company." Duke checked the ammo in his pistol then holstered the gun.

They were here.

But "they" was only one person.

Lam?

Duke checked all of the surveillance inputs and the CCTV links.

Nothing or no one else registered.

The warning was coming from the ground sensors on the trail, and then only from a solitary intruder. He could kick himself for not rigging video along the woodland trails. But he'd had only so much time and so much money.

Whoever it was that tripped the ground sensors progressed at a speed that neither suggested someone sneaking along nor acting in a hurry. He was tempted to detonate one of the Claymores anyway, but held off. What if it was just a hiker or a neighbor hunting mushrooms? Plus the blast would bring all kinds of unwanted attention.

Shit!

Duke grabbed a set of comms from the table and said to the guard, "Watch the monitor, and radio only if other sensors go off. Do not come out without my say-so, unless you want to get shot by mistake."

Duke hoisted on the ammo vest and tactical gear, grabbed the M4A1 carbine, and left the cabin.

Whoever was crossing his property picked a bad night for a stroll.

They were nearly to the end and not dead yet.

Billy Ray's legs felt like rubber. His one worry now was tripping over an exposed root on the trail and spilling the three of them on the ground.

Had it been *his* defensive perimeter, he would've chosen *not* to light off the grenades or a Claymore to counter a single *potential* combatant.

Aside from wasting valuable ammo and time resetting the traps, the noise would wake up the whole countryside.

Nor was it lost on him that he was risking all their lives presuming to know Duke's mind, or that the cartel hitman had any conscience at all. One should never underestimate the enemy, nor overestimate him.

According to Dodd, there were no listening devices deployed on the property, only video and ground sensors. Still, Billy Ray ordered absolute radio silence until after they were well beyond the geophones.

Lam was having no trouble in the makeshift stirrups. Even Tafoya was surviving her upside-down batwoman role, and doing so without uttering a single complaint, which likely meant she was banking it for later.

Billy Ray took a few shaky steps beyond the final ground sensor and came to a halt.

He whispered, "End of the line, folks."

Tafoya secured her pistol and extended her arms to the ground. Lam released her legs and she cartwheeled to her feet with a silent *Ta-dah!*

Lam was next, removing his feet from the stirrups. Then he squared his stance, adjusted the ruck on his back, and nodded his readiness.

Billy Ray was thankful not to have lost anyone, so far. The worst part about their circus act was knowing the night was bound to get ugly.

The only easy day was yesterday.

Duke fitted sound-amplifying headphones over his ears and dialed up the sensitivity. Then he donned night-vision goggles and went hunting.

He didn't get far.

The guard's voice blasted in his ears. "Spot anything yet?"

He'd commanded the imbecile to monitor the security inputs and only make radio contact if more sensors were tripped.

Duke could only wonder why Hector would put such a dunce in charge of the pipeline, someone with no military training or discipline.

Maybe it was on purpose, to rub Duke's nose in shit and make him work harder for his job back.

But now Hector's orders were to eliminate him all together.

We'll just see about that.

<==== PIPELINE ====>

The guard said, "Hey, dumbass, are you there?"

"Unless you have something to report, stay the hell off the radio."

Smiley obviously didn't like being told what to do, especially by an underling. Finally, the radio went silent.

Duke raised the carbine in a tactical stance and resumed the hunt.

The moon had set. The night was dark. And dawn was still four hours away, plenty of time to shoo off a lone trespasser.

He knew every inch of his property and had rehearsed battle scenarios numerous times.

He'd always known *they* would come for him. And whether they turned out to be the long arm of the law or a rival cartel hit squad, made no difference. He could not and would not allow himself to be taken alive.

A single trespasser should be simple enough.

They took a knee, placing their backs toward each other and scanning the woods with their night-vision devices—ones not available to anyone outside of the K-KEY Group.

The new technology made the surrounding woods appear nearly as bright as daytime, and did so without the green glow of traditional scopes, instead employing tiny cameras mounted on the Kevlar skullcaps displaying visual input directly onto the lenses. Furthermore, the goggles covered the eyes and mouth like scuba masks, while the respirator silenced the wearer's breathing, supplied enriched oxygen when a shot of adrenaline was called for, and housed two-way radio communications.

It felt to Billy Ray as though he was walking around with a television set strapped to his face forcing his brain to trust in virtual truth.

He still preferred his good ol' mark-1 mod-1 eyeballs. Still, there was no denying the tactical advantage the masks provided to a warfighter.

Dodd reported, "Cabin door opening . . . one body exiting."

"ID?" asked Billy Ray.

"Height, weight . . . matches Duke."

"He's taking the bait," Rebecca said, monitoring the team from back at the Meauwataka store.

Lam stated, "Betting on Duke's morals could've gotten us all blown into little pieces that even tweezers couldn't pick up."

"I've had experience with sociopaths and psychopaths," Rebecca replied. "In my professional opinion, Duke is neither . . . turned to the dark side perhaps, but he's not crazy."

"Sorry, Lam," Billy Ray offered. "Once I saw how he and I shared a few common traits, I believed it was a gamble worth taking."

"Well, it worked," Tafoya chimed in.

Perhaps, Billy Ray thought. *There were no guarantees in war.*

They waited for Dodd to signal the start of the operation. Then their single blip on Duke's security monitors would become a swarm of fireflies.

Something moved!

A doe and its fawn stepped onto the tiny game trail in full view. Their bodies glowed fluorescent green in Duke's night-vision goggles, like alien creatures from another planet. Both animals stepped cautiously hunting for their evening meal of acorns and fresh grass.

But it was clear by their manner they hadn't been spooked.

Duke continued on his way, scanning the woods as he progressed.

He was nearly within visual range of where the intruder should be. He expected to spot a flashlight or headlamp soon.

And if he didn't?

He tightened his grip on the M4A1 and kept going. He raised it to a combat grip, swinging the weapon always left to right, looking down the barrel and then lowering it. He repeated this process with every step he took, employing standard target search technique.

Dodd's voice came through their earpieces, "Target to the north of you and closing on your position."

As the crow flies, they were still about four hundred yards from the cabin and in the thick woods.

And yet, Duke had cut the distance to their position in half, and did so silently.

For Billy Ray, that meant the enemy was adept at night ops, and likely also equipped for the darkness.

He reviewed the mission with Lam and Tafoya.

He reviewed the mission with Lam and Tafoya.

"Our first priority is to spook the enemy and draw them away from their stronghold. Then we'll fool them into wasting ammo. As long as it's dark, we're invisible in these suits. So when the shooting starts, just stay calm, hug a piece of dirt, and keep moving in short bounds to each new position indicated on your mask lenses."

Dodd flashed each person's first coordinates across their masks.

Billy Ray continued, "The Admiral will let us know when it's each of our turn to be a firefly. Expose yourself, zip up, and keep moving westward to the rendezvous point down in the dry creek bed."

Again, Dodd responded by posting a map on their mask lenses.

"As you see on your displays, the creek snakes past the cabin. We'll reassess the battle at that point before making our final assault."

Billy Ray looked at Lam and Tafoya. His helmet cams showed two black-clad forms with solid masks where human faces would be.

"Any questions?"

Tafoya said, "I better get wads of Benjamins for this!"

Lam chuckled.

It was the first Billy Ray heard him react to Tafoya's brand of humor.

That was a good sign.

It showed the team was pumped up and ready to go.

But it also meant the last thread of their group dynamic was tied up nice and tight.

Billy Ray said a quick prayer.

Now there were no loose ends—

Only fate.

13

It was time.

"Weapons," Billy Ray ordered. "Safety's off."

"Check," Lam said.

"Me too, check," Tafoya reported.

"You ready, Dolittle?"

"On your mark, Wolverine."

Billy Ray counted down from three and said, "Mark."

"GO, GO, GO!" Dodd ordered.

Quickly, quietly, three shadows scattered toward their first postings. Then at random intervals over the next minute, Dodd called each team member's name.

Billy Ray, Lam, and Tafoya, took turns opening their light-canceling suits to expose a portion of their bare skin to the infrared cameras mounted about the property—literally flashing the enemy!

Then they zipped up and hustled to the next coordinates typed on the computer lenses of the masks.

Duke heard movement through the amplifying head gear, the sound soft and precise.

He looked around. But nothing showed in the luminescent brightness of his goggles.

It was probably one of the smaller forest creatures rustling through the undergrowth: raccoons, possum, even turkeys, all plentiful in the area.

He plodded forward along the tiny game trail that only he and God's critters knew about . . . move, stop, search . . . listen. Then repeat.

The guard broke his silence, "What the hell?"

So the idiot wasn't asleep after all.

Duke stopped his progress. "What is it this time?"

"Hold on!" the man said.

Duke cursed. *But the guy was excited about something.*

As he awaited smiley's sitrep, a tiny flash of light caught his eye. He turned in response. The light was brief, and typical of Northern Michigan, the trees too thick to allow a clear line of sight.

Then another flash lit on his left flank.

Duke turned. The light extinguished.

There was a third flickering light to starboard, accompanied by a zipping sound in his headphones.

<====== PIPELINE ======>

But each time the lights vanished before he could get a bead on them.

Duke was about to join the guard's strong language when smiley came back on the line. "Your woods are haunted!"

"Be specific," Duke commanded.

The guard was spooked. "The infrareds are flashing heat signatures, like ghosts, or giant lightning bugs . . . there one moment, gone the next."

"What about the visual spectrum?"

"Nothing," the guard replied.

"That's impossible!" Duke forced, but heard doubt in his voice.

"Holy hot shit!" the guard yelled in the earphones. "It *IS* a ghost! And she just showed me her tits!"

Three lights flicked on and off at nearly the same instant, but all at different points in the woods than before.

Was this some kind of joke?

He lifted the M4A1 and switched the assault rifle to full-auto.

The guard yelled in panic, "There they are! Kill them!"

Duke sprayed a hail of bullets at the lights, sweeping side to side, draining an entire magazine and then another.

He slapped fresh ammo into the gun and prepared to fire again. The lights vanished.

Duke looked down at his feet. He hadn't moved. Bad tactics—

Duke! Move!

He took off running along the game trail in the darkness, scanning the woods as he went, finally pulling up behind the trunk of a downed tree.

After a quick breath, he lifted the gun over the tree and peered through the scope.

There it was again on his left flank!

A single light blinked on and off.

Duke pivoted and let loose a burst of automatic gunfire into the area.

Immediately, another light shined on his right flank, closer than before. He fired at that one too.

Then a third straight ahead, only forty yards away this time. The M4A1 jumped in his hands as another volley of hot lead streamed toward the glowing anomaly, but to no effect.

Was it ball lightning? Swamp gas?

Then the vision of a talking dog came to mind and the hairs prickled on the back of Duke's neck.

The question changed—

Not what but WHO!

Duke plugged a grenade into the M203 launcher and pulled the trigger. A distinctive *THUNK* sounded as the round left the chamber.

Billy Ray was well-aware of the sound made by a Colt M4A1. He knew its range and its compliment of ammunition. He also knew what any good warfighter worth their salt would have attached beneath the deadly assault rifle—an M203 grenade launcher.

So after taking his turn flashing his skin and not drawing any gunfire, he knew what was coming. In fact, he would've done the same thing.

Billy Ray paid no mind to stepping carefully now. A world of hurt was coming his way.

He took off at a dead run, crashing through brush and briars, hurdling over downed trees, and then diving headfirst over the edge of the creek bank a mere second before the night went boom!

Shrapnel zinged through the air, ripping twigs and leaves to shreds before smacking into the surrounding tree trunks.

Sucking wind after his narrow escape, Billy Ray announced over the comms, "The gig's up. Get to the creek, now!"

Lam and Tafoya acknowledged the order.

Dodd said, "I'll provide a distraction."

A moment later, the countryside was bathed in music, treated to an exceedingly loud version of Souza's "Stars and Stripes Forever."

If gunfire and grenades didn't manage to piss-off the neighbors, surely blasting music would. The ear-piercing sound came from Dodd's drone flying overhead, emitting harmful noise from a sonic weapon called a Long Range Acoustic Device mounted beneath the unmanned plane. LRADs had proven effective for repelling pirates at sea, and even causing belligerents on land to scatter with hands held tight against their ears.

Billy Ray could just make out Tafoya shouting over the earbuds.

"Ahhh! I can't hear my face!"

"Dolittle, do something!" Billy Ray ordered.

A pain-filled second later, the music was redirected to the spot where Duke now stood.

Duke dropped his gun and pawed at his headphones, frantic to switch them off. The quick reaction saved one of his eardrums, but not both.

Blood and fluid trickled down his neck.

Then an intense feeling of vertigo swept over him, causing him to puke the contents of his guts: whiskey, pills, and crackers.

The dizziness passed and Duke retrieved his weapon. He pulled a star burst round from his tactical vest and jammed it into the grenade launcher.

<===== PIPELINE =====>

He didn't need to see the drone circling overhead. He needed only point at the music and fire.

Another THUNK.

The sky lit up, illuminating a bird-like form. Duke quickly jammed an HE round into the launcher and pulled the trigger.

The grenade caught the unmanned drone in its destructive wave and blasted the airplane apart.

Fiery pieces of the craft fell from the sky and instantly ignited fires in the tinder-dry leaves and pine needles.

Then Duke took cover.

Lam joined Billy Ray and Tafoya down in the creek bed.

Having scampered farthest after their firefly ruse, Lam was out of breath. That didn't prevent his usual deadpan, however.

"There goes the neighborhood!"

"And half of God's Green Earth," Billy Ray added, appreciating a battle buddy like Lam.

Tafoya said, "Good. Because this *señorita's* done flashing her assets!"

Billy Ray pulled off his mask, so did Lam and Tafoya. The bright fires rendered night-vision technology worthless. Neither would their techy leotards work for keeping them invisible.

The high-tech part of the mission just went low-tech—eyes and ears, brains and brawn, sneaky stealth.

"So much for a battle plan," Billy Ray said. "Let's reassess."

Dodd replied, "I meant to give you all cover, not blow it."

Billy Ray countered, "A forest fire presents new opportunities."

Lam looked around. "This reminds me of the Piney Woods back home. And as any Texan knows, pine trees go up like Roman candles."

"Time's running out," Dodd proclaimed. "The locals in these parts respond quickly to fire."

"And bring the fire department," Tafoya said.

"They could then become targets," Lam added. "And a way out for Duke during the confusion"

Billy Ray asked Dodd, "What about the *other* responders?"

Dodd didn't answer—his silence an admission.

Lam knew what Billy Ray was referring to, having had to bargain with Dodd in a similar situation before. "Is that really necessary, Admiral?"

"Yes, Agent Lam. Before the drone was attacked, its sensors discovered an anomaly beneath the cabin. The analysis is conclusive. That *special* septic tank Duke installed doesn't hold human waste."

"The missing Rapture!" Lam exclaimed.

"Likely," Dodd replied. "But others will have to confirm that."

"But the FBI—"

Dodd cut Lam off. "No police."

Tafoya didn't get what all the talk was about. But Rebecca did.

For the first time in a long while, her voice came over the earbuds, "Get out Billy Ray! The Admiral called in a kill squad. You three have less than thirty minutes before those flying saucers do to you what they did to those Korean terrorists last year."

It was East Texas all over again! Billy Ray thought.

Dodd made no attempt to defend his actions. Instead, he said, "Not to worry. You have IFF built into your masks."

Billy Ray and Lam stared at each other—without their masks on!

Tafoya caught their concern. "IFF?"

"Identification Friend or Foe," Billy Ray explained. "If an interrogator doesn't receive our signal IDing us as a *friendly*, we get painted red and dead."

"And with what's coming, that would be very bad," Lam added.

Tafoya looked confused.

Lam explained, "You know that news story you told me about where UFOs were spotted over Grand Haven?"

Her eyes narrowed. "Yeah, and you laughed at me."

Dodd ended discussion of a state secret. "For the sake of argument, let's just say they're *identified*."

Tafoya said, "What about us, how will *we* be identified?"

Billy Ray pointed at the now-useless night-vision masks. "We won't."

He thought back to the ordeal at the Texas Waterland Family Park a year ago, and how a dog collar around his neck had saved their lives.

"I'm not leaving," Lam stated emphatically.

Tafoya said, "Me neither."

"Billy Ray . . ." Rebecca pleaded. "You have to get out of there!"

Billy Ray checked his watch. A full minute had passed, plenty of time for Duke to regroup. Already the fires from the downed UAV had grown.

"Thanks for the heads up, Rebecca," Billy Ray said at last. "But I'm staying. It's time we put an end to the Gallina cartel once and for all."

It wasn't lost on Billy Ray that it was love in Rebecca's heart begging him to end the mission.

To her credit, she accepted his pronouncement like a soldier—

No more talk.

"Dolittle?" Billy Ray used the codename to signify serious business.

"Yes, Wolverine?"

<===== PIPELINE =====>

"How many flying machines?"

"One."

"Manned or unmanned?"

"Manned."

"Hold them off," Billy Ray ordered.

"It not's like Texas. I don't have control."

So the truth comes out at last.

Billy Ray pressed, "Maybe *you* don't but POTUS does. And I'll bet since you declared this a *military* operation, we've been airing live on the Situation Room television."

"State your point, sailor," Dodd said.

"I don't know what trouble is brewing among your group. And frankly, I don't give a damn. But unless you want three dead *friendlies* on your hands, then that spacecraft better hold off-station. Because just like in Texas, I *DO* have control!"

Dodd's pause meant Billy Ray had hit a nerve—

Maybe lots of nerves.

"What if you don't?" Dodd said finally.

"Then we're all dead and it won't matter. Now will it, Admiral?"

A woman gasped over the com line. Billy Ray couldn't tell if it came from Tafoya or Rebecca.

But if he had to guess . . .

Suddenly, a new voice announced, "Standby for The President."

Billy Ray and Lam looked at each other. They recognized the voice as Lam's former boss, Chris Dreyfus, once the SAC of the FBI's Dallas Division before POTUS hired him away to serve the K-KEY Group as their legal counsel.

Or so Lam had told Billy Ray.

Then a voice came over their comms that most of the inhabited world would recognize. "Mr. Jenkins . . ."

"Roger, sir?"

"How much time do you need?"

"The devil doesn't wear a watch, Mr. President."

"A guess then."

Billy Ray made a mental calculation.

The fires from the downed airplane were increasing at an alarming rate. Duke was still out there, hunting them hunting him. Plus there was still the cabin and what lay beneath it.

Realistically, he'd like to request a full week.

"One hour, Mr. President . . . unless our radios go silent. In which case, blow this place all to hell, because I'll already be there waiting."

"An hour then, Mr. Jenkins, not one second more. Now go to work and complete your mission."

POTUS was gone.

Billy Ray faced Lam and Tafoya, his look plain—new reality new plan.

War was like that.

"Here's what we're going to do."

"Answer me, asshole!" The guard was yelling in Duke's earbuds. "What's going on out there?"

Duke hadn't heard the idiot at first—he hadn't heard anything in fact. His left ear was wrecked and the right one just now ending the god-awful ringing.

He looked around at his property.

Small fires burned everywhere. Soon they would be big fires. Soon after that, all would be lost.

Ghosts my ass!

Duke had no idea where the enemy was, or who and how many. Lam, he assumed, plus that magician who had seemed to be inside his head, knowing his thoughts, always a step ahead.

He was about to change that.

Duke tossed away the goggles and headphones. The crackling fires burning in the forest, rendered the equipment useless. Now he'd do what his father had taught him to do in the forest—hunt.

Duke checked the M4A1, it was out of bullets and grenades. Going back to the cabin for more ammunition would further doom him.

He answered the guard at last, "Set off all of the booby traps."

"All?"

"Just do it! The mines, everything, NOW!" Duke yelled.

It was time to unleash the fires of hell!

Billy Ray had drawn the enemy out and then gotten them to overreact.

Now victory would be supplied by the enemy themselves, or should be. Nothing came easy in war, especially from a desperate foe.

Or two warriors who thought alike.

Proof of that came a moment later when twenty or more explosions began ripping apart the north woods.

All of the grenades rigged along the geophone-lined trail, and several more strategically sited, began blowing one after another, severing the tree trunks to which they were lashed.

<===== PIPELINE =====>

Fifty-foot-tall pines and oaks toppled in all directions, in turn knocking down additional trees, like killer dominos crushing all in their path—deer, raccoons, turkeys . . .

And nearly three operatives of the K-KEY Group.

The mayhem was capped a moment later by four earth-shattering blasts from the land mines. The Claymores shredded the areas in their kill zones with thousands of small projectiles and ear splitting thunder.

The area looked like the devil's playground.

If not for the fact Billy Ray, Lam, and Tafoya were hunkered down in the hollow of the dry creek bed, they would've been pulverized by the shockwaves, peppered with a zillion bits of shrapnel, flying rocks and wood splinters, or mashed into human paste by the falling trees.

And still the fires grew!

Duke crawled out of the shelter of a hollowed-out Maple tree.

He needed to move.

He was done defending the indefensible, done with giving a damn about saints and sinners.

He'd been both.

And though he hadn't held a general's rank, he had been the chief enforcer of an international crime syndicate. And yes, he'd been good at his job—damn good!

It was Hector who'd been the fool.

Still, Duke had nobody to blame but himself.

He'd chosen the wrong turn in life. And now that road had reached a dead end.

But he wasn't done yet.

He would take Lam and the mystery man to hell with him.

Billy Ray didn't like it, but he'd chosen to divide his forces.

He sent Lam forward to assault the cabin, while he and Tafoya ferreted out Duke.

The problem was they were being hunted now too, he was sure of it.

Furthermore, they were out of time. Local law enforcement, firemen, and curious neighbors were surely on their way.

Having lost the drone, they no longer owned the advantage of tracking Duke in the woods.

Their *gee-whiz* equipment was useless now, though fortunately, they still had comms and little more.

POTUS and the K-KEY Group weren't contributing further assistance beyond observing. And for whatever reason, they were just watching from their safe, cozy seats. And Dodd's role as the Great Oz, pulling levers and pushing buttons from behind his secret curtain, was done.

Why that was, Billy Ray didn't yet know, and Dodd wasn't telling.

The team was on their own. Opposing forces were more equal now, left to do battle the old fashioned way—

Gutting it out.

Lam made it to the cabin without incident.

After casing the entryway for tripwires and traps, he hailed Dodd, "Going in now, Admiral."

"I'm blind here, Agent Lam, so watch your six."

"Roger that."

Lam entered the structure, again meeting no resistance.

He cleared each of the rooms all the while remembering Tafoya holding up two fingers for how many people would be inside.

She may have been correct, because the place was deserted.

The cabin—house actually, was well-built with an easy floor plan. The interior was painted in bright colors. Soft pillows filled a cozy sofa. And a checkered cloth covered the dining room table.

But the style seemed more appropriate for someone's grandmother than a fearsome killer like Duke.

Next, Lam made his way down to an unfinished basement. With his gun at the ready, he flipped on the lights.

The entire space was nothing but bare concrete floors and walls. However, built into the middle of the far wall was a hatchway door, like those normally found on ships and submarines.

A tornado shelter? An armory, perhaps?

He radioed Dodd. "I've found something, Admiral. Those blueprints you have of Duke's cabin, what do they show for the basement?"

"Wait one." Dodd was back a moment later. "There is no basement."

"Curious, I'm actually standing in one and looking at a steel door built into the foundation wall."

"Good work, soldier," Dodd said.

"Thank you. But with all due respect, sir, I'm not a soldier. I'm a—"

The lights went out. This time it wasn't Dodd being cute though.

Then Lam felt it more than heard it—a strange humming sound.

He knew exactly what it was!

<===== PIPELINE =====>

Billy Ray climbed out of the creek and onto the trail. Tafoya followed.

Then he led her through a burning forest searching for Duke.

A burning pine tree fell across the path forty yards ahead, and flaming embers rained down from the dark sky above.

Then unexpectedly, Duke appeared out of the dark woods, leaping over the blazing pyre like the devil dancing through hell.

Billy Ray let loose a burst of automatic gunfire from his H&K UMP.

The long volley of .45 caliber rounds chased after the big man.

But none caught flesh before Duke disappeared into what little darkness there was due to the blazing fires.

Billy Ray had guessed correctly, Duke was an adversary worthy of respect. Now the tables were turned, he was reacting and wasting ammo.

A scream behind him!

Billy Ray spun around to find Tafoya about twenty feet behind, tangled in the arms of a man dressed in a gray security guard uniform.

She was giving as well as she was getting, but only for the moment. The man was bigger and stronger, and soon gained the upper hand.

Billy Ray let the machine gun drop on its strap and pulled the SOCOM pistol. He aimed, but couldn't get a clear shot because of the tussle.

The security guard managed to get an arm around Tafoya's neck from behind. He brought a big SIG Sauer pistol to bear against her temple and shouted, "Drop your weapon!"

The last thing Billy Ray would ever do was drop his weapon.

Evil made no bargains.

In fact, the guy had a problem. If he did shoot Tafoya then Billy Ray would gun him down.

He took steps toward Tafoya's captor.

"Stop or I'll Shoot!" the man warned.

"Pull that trigger and you're a dead man."

Tafoya didn't say a word, but her eyes got as big as dinner plates.

Billy Ray stared at her for a long moment, getting her to focus on him. Then he glanced at her belt and back up at the security guard.

Tafoya blinked to indicate she understood Billy Ray's intention to distract the man, and for her to go for the tactical knife on her belt.

Billy Ray said condescendingly, "You have a big challenge, buddy."

"Oh yeah?" the guard shot back. "Yours is bigger, dumbass."

Billy Ray took another step, still attempting to get a clear shot.

Just then something caught his attention, something coming out of the flames on the trail behind Tafoya and the gunman.

It was Duke.

Lam flipped up the dogs on the steel hatch.

Before opening the hatch, he said a prayer, in case it was booby-trapped. It wasn't.

Then he held his gun at the ready and shined the mounted flashlight into the space beyond.

Amazingly, Duke had built the cabin around a fully-intact chemical tanker—still on its wheels!

Lam spotted a pumping station for extracting the drug from above, just as one would expect for a special 'green' septic tank.

He'd been in Michigan for months. And finally, here was the Rapture, the last of the deadly poison from Texas.

Time to destroy the drug.

Lam radioed Dodd. "Located the Rapture. Attaching explosives now."

"Belay your last, Mister," Dodd ordered.

"What!"

"You heard me, Agent Lam. You'll not place explosives in that house."

"But—"

"Others are on their way to collect the missing drugs."

Lam was reminded what that meant as the humming noise grew stronger. He imagined electricity going out across Wexford Country. Still, he could hardly believe what he was hearing from Dodd.

"This poison needs to be destroyed!"

Dodd took a moment before answering. "Stand down, Agent Lam. *They* will dispose of the Rapture appropriately."

Then Lam remembered how this wasn't a closed operation, that others were listening, observing . . . *planning?*

He had never fully trusted Dodd and the K-KEY Group.

More to the point, he didn't trust any group or politician who operated outside of the Constitution. Now he had even less reason to trust.

What were they up to?

Lam's thoughts were interrupted by the sound of a mighty crash from the cabin above. Then smoke began filling the air a moment later.

He had to get away now!

But first, there was one more thing he had to do.

Duke was no fool, Billy Ray saw.

Rather than approach from directly behind on the trail, the big man circled through the woods, using the cover of the trees, flanking Billy Ray, and even making eye contact as he approached.

<===== PIPELINE =====>

In a flash, Billy Ray had the H&K UMP pointed at Duke, ready to fire from the hip, while still maintaining a steady aim at the security guard with the SOCOM pistol.

He was caught in a crossfire!

Life and death would be determined by who fired the first shot.

It would be either him or Tafoya left lying on the ground beside the corpses of the enemy.

He was no trick shot artist, but didn't need to be to kill Duke with the machine gun. It was the headshot to the guard to save Tafoya posing the catch-22. If his aim was true, the guard was dead meat—but then he'd be gunned down by Duke!

They were in need of a miracle.

That miracle came, and in a most mysterious way.

After making eye contact with Duke, Billy Ray had raised his gun. Duke, however, did not. Instead, the big man kept walking toward the gathering. He held a Viet Nam-era pistol down at his side.

Finally, Duke halted ten paces away on Billy Ray's right flank.

The act seemed so curious and tactically bizarre that Billy Ray held off gunning Duke down. There'd been something noble in the man, regardless of his criminal reputation. And he seemed to be approaching the standoff as a brother-in-arms. Gone was the assault rifle Billy Ray had heard earlier. Still, he was no fool, either, and kept a sharp eye on Duke and steady pressure on both gun triggers.

Thus began an awkward silence. Everyone seemed frozen among the crackling flames. Finally, the guard shouted, "Shoot him, you idiot!"

In the glow of the fires, Billy Ray saw the lines around Duke's mouth grow taught. Then Duke looked away with disdain from the guard and addressed Billy Ray. "Fooled thrice . . . Military?"

"Former. And you?" asked Billy Ray.

"A little. But mostly a callous father who knew how to hunt, and hurt."

Billy Ray nodded at the pistol in Duke's hand. "Nam?"

"Yes. Human game. Had he died there my life might've been different."

The man holding the gun to Tafoya's head went apoplectic. "What kind of a hitman are you!"

Duke responded, "I only have one bullet left."

The guard continued his rant, "I can't believe this! You're a dumbass, just like your faggot boyfriend, Tito. Now shoot this bastard!"

The muscles around Duke's mouth tightened at the taunting. But again he ignored the guard, letting the big pistol hang by his side.

Billy Ray held off pulling the trigger, too.

"What's your problem? Shoot him, asshole!" The guard yelled.

Duke looked away from Billy Ray and straight at the guard. Then he said with an icy voice, "You remind me of my father."

"Was he an asshole, too?" The guard smiled.

"Yes!" Duke drew the pistol from his side like an Old West cowboy and blew the man's head off. At the same instant, Billy Ray's reflexes acted. He pulled the trigger on the UMP and stitched three holes across Duke's chest. Duke and the headless guard hit the ground at the same time.

Billy Ray moved quickly to Duke's side and knocked away the Colt pistol. As he did so, he noticed a series of notches carved into the handle.

Lam came running up and threw his arms around Tafoya just as she fainted, covered in brain matter and skull fragments. He lowered her to the ground and then joined Billy Ray and Duke.

Duke fought for breath. Pink froth bubbled from his mouth. He saw Lam and said, "Mariposa . . . Webster Power Plant. Take her home—" Duke's body spasmed and he coughed up crimson blood.

"Hold on!" Lam shouted.

Duke forced his final words, "Home. . . where butterflies are born!"

At that very moment, large explosions filled the night air, and then massive blazing trees crashed down on Duke's cabin.

Tafoya struggled to her feet. "Why did he save us?"

Billy Ray stared at the dead man's still form. He noted the echo of the explosions rolling through the wilderness, like a salute to a fallen warrior.

"He didn't. Duke saved himself."

As Lam helped steady Tafoya, she asked, "And what did he mean about butterflies?"

"Always the reporter," Lam said. "C'mon, Tami, let's get out of here."

The three of them walked out of the burning forest, exiting their own hell of death, the stress of combat, and the raging fires.

They left behind a lonely house on a hill.

As they arrived at their vehicle, Billy Ray said, "Hey Army, I heard Dodd order you *not* to set charges inside the cabin."

"Affirmative, Navy. But he said nothing about blowing up the nearby trees, which just so happened to be on fire, and might topple onto the cabin and destroy that tanker of Rapture."

"Geez, Lam. Who taught the Army how to fell trees? You're supposed to attach the charges on the other side of the trunks."

Lam shrugged. "Whoops. My bad"

The deep pulsating hum filling the night air ceased. Then America's not-so-secret next-generation aircraft, hovering above Duke's destroyed property, rose into the sky and shot off toward the east.

The battle was over.

<===== PIPELINE =====>

PART THREE

A Good Day To Die

14

When dawn arrived, nothing remained of Duke, the cabin, or the missing ten thousand gallons of Rapture.

All had burned up in the fires.

It was being called the Great Meauwataka Fire, and it would consume nearly thirty thousand acres of prime forestland and dozens of hunting cabins before finally being extinguished.

Miraculously, no deaths were reported, not even Duke and the guard.

Details were sketchy on the possible cause of the fire, or why it had continued to burn so stubbornly. An unknown accelerant was suspected as the prime culprit. Although theories on what started it ranged from freak summer lightning, to a blown electrical transformer, or even one of the growing number of meth labs popping up in the national forests.

Local residents reported hearing explosions. One man driving home from a tavern, called 911 to report seeing a UFO. Authorities dismissed the man's story, arrested him on suspicion of drunk driving, and hauled him off to jail.

Someone in the media claimed that the trees themselves could've been the source of the loud noises, stating in a news article that ". . . as volatile pine resin ignited, superheating the moisture inside the trees, like steam in a pressure cooker, they blew themselves apart."

But most locals baulked at that theory, too, settling with the notion the government was hiding something, as usual.

And because the devastation ranged over such a large and remote area, investigators didn't expect a final report anytime soon, if ever. The Meauwataka fire would likely remain one of those unsolved mysteries.

The team returned to the general store to gather Rebecca.

Before leaving, Dodd compelled the owner to sign papers ensuring his silence. Billy Ray argued that Bruce was owed a sizable reward by the government for information that led to Duke's capture or conviction.

Dodd responded that Duke wasn't captured *or* convicted, so technically no money could be paid out. To which, Billy Ray offered to go *apprehend* a bucketful of the man's ashes so Lam could read it the Miranda rights.

Dodd finally relented, realizing it was a no-win battle, and ended their radio contact.

Bone tired, covered in soot, and smelling barbequed, the team climbed into the big Ford and drove back to the beach house in Holland.

Upon their arrival, everyone scattered to a shower to rid themselves of smoke and filth and death.

Afterward, the men and women went to their separate closets for fresh clothes and some beef jerky and chocolates.

The gummy bears went untouched, Billy Ray observed.

Then he remembered Lam's daughter Katie, and assumed the hard-nosed Fed's personal algorithm included purchases made for her.

They gathered briefly in the kitchen where Lam and Tafoya packed sack lunches together and hustled off to join the raid in Muskegon.

Billy Ray couldn't fault Lam for wanting first dibs on cuffing Hector Gallina. Nor did he wish to see Tafoya denied the chance to capture the moment on camera. They'd earned that right.

Furthermore, he and Rebecca were thrilled for their friends, that they'd come to accept one another as teammates, and potentially more.

Now it was their turn.

They had the mansion all to themselves—all twenty-thousand-square-feet of it. And even though they stood in Billy Ray's favorite room, the kitchen, he actually didn't feel like eating.

Instead, he looked into Rebecca's tired eyes. "I know a wonderful cabana with our name on it."

Rebecca seized his hand.

This time it was she who led the way across golden sands to the soft cabana mattress . . . pleased to be in each other's arms—

Thrilled to be alive!

There'd been death, but they did their jobs. The Texas affair had followed them both for an entire year.

Thankfully, it was finally over.

The bright sun had a disinfecting quality, as did the gentle breeze and waves lapping on the shore.

After making passionate love another joyful time, they fell fast asleep, nestled in each other arms.

Again the barn was used as a command center.

This time, however, SWAT vehicles replaced farm tractors. And the rows of chairs filling the center area, were occupied by three teams of FBI agents receiving a final, pre-mission intel briefing.

Afterward, the agents broke into squads to discuss their assignments for what would be the second major action in Muskegon in two days.

<==== PIPELINE ====>

Due to the sprawling grounds of the Norman Webster Power Plant and Paper Mill, and because the facility was situated along a quarter-mile of the Muskegon Lake shoreline, which also bordered Lake Michigan, assaulting the cartel stronghold would require a full complement of sea, air, and land assets. SWAT team coordination would be imperative.

In Lam's opinion, they weren't storming a donut shop and wished for more SWAT members. But there hadn't been time. The operation had to be marshalled in haste for fear that Hector Gallina would be tipped-off to the Meauwataka battle and try to escape justice down a hidey-hole like Saddam Hussain did.

Every agent within two hundred miles was ordered in. Reinforcements were on the way from neighboring states. But unfortunately, they wouldn't arrive on-station until nightfall—a good six hours away.

Moreover, they would be conducting a risky daytime raid, which by Special Weapons and Tactics doctrine, was not the optimum condition for assaulting an armed compound. Daylight only served to level the battlefield for the bad guys.

Nevertheless, the assembled agents were up to the challenge of bagging one of the worst criminals defiling the planet—Hector Gallina, and putting an end to the Gallina family cartel.

Blueprints showed a million square feet of paper mill facilities.

A labyrinth of tunnels snaked below the company's grounds. Meanwhile massive pipelines traversed the property aboveground, with some of the pipes reaching far out into Lake Michigan.

Lam couldn't help noticing how eerily similar the massive feed pipes of the Webster power plant were to those in Port Sheldon, where the body of the third Jane Doe had washed ashore.

Was it by chance, destiny perhaps?

Maybe both, Lam concluded.

Duke's dying words had been to find the butterfly at the Webster plant. He and Tafoya had then solved the riddle on the drive to Muskegon. It was the birthmark that had caught their attention at the Port Sheldon crime scene, the one shaped like a monarch butterfly.

Thanks to Duke, they even had a name, Mariposa.

After a call to the Spectrum hospital by Agent Tompkins, Tafoya's camera equipment was delivered to the barn. It was her photo of the deceased Mexican woman that was uploaded, printed out, and passed around to the strike team, along with a headshot of Hector Gallina.

Furthermore, the county morgue confirmed that Jane Doe's body had been discovered missing from its storage drawer, and then replaced with the brutalized remains of the missing night watchman.

Complicating matters further for striking the Webster facility, was the constant flow of railway cars rolling in and out of the power generating plant, each heaping with black coal to feed the voracious fires that produced steam and electricity for the mill.

Their surveillance confirmed the presence of at least two dozen men armed in gray uniforms patrolling the grounds with Kalashnikov rifles and machine guns. Additionally, cartel snipers were positioned atop the main power plant, as well as along the catwalks on the twenty-story tall smokestacks. Intel identified at least 10 snipers armed with lethal Dragunov SVD rifles, effective out to 800 yards on a human target.

Again, the Muskegon Police Department would play a critical role assisting a federal raid inside their city. The MPD would first issue a news bulletin to the press about a broken gas main and orders for immediate evacuation of all homes and businesses in the area.

Then quietly, amid the panic, squad cars would block all routes leading to and away from the Webster Plant along Lakeshore Drive.

From the water, the Coastguard would help by clearing Muskegon Lake, as well as block access through the channel into Lake Michigan.

The big SWAT vehicles were the most conspicuous, and needed to time their arrival simultaneous with the air assault and helicopter fast rope insertion teams. Once the air team exterminated the enemy sniper threat, and the ground force teams assaulted the property, then Lam's five-man team would get the GO order to find and arrest Hector Gallina.

That was the plan anyway, a large and complicated plan. Predicting the outcome once the shooting began was impossible.

Lam hardened himself to expect the worst.

He looked at Tafoya. Instead of a silenced pistol like the one she'd carried during the battle in Meauwataka, she was armed with her favorite weapon—a camera. Only after a great deal of lobbying, and then threatening to resign, was Lam successful getting Tafoya on the team, though not a single person had agreed to let her accompany the raid, especially Agent Tompkins. So Dodd was compelled to take the matter all the way to the top in D.C. Only after a phone call from the Attorney General, did Tompkins finally give the nod.

Lam hoped he wasn't making a huge mistake.

But Tafoya had more than proven herself in battle the previous night. She was a warrior. Also, it was probably easier to beg and cajole and threaten to quit the Agency, then get Dodd to ask POTUS to command the AG to order Tompkins to allow Tafoya on the team, than had he simply told her she couldn't come.

He was starting to like that about her.

<=== PIPELINE ===>

A gray-uniformed guard rushed past the two men holding their Uzis outside of Hector Gallina's office door.

"*Jefe!* I think we're about to be visited," the man reported.

Gallina ignored the peon, concentrating instead on the lovely bare-chested Latina girl providing him a soothing back massage.

She'd been a gift from the mayor of a small village in the State of Oaxaca, one of nine daughters. Unable to feed them all, or protect them, the mayor had offered up his fifth daughter. Hector refused, choosing the seventh daughter instead, who was prettier and much younger, barely having reached menstruation. For this, Hector had shown his generosity by allowing the mayor to keep his job and feed the rest of his family.

The Catholics, Hector thought. *Thanks to them, he'd never be out of human product.*

The guard echoed his alarm with a little more volume. "The Muskegon *policia* have evacuated all neighborhoods surrounding our facility. They've even moved the lake traffic away from the area."

Hector waived a well-relaxed arm. "Check your television. There's been a gas line rupture. Besides, what could the local authorities ever do against us?" Hector nodded at the girl. "What did authorities do for her?"

"But—"

Hector cut the guard off. "Where's my idiot chief of security?"

"He hasn't reported in, *Jefe.*"

Hector made a mental calculation: ten hours. He'd ordered much for his head of security to accomplish. Furthermore, there was no cellular service in the north woods.

Still, that idiot should've made contact by now.

Hector wondered if he'd been too hard on Duke, then quickly dismissed the idea.

Duke had needed to be taught a final lesson. When the man he'd trusted since the early days had let him down again and again, death could be his only verdict. Anything less would send the message that Hector Gallina was soft and could be taken advantage of by others.

Duke should be dead by now. It would serve as a lesson to the rest of his cartel, failure would not be tolerated in the *Family,* not by anybody, even someone with Duke's abilities and special talents.

Nothing personal, just business. Blood in, blood out—

Except his, of course.

Hector dismissed the guard with a wave of his hand.

Then firm teen breasts resumed rubbing against his aching back, easing the pain of one so burdened as himself.

John Sattgast, producer for the Mid-Western News, bolted up straight in his desk chair. He stared bewildered at a bundle of facsimiles just handed to him by his executive assistant. The documents were unsigned and had no address, not even an originating phone number. It was as if the fax machine magically came alive and spit out the sheets of paper.

What he now held in his shaking hands was pure dynamite!

Not since the Watergate scandal under the Nixon administration had there been a political hot potato of this magnitude—one that could blow the roof off the White House. It could shake the nation to its core.

Was it all true?

True or not, there was no time to waste validating the information. He had phone calls to make—important phone calls . . .

Once his hands stopped shaking.

Four UH-60 Black Hawk helicopters approached the Webster property from the west: two sniper teams, two air assault rope teams.

Fitted with low noise technology and other stealth compliments, the menacing birds flew single file from off the big lake, and then through the Muskegon channel barely clearing the masts of sailboats. They were coming in NOE—Nap of the Earth flight plans.

Men in black uniforms, newer assault-rifle proof Kevlar vests and military grade helmets, tactical gear and weapons, sat in open doors on the helicopters. These FBI airborne assets proceeded east across Muskegon Lake, flying NOE only meters above the water before peeling away to their assigned positions.

The sniper team helicopters were ordered to loiter on-station some twelve hundred yards from the target. While, the rope teams positioned themselves in a direct line of the noonday sun.

When ordered to do so, the sniper birds would elevate and take out the cartel shooters on the smokestacks, catwalks, and rooftops. Then seconds later, the fast rope insertion teams would drop down to secure the approach points for the big SWAT vehicles storming into the main commons to disgorge its heavily armed assailants.

Lastly, the fast boats would strike shore with three additional SWAT teams to cut off any thought of a water escape by Gallina.

The sea, air, and land assault would combine to yield ninety seconds of shock and awe. After each unit leader finished checking in, Tompkins began the countdown.

T-minus 1 minute . . .

Billy Ray bolted upright from his sleep. A cold sweat covered his brow.

"What is it?" Rebecca said, startled by the sudden movement.

"Something's wrong." Billy Ray looked all about them, up and down the beach, then off to the horizon on Lake Michigan.

"Is it Johnny and Tami?" Rebecca asked.

"Maybe, I'm not sure. It feels more like I'm being watched."

"Dodd?"

"I don't know."

Billy Ray had learned to trust his instincts long ago. Paranoia saved his life a number of occasions. But these signals were difficult to discern.

Sometimes the feeling he got was sublime, a whisper to his soul. Other times it was more direct, hairs standing on the back of his neck, his skin crawling. Coming out of a deep sleep, he labored to interpret the threat.

Rebecca wrapped her arms around him and the fright abated, slightly.

Perhaps it had been past traumas replaying in his sleep, nameless battles, faceless corpses. As with so many warriors, dark currents flowed within . . . deep, unfathomable—pulling him downriver.

Still, he couldn't shake the feeling that he was being stalked, and that it wasn't related to Dodd or the pervasive government surveillance.

It was something else . . . something very, very evil.

And it was coming for him—and him alone.

This time they did not make love, nor take a dip in the lake.

Billy Ray opted to get dressed, Rebecca likewise.

They had to move.

A figure dressed in full black burqa to cover ruined skin, lowered a powerful set of binoculars.

Somehow, the man being spied on seemed to take notice.

Then the burqa-clad stranger shifted the speed boat into gear and motored away from the beachfront mansion.

"GO!" Agent Tompkins gave the command.

The helicopters performed a deadly aerial ballet—

SWAT vehicles rushed in according to plan—

Fast boats stormed ashore—

The *GO* order for the foot teams would come next.

If Gallina was on the premises, as present intel indicated, there would be no escape.

Finally, amid automatic gunfire and explosions, Lam and Tafoya's turn came. They rushed to their first objective, a tunnel at the south end of the Webster facility.

Then they began their search for the butterfly girl.

Being underground, there was no noise of the battle raging above. Lam could only gather fighting was fierce by the radio traffic. His team completed a search of the first tunnel, then another, and yet another.

Finally, Lam halted his team. "Where would Gallina hide the body?"

The agent beside Lam said, "I'm still wondering why Gallina took the dead girl in the first place. What's so important about a decaying corpse?"

Tafoya spoke for the first time. "Damn! That's it!"

"What's '*it*'?" Lam asked.

"*Decaying.* Is there an employee cafeteria in the main building?"

Another agent, echoing the ill feelings toward Tafoya's presence, most notably her being a TV news reporter embedded on a SWAT operation said, "You hungry already?"

Tafoya rolled her eyes. "Did anyone check the refrigerator?"

Lam radioed the change of plans then motioned for the team to follow.

The refrigerator!

Why didn't he think of that?

Sattgast ended his conference with the corporate office.

He was given the go-ahead. To lose out on scooping the story of the century could sink their fledgling news station. Conversely, it could vault them past their competitors too in the never-ending campaign for ratings and huge sponsorship dollars.

In five minutes, the station's most senior anchor would interrupt normal television programing with the hottest breaking news to burn the airwaves in over forty years:

The President of the United States, in concert with a secret cabal, has suspended the nation's Constitution. Backed by the heads of the military industrial complex, the media, banking and retail moguls, the nation's most feared intelligence group has been turned on its own citizens . . . .

And so the report would go across the airwaves.

As he stood next to the station's large studio camera waiting to give the *GO* signal, Sattgast wondered if there couldn't be more to the story.

Why would POTUS do such a thing?

With a still-trembling hand, he counted off five fingers and pointed at the station's top news anchor.

And the story went *live.*

<===== PIPELINE =====>

15

As Lam and his team exited the tunnel to ground level beside the main office complex, they were warned to take cover.

Barricaded inside a metal pillbox high atop one of the smokestacks, a .50 caliber M2 Browning machine gun rained copper jacketed hell on the SWAT vehicles. Supersonic rounds of armor-piercing steel tore through everything in their path like hot rocks passing through soft bread.

Help came in the form of a 76mm artillery shell, fired from the deck of a US Coast Guard cutter standing off-shore on Lake Michigan.

Suddenly, the upper half of the smokestack vaporized, sending large pieces of the stack falling to earth.

A stunned quiet ensued, except for the shouts of squad commanders and police sirens.

But no more guns.

The battle at the Norman Webster Power Plant and Paper Mill on the shores of Muskegon Lake terminated as quickly as it had started.

En route to the employee cafeteria, Lam received word that Hector Gallina had been captured in his office without a shot being fired.

He was patched through to the apprehending team leader and could hear Gallina demanding to be read his Miranda Rights or be set free. The scumbag was claiming his innocence and rambling on about how there was no evidence linking him to any crimes, and certainly not ones warranting such a gross overreaction by the federal government. Furthermore, the security force protecting the facility had been contracted from a private firm, to which he claimed to have no connection, and for the FBI to take matters up with them—

Technically, Gallina was correct, Lam thought. And presently, there was no solid evidence linking the cartel boss to crimes sufficient to put the bastard away for any meaningful length of time.

Then Lam opened the cafeteria's large walk-in refrigerator and all that changed. Behind a false wall, the team found all they needed to throw the book at Hector Gallina. There was the Mexican girl's body bundled in a white sheet, her face angelic and peaceful in death except for the open gash from her left ear to her right ear.

Lam left Tafoya and two agents behind to take photos and secure the crime scene until a forensics team arrived. Then he went to join his colleagues and a ranting, despicable Hector Gallina.

A hush fell over the room as Lam entered.

With dead fish eyes, Gallina watched him approach.

"Hector Gallina, you're under arrest—"

"On what charge?"

"Killing butterflies!"

Before Lam could read the Miranda warning, he was stopped when an agent from one of the search teams entered the room.

Though the man was a seasoned veteran of the FBI, tears formed as he reported, "We found secret holding tanks inside of coal cars filled with women and children . . . suffocated . . . bound for the furnaces—" The tough agent failed to complete his report and left the room.

Lam turned back to Gallina.

The long scar on the man's face twitched.

The news anchor finished his report, and then regularly scheduled programming resumed.

Immediately, the newsroom phones began ringing off the hook.

Sattgast was thrilled!

The Mid-Western News had scooped them all: Fox, CNN, NBC, and the rest of the media alphabet.

He'd done his job, as a professional journalist and as the production manager of the hottest television news program on the air.

Maybe his star would rise among the echelon of top TV producers, perhaps all the way to New York.

However, he couldn't shake the feeling that he'd just fired the first shot that would change the world.

He also hoped that he'd done the right thing.

Billy Ray and Rebecca entered the mansion dressed and ready to go.

But go where?

He dialed Dodd's phone number.

There was no answer nor any indication he could leave a message.

He checked the cell phone power and signal strength. There was an adequate amount of both.

He dialed again. Same result.

Never had he telephoned Dodd and not gotten through.

He called Dodd's name out loud, but got no reply, and the kitchen lights stayed lit. Then he walked over to the dog dish. The water bowl was full and a tasty dog treat left untouched. There was no Augie either.

Next he searched through several rooms until locating one of the interior surveillance cameras. Its power indicator light was off.

Billy Ray's skin began to crawl.

The high school tour at the Paladin Nuclear Power Plant ended.

Rasul and his classmates approached the Radiation Portal Monitor to be screened before exiting the facility. The RPM could detect extremely small levels of radioactivity.

Rasul hoped he'd sprinkled enough of Qasem's powder in everyone's food and drink. He also hoped nobody noticed the absent ballpoint pen he'd carried into the building.

Certainly, he was about to find out.

The group lined up at the portal machine. Rasul was first to enter.

A red light strobed and a bell sounded.

The startled security guard had Rasul step back. The light went out and the alarm stopped. The guard was eliminating the chance of a false-positive reading.

Rasul was motioned forward again. And again the red light flashed and the bell sounded.

This time, the guard whipped into action and pressed the call button on his shoulder mic. "We have a possible human contamination event."

Within seconds, additional uniformed personnel arrived, as did a woman in a business suit accompanied by a man in a white lab coat and carrying a yellow box and wand.

The lab technician scanned Rasul and said to the woman, "cobalt-60."

"Not again—" the guard began to say before the woman raised her hand to squelch further comment.

Within moments, the entire group of kids, two teachers, and a female parent chaperone were tested and then herded off to a side room.

They were asked to wait while a special team of paramedics were called. They were also told not to worry, it was only a precaution.

Rasul looked around the padded room. He knew exactly what it was, a lead-lined containment cell.

Now they were all victims of contamination.

Qasem's choice of cobalt-60 was genius due to it being a byproduct created within the Paladin reactors then sold to medical suppliers and research institutes. The manipulation worked because of the prior leaks of radioactive water into Lake Michigan. It was the poor safety record that came to doom the aging facility.

Comically, by the time investigators determined the cobalt-60 had not actually originated in Michigan, but from a stolen shipment in Mexico, it would be too late.

"Allah be praised," Rasul whispered under his breath, thankful to be a tool for Jihad.

Hector Gallina and his bodyguards were led away with their hands behind their backs in cuffs. Some of the agents who had witnessed the bodies in the coal cars may have put their shiny new bracelets on a bit too tight. If it was up to them, and not the law, those cuffs would never come off again, ever.

On the way out the door, the cartel boss turned back to Lam and said, "You're making a big mistake. You need me."

Lam stepped close. "I need predators like you and your dead father like I need rabies." Lam turned to the agents escorting Gallina. "Now get his skunk ass out of here before I blow his brains out!"

At the mention of his father, a pained look crossed Gallina's face.

Tafoya had entered the room moments earlier to tape the reading of the Miranda warning being given to Gallina. She raised her camera and snapped a perfect photographic portrait of Hector's shocked face at the very moment Lam mentioned the deceased Angel Gallina.

After an hour-long task force meeting the mission was declared over. Crime scene investigators would take it from here, possibly for weeks gathering so much evidence.

Lam went looking for Tafoya. He found her inside of the cafeteria refrigerator standing next to a closed body bag and the same medical examiner as when they'd first met at Pigeon Lake.

Tafoya turned at hearing his approach. Tears filled her eyes.

Lam stepped next to her and took her hand.

She allowed the gesture and said, "I want to take her home, Johnny."

"But where's home?"

"Duke said 'where butterflies are born.' I think I know where that is."

Lam looked up at the M.E., his request communicated without words. The man nodded.

Billy Ray telephoned for a cab.

He had a powerful feeling they needed to get away from the beach house, that something had gone terribly wrong, and lots more was close behind.

Dodd's cell number continued to go unanswered.

He helped Rebecca into the back of the cab, then slid in and pulled the door shut.

The car radio was tuned to a talk radio program. He wasn't much of a news buff, mostly because he tended to get deployed when events turned sour. Until then, he preferred the joyful bliss of ignorance.

<=== PIPELINE ===>

This time, however, the topic caught his attention, Rebecca's too. Even the cabbie appeared preoccupied by the report, as the nasally-sounding host ranted on about how the government went too far—

". . . and what good was the nation's Constitution if the President was going to ignore it anyway? America already cast off the yoke of one oppressive monarchy in its history, and it damn sure didn't need a new one!"

Then the talk show host primed his listeners with a rhetorical question. *"Could a shadow government really be ruling the United States?"*

It sounded like nonsense to Billy Ray, until a name came over the car speaker that nearly launched him through the roof. As bumper music rose to indicate an impending commercial break, the host said, *"After a word from our sponsors, I'll tell you who this K-KEY Group really is!"*

Billy Ray and Rebecca stared hard at each other.

It was crystal clear to them now.

They'd been shut down.

Sattgast pulled himself away from his desk and walked to the window.

From the fortieth floor of the Mid-Western News headquarters on Wacker Drive, he had a clear view of Chicago's famed Loop bridges along the Chicago River.

The view from his office was worth the long hours at the news station.

Standing in crumpled clothes, not having slept in over twenty-four hours, and an empty stomach, save for gallons of coffee, he let out a breath and smiled.

They'd done it . . . they'd scooped the big networks once again.

The news cycle was just that, a cycle. Bad news tended to come in bunches. And his MWN station was getting dealt aces!

His computer chimed, signaling yet another news flash, ending his momentary break from reality.

This particular news cycle was shaping up to be a turbulent one, with no change for the foreseeable future, much to the glee of the company executives, of course. He'd already canceled plans to attend a Cubs game against the cross-town rival White Sox. Too bad, too. He had a feeling this could finally be the year that the Cubs' broke the Curse of the Billy Goat. He'd also been compelled to send his wife and kids on to their vacation home for the weekend without him.

Bad news meant good ratings. And good ratings attracted advertising dollars Which, in turn, translated into profits for the company and its shareholders. And finally, sizable paychecks for Sattgast and his staff.

Meaning—unless people were fed a steady diet of doom and gloom about market crashes, government spying, beheadings, wars, rumors of wars, and the like, to keep viewers glued to the tube, how would they ever learn about the sponsors' newest line of cars, weight loss products, or erectile dysfunction drugs?

Such was the media's own *curse,* Sattgast lamented.

He returned to his desk and the latest news flash.

The newest item dealt with a group of school kids being contaminated by radiation on a field trip to a nuclear plant in South Haven, Michigan.

Sattgast studied the information very carefully.

Ironically, the incident happened only a few miles from his Lake Michigan cottage where his wife and kids were staying the weekend.

Although medical authorities claimed the level of radiation exposure posed no long-term negative effects, and the children were expected to make a full recovery, the matter proved to be the final straw for a public weary of continued safety violations at the aging facility.

Protestors were arriving in chartered buses to lay siege at the facility. Dozens of news reporters and camera trucks had descended on the area. The local sheriff was forced to call in state police to help maintain order.

Leaders of the protest group and angry citizens were calling upon the federal government to cease operations at the nuclear plant and then remove all nuclear fuel from their shores. And do it now!

To the government's credit, a spokesperson for the U.S. Nuclear Regulatory Commission, whose motto was *Protecting People and the Environment,* issued an official statement that pleased the protestors:

> "Due to the plant's poor safety record, and out of an abundance of caution, the Commission has revoked the plant's operating license and issued a cease and desist order. Beginning immediately, all generating activities will close at the Paladin plant and radioactive materials and byproducts shipped to a 'safe' facility."

Sattgast gave a sigh of relief at reading the statement. Certainly the world didn't need any more Fukushimas or Chernobyls.

Due to the government's swift action, the end of the Paladin Nuclear Plant wasn't being measured in years but in days. The first transfer of the most-radioactive materials was scheduled and transport arranged.

Sattgast made a note to call his realtor. Surely, properties near the nuke plant could spike in value. So why not get a piece of the action.

He handed the report to his secretary, who passed it to the newsroom writer, who transcribed it to a teleprompter, which was rolled in front of an anchorman, who would read the breaking news after a sponsor break.

<== PIPELINE ==>

Sattgast was about to leave when his computer pinged again. And again a startling news story appeared, something about the capture and arrest of a Mexican drug cartel kingpin in Muskegon, Michigan.

What the hell was going on up in the Wolverine State?

He decided not to add the cartel story to the 'breaking news alert.' Instead, he dialed his research staff for a report on cartel activity in the U.S. No use offending the Hispanic population, their votes are important.

Sattgast's stomach growled reminding him it was lunchtime. He rose to go— All at once, the streets below went crazy. Police sirens erupted, strobe lights appeared from every direction, and dozens of squad cars raced to block intersections. Within seconds, all city traffic was halted and a solid ring of red and blue flashing lights surrounded the Willis Tower.

Then Sattgast's own building's alarms sounded and his secretary rushed through the door. "John, it's another bombing! Get out now!"

Looking across at the majestic skyscraper, Sattgast could only think of one thing—*9/11*. Then he turned and ran.

"Where to?" the cabbie asked.

Billy Ray didn't actually know. Two attempts to reach Dodd had failed. Worse still, an automated message said the number was out of service.

Calling Lam and Tafoya proved fruitless, as well, going to voice mail. Undoubtedly, they were still involved in Muskegon.

He was saved from answering the cabbie by his ringing cell phone.

It was Lam. "We got the bastard!" referring to Gallina. "And you guys?"

"Good work, Army! We're leaving Holland . . . I think we've been fired."

"How so?" asked Lam.

"E.T. phoned home and nobody answered."

"Strange. Let me try." Lam was back immediately. "Get to the barn, Wolverine. We have a major emergency."

"Roger that, Lover Boy."

Before Billy Ray could give the cabbie a destination, the nasally guy on the radio interrupted a fruit tea commercial with a breaking news alert.

"This just in, folks . . . only minutes ago, a terrorist group tried to blow up the Willis Tower in downtown Chicago. Authorities killed both bombers before they could detonate their devices. It's reported that the terrorists were using radioactive dirty bombs—"

Billy Ray and Rebecca stared at the Pakistani driver.

"Hey, don't look at me," the cabbie said. "I love America."

"Let's go," Billy Ray replied. "Head east, I'll guide you."

His skin was crawling again.

16

The "barn" was getting a good deal of use, Billy Ray concluded as he entered the super-secret facility. This time because the order to disband the federal taskforce after raiding the Gallina compound was rescinded.

All special agents and contractors were ordered back to the fusion center to await further orders from D.C.

Billy Ray and Rebecca sat just as the briefing on the terrorist bombing in Chicago began. Lam had been designated by the Director of the FBI to act as the Special Agent in Charge.

"The matter's still fluid, as you can imagine," Lam began and then explained how two al-Qaeda operatives, a young black woman in her twenties and a middle-aged disabled white male in a wheelchair, had positioned themselves at opposite sides of the Willis Tower intent on detonating two extremely powerful and sophisticated devices containing C-4 plastic explosives and various forms of projectable materials to cause maximum carnage. Also, for the first time on American soil, radiological material made up part of their bombs.

But thanks to an anonymous tip phoned into the Chicago Police, SWAT team snipers were able to arrive in time and eliminate both terrorists before they could actuate their detonators.

A dozen hands shot up in the crowd.

Who was the tipster? Had anyone claimed responsibility yet? Did the bombs match known types used in Boston or elsewhere? What could be deduced from the dissimilarity of the suspects to those of typical Islamic terrorists, and were common profiles no longer valid?

Billy Ray didn't envy Lam. His friend was neck deep in a gator swamp holding a bucket of chicken.

They'd talked briefly before the meeting. Lam said that his old boss Chris Dreyfus was no longer answering the K-KEY Group phones either.

Regardless of the reason, they'd been cut loose, and at the worst time.

In that case, at least Lam had the Bureau to fall back on. Whereas, Billy Ray was strictly a military Special Ops dude, and a civilian to boot. He'd simply melt back into society . . . or head into the High Sierras.

So if the paradigm had truly shifted, as Dodd claimed in his recruiting speech at the hospital, and radical Islamic terror cells were active in America blending in with everyday common people, then civilian law enforcement would be ill-equipped to battle such an asymmetric threat.

Dodd's pitch for him joining the K-KEY Group centered on America being under attack—that defeating an enemy hell-bent on destroying the U.S. and slaughtering its citizens, was a job for warriors.

<== PIPELINE ==>

Billy Ray found himself in agreement with Admiral Dodd.

As good as the nation's law enforcement was, it would take more than federal, state, and local police to combat an army of terrorists. Cops were ill-equipped and not trained for this type of warfare.

The nation wasn't fighting a crime wave, it was facing the specter of all-out asymmetric warfare—

And pure evil.

Yet, where was Dodd?

Was the outing of the K-KEY Group preventing POTUS from acting to save the country, similar to when a previous president's power to act had been stymied by sexual scandals in the White House? What about the suspension of Posse Comitatus? Where did it stand and who held the reins of power?

Billy Ray looked at the men and women gathered around him. They'd just brought down a vicious cartel boss and his band of cutthroats. Each person present deserved a vote of gratitude from the nation they served with honor and integrity, and most of all, bravery.

Next he looked at Tafoya and Rebecca sitting next to one another: Tafoya taking notes on a steno pad, Rebecca listening intently to Lam's briefing. They too had acted bravely, common people performing uncommon acts of valor.

And then he thought of himself—*alone again.*

The country was facing an existential threat from Muslim Terrorists. Jihad was rising within the nation's borders. Lone wolf killers presently, but surely much more to come. Jihad was no longer just a foreign word, it was within the gates.

The bottom line . . . terrorists had just given notice that they'd use any means necessary to destroy the country—nuclear, biological, and others.

The enemy was well-versed in America's morals and the high value to having a free and open society. They had no such constraints. Al-Qaeda followers are experts at irregular warfare and manipulating its target.

It was now more imperative than ever before to track down and destroy these soldiers of Allah no matter what, no matter where, and yes, no matter how.

Billy Ray recalled Dodd's admonishment about freedom.

Given that the stakes for every man, woman, and child in America was life or death, he was now inclined to 'pretend.'

Billy Ray rose from his chair. All eyes turned to him.

"It's a ruse."

"What do you mean, Jenkins?" Lam asked.

"The attempted bombing . . . it was a red herring."

Agent Tompkins came to Lam's defense. "How can you be so sure?"

"I can't," Billy Ray admitted. "But your question shouldn't be *whether*, but *why*. So I'll answer that instead. This country is in a battle for its very existence. It's not motive that matters here, but purely an objective."

"Please explain," Tompkins said.

Billy Ray did so. "We must not mistake terrorists for criminals. They're the dogs of war, skilled in asymmetric warfare. If we are to win this fight, we must think like them. I'm betting the nuclear material found in those bombs is not the end, it's only the beginning."

Billy Ray looked back at Rebecca.

Her face had turned white as snow.

By the following day, the nation's news media had suspended normal programming to report on the Chicago attack by an al-Qaeda terror cell, ". . . Or one of its vile offshoots."

Church pastors and clergy led their congregations in thankful prayers that, once again, God had spared America from a terrible fate.

The President's Press Secretary, a man skilled at talking while saying nothing, made an appearance to calm the nation.

He reported the government was "hot on the trail" of those who perpetrated the *failed* attack on the Willis Tower, and that Lady Justice "wouldn't rest" until the criminals were apprehended . . . but due to the on-going investigation, further comment would be ill-advised.

Daily questioning from the assembled White House press corps received the same response.

By week's end, and with no word on who was responsible for the attempted bombing, public patience evaporated.

Finally, using his spellbinding charm and the dramatic backdrop of the Oval Office, the President of the United States addressed the nation.

For thirty minutes, POTUS outlined the nation's historical reaction when facing challenges . . . its creed of banding together, one and all, laying aside personal differences to face the present challenge as "one people." Then he implored the nation to remain calm and trust its elected government and its agents as they sought "Justice for all and to root out those who would do harm to our nation and its citizens."

Noted by most press correspondents, the speech did less to calm the nation than it did to advance the man's appeal in the upcoming elections. It was short on detail, long on platitude. Some people believe that Washington D.C was built on a swamp, but most today know it's built on hot air!

<==== PIPELINE ====>

So either POTUS was holding his cards close, or the government had no hand . . . the nation simply got lucky in avoiding a black swan event capable of turning politics on its head.

But for many citizens, the refusal to name and blame was irksome and showed weakness. Two times America had been attacked by Islamic radicals, not counting lone wolf incidents and near-misses.

Failing to retaliate would invite a third strike.

For as horrific as the 9/11 World Trade Center terrorist attack was, with thousands of lives lost or sorely disrupted, and billions of dollars in damages, it could have paled next to Chicago suffering a nuclear event.

People were taking to the streets to protest the country's tepid leadership. They were suspicious of bread and circus promises, and cynical of the rosy narratives and blithe attitudes by their elected officials.

Citizens were tired of appeasing the nation's enemies, and offended by acts of terror designated as "workplace violence" instead of calling it what it was. Most of all, people were tired of the smoke and mirrors show that our government excelled at.

The party was over. The secret was out.

Islamic terrorists were operating on American soil.

Their aims, their goals, and their declarations were plain—they'd declared a religious war and everyone knew it, especially other Muslims suffering terribly under the knife of its radical fringe. But more than just a religion, Islam was a government, a total way of life. Radical Islam forced an unyielding theocracy on its adherents, and death to all the rest.

Most dangerous of all was that ideology could not be defeated with guns and bombs, but only by the sharp sword of truth.

Already, many grassroots Americans were beating the drums for a change in the November elections, demanding a new direction, and new leaders willing to exercise America's great power and to promote its Judeo-Christian values.

Sensing a mounting storm, groups usually protective of the President and his party began allowing some uncensored criticisms and distancing themselves from him. Media outlets of all stripes fell in lockstep with the public's discontent, fanning emotions to compete for network ratings, even manufacturing news to drive a favored narrative.

There was no denying the nation had dodged a bullet with the Merc incident. And consequently, national polls began trending badly for the current administration and its candidates.

However, history suggested such hysteria would be a flash in the pan. Public fear and anxiety would ebb eventually. And folks would go back to their usual concerns.

So POTUS was advised to stay the course.

A second week passed, then a third. And history proved correct.

The speculation that had earlier run rampant of who was responsible for the Chicago attack, played itself out. Conspiracy theories filling the internet returned to usual subjects like alien abductions and who killed the Kennedys. Police stations saw relief, too, as the anonymous tips swamping their lines fell to a trickle. People all across the nation gathering around water coolers, coffee shops, and pubs who debated the bombing, simply tired of "yesterday's news" and got back on celebrity rumors and sports teams.

The feared act of citizens turning on one another, suspecting their neighbors and those with questionable citizenship, waned. Even the sign placed at the edge of one Arizona town that read *America, love it or self-deport!* was pulled down.

And finally, the pundits on talk radio who'd been thumping their chests daily, like Kong in the jungle, with I-told-you-so's about "terrorists living amongst us" turned their ire on other matters.

In the end, the Commander-in-Chief was lauded for having shown restraint in the face of a dire threat to the nation. His media support returned stronger than ever.

And his poll numbers rose.

The trail had gone cold, Lam concluded, setting down the intel reports.

Additionally, neither the man nor the woman fit any of the FBI's typical profiling for Mideast terrorists. In fact, investigators had thus far failed to connect them in any way to the teachings of radical Islam let alone a terrorist cell, or each other.

Yet they weren't lone wolf operators either.

Someone pulled their strings. Someone made sure they were trained, equipped and had current intel on their designated target.

But who?

In a typical terror cell structure, the man and woman would have no knowledge of each other, operational or otherwise.

Yet Lam still found the disassociation bewildering.

The male bomber had been a decorated Iraq War military veteran, distraught over his disability caused by a roadside vehicle borne IED. Investigators tracked down the makers of the man's motorized wheelchair, a company who graciously donated critical equipment to countless injured vets. But someone modified his personal chair sometime after delivery.

<===== PIPELINE =====>

Nor could the FBI determine a motive for why the U.S. military veteran would want to take the lives of so many of his fellow countrymen.

As for determining the mindset of the young African-American woman, that proved even far more frustrating. She'd acted with extreme cunning by faking her pregnancy. Even her mother bought into the her claim and was excited about becoming a grandmother.

Thus far, investigators could only determine the prosthetic belly had been purchased over the internet by an anonymous person in Florida using a stolen credit card, and that the package was delivered to a vacant house. The answer to how the device found its way to Chicago was still being sought.

As with the disabled veteran, nothing in the woman's background linked her to al-Qaeda, ISIS, Al-Shabab or any other known radical groups. The only similarity between the two bombers that FBI profiler psychologists could determine was both had been distraught.

The woman's emotional state was critically altered when as a teen mother she witnessed her toddler ripped apart in a hail of bullets in an extremely violent drive-by shooting in St. Louis, Missouri. No one was ever held accountable. Then some months later, she'd moved to Chicago to be near her family and attend junior college.

The male's profile was similar in that his bright future was forever altered by a violent and mindless act. Once a popular high school track star before joining the Army, his life was changed in an instant by a VBIED. The loss of his legs, as well as severe PTSD, contributed greatly to his mental sense of order. He felt emotionally numb, had memory lapses except those times he relived the moment of the explosion and he withdrew from people he had previously loved and had been loved by.

Lam finished briefing Billy Ray and Rebecca in their hotel suite near the Grand Rapids airport.

"Someone got to them," Billy Ray concluded.

"Someone expert at manipulating vulnerable minds," Rebecca added.

For the past days, Billy Ray and Rebecca had spent their time scouring the internet for any small bit of information on terror incidents in the United States, especially homegrown radicals describing themselves as jihadists. They were even granted access to top-secret labeled documents on foiled al-Qaeda attacks not known to the public.

They hoped to discover patterns and coincidences, anything out of the norm with known al-Qaeda recruitment methods.

In some cases, Rebecca concluded the identified perpetrators had acted as copycats, frightening for its own dark reasons. A few other terror acts were carried out by angry dudes in prison, who turned righteous to ease their incarcerations, or who were being ordered by gangs requiring murder to secure their membership.

But in the end, Billy Ray and Rebecca failed to make connections between the profiles of the Chicago bombers and the people described in the news accounts or the classified white papers.

Billy Ray did discover one possibility, however. He recounted the story to Lam and Rebecca about a hijacked garbage truck in Mexico a year earlier that was transporting outdated radiotherapy equipment to a contaminated materials waste center.

It never arrived.

Authorities discovered the truck sometime later, but the canisters of nuclear material were gone.

The radiotherapy machines had contained radioactive cobalt-60. It was the very same material used by the Chicago bombers. Over time, nuclear forensics could reveal the age, origin and history of the Chicago material by using the isotropic characterization of the stolen materials. Then they'd know for certain.

Lam confirmed that region of Mexico was known to be under control of the Gallina cartel. So it could be that the cobalt-60 was linked to them. Though it didn't make sense for a drug cartel to switch to terror tactics. There was no money in it, unless they were missing something somewhere.

There was a knock at the door.

It was Tafoya. "Miss me?"

"Nope. We slept like babies," Billy Ray thought of the beach cabana.

"More like rabbits," Tafoya teased, joining them at the table.

She'd spent the previous days doing what Tami Tafoya did best, investigative reporting for her TV station, and now for the entire nation. The present news cycle was keeping everyone busy poking the bushes for answers. As it turned out in any investigation, each answer only surfaced more questions.

Billy Ray noticed Lam casting the exquisite Cubana a genuine smile. Clearly, a sense of fondness passed between the Fed and the reporter.

What a turnaround, he thought.

Lam resumed the talk at the table.

There'd been an article in the Grand Rapids Press and South Haven Tribune, pushed below the fold due to the "failed" Chicago bombing, about the poisoning of a high school kids touring at the nuclear power plant near South Haven.

"That, too, involved cobalt-60," Lam pointed out. "The stuff seems to be everywhere."

<==== PIPELINE ====>

Rebecca said, "Actually, cobalt-60 is a very common material used throughout our society, especially in the treatment of malignant diseases, as well as its wide use to eliminate organisms from pharmaceuticals such as ointments and solutions." So yes it is almost everywhere".

Tafoya showed her surprising breadth of knowledge too. "It's also used in industry to check metal parts for weakness, and in blast furnaces to measure their performance. Moreover, cobalt-60 is a byproduct created in nuclear reactors, such as the Paladin plant where the kids were exposed. So yeah, it's everywhere."

Lam let out a low whistle.

"Incidentally," Tafoya continued, "the Paladin plant was just ordered closed by the regulators and all its radioactive materials shipped out of Michigan."

Billy Ray threw up his hands. "So where does all of this leave us, the 'A' team?"

Lam said, "My guys are throwing everything they've got at this case. But I'm afraid the trail's gone cold."

"Same on the psychological profiling front," Rebecca agreed.

Tafoya let out a long breath. "Same here, nothing new to report."

"Dodd picked a shitty time to cut us off," Billy Ray carped.

Over the days after losing contact with Admiral Dodd, the four of them had continued to operate as a team anyway.

But a body needed a head.

Billy Ray felt guilty for having been so impatient with Dodd. He'd gladly welcome his friend's long-winded answers now.

They'd hit a solid brick wall.

Qasem sat beside Tariq at the computer, watching his young genius' fingers fly over the keyboard.

"How can you be sure the Americans won't discover your Arab nose poking under their tents?"

Tariq looked up from the monitor. "Because my nose is already inside their tents, thanks to some very sloppy cyber security by a high-ranking government official."

"Explain," Qasem ordered.

"You're aware of Trojan Horse viruses, how they present one thing but deliver another. Well, mine is more like an earth worm, routing through scores of countries to cloak my identity. I've been tunneling into their tents for years creating secret access ports and storing code for a future time."

And that time had come, Qasem thought.

"And no one suspects your intrusion?"

"I'm absolutely 100% positive," Tariq said, then paused the cursor at a line of computer code and faced Qasem. "Only my superiors were aware of my presence. But I never knew who they were. Plus I kept hands off the king's treasures . . . so many secrets for the plucking, like low hanging fruit—military, industrial, banking. But my unquestionable orders were to create portals only."

Qasem placed a hand on Tariq's shoulder and squeezed. "It was good of you to always be obedient. For it was I . . . I am your commander."

Tariq pulled back, startled. "But how? We're from different worlds, me a Sunni Arab and you from Iran. Our peoples have battled each other for centuries."

Qasem released his hand from Tariq's shoulder.

Tariq studied Qasem. "Who are you really?"

Qasem chose not to identify his true name nor explain how the illusion had been achieved.

"You need only know one name, Allah. We Muslims have been cutting each other's throats for too long. Is this what you think our master wants?"

"I imagine not," Tariq replied feebly.

"But that's exactly what America wants us to continue to do to each of our brothers. The time has come for Sunni and Shia to unite against the true enemy of Islam." Tranquilly he asked Tariq, "Are you with me, my brother?"

Tariq felt Qasem's eyes bore into his soul, He knew a wrong answer would end in his quick death. He also knew Qasem was right. Should Islam remain divided, America and its Western allies would never be defeated.

"Yes, Qasem, I'm with you."

Qasem nodded. "Then *you* may now actuate the command we have trained and lived for."

Tariq did as ordered, without hesitation. He felt honored to be the one chosen to change the world with a simple key stroke on a computer.

A new screen appeared with tabs showing the headings of several U.S. government agencies and links to the Great Lakes commodities suppliers critical for the mission. The malware then made the terror cell appear as legitimate wholesalers and issued the appropriate documents and validated purchase orders.

Qasem was pleased. Now the next phase of their operation could proceed, which entailed commandeering a lake freighter and filling it with all of the volatile bomb ingredients, including high-level radioactive waste transiting from the shuddered Paladin plant to a facility in Wisconsin.

<==== PIPELINE ====>

Once the nuclear materials were added to the thousands of tons of explosives, their ship would become a bomb unlike any the world had ever seen. It's blast effects would resonate around the world. Along with a contingent of Iranian Quds Force commandos aboard, whom Qasem had trained personally, his ship of death would steam south on Lake Michigan, and then up the Main Stem of the Chicago River into the heart of the Windy City—nay, the heart of America!

Moreover, the ship he chose would enter the kill zone to the jubilant applause of its victims while the whole world watched on television.

Qasem let out a long breath.

This would be his final mission. He expected to die.

In one way or another, his whole life had prepared him for this day of private glory and entry into paradise. With him there would be no silly martyr's anthem or poor quality video spouting invented motives for killing infidels. He was a professional career soldier, not a crazed murderer.

When the time finally came to trigger the bomb, he would simply praise Allah . . . and open the gates of hell for the infidels!

Qasem could almost taste his reward in paradise, his nestling in the arms of virgins while beholding his plan unfolding on the sinful Earth below—his pleasure at seeing the demise of the Western World, and America's great reckoning—the carnage visited upon all of Allah's true enemies as the wages of sin.

As in Europe, the United States would be invaded along its unguarded borders. And then the clown car act of its leaders scrambling to halt the inevitable would begin.

A true Divine Comedy!

Destroying the most powerful nation on the planet would be born from deep within. Sleeper cells secreted into the United States over many years, would sabotage key utilities and transportation assets, then topple the border walls for the great hordes—poor Latinos from Central and South America escaping their own desperate hell, flushed from their homes by conspiring drug cartels, flooding across the threshold, and trampling the garden of El Norte.

And blood would flow freely in the streets, ". . . as high as a horse's bridle" as society spins out of control—race riots, criminals ambushing cops to settle old scores, atheists crucifying Christians and Jews, zombie drug addicts attacking the weak and vulnerable, everyone shooting at everyone else. Neighborhoods in flames.

Utter chaos!

In a rush to save themselves and their lands. The Fifty States would declare independence from a federal body who failed to protect them.

And then a great nation by virtue of its union, would break into pieces, mere islands defending against a rushing sea of invaders.

The lessons of Troy, Jerusalem, and Rome gone unheeded.

Such had always been humanity's path—a people banding together, growing great by common faith and unity, enjoying prosperity for a time, until greed and apathy, self-importance and indulgence, gnawed at their honor and virtue—weakening, fraying, and dividing a once-great people.

And finally collapse, supplanted by the next group wanting a turn.

Qasem's plan accounted for this universal truth.

And this time, the next in line would be Islam and it's true faith. The leaders in Tehran were moved to tears upon learning of his design—making Iran a world superpower, again, and Shia Islam the master of all men's souls on planet Earth.

The most secretive part of his scheme, however, was how the Sunni wing of Islam would be destroyed, and the great rift in Islam healed. The other 71 sects would also be wiped from Allah's eyes as an abomination to his glory. Then the one true faith would be unified at long last.

But first, the Sunni savages of ISIS, Boko Haram, and others, would fulfill their function as Iran's unwitting attack dogs, occupying America's attention—an insurgency nipping here, biting there . . . distracting, like a shiny object to a cat.

Meanwhile overseas, ISIS would play the role of flushing dogs herding millions of Muslims like starved cattle from their war-torn homelands into the soft belly of Europe.

Overwhelmed, America and its allies would beg Iran's help putting down the Sunni dogs. Their presidents and prime ministers would scurry to Tehran's front steps imploring the Grand Ayatollah for his spiritual authority, and to return prior favors.

Then would the Islamic Republic of Iran rise to preeminence as the king of the south and send these Christian infidels to their northern homes with their tails between their legs, leaving America to stand alone.

And when the dates and times predicted in the holy writings arrived, then would Rasul's true identity be revealed to the world: as the one who was in times of old and is again . . . a man-child born of a Sunni mother, sired by a Shia father. The prophesied redeemer—The Mahdi.

Upon seeing Mahdi revealed on every television screen and computer, hearing the news over radios and cell phones, or heeding the sonorous call of the *muezzin,* Muslims the world over would cast themselves to the ground in supplication and unity.

But for all others, arriving like a thief in the night, the Judgement Day!
And the rebirth of the Persian Empire.

<=== PIPELINE ===>

The team was disbanding. After checking them out of the hotel, Billy Ray joined Rebecca under the portico to await the airport shuttle.

Earlier, she'd proposed that he come live with her in Washington State, and he accepted. Though he'd insisted traveling cross-country at ground level, instead of by air. Probably because he'd been made to jump out of so many perfectly good airplanes. Though this time he'd forego the long walk and ride a Harley.

Rebecca made a sad face but said she understood, and that his later arrival would allow her to clear a month-long patient backlog.

Plus Billy Ray had made a promise years ago to an old SEAL teammate he wished to keep before arriving in Seattle. It was rumored that *Snake* was hiding out somewhere in the High Sierras.

Better than a prison cell for ten years, Billy Ray thought.

As for their friends, Lam had been ordered back to Dallas and would depart after wrapping up business in Grand Rapids. While Tafoya was pure Michigan, and in hot demand with her star rising fast at the television station. She'd even been offered the anchor position on the evening news—a big fat cherry for any media professional!

The two had talked about getting together for a trip to Mexico at some point, but were unsure when.

The only thing certain for everyone was they felt sad for the parting.

The shuttle arrived. Lam had volunteered to taxi Billy Ray and Rebecca to the airport, but they'd politely declined. After hugs and handshakes, they boarded the shuttle for the airport and were off.

Lam and Tafoya stood side by side, waving at their friends.

Finally, they turned and faced each other to offer their own awkward goodbyes. They were quiet for a spell, searching each other's faces.

It was time to part ways. Maybe in days past they both would have welcomed it. But that had changed.

"Will you call me when you get to Dallas?" Tafoya asked softly.

"Yes," Lam kept it short, probably too concise . . . too cold.

He wasn't much on small talk, especially with women. And especially with a woman he'd come full-circle with, from annoyance to . . . *to what?*

Lam wasn't sure.

Or maybe he *was* sure, but was just being pigheaded, unwilling to admit how much he'd grown to respect Tami Tafoya.

How much he enjoyed her company.

And how much he would miss her.

17

The President's security team gathered in the White House Situation Room, nicknamed "The Woodshed" by Capitol Hill staffers.

On this day, however, the people awaiting the President's arrival in the smallest of the three conference rooms did not comprise his usual National Security Team, at least not the one known to the public. Instead, they were the five heads of the K-KEY Group.

And they were tense . . . very tense.

The Assistant Director of the WHSR signaled the President's arrival by fogging the privacy windows.

"Thank you, Mr. Ronin," POTUS bid his assistant.

The K-KEY Group rose to their feet.

The President etured them to their seats and went to the head of the table. "Gentlemen . . . and Lady," he nodded to the lone female whose name badge displayed the single letter *V*. "Let me start by thanking you all for your contributions and devotion to our nation's safety."

The group nodded almost in unison.

"The last we met, I imposed a temporary halt to all K-KEY Group operations in order to find the traitor within our ranks. I presume you all came ready to report your findings." POTUS motioned to V. "If you would go first, please."

In a monotone delivery, V said, "Our fleet of Low-Frequency Acoustic Levitation vehicles have been ordered back to the subterranean bases."

"Do you mean our go-fast machines?"

"Yes," V replied, unmoved by the President's phraseology.

"Please continue," POTUS ordered.

"Computer systems, security protocols, and all personnel have been fully audited. I can report with absolute certainty that the security breach did not come from my people."

The next two K-KEY Group members offered their findings.

The first man headed the world's largest telecom company, while the second man steered a vast media and entertainment empire. Both succinctly denied security breaches at their respective companies.

The same was claimed by the next member of the K-KEY group, the world's first trillionaire.

Robin Getz, of Getz Enterprises, had made his obscene fortune pioneering the world's largest internet store that sold nearly every item and service known to mankind. But it didn't stop there. Contributing immeasurably to Getz' financial success was his company's use of Predictive Modeling Algorithms, or known as PMAs..

<===== PIPELINE =====>

Around the clock, every single day, year in and year out, the personal likes, habits, and preferences of over three billion consumers, nearly half the world's population were tracked by Getz Enterprises, and then sold to tens of thousands of on-line and on-air advertisers, bulk mailers, and pollsters.

Getz knew what individuals wanted a full month ahead of them opening their wallets. He knew a person's behavior better than they did, knew where they lived, even for whom they would cast their votes.

Then Getz sold that information over and over and over again.

Unlike the K-KEY members who oversaw publicly traded companies, Getz' fiduciary responsibility was owed to just one person, himself.

"Not I," he said.

That left the final member of the K-KEY Group, its founder, Admiral John Dodd. He studied the face of each member, and then the President. These few souls controlled each of the main pillars of American society: telecommunications, a complicit media, PMAs on most every individual, and lastly, POTUS' command and control of the military.

He'd formed the K-KEY Group after witnessing America's enemies successfully exploiting the Republic's economy, morals and rule of law to their own advantage.

But now, seeing the lack of virtue among the nation's leaders, he worried about suspending the Constitutional checks and balances on the Federal Government that was specifically designed to protect its citizens.

No one was incorruptible.

What if America's immense power fell into the wrong hands?

POTUS said, "Admiral, you head the research and development sector of our group, as well as all tactical operations. Might the traitor have come from within your ranks?"

"Mr. President, my investigation is on-going. As you can imagine, I have assets in deep-cover situations. Therefore, I can neither confirm nor deny whether anyone under my command has turned against us."

All eyes stared at Dodd.

"But it is possible," the trillionaire suggested sternly.

"Yes, Mr. Getz, it *is* possible. It's just not probable."

Dodd felt sick that someone inside their organization had betrayed them. He'd severely vetted every human asset prior to their joining the K-KEY Group by utilizing the most sophisticated means available. And yes, that included everyone sitting at the table today. So who could have defeated truth serums, multiple lie detector tests, and exhaustive background checks?

Nobody!

Yet the fact remained, someone *had* penetrated their ironclad security, and was very near to exposing the most powerful consortium of political, financial, and military leaders since Hitler and Stalin.

The panic among the K-KEY Group was palpable. And for good reason. Exposure would spell an end to their prominence *and* fortunes––if not their freedom.

It didn't matter that the K-KEY Group utilized secret technologies and cut Constitutional corners solely for the good of the country. Voters would never consent to any group claiming *Authority Over All.*

The media mogul spoke, "Our surveillance efforts have enraged the nation. My editorial boards won't hold their tongues much longer about domestic spying, and neither will my stable of movie actors."

The telecom titan pitched his gripe. "Phone sales will plummet if customers learn how their every conversation is being recorded and then stored in black program computers. I could be ruined!"

Murmurs filled the room, with the exception of V, who remained mute and unreadable. And for good reason. Her constituents would win either way. Companies that produced war machines always did.

Getz was a straight-talker. "Mr. President, if voters learn you signed a Presidential Directive suspending the Constitution, they'll jam that pen so far up your ass it will take a team of spelunkers to find it. It would be good of you to remember that although we put you in office, we can't guarantee against others taking you out."

"Is that a threat, Mr. Getz?"

"No. It's a fact."

Finally, POTUS cast a look at Dodd as if asking, *Et tu Brute?*

"With all due respect, Mr. President, stopping that terror cell in Chicago wasn't accomplished by *our* efforts. The tipoff came from a concerned citizen, followed then by the prompt action of civilian law enforcement."

"Are you suggesting the K-KEY Group is no longer needed?" POTUS said, sounding hopeful at finding a way out of the current mess, and dissolving a group inherited from the previous administration.

"Just the opposite, sir. I believe we've been duped."

Getz objected, "But the terrorists were killed before they detonated the dirty bombs, and the cobalt-60 stolen in Mexico has been recovered."

Dodd countered, "My forensic people say each of those bombs were incorrectly wired and wouldn't have exploded anyway. Secondly, not *all* of the cobalt-60 was accounted for. One gram is still missing."

"Insignificant. Hardly worth our concern," the media baron opined.

"What if the terror plot was supposed to fail? What if it was a Red-Herring to send us running in the wrong direction?" Dodd voiced.

<===== PIPELINE =====>

The telecom titan snuffled. "It wouldn't be the first time those al-Qaeda boobs bungled. There was that shoe bomber, and then the dumbass with the exploding underwear. What a joke!"

Dodd countered, "Maybe the terrorists want us to think they're boobs and that we're totally in control?"

No one in the room, besides V perhaps, was buying his argument.

The media guy switched lanes. "With the Texas matter over with, let me veer attention away from us. I'll have my editors press a few hot-buttons, like cops killing black kids, the war on women, climate change, stuff like that—works every time."

Dodd didn't like the way the meeting was going.

Excluding V, the members were getting cold feet in the War on Terror, worried more about profits and reputations than keeping America safe.

It was time to state his case.

"Mr. President, removing our attention from the al-Qaeda threat would be a mistake. Just this morning, my people detected intrusions into some of our federal computer systems, including the Department of Energy. It could be a cyber-attack. A second terror event may be imminent."

Getz said, "Words like *may* and *might* don't sound convincing, Admiral. Everybody's getting hacked these days."

Dodd figured Getz would know, being the greatest offender of them all, insidiously collecting minutia on everyone through social media and merchandise barcodes. "Then what would convince you, Mr. Getz, *successful* terrorists? Our job is to prevent attacks." Dodd pressed, "One of my tactical teams may be onto something in Michigan . . . something that could flush out the enemies within the gates."

"You mean those Texas hillbillies, the ex-con and the FBI guy, plus their hotties you used my retail algorithms for?" asked Getz mockingly.

"Yes," Dodd said, needing to bite his tongue.

Having heard enough, the media mogul weighed in, "Mr. President, I propose we implement your plan, effective immediately."

Dodd didn't know what "plan" the media guy was referring to. Had the others gone behind his back?

POTUS raised his hands for calm. "The al-Qaeda plot has been foiled, regardless by whom. We can all breathe a little easier now."

"I disagree, Mr. President," Dodd said. "There remains an imminent crisis. We need to push on."

"Crises pose opportunities," POTUS countered. "But make no mistake, Admiral. I shall push on to other 'enemies within the gates,' as you call it, like banning assault weapons, global warming, racism, and income inequality."

POTUS' words were a stark reminder that the Commander-in-Chief was also the political leader of the nation.

"The country cannot have its President tarnished by rumors. So my press secretary has prepared a speech for me to reassure voters that the Chicago matter involved mentally ill citizens, not foreign actors. And that the rumors of domestic spying arose from internet crackpots."

"But that's not entirely true, Mr. President."

"Be that as it may, Admiral, it buys my security team time to discover those behind this appalling crime." The President stood and pressed a button on the table. "If you will excuse me, I have a teleprompter to read."

Dodd stood up. "Mr. President—"

POTUS halted at the door. "Yes, Admiral?"

"Islamic terrorists *are* behind this and won't be stopped by words or wishes. You want peace, we all do, but America must beat its plowshares into swords, before it's too late. Therefore, I'm requesting in the strongest terms possible that you allow me to take the fight to the enemy."

"Negative. That was not what I promised America when elected."

"But voters weren't informed of the true dangers facing the nation. They were told all was well. If we lose this fight, your legacy won't be that of a peacemaker but a man out of season—the *premature* President. The man who let National Security slip through his fingers."

The small room fell silent, even activity in the main SitRoom ceased. POTUS wasn't known for taking kindly to challenges to his authority.

"I beg to differ, Admiral. History applauds peacemakers." The President cast Dodd a cold look. "In case I was not perfectly clear before, your group is to stand down . . . indefinitely."

"Then I feel it necessary to resign my commission," Dodd stated.

"As you wish. I shall expect your resignation on my desk by first thing Monday morning." The President widened his gaze to the group. "Mr. Ronin will see you out."

The meeting ended.

Halfway across the country, another meeting was concluding.

Hector Gallina had just made a decision that could kill two birds with one bullet—gaining his freedom and getting the pricks who betrayed him.

He pushed his chair back from the metal table and stood.

Gallina lit a cigarette and paced the concrete floor inside the stark conference room of the Muskegon Correctional Facility.

Gallina's progress was tracked by the armed prison guard posted in front of the door.

The other two people watching him pace the small room. His lawyer sat ramrod still, awaiting his boss' directive. The other attendee was the lead investigator for Michigan's Western District of the Federal Public Defender's Office, Julio Camacho.

Gallina halted in front of the only window in the room, a one-way mirror, and studied his reflection.

Camacho capped their earlier conversation, "That's exactly how it's done, Mr. Gallina. If you possess information you wish to share with the FBI, I can make the call."

Gallina blew a cloud of smoke against the mirrored window and watched it mushroom.

"Will the Feds deal?"

"That'll depend on the information and its quality."

Gallina turned around and stared at his lawyer, a portly Hispanic with a Van Dyke beard and bulging eyes.

The man nodded.

Gallina tossed down the cigarette and crushed it out with his foot.

"Make the call."

Lam's cell phone rang.

A man asked, "Agent Lam?"

"Who's calling?"

"My name's Julio Camacho. I'm the lead investigator in the case against Hector Gallina . . . on behalf of the defendant."

Lam was caught off guard by the call. Surely, there was no shortage of evidence linking Gallina to a dozen capital offenses.

His annoyance flashed. "What do you want?"

"The *defendant*," Camacho accentuated the word to show their contrasting roles in the justice process, "wishes to share information."

"Then phone the Michigan SAC."

"Mr. Gallina requested you and you only."

"Oh really! Tell him to go f—"

"It's about Chicago," Camacho interrupted. "He claims to know who's behind the attack . . . and where they plan to strike next."

It sounded like Gallina was trying to pull a fast one.

"Outa' my league," Lam said. "Contact Homeland Security."

"I did, Agent Lam. You'll be hearing from them shortly. This is merely a courtesy call."

Lam caught the seriousness in Camacho's message.

It was no joke.

"Just say when and where, I'll be there."

Camacho provided Lam the time and place.

Billy Ray and Rebecca finished their coffees at the Starbucks inside the Grand Rapids airport and walked up the ramp to the TSA checkpoint.

Just then, a familiar voice called out their names.

It was Lam, and he was walking swiftly toward them lifting his FBI badge in plain view for the TSA Agent.

"I'm glad I caught you."

"What's up?" Billy Ray asked.

Lam grabbed Rebecca's luggage. "We need to get back to the coast. I'll explain in the car."

Rebecca said, "What about our airline tickets?"

"I'll have them cancelled and your card reimbursed."

"You can do that?" she wondered aloud.

"What better way to use my *Authority Over All*."

The drive from Grand Rapids to the Muskegon Correctional Facility was spent with Lam informing Billy Ray about Hector Gallina.

"How can you be sure Gallina's not yanking your chain?"

"He gave a bunch of details that hadn't been made public."

"Such as?" Billy Ray asked.

"He hired four Mexican men to run his company's IT department."

"Oh yeah?" Billy Ray could guess where this was going.

"Yeah," Lam admitted. "Turns out the men weren't Latinos after all. Furthermore, Gallina claims the men serviced more than just the mill's computers. They hacked banks and credit card companies. He swears knowing nothing of the illegal activity until the morning of our raid."

"What a load of bull," Billy Ray said.

"Obviously," Lam agreed. "But I confirmed the intrusions. Millions of dollars were stolen and never recovered."

"What do you mean they weren't Latinos?" Rebecca inquired.

"Gallina claims to have proof the men were Middle Eastern, and that they also kidnapped and killed three of his female employees, who just so happen to be the Jane Does I told you about."

Billy Ray said, "That's all stuff for cops. What's it got to do with me?"

"Gallina claims the men are al-Qaeda terrorists."

"Chicago?" asked Rebecca.

"Yes," Lam replied. "Chicago and much more."

<===== PIPELINE =====>

Hijacking the century-old Edmund Challenger freighter went smoothly. Piracy was virtually unheard of on the Great Lakes, especially when the pirates are wearing Coast Guard uniforms and brandishing legal search warrants, instead of swords and eyepatches and yelling *arrrrg.*

Months ago, Qasem had chosen the old "laker" for two reasons: its maritime life as a bulk carrier on the Great Lakes had come to an end, and was scheduled for one final voyage before its storied life was done.

Moreover, the Edmund Challenger was the only freighter allowed up the Chicago River into the heart of Chicago due to its shallow draft.

Built several years before the ill-fated Titanic, the Edmund Challenger was the last steam-powered ship working the Great Lakes.

The ship never failed to draw curious Chicagoans to the riverbank to watch the eighteen bridges rise to accept the 562-foot length.

Everyone knew to hold their breath and place their bets whether the behemoth would squeeze successfully through the downtown area, and steam up river between the densely packed buildings and skyscrapers, without causing disaster.

The freighter was despised for leaving a trail of malfunctioning bridges in its wake, and stalling Chicago traffic for hours. For this, it had come to be labeled by Chicagoans as "The Jinx Ship."

It was that dubious aspect of the old laker which intrigued Qasem—
And the Edmund Challenger would prove a jinx one more time!

The first test of Tariq's computer virus proved successful as Qasem's Iranian commandos presented a signed warrant to search the Challenger for suspected drugs. After just twenty minutes, and without firing a shot, or a radio distress signal being sent by the crew, the ship was theirs.

Next, they headed east to rendezvous with a *laker* hauling fertilizer. After producing the *"legal"* paperwork, thousands of tons of ammonium nitrate, or AN, was transferred into the holds of the Edmund Challenger., then the fertilizer ship crew was rounded up, blindfolded, and put aboard the Edmund Challenger.

The liquid fuel component of the bomb came next. They steamed south to an off-shore fuel facility where, once again, Qasem presented proper identification and purchase orders. After two carful hours, a half-million gallons of nitromethane racing fuel, or NM, safely joined the fertilizer in the belly of the Challenger, as did the lifeless bodies of three American fuel technicians. Their throats were cut to ensure their lasting silence.

Qasem could only smile at the ease with which the first two bomb elements were obtained. But Allah did not allow his true servants to gloat.

What happened next nearly ended their holy mission before it got started.

Although the purchase order for the liquid propane was in order, the captain of the gas hauler wondered aloud why a full cargo of combustible propane would ever go aboard a cement ship. There had to be a mistake.

At the instant the man lifted the ship-to-shore phone to confer with his superiors, Qasem drew his pistol and put a bullet in the captain's head. Then the boat's entire crew was rounded up at gun point, bound, and put with the other hostages aboard the Challenger.

Piracy may not be known on the Great Lakes, but ghost ships were.

After offloading more than a thousand LP tanks, and then mopping up all evidence of the ship captain's murder, the vessel was set adrift.

Back aboard the Challenger, Qasem ordered the largest LP tanks fitted with remote detonators and lowered into the holds with the ANNM. And then his explosives team crafted dozens of improvised artillery using the camp stove-size canisters, just like the *hell cannons* being used in the Syrian war.

Finally, in a devilish move to create a mission failsafe, Qasem ordered his soldiers to ring the Edmund Challenger with the remaining propane tanks and then standby to open the valves to create a gas cocoon.

The Edmund Challenger was now a ten-thousand-ton fuel bomb, primed and ready to destroy the infidels. Furthermore, if anyone dared get close, his men would loft hell cannon rounds without fear of return fire. And should the Americans use their missiles to try and stop the ship, the volatile gas cloud would make them masters of their own doom.

Qasem was tempted to steer a straight course to Chicago, and lay waste to one of the great cities in the world. The amount of death and destruction would be inconceivable.

But that wasn't enough!

America's punishment must be an example to all mankind.

He would now add high-level nuclear waste to Allah's bomb.

It was for this final element that Tariq's ingenious computer program was mostly intended for—pirating the nuclear material transiting from the shuttered Paladin power plant over water to Wisconsin.

Qasem looked at Tariq as his young lion held a finger above the *enter* key on his computer.

Their eyes met.

Then almost imperceptibly, Qasem nodded.

Tariq's finger came down on the keyboard and the computer screen began scrolling rapidly, issuing a series of pre-programmed commands.

Tariq's intrusion started first inside of an unsecure server owned by a senior diplomate at the U.S. State Department.

<===== PIPELINE =====>

Then the long journey through the wormhole began . . .

The worm in this this case was a *nuclear safety inspection order* originating from the International Atomic Energy Agency, headquartered in Vienna, Austria.

After Vienna, the line of authority ran through the United Nations to its regulatory agency whose responsibility was the safe carriage of high-level radioactive wastes on board ships plying all waterways of participating member states, of which the U.S. was a signatory.

That agency was known as the International Maritime Organization,

The IMO routed the inspection notice to the U.S. Department of Energy, who in turn forwarded the request to the National Nuclear Security Administration.

The NNSA then notified the Office of Secure Transportation of the mandatory surprise inspection.

And finally, the OST radioed its armed couriers aboard the purpose-built container ship ferrying the massive nuclear waste containment casks across the waters of Lake Michigan.

Although annoyed, the OST agents halted their ship and ordered the crew to stand by for inspection.

18

Lam parked the Ford Expedition near the southeast gun tower at the Muskegon Correctional Facility and turned to Rebecca.

"Women aren't allowed in the cell blocks. You'll have to wait in the warden's office."

Rebecca's jaw tightened. "A gal could get a real complex hanging out with you two."

Billy Ray knew how much Rebecca hated being excluded.

Neither had she hadn't liked being left behind in Meauwataka either.

But his keeping her back had had another side to it. He was in love with her and wanted her to be safe.

He'd already failed to save her sister, and pledged never to repeat that failure again.

"Leave the keys," Rebecca said sounding dejected, "I'll wait here."

As Billy Ray moved away from the vehicle, he noted sunlight reflecting off the scope of a rifle in the guard tower, tracking their every step.

"It's obvious to me, Navy," Lam said approaching the prison entrance.

Billy Ray hushed the ghosts of his past. "What's obvious?"

"You're protecting her."

Billy Ray didn't answer.

"Let me give you one word of advice, Jenkins."

"Is it Army advice?"

"Well, maybe it is."

"Okay, hit me," Billy Ray said.

"Marry the girl. Settle down. Have kids. Get chubbier. In other words, GET A LIFE!"

"You said one word, Lam. That's a whole list."

They reached the correctional facility door. Lam stopped. "You know what I mean, my friend."

Yeah, Billy Ray knew exactly what Lam meant.

But with his love for Rebecca also came the fear of losing her.

The USS Silversides prepared to launch on a historic journey, its second such journey, in fact.

The first time out of the gates for the Gato-class submarine was August 1941, leaving from California's Mare Island Naval Shipyard to join World War II in the Pacific Theater.

<===== PIPELINE =====>

Now 75 years later, long after the legendary submarine's service had ended, the boat would embark on another improbable journey.

This time for peaceful purposes. Or so its voluntary crew supposed.

The Silversides was the cornerstone exhibit at the Great Lakes Naval Memorial & Museum in Muskegon, Michigan. It had taken scores of sponsors, and then thousands of man-hours from submarine enthusiasts and old-time sailors dedicating themselves to restoring the vintage boat to full functionality.

And they'd accomplished it!

Their mission was complete, or nearly so. There remained a final day of sea trials prior to the submarine taking up station at the Grand Haven Coast Guard Festival to serve as the main attraction.

The Silversides' crew consisted of twenty-nine volunteers, which fell far short of its wartime contingent of six officers and fifty-four enlisted crewmembers.

The babe, and only female, of the mostly-aged group of men, was a twenty-something buxom blonde named Tina. She was a petty officer in the "new" integrated Navy, and a testament to just how much times had changed for U.S. submariners.

Meanwhile, the jalopy of the bunch was an old sea dog named Creed, who'd seen action in the *silent service*. Now bumping up against the century mark in age, Creed was the lone submariner from WW-II. Therefore, designating him to act as the boat's Executive Officer turned out to be a no-brainer.

Commanding the Silversides was an active duty naval officer completing his final years in the "modern" underwater force, Captain Mike Rinard. Ever since childhood, Rinard's personal study had been the history and evolution of submarines, from ancient times to the American Civil War, through those of the First and Second World Wars, up to his present command aboard a modern Trident *boomer.*

Though for all Rinard's skill at commanding nuclear submarines, it was another sailor among the Silversides crew who possessed the most experience operating *diesel* boats, and an old salt if there ever was one. Retired master chief petty officer Scott "Torch" Terrill was a veteran of both the Korean and Viet Nam Wars. Torch was a "sailor's sailor" and bellicose in nature and profane of a cusser as could be found on the water, or below it.

Torch's most distinguishable characteristic could be seen jammed in the corner of his mouth—a soggy unlit cigar. Furthermore, master chief Terrill was one of a diminishing number of souls who could run a diesel submarine. Unsurprisingly, he was assigned Chief of the Boat, or COB.

Filling out the crew were men from every decade of the Silversides' existence. One by one, they boarded, stopped to salute the nation's flag, and then went below to store their gear and attend their duty stations.

Rinard, Torch, and an old sonarman named Colon, remained topside to direct removal of the gangway and mooring lines. They watched as a tug inched next to the Silversides and prepared to nudge the football field-long submarine into the Muskegon channel and out to open water.

Once Rinard got a final boat readiness report from Creed, they would shove off.

Below decks, Creed inspected the Silversides one last time, ducking through hatch after hatch, and making final checks before getting underway. He paused next to the Silversides' big Fairbanks-Morse engines that powered the generator and charged the two 126-cell Sargo batteries. The sights and sounds and smells of the boat were just as satisfying as they'd been seventy-plus years earlier. In fact, he felt like a kid again—they all did.

Because for one damn glorious week, a handful of old warriors were getting the chance to ignore aches and pains and old-men issues, and put to sea again. Sailors belonged to the sea and the sea to them.

Creed determined all was in order. He radioed his report to Rinard and then gripped the vertical ladder to head topside through a hatch that he remembered used to be a little bit wider. He was also a little bit thinner back then.

Pain shot through his gnarled, arthritic hands. His aged legs felt rubbery. But he forced himself to climb anyway. Each rung seemed a greater distance from the last as he cursed his old bones to action.

As Creed climbed toward the bridge, he couldn't help thinking of his four daughters, themselves now senior citizens. They would've pitched a fit seeing him shimmy up the vertical ladder. But he would've blown off their objections. Despite complaints from withered muscles and stiff joints, he felt more alive than he had in many years. And even should something happen, he could imagine no better way to leave this world— at sea doing his duty.

Anything was better than wasting away.

Creed surfaced into the fresh air on the bridge and joined Captain Rinard and the others.

As he scanned the excited crowds lining the pier, a memory flashed before his dimming eyes. It was his proud parents sending him off to sea for the first time, their faces a mix of jubilation and apprehension, wondering if their son would return victorious . . . or not at all.

<≡≡≡ PIPELINE ≡≡≡>

Captain Rinard acknowledged Creed's arrival then gazed the length of the Silversides. His eyes came to rest below him at the rows of Japanese flag decals pasted on the sail. Each one represented an enemy ship confirmed sunk during World War II. He noted one empty space among them where a last battle flag decal could fit.

Thankfully, there'd be no war on this journey.

Finally satisfied the boat was ready to shove off, he turned to Creed and said, "As the honorary XO, you may give the order."

Creed nodded, put the radio to his mouth, and gave the command.

The tug gave a long blast of its horn then reversed its engines.

For the first time in generations, the USS Silversides moved from its comfortable lair and put to sea.

The crowd erupted! Hands clapped. Flags waved.

Cameras flashed.

The USS Silversides moved from the shadows of history as a museum piece into the Muskegon channel, and finally toward the open waters of Lake Michigan.

Colon left the bridge and descended into the boat to take his place at the sonar station. He slipped on a pair of headphones, switched on the passive listening equipment, and waited to be called on to aid the boat's navigation after clearing the ship channels.

Torch, Creed, and Rinard remained topside watching the tug fall away, and then leaving the Silversides to its own heading . . . and old mariners to their thoughts. Yet, if they'd only known how wrong Captain Rinard was about filling that last decal space.

And how close they would all come to perishing.

Thirty nautical miles northwest of Muskegon, well beyond prying eyes on the open expanse of Lake Michigan, Qasem paced back and forth on the bridge of the Department of Energy ship, a vessel built purposely for transporting high-level radioactive waste.

He was careful to avoid the puddles of blood but could do nothing about the slaughterhouse smell in the summertime air.

The captain of the DOE vessel and the Special Agent in charge from the NNSA's Office of Secure Transportation had received secure radio confirmation ordering a surprise inspection by the International Maritime Organization. The OST agents were trained and equipped to "deter, surprise, and delay" even the most aggressive adversary. But when the stand-down order came by way of official channels, there was little they could do but cooperate.

And now would come the greatest heist in American history.

Appropriately disguised as a UNIMO safety team, Qasem and his men met no resistance aboard the DOE ship beyond presenting their ID's and "official" paperwork.

The DOE Captain and OST agents never saw it coming, as Qasem's handpicked fighters, among the very best in the Iranian Revolutionary Guards, spread throughout the ship conducting the "inspection." Within minutes, not a living soul remained of the ship's contingent.

The radioed messages, brass badges, and "official" paperwork, even the nuclear inspection notices, were all owed to Tariq's clever handiwork. Furthermore, the war planners in Tehran were ecstatic with the results.

Ironically, the most critical portion of their mission turned out to be the simplest to implement. The reason—

Institutional arrogance, Qasem concluded.

The American nuclear energy industry had long gloried over its sixty-year record of near-perfect performance. And rightfully so.

But much had changed over six decades. The nation's bureaucracies had swelled. Administrators grew lazy, more concerned about their own rising stars than minding the store. Praise and high marks came to be expected rather than earned. And nepotism dulled the edge among active personnel, with loyalty ensuring its continuance.

Costs rose, budgets ballooned. And a complete faith in technology came to replace trust in dedicated employees. Whistleblowers received harsh treatment, their lives often ruined. None dared criticize.

Yet the narrative remained the same—all was good and Americans were *safe.*

That stellar sixty-year record was about to be shattered.

For the rest of the morning, Qasem directed the transfer of four truck-sized, cylindrical nuclear material containment casks into the holds of the Edmund Challenger.

At last, twenty-five tons of high-level radioactive waste joined the ammonium nitrate, nitromethane, and propane gas tanks.

It was now time for the group of men Qasem selected to perform their final mission in the flesh. Their sacrifice to Allah would be the breaching of the nuclear casks prior to detonation of the massive ship bomb.

Once exposed, no amount of potassium iodide would save these brave martyrs from a ghastly and excruciating death.

Before casting off from the DOE ship, Qasem ordered the tracking beacons removed from the storage casks and tossed among the dead agents. Then the ship's sea valves were opened and the vessel sent to the bottom of Lake Michigan.

<=== PIPELINE ===>

Back underway aboard the Edmund Challenger, Qasem entered onto the bridge and lifted the ship's 1MC to his mouth.

His voice issued loudly from every speaker. "The time has come my brothers to bring down the Great Satan. We shall make the world free and Islam victorious at last. Afterward, we shall all meet in paradise and look upon the face of Allah."

Qasem returned the microphone to its cradle and turned to face Bashir and Tariq.

His young *shahid* stared at him, wild-eyed, anxiously awaiting the instructions to the helm. Anxiously awaiting the order to put their killer ship on a collision course with their destiny—

Nay . . . the world's destiny!

After clearing security, Billy Ray and Lam were escorted into a narrow chamber with a one-way mirror that looked into an interview room. It was sparsely furnished with metal Steelcase furniture.

There were two Hispanic men in the room awaiting Gallina's arrival. One was a portly man in a cheap suit, the other tall and handsome.

"A nickel says the fat guy's the lawyer," Lam observed.

"You should know, Army," Billy Ray said.

Acting insulted, Lam eyed Billy Ray.

"Look who's talking. Have you seen yourself in a mirror lately?"

"No. Why do you ask?"

"Because you're looking quite lawyerly yourself these days."

"Just because I don't get up at oh-dark-thirty and run around the city for no good reason like you Green Berets."

"No, you'd rather walk to Seattle. Try jogging it next time, Chubby."

"Score one for the Army," Billy Ray said, turning attention to Gallina.

Just then the tall Hispanic guy turned and faced the one-way mirror, then motioned them toward the door.

They met briefly outside where Camacho introduced himself and then added, "Mr. Gallina is prepared to offer the government information he hopes will show his good intentions and help clear his name."

Lam introduced Billy Ray, though left off the military part, then asked Camacho, "Do you really think Gallina is innocent?"

Camacho chose his words carefully. "He is until proven guilty. My role is to ensure due process."

Lam sat in a chair opposite Gallina and the fat lawyer.

Camacho and Billy Ray remained standing, while a prison guard manned the door.

For nearly a minute, no one spoke while the lawyer fumbled through an expensive briefcase.

Like two prizefighters before a championship bout, Lam and Gallina stared each other down. As for which man would make the other blink first, Billy Ray put his chips down on Lam.

The lawyer finally found what he was looking for and slid a single sheet of paper across the table to Lam.

"Señor Gallina's statement."

Gallina broke the silence. "I'm innocent of all charges."

"Tell it to the judge," Lam said coldly. And then without taking his eyes off Gallina, he lifted the document, wadded it into a ball, and tossed it on the prison floor.

The lawyer's mouth dropped open.

Camacho took a step toward the group.

The prison guard shifted.

Billy Ray, however, didn't move. He knew Lam all too well.

Lam leaned forward. "Don't waste my time, you maggot. You got something to say, then say it to my face!"

At the provocation, the patina of innocence left Gallina.

Lam pressed, "You're a human trafficker. That makes you the worst kind of scum. You enslave people, just like your disgusting daddy did."

At hearing his father referred to in the past tense, Hector Gallina said icily, "She's pretty. You must be a proud *daddy* yourself."

Gallina nodded to the lawyer, who then withdrew a red manila folder from his briefcase and slid it across the table. Paper-clipped to the front of the folder was the picture of a young girl with dark hair, chocolate brown eyes, and a pink Rainbow Brite shirt.

Lam blinked.

With lightning reflexes, Billy Ray snatched the folder off the table while Lam's mind remained elsewhere.

Billy Ray grabbed Gallina by the throat. "Where'd you get this?"

The prison guard came forward, drew his weapon, and ordered, "Step away from the inmate. Do it now!"

Billy Ray might as well have had cotton balls in his ears. He shouted at Gallina, "Where'd you get this!"

"Let go of the prisoner!" the guard repeated, more forceful this time.

Lam recovered, and then stood and presented his *Authority Over All* badge. "Stow your weapon, officer! This is a matter of National Security."

The guard hesitated, a testament to good training and strong sense of duty, and also never having seen such an ID before.

The gun lowered.

<== PIPELINE ==>

Billy Ray released the chokehold.

Gallina was no pussy. Rather, his criminal mind sensed a change in the game, and brand new rules.

"I got it from a freak dressed in black . . . mask, gloves, the whole bit. And his voice was mechanical. He said he'd worked with my father."

"What do you mean by 'mechanical'?" asked Lam.

"Electric voice box. We named him *El payaso negro.*"

"The black clown," Camacho interpreted.

"Where is he now?" Lam asked.

Gallina shrugged his shoulders.

Now it was Billy Ray who blinked as he stared at the folder. The words were written in Korean—Operation Blood Star.

But that was impossible! No one survived the battle at the Texas Waterland Family Park. Dodd's flying machines had made sure of that, obliterating all traces of the enemy fortress with laser weapons. Even the underground command center and drug labs were pulverized by Wiggins' self-destruct bombs.

Only he, Lam, and Rebecca got out alive. Afterward, the feds declared the park a National Security Area and locked the place down tight. Although, Billy Ray recalled Lam having observed two Asian men dressed in *black* business suits departing the facility prior to its obliteration. Could one of them be responsible for the red folder? After all, Angel Gallina had successfully redirected a shipment of Rapture to Michigan. At least some evidence escaped under the government's nose.

Billy Ray shook off the fog of war.

They had to end the Texas matter once and for all; even though they thought they had by destroying the Rapture at Duke's cabin and arresting Hector Gallina. But once again, the *patrón* spoke from the grave. And now Angel Gallina's evil spawn sat before them negotiating deals.

Lam snatched the Blood Star folder from Billy Ray's hands and waved it in Gallina's face. "Do you think this is your bargaining chip?"

Gallina didn't respond.

Lam put a finger an inch from the cartel man's nose. "If you or your goons go anywhere near my daughter, I'll kill you!"

In response to the enhanced interrogation, Camacho stepped to the table. The guard's hand went back to his weapon. The fat lawyer sat petrified in his chair.

Gallina vaulted from his chair. "Then tell me who killed my father!"

Billy Ray moved between Lam and Gallina.

"I did!" he said coldly. "I sent an RPG into the side of his white limo."

Gallina stared hard into Billy Ray's eyes. His jagged scar twitched.

The room went deathly silent.

Finally, Gallina did something entirely unexpected. He formed a broad toothy grin and lowered himself back in the chair. Then he said, "Relax, G-man, I don't hurt little girls. Nor did I have anything to do with the dead ones you found washed up on the beach. But I know who did." He pointed. "That folder is a gift. Now sit your *culo* down and listen to what I have to say . . . before it's too late for us all."

Gallina had regained control, even from a prison cell.

After POTUS exited The Woodshed, the Media mogul and telecom king did so too, anxious to return to their royal courts.

Then the trillionaire departed to go do what trillionaires do. But since the world had only one, Dodd could only guess what that might be.

That left Dodd and V alone in the room, the only K-Key members whose paychecks were signed by the U.S. Treasury.

They stared across the table at one another. V's face was a blank slate, hard and unreadable. Dodd knew her thoughts. He'd recruited V at the inception of the secret group. She'd originally been the lead scientist on the development of the tactical laser weapons employed on the "go fast machines," a program that she now directed.

They needed to talk. But it had to be some place where they wouldn't be overheard. The walls in this entire building had big ears.

So rather than speaking out loud in the conference room, Dodd blinked his eyes three short *dots,* three long *dashes,* and three short *dots.*

V caught the SOS signal. Then she nodded and left the room.

Billy Ray and Lam left the prison.

There was no joking this time. Instead, each man concentrated on the information just received from Hector Gallina.

And it was frightening.

Lam phoned the FBI Director to report a terror event was imminent, one involving weapons of mass destruction—dirty bombs.

In turn, the FBI Director contacted his superior at the DOJ, who then informed Homeland Security, and so on up the chain of command.

Thirty minutes later, POTUS summoned his political advisor and the "normal" security team to the Situation Room to begin his sworn duty of defending the nation. But what the President and his advisers could not know, due mostly to disbanding the K-Key Group, was that they were already too late.

<===== PIPELINE =====>

Rebecca had seated herself behind the wheel of the big Ford. Upon seeing the men approach, she started the engine.

Without argument, Lam let himself into the front passenger seat of the SUV. Billy Ray took the back.

"What happened, guys?" Rebecca asked. "You look like you stared death in the face."

"We did . . . or are about to," Lam replied.

Rebecca looked back at Billy Ray, who merely nodded in agreement. "Where to?" she asked.

Lam thought a moment. "The Coast Guard station on Beach Street."

"Where's that?" Rebecca asked.

Lam pointed west. "That way. Stop when you get to the water."

Rebecca rolled her eyes then shifted the vehicle into gear.

They left the Muskegon Correctional Facility and wound along the tree lined road exiting to South Sheridan Drive.

Suddenly, all power in the vehicle quit and the engine died.

"Hey! What'd you do to my new rig?" Lam complained.

"Nothing," Rebecca said as the vehicle coasted to a stop.

"Shoulda' bought a Chevy," Billy Ray said from the back.

All at once, a deep resonating hum filled the cab and an ominous shadow passed over the Ford.

Rebecca threw her hands over her ears, but that did little to stop the physical sensation she felt deep in her bones.

Then a machine she'd seen do terrible things in Texas appeared—a saucer-shaped craft. The object stopped in midair in front of them then lowered to the ground.

The humming subsided, then a hatch opened and a ramp extended to the tarmac. But instead of a Martian stepping forward, an Australian shepherd dog ran out of the craft with a Frisbee in its mouth.

"Augie!" Rebecca exclaimed.

Next came a short, energetic man toting two large metal suitcases. It was Egolf, the mysterious K-Key Group operative.

Lastly came a tall man with broad shoulders. He had short-cropped silver hair and owned the kind of smile that must've been sown on at birth.

"Dodd...?" Billy Ray said quizzically.

"But his legs—!" Lam began to say.

They exited the car and met the non-Martian beings in the middle of the road.

Then without a whisper of a breeze, only the near-debilitating hum, the nation's newest secret weapon defied gravity by lifting straight upward, and disappearing in the blink of an eye.

Billy Ray lowered his eyes from the sky to meet those of his former SEAL commander.

"Dolittle, you've sprouted legs!"

Dodd tapped his pants. "Newest thing in prosthetics. I borrowed the electronics from the Marine Mammal Augmentation Program. Wait 'til you see what these babies can do."

Dodd pressed a button on a wrist-worn computer, and to everyone's astonishment, he grew a foot taller!

"And I can outrun Usain Bolt," he boasted then touched his wrist and shrunk to normal size. "If the field tests pass muster, we'll outfit our wounded warriors. There'll be arms and hands coming online, too."

Lam pointed to Augie the talking dog. "Do you have singing horses? They could form a dog and pony show."

"No chimeras here, Agent Lam," countered Dodd. "Any dog owner can tell you what their pets are saying. I merely recorded Augie's desires. His own sounds actuate a throat mic and are played back in English."

Billy Ray shook his head.

Dodd never ceased to amaze. Ask him the time and he told you how to build Big Ben.

Lam busted up the party.

"Can we quit with the Six Million Dollar Man stuff, evil waits for no one," he said and then headed for the vehicle.

As if on cue, the last traces of atmospheric resonance from the saucer ended and the Ford's big engine roared back to life.

Egolf wasn't big on chit-chat, either, and followed Lam to the SUV.

Billy Ray ended the pow-wow and left Dodd standing in the middle of the road mumbling something about fine-tuning the gravity-canceling frequency exchangers on the L-FALVs before the next lunar . . .

A big smile crossed Billy Ray's face. He hadn't the foggiest idea what Dodd was talking about, but he was damn glad to have his old friend, and SEAL Team Commander, *standing* by his side again.

Some guys used downtime for screwing off, John Dodd invented—a scientist by day, warrior by night.

This much Billy Ray knew, though. When the battle got hot, there'd be no long-winded explanations. Only Dodd's clear-headed leadership.

And one team.

<===== PIPELINE =====>

19

Qasem ended his final contact with Tehran.

Often, a hunter only got a single shot at its prey. And for a beast as powerful as America *this* was that one shot.

The *GO* order was given. Then the Supreme Leader had commended him on a successful mission. Though true to Qasem's reputation, he cautioned his leaders to hold off firing their pistols into the air until the job was done and they saw a fiery cloud over Chicago on Al Jazeera news. He'd always insisted of himself and of those he commanded that success would only be measured by results. Should America still stand on the morrow, it would mean but one thing, he failed.

Qasem tossed the secure telephone over the side of the Edmund Challenger and watched it sink beneath the waves.

He was on his own now—one man, one mission, one God.

There would be no turning back now.

There was only going onward to glory . . .

And then paradise where he could touch the face of Allah.

Lam drove the team to the small Coast Guard station situated at the mouth of the Muskegon channel on Beach Street.

Egolf worked on a laptop computer in the front seat during the ride, while Billy Ray and Dodd occupied the middle row—Billy Ray gathering his thoughts, Dodd dialing God only knew on his *special* phone.

Actually, Billy Ray knew what the device was, a tactical satphone. He merely enjoyed teasing Dodd about being so techy. And then in turn getting no end of ribbing for his still owning a flip phone.

Rebecca, bless her enduring patience, volunteered for the way-back in the SUV WHERE she petted Augie and observed her surroundings.

Minutes later, Lam turned in at the Coast Guard station and parked.

No one exited. There would be a quick sitrep first.

Dodd finished his calls, including one to get the ETA for Tafoya's news station helicopter. Then he had Egolf replay Gallina's interview.

After the recording ended, Billy Ray said to Dodd, "I presume your all-powerful group is mobilizing its response teams."

Dodd was saved from answering the question by the *whoop whoop* of rotating helicopter blades and Tafoya's arrival.

To avoid being sandblasted, everyone remained inside the Expedition until the helo powered down.

Tafoya never tired at the thrill of riding in the news station helicopter. Neither did she mind getting her hair a bit mussed by the Mickey Mouse ears and microphone.

The muss was worth the fuss.

She hadn't been briefed on the nature of Dodd's request, only that it involved national security. Hell, she could've guessed that much.

But whatever it was, she was game.

In for a penny, in for a pound, as her *abuelo* used to say.

She felt a tingle of excitement for another reason, too. She would get to see Johnny again. They hadn't made a date for Texas yet, so getting together so soon was a wonderful surprise.

A short minute later, the helo touched down at the Muskegon Coast Guard station, sited at the north end of the pristine Pere Marquette beach. The chopper powered down and Tafoya exited.

She was tempted to rush straight over to Johnny, but checked her inner-schoolgirl. What's more, the big SUV was chock-full of people and critters and stuff, like the Griswolds out to save the world or something.

The doors opened and everyone spilled out, including the talking dog from the beach mansion sticking close to Rebecca's side. Considering the pooch's vocal *abilities,* Augie likely had a canine crush on Rebecca.

Next came a hyper fellow lugging large matching suitcases. He was joined by a tall man owning the same face that had appeared on the theater screen—Oz or Dodd or . . . Tafoya decided to show respect and go with *Admiral.*

Finally, Johnny and Jenkins left the vehicle and headed her way. Their looks were more dour than Tafoya had ever seen them; no lampooning, just business.

They met in the middle of the parking lot. Lam looked at Tafoya first then turned and scanned the deserted lot.

"Where is everyone?"

"Grand Haven, at the festival," she replied.

Billy Ray said, "I hope they left a key under the mat."

Tafoya rolled her eyes. "It's not *that* deserted."

Dodd walked briskly past the group and said, "Quit jacking your jaws, the Coast Guard duty officer is waiting for us."

Tafoya almost called Dodd a name beginning with the letter 'D' again.

"So much for getting Dodd's drink recipe," Lam said.

"Brevity is the soul of wit," Billy Ray concurred.

"He's in command mode now," Rebecca opined.

Then they all turned and trailed after Admiral Dodd like new recruits.

Chicagoans began roping off spots along the Chicago River.

At 4 p.m. Central Time, the good citizens of Chicago would witness a truly historic event, the return of the last steam powered lake freighter plying the Great Lakes, the Edmund Challenger.

Since 1906—five years before the launch of the ill-fated Titanic—the six hundred foot-long freighter had set sail from its Chicago homeport for destinations throughout the five Great Lakes, often to sneers and jeers of motorists stopped dead while the city's eighteen bridges raised to accept the massive vessel. Worsening commuter inconvenience further still was the problem of the bridges getting stuck open for hours, for which the folks of Chicago dubbed the Edmund Challenger a "jinx ship."

But this time when the bridges lifted, it was expected that even angry motorists would applaud the delay—

Because it was going to be for the last damn time!

They were met by Chief Petty Officer Gary Miller and escorted into a conference room with tables, chairs, dry erase board, and a flat screen television monitor on the wall.

Egolf got to work immediately by interfacing his laptop computer with the large wall monitor and firing up a PowerPoint presentation.

Dodd stood beside the monitor, and had only just begun briefing the team, when a thunderous roar filled the room, then abated a moment later. The sound had come from the skies above Muskegon.

Tafoya goaded Dodd. "Was that one of your alien motherships?"

Chief Miller took the bait. "Sorry, ma'am, there's no such thing as flying saucers. That was a T-38 Talon practicing for tomorrow's airshow in Grand Haven."

Egolf tapped his keyboard. "A contingent from the 12th Flying Training Wing headquartered at Joint Base San Antonio–Randolph, Texas."

"Geez, not more Texans!" Tafoya griped.

"A trainer?" asked Billy Ray. "What happened to using Thunderbirds or the Blue Angels?"

Dodd gave one of his shortest answers to date. "Budget cuts."

The group sounded a collective Ohh.

Dodd resumed the briefing, rehashing the same intel they'd started with—meaning there was nothing new, implying they needed more, or else their ass was grass and the terrorists owned the lawnmower.

"If not for Gallina, we'd be sucking our thumbs," Lam said. "My chips are on al-Qaeda terrorists prepping to explode a bomb on American soil."

Billy Ray said, "If that's all we got, then we're still milking ourselves."

Tafoya asked, "Where are these terrorists supposed to hit us?"

Egolf filled the monitor with a map of the Midwestern United States.

Dodd pressed a finger on the City of Chicago. "Someplace with lots of people, like at the Boston Marathon . . . maybe the Navy Pier."

"What about those MERC towers?" asked Rebecca.

"It's doubtful now," Dodd said. "Terrorists prefer soft targets. After their Willis Tower failure, security is tight as a drum."

"What failure?" Lam questioned. "I thought that was a red herring."

"Still under debate," Dodd replied dismissively.

Lam shot back, "So is how lint balls get in my belly button, Admiral. But they turn out to be real."

Billy Ray caught the strangeness to Dodd's answer, too, as if the Admiral knew more than he was telling. He put them all back on point.

"The Navy Pier suggests a water threat."

"One if by land, two if by sea," Egolf quoted Paul Revere.

Rebecca pressed for more intel to help her profile the enemy, "If by water then how? Speed boats?"

"Most likely," Dodd replied. "Al-Qaeda did it before attacking the USS Cole in Yemen with rigged fast boats."

Tafoya joined the *debate*. "But there are thousands of boats out on Lake Michigan. How can we know which one?"

"Maybe Gallina screwed us for killing his father," Lam thought out loud.

Dodd had no words to offer, only a slight drop of the head and a shrug of the shoulders.

Billy Ray wasn't used to seeing his commander shrug off anything. In fact, nothing had seemed right with Dodd from the very beginning, going back to their first discussion at the hospital.

It was time for truth.

"Why are we here, Dolittle?"

"Come again, Wolverine?"

"Why are we so deep in the dark on a threat that could spell death to millions of Americans? Actually, I'll cut to the chase. Why are *you* here? Our calls went unanswered, and then one day you just drop out of the sky."

Lam piled on. "By the way, Admiral, you didn't answer Jenkins earlier. Are your people coming or not?"

The look on Dodd's face was instantly recognizable, at least to Billy Ray. He'd seen it before, in South America, when their four-man SEAL team became trapped and Dodd learned there'd be no Quick Reaction Force deployed to extract them.

<== PIPELINE ==>

Two brave men had paid the ultimate price on that mission, and all because some desk jockey got cold feet. Only by a miracle did he and Dodd got out alive.

Billy Ray looked hard at Dodd. "We've been cut off again, haven't we?"

Lam stepped forward. "What's Jenkins talking about? Tell me your all-powerful group is mobilizing its teams. Because I damn sure know my FBI agents haven't been given any green light yet!"

Dodd glanced at Egolf then at the group. "We've been shut down."

Incensed, Billy Ray said, "Tell me I didn't just see you skipping merrily out of a flying saucer on a new set of designer legs."

"L-FALV," Dodd corrected. "They've been ordered back to base."

"Mind putting that in English," Lam demanded testily.

"The vehicle you saw, and are forbidden to speak of, operates on a principle of low-frequency acoustic levitation." Dodd noticed blank stares and abbreviated his answer, "They cancel gravity—"

Billy Ray cut him off, "I'm not talking about your damn toys!"

Dodd was speechless for a moment, seemingly contemplating a specific answer . . . or maybe choosing whose side he was on.

Finally he said, "POTUS shut down the K-Key Group, indefinitely. Is that plain enough for you? You all heard it on the news, someone exposed us to the press." Dodd shot an accusing look at Tafoya. "And now his political team is circling the wagons to save his administration, and make sure he wins the next election without a scandal."

"'Save the President?'" Tafoya mocked. "What about the rest of us!"

Billy Ray pressed, "Let me get this straight, Dolittle. A shit-storm's about to hit America, people dead or sickened by radiation, and the President just grounded our best assets?"

Dodd snuffed. "So *now* you like the K-KEY Group and all the spying."

Rebecca spoke up. "That's not fair, Admiral Dodd."

Billy Ray zeroed in. "But I still don't get it. Why are *you* here?"

The room went quiet. Everyone stared at Dodd.

"I resigned."

Lam retrieved his K-KEY Group ID from his jacket, tossed it on the table, and said, "Years of government surveillance, a national dragnet, miracle machines, laser weapons, and Spec-Ops teams . . . all sold to the country on the promise of keeping us safe. And now, when it's needed most, nothing's available because some damn politician needs to protect his legacy. Does that about sum it up?"

Dodd remained mum.

Billy Ray asked, "What the hell was it all worth then, Dolittle? We were probably *safer* when we fended for ourselves."

Actually, Dodd didn't have a good answer for his team. But the one thing he did know was that from time to time leadership faltered, a nation was tested, and its people are reminded of how much freedom really cost, in both blood and treasure.

This was such a time.

America was about to be tested as it never had before, and by an enemy whose depravity was rarely matched in human history—

PURE EVIL.

And yet, in the darkest hour, deliverance would not come by way of a shadowy body like the K-KEY Group. Nor would the country's politicians and bureaucrats man the ramparts and dig trenches. Because the federal government was not flesh and blood. It was an institution, at whose altar too many for too long had placed their trust in cures that only they as citizens could fix—one man, one woman, one home, one church, one block, one town at a time.

Only from them could a nation be *unified* and made durable.

Sadly, that boot-strap truth had long since been swapped for sugary promises of prosperity and safety for all, a modern equivalent to Rome's bread and circus. Realistically, no government could make men free, only the opposite. Freedom was imbued, gained by capture, and preserved in struggle. Or it was lost.

Amid the silence and stares in the tiny Coast Guard station, Dodd felt guilt pressing down on his shoulders.

Because *he* represented the government.

And he'd just told his team their government wasn't coming.

After having the daylights scared out of everyone the previous weeks, Sattgast was glad for the chance to produce a lighthearted story on the final voyage of the century-old Edmund Challenger.

The ship had always created a stir when returning to its Chicago home port, and was likely to do so again.

Already, thousands of Chicagoans lined the riverfront to welcome the massive freighter and participate in a moment of history. Members from the Chicago historical society had erected information booths to laude the fact that the Edmund Challenger was launched five years before the Titanic, and then outlived the doomed vessel by more than a century.

Vendors were out in force selling Edmund Challenger T-shirts, mugs, banners and whatever else. Businesses were letting employees off early. Bookies were even looking to turn a buck on the whole affair, tempting bettors with decent odds for another Edmund Challenger disaster.

<=== PIPELINE ===>

If nothing else, the city knew how to party. All of downtown Chicago was taking on the air of a street fair.

Sattgast ordered his cameras set up at key viewing sites to capture the event. The raising of the Loop bridges on the Chicago River, flowing as it did between the numerous and massive skyscrapers, would make for spectacular viewing on the nightly news—not to mention a financial boon from the station's many advertisers.

So whether it was to be scenes of joyous Chicagoans celebrating in high fashion, or a million snarling commuters foiled by faulty bridges in what could only be described as a modern-day buffalo jump, it hardly mattered. Pain was gain in the news business; controversy drove ratings.

Sattgast hoped for the former, of course.

But either way, his Mid-Western News cameras would capture the moment for the world to see. And MWN ratings would be off the charts!

"I'm one of you now," Dodd said.

Tafoya rolled her eyes. "Whatever," she mumbled.

Lam shook his head while staring at the ID with POTUS' face on the front, realizing it now held as much influence as an expired library card.

Rebecca got her Texas dander going. "Cowboy up, y'all! If America is in danger, then we don't need permission, we need action."

"I agree," Tafoya said. "We can't just wait for the cavalry to save us. What if they're too late?"

"Or not coming at all!" Lam remarked tersely.

Egolf chimed in a rare comment, "That's precisely why we're here."

Just then, Lam's phone rang, interrupting the meeting.

"It's headquarters. I'll take the call outdoors, if you all don't mind."

The others watched Lam exit the conference room.

"So now what?" Tafoya asked.

Billy Ray beat Dodd to the answer, "So now we're on our own."

"As bleak as that may sound," Dodd said, "Jenkins is right."

"But where do we start?" asked Rebecca. "The terrorists could be anywhere on the lake and using any one of a thousand boats."

Lam came back in the room. His Blackberry phone was still in his hand and his arm hung limp at his side.

Evidence that the team just caught their first break came by way of the blood draining from Lam's face.

He cleared his throat.

"It's worse than we thought . . . not speed boats. The sons of bitches are using freighters!"

Because the Edmund Challenger cargo holds were so heavily laden, the ship's Skinner Marine Uniflow 4-cylinder reciprocating steam engines labored to meet the ship's demands, pushing man, metal, and material through deep blue green waters toward home, for the last time.

Yet, the Challenger's crewmen over the years had always likened the massive ship to a draft horse sensing its barn and bucket of oats. Nonetheless, the current pace would delay arrival in Chicago by nearly an hour.

Qasem cursed in Persian.

What a shame it would be if their holy mission failed by way of a simple technicality.

Bashir had suggested jettisoning some of the ship's fuel oil to reduce weight. But that would only lead an oily trail straight to them. Since their piracy was yet undetected, the fuel idea was beyond idiotic.

Losing minutes arriving on target was actually the least of Qasem's worries, though. The greater concern was how low in the water the Edmund Challenger was running, and whether it could safely navigate the Chicago River without grounding before reaching its desired downtown target area.

His engineers had properly estimated the weight of the nuclear casks. However, they'd overlooked a one simple matter, the ship's legitimate cargo. Many thousands of tons of cement was the culprit for the ship's added displacement. Plus it caused a dusty mess, coating everything and everyone it touched.

Stopping to off-load the cement at the two remaining customers on the Challenger's schedule would add hours to their arrival time. That was unacceptable, since the bomb's placement on-target was calculated to coincide with Iran's scheduled medium range ballistic missile launch in the Middle East, secretly meant to draw the world's attention away from Chicago.

But one man's problem is another man's solution, Qasem thought.

As it turned out, Tariq was overjoyed when learning of the powdery cargo, and claimed the cement dust would form a giant cloud during the explosion and vastly add to the spread of radioactive contamination. Afterward, the aptly named Windy City would aid in its own destruction as its robust air currents carried the irradiated death cloud far and wide to coat every surface, be inhaled by every living being, and then harden into concrete when exposed to moisture.

Qasem shivered at the glorious prospect he had been handed.

Allah's vengeance had no equal!

<== PIPELINE ==>

Qasem ordered the only solution left to lift the ship, pumping out the ballast tanks. He was gambling that recent rains had swelled the Chicago River sufficiently to prevent the ship from grounding. Then with Allah's help, he would ram the bomb into the beating heart of the Great Whore.

Qasem had Tariq radio ahead to cancel the ship's remaining stops.

Then he said, "After that, release the rest of your Trojan horses."

All would be over soon. And the world would never be the same again.

Lam walked to the map on the TV screen and then briefed the group.

"Here's what I got from headquarters. There've been two separate incidents on the Great Lakes this morning involving freighters. The first involves an Indiana firm claiming one of their freighters disappeared."

"As in *poof?*" Tafoya asked.

"Maybe," Lam said. "The company has been unable to raise the crew on radio or cell phone. The bulk carrier's last location was here." Lam touched a spot twenty miles east of Manitowoc, Wisconsin, smack dab in the middle of Lake Michigan. "It could just be equipment failure, but it does raise some eyebrows."

"The Lake Michigan Triangle strikes again!" Tafoya said sarcastically.

Rebecca asked, "What about pirates?"

"Unheard of on the Great Lakes in modern times," Dodd replied.

"Weather conditions?" Billy Ray looked at Egolf.

Egolf checked the Great Lakes Weather Service forecast. "Nope, clear sailing everywhere."

"And the other ship?" Dodd asked.

"That incident is far more out of the ordinary," Lam answered. "An actual mayday came from a freighter on Lake Huron, near Mackinaw Island." Lam tapped the map. "Right about here."

"What do you mean?" asked Billy Ray.

"The mayday lasted only four seconds, then a male voice spoke a phrase in Arabic. After that . . . nothing."

Strange indeed, Billy Ray thought. "What was the phrase?"

"Assuming a correct translation, the man said, 'PANTHER-3-E'."

Dodd showed a startled look.

Rebecca cut in, "Sounds like code, but code from who and to who?"

"Don't know yet," Lam said. "Our analysts are still chasing it down."

The entire group went silent for a moment, processing the information.

Finally, Dodd said, "Tell me about the ships, Agent Lam."

"The first one carried fertilizer, ammonium nitrate, to be exact."

"And the second ship?" Billy Ray asked, already thinking ahead.

"A gas hauler," Lam replied. "Liquid propane."

Something was missing. Billy Ray thought.

"Lam, Does the FBI know of any large purchases of fuel oil."

"I know where you're going with that, Jenkins. The answer's no, not fuel oil. It was a half-million gallons of nitromethane."

"Bomb-making ingredients!" Dodd sad. "So that's how they'll do it!"

"Sorry, but I don't get it," Rebecca said.

Ever the human encyclopedia, Tafoya said, "You know about the Oklahoma City bombing in 1995, right?"

"Ya . . .?" Rebecca said.

Dodd took it from there.

"The bomb that destroyed the Alfred P. Murrah Federal Building, and a large part of the downtown area, was a rental truck filled with ammonium nitrate and racing fuel, plus liquid propane for added brisance. Now imagine a massive freighter instead of a truck. Thousands of tons of the stuff instead of pounds. The devastation would be unimaginable."

Billy Ray noticed blank stares. "Brisance is the shattering capability."

Rebecca said, "But what harm would come by blowing up a ship in the middle of Lake Michigan? There isn't much to shatter out there."

"Indeed," Dodd said. "An explosion on open water is meaningless. Unless—" He swallowed hard. "Everyone, get busy finding that ship!"

Dodd hurried off to dial people who likely didn't exist.

Everyone else went to work.

Lam got on his Blackberry to consult with FBI HQ. Egolf banged the keys on his computer. And Tafoya called up her media contacts.

Billy Ray and Rebecca got busy, too, detailing their thoughts on yellow legal pads.

Rebecca filled the first page on the legal pad with forensic details, intel facts, and bits of Gallina's testimony. Then she flipped to the next sheet and formed a psychological matrix for the eldest of the four terrorists identified by Gallina.

A profile took shape—their adversary was someone devoted to death, employed mayhem as a strategy, showed little if any emotion, possessed the calm demeanor of a priest, and had the charisma of a military general. Above all, he was someone who welcomed his own death.

Billy Ray's task was to create a list of tactical assets for combatting the terrorists and sinking a 600-foot long freighter filled with two million pounds of super high explosives.

After five minutes, he still sat staring at a blank page. The reason was simple—there wasn't much to choose from.

<====== PIPELINE ======>

The bulk of the Coast Guard was tied to a pier in Grand Haven, crawling with festival-goers. Most of the surrounding police forces were busy with festival crowds and weekend partiers in their own locales. Regardless, neither institution was equipped to battle terrorists aboard a massive floating bomb. Moreover, there still remained three paramount questions: which ship, what target . . . and why no K-KEY Group.

Their backs were truly against the wall this time. Without the aid of warfighting machines, their tactical options were chillingly few.

Billy Ray felt his stomach tighten.

"I may have something," Tafoya announced after ending a call with a media contact in Chicago. Everyone stopped to focus on her.

Dodd entered the room accompanied by the Coast Guard duty officer. "What is it, Tafoya?"

"I'd forgotten all about the event this evening in Chicago."

"What event?" Lam said.

"The final voyage of the Edmund Challenger . . . a good portion of the city's population is gathering at the Chicago River to watch the massive freighter end a hundred years of service on the Great Lakes. Local bookies are taking bets the ship will live up to its reputation."

Billy Ray looked at his watch. "Skip to where they kiss, Tafoya."

He wondered if the real reason Dodd chose the newshound for the team was their shared fondness for encyclopedic answers.

Chief Miller, spoke up, "They call it 'The Jinx Ship' for causing the river bridges to jam and snarl downtown traffic for hours."

Egolf played a YouTube video of the Edmund Challenger on the TV monitor. It showed the freighter steaming past the Navy Pier, then up the Chicago River under a line of raised bridges into the heart of the city. Giant skyscrapers lined the riverbanks like concrete and glass sentinels.

Billy Ray froze. Lam's face lost its mocha color.

"Chicago!" they voiced simultaneously.

"Al-Qaeda's signature—a double-wave attack!" Rebecca added.

Dodd turned to Chief Miller. "Radio that ship. I want its location, speed and course setting, now!"

"Yes, sir!" Miller hurried from the room followed closely by Egolf.

Dodd had a really bad feeling that it was already too late.

He cursed himself . . . and his politician-first Commander-in-Chief.

How could they have been so shortsighted? Or worse, have chosen political goals and personal legacy above national security!

He left the room to call the one person he trusted most among the now-defunct K-KEY Group, the only woman among its elite membership.

He hoped V was still picking up the phone.

20

Rebecca glanced up from her notes to find Billy Ray staring at her.

"Done already?" she asked.

"Unfortunately." He made no attempt to mask his concern.

"Well, I'll show you mine if you show me yours," she batted her eyes to tease him.

Billy Ray attempted a smile and then rotated his notepad.

There wasn't much there, merely a short inventory of the team's weapons, and the six names of their team comprising the available personnel. He'd begun to list tactics and methods, but left that undone.

Instead, he'd skipped to the bottom of the page and scribbled two letters with a circle drawn around them.

Rebecca showed her page, too. It was filled top to bottom, and it also had a circle at the bottom with a single word inside.

Then she took a moment to study the man she was in love with.

Billy Ray was country-strong and had no quit in him. But his true thoughts were flashing across his face like a neon sign—CONCERN.

The rising tide of doubt, she concluded.

"Billy Ray, we're going to make it. We'll find these people and stop them."

"How can you be so sure?" he challenged.

Rebecca pointed at the word circled on her notes. It read ALONE.

"Huh? Who's alone, me?" Billy Ray asked.

"The enemy."

Billy Ray met Rebecca's eyes directly. "But according to Gallina, the leader of the terrorists has three cell members helping him, and only their leader knows how many others. But I'd bet it's considerable."

"I know what you're thinking, darling. What are their numbers, what weapons do they have, and what is their training." She pulled Billy Ray's page close to her. "But there's one particular fundamental that surpasses bombs and bullets. It even surpasses an individual's will to win."

Billy Ray's worry lines softened.

She had his full attention.

Having endured the rigors of SEAL training, a nearly impossible task, then multiple extreme missions around the globe, Billy Ray knew about a man's will to succeed.

"What might that be?" he asked.

Rebecca nodded at the circle at the bottom of his notes. "I'm guessing the letters 'CP' on your page stand for 'Common People.' Am I right?"

Billy Ray sat more straight. "How'd you know?"

<== PIPELINE ==>

"I heard you use the term earlier, and it fits. I've seen how resourceful you are, how you play the hand you're dealt and rally people around you."

Billy Ray listened intently.

"I witnessed it in Texas with Larry Bell, with Gus Heavenor, with that goofy newspaper reporter, even with your lady friend, Eva. And then there was Jonesy, the Korean War hero."

"But I didn't believe Jonesy," Billy Ray objected.

"You did eventually. And you even trusted me to fight, too. It was because of your leadership and pure ingenuity that WE beat a madman and his trained commandos, not to mention Gallina's cartel thugs."

Billy Ray remained silent, reliving those final moments in Texas.

"Okay, so the government's not coming this time. Or if they do, it'll be too little too late. That's one given fact in this mission. So yes, the chips are down, my love. But we're not out of this yet, not while we have *our* team and millions of potential heroes all around us—moms, dads, factory workers, carpenters, your pest guy Deano, computer nerds, teachers, firemen, police . . . you name it.

"And yes, most lack military training. But the key is that they're willing to give what it takes to get the job done. Every one of them, *common people,* capable of uncommon acts of valor, if we but trust them."

Billy Ray sat taller in his chair.

"We'll win this fight, sweetheart, just like we did in Texas. We just need to find our *own* way."

Billy Ray stood, rounded the table, and took Rebecca in his arms. "That's the best damn pep talk I've ever heard. I feel like I could take on the bad guys all by myself."

"No you can't." She nodded at her notes. "That's what *he's* doing, the leader of the terrorists. He's fighting alone, ordering a group instead of leading a team. This enemy's profile isn't like my father or Wiggins. Roy Payne was born a psychopath, and Joseph Wiggins probably became one. But this al-Qaeda terrorist is different."

"Sounds like our guy is anything but a madman," Billy Ray agreed.

"Correct. And I'm not sure he is al-Qaeda even. A believer yes, but he is mature, patient, confident, and probably a genius in his own right. But I see one major fault with him."

"What's that?" asked Billy Ray.

"His beliefs constrain him to a single course of action—death. All of his decisions will be made to that end. Predictability is his weakness. We need to find a way to exploit it, get him to make critical errors to throw him off course. Or if needed, make him stick to his single-minded action. It can work both ways. I saw my father's shifting sands enough to know."

Rebecca's assessment matched with the teachings of the greatest military strategist of all time, Sun Tzu. Of the thirteen chapters in Sun Tzu's The Art of War, the man in Rebecca's profile nailed twelve of them. From planning and preparation, to intelligence and surprise, this terrorist mastermind had left nothing out, save one critical element—flexibility.

Radical Islam's mandate was to kill infidels. Contrastingly, Chinese rulers sought subjugation. The rigid ideology of Islamic terrorists didn't train for or allow for free thinking, only adherence to its creed and control by a single man with authority over all.

The parallel between their tormentor and America's present command environment wasn't lost on Billy Ray. The nation's political leadership seemed to have gone blind to what made the nation great in the first place, a belief that the whole was greater than the sum of its parts.

Rebecca drew tight in Billy Ray's arms. And her next words put a cherry on his thoughts. "We have more than faith. We have each other."

Billy Ray squeezed her tightly. "I've never been more thankful to have you by my side than right now."

They held each other, enjoying a private moment before—

The door opened and in paraded the rest of the team.

"Save that stuff for the winner's circle," Dodd said.

Billy Ray released Rebecca. "Spoken like a man with a plan."

"The beginnings of a plan, anyway," Dodd said. "I expect you all to fill in the rest. That's why I pay you the big bucks."

"What big bucks?" Tafoya balked. "I haven't seen a single dime for flashing my breasts."

"Can it, lady," Dodd said. "You did it for your country."

"Gee! What next, free lap dances?"

Lam cut in. "I'd say we're flying by the seat of our pants, Admiral."

"Funny you should state it that way, Agent Lam," Dodd said.

Everyone showed curious looks. Then a second later the same loud roar they'd heard earlier filled the room.

Dodd turned to Egolf. "Make the call."

It became clear to the group what Dodd meant.

"Yes, the United States Air Force."

"But it's just a single plane," Lam remarked.

"And probably not armed," Tafoya added.

"Beggars can't be choosy, folks. And that single plane can cover a lot of open water." Dodd replied.

Billy Ray wondered if Rebecca's talk had been piped throughout the building, because Dodd was sounding damn glib for a man up to his ass in alligators.

<=== PIPELINE ===>

Air Force Major Millicent Von Ryan thought of her father. She always did when flying upside down.

She was six years old the first time daddy belted her onto his lap and soared across the Kansas countryside in the family's crop duster.

Then upon returning home, daddy flipped the plane over while passing above their family farmhouse so young Millie could wave down at her dear mama.

The frightened look on her mother's face had never left Von Ryan. Neither had the tongue-lashing her father got that day for his wild stunt.

But the seed was planted. From that moment on, Millicent Von Ryan knew exactly what she wanted to do with her life—

FLY!

The callsign embossed on her helmet read *XXPRESS*. The name honored her daddy's favorite movie, while the double-X denoted the female chromosome. Mostly though, it just meant she loved going fast and flying high.

Von Ryan entered her final practice run above the long, uninhabited stretch of beach north of Muskegon. The next day, she would perform her stunts for real above thousands of cheering people gathered at the state park beach in Grand Haven.

As she neared the North Muskegon State Park, she noticed a group of beachgoers had gathered and formed themselves into the shape of a heart. So just as she'd done thirty years earlier while passing above her mother, she inverted the jet and waved to the family below.

Coming out of her pass, she rolled upright and went full throttle into the clear blue heavens, forever grateful for that first plane ride years ago.

"Thank you, Daddy," she whispered into her helmet mic.

"You're welcome," a strange voice replied.

"What the—!"

The voice continued, *"Major Von Ryan?"*

"Affirmative." She checked the radio frequency on the Up Front Control Panel. It was correct. "This is a military channel. ID yourself!"

"Wait one—"

Then a different man said, *"This is Admiral John Dodd. I've been authorized by General Tatam to communicate with you directly."*

"Air Force Chief of Staff Tatam . . .?" Von Ryan felt growing frustration.

"Yes, Chad Tatam."

"Is that so, Dodd, or whoever you are? Then put him on the line."

"Major, You may refer to me as Admiral or Sir," Dodd commanded. *"General Tatum is unavailable, as he's en route to the White House."*

"What about my commanding officer—"

"*SHE has also been so ordered,*" Dodd emphasized the gender.

The man had that pegged, too, Von Ryan thought.

"What's so important that the Navy feels compelled to interrupt my air show preparations?"

There was a pause. Then Dodd said, "*An al-Qaeda attack is believed imminent. You are the nearest asset to the terrorists.*"

Von Ryan leveled off at ten thousand feet, reduced her air speed, and said, "Cut my orders, Admiral. You have my undivided attention."

Dodd provided Von Ryan two GPS coordinates to pass over and put eyes on target. The first location was one Lam had just been informed of, a U.S. Department of Transportation ship transiting from West Michigan to Wisconsin. The DOT vessel carried nuclear waste material and, according to Lam's source, was presently participating in a United Nations inspection.

The second coordinate was the last-known position of the Edmund Challenger, their best guess for the ship hijacked by the al-Qaeda terrorists.

Dodd handed the headset back to Egolf to monitor Von Ryan's progress. Then he turned to Billy Ray and Rebecca and asked, "What have you two come up with?"

Billy Ray nodded for Rebecca to go first.

"With the information you provided, I can say our bad guy doesn't fit the usual profile."

"Not a psycho?"

"Definitely not, nor is he a sociopath . . . or even an actual terrorist."

"What then, Ms. Payne?" Dodd pressed.

"A patriot."

Tafoya said, "He sounds crazy to me. Patriots don't murder people."

Billy Ray came to Rebecca's rescue. "True believers don't consider their cause to be murder. If you need a historical example, think of the Christian Crusades, or more recently, the firebombing of German and Japanese cities in WW-II, or finally, the atomic bombs dropped on Japan."

Lam said, "If you're correct, then this al-Qaeda leader may have a greater goal than scaring the crap out of people. Maybe he's achieving someone's national interest. But who, ISIS?"

"Not ISIS," Rebecca said. "That group is rank with insanity. Think on a bigger scale without the apparent insanity."

<=== PIPELINE ===>

Egolf interrupted the discussion. "Admiral, the Major's reporting in."

The team quieted and Von Ryan's voice filled the room loud and clear. *"You sure about those coordinates? Nothing here but deep blue sea."*

Egolf scrambled to confirm the GPS numbers and nodded.

Dodd said, "Tune your receiver to the following wave length—"

He gave the frequency for the radio transponders on the DOT ship.

A moment later, Von Ryan said, *"Getting a faint signal. What's it from?"*

"The ship you say is nowhere in sight. It was carrying containment casks of spent nuclear fuel."

Several moments passed then Von Ryan said, *"That's strange. I'm picking up signals directly below me. But I repeat . . . there is no ship."*

Dodd's face went pasty white.

Lam's jaw dropped. "Mother of God!"

Dodd slapped his satphone to his ear and hustled out of the room.

Billy Ray knew exactly what just happened—the game changed.

A massive lake freighter had been converted into a giant bomb. Worse still, that bomb now contained the deadliest material known to man.

He shuddered.

The end of days had come so sudden.

For the second time in an hour, General Tatam finished a conversation with his old friend and colleague, John Dodd.

It was a short conversation—*one that made his blood run cold.*

Tatam said to his driver, "Step on it, Master Sergeant." The uniformed driver actuated the light bar in the vehicle's grill and punched the gas.

Next, Tatam dialed the White House using his secure car phone.

Thankfully, he got cleared-in to someone he knew, given that it was the weekend and most of the President's National Security Team had left town to speak at fundraisers or attend to their families, thus leaving more junior personnel in charge.

"Situation Room, Assistant Director Ronin," the voice answered.

After identifying himself and providing the correct numerical code, Tatam said, "Agent Ronin, is POTUS in residence?"

"Yes, but the First Family is packing for their vacation."

"Get word to his Chief of Staff immediately that a terror event is imminent or likely already in progress. Then notify the Security Council. This is an all-hands-on-deck situation no matter where they are. I'll stake my stars on it."

General Tatam hung up the car phone and sat back in the seat.

He'd never been a praying man . . . until now.

By the time Dodd returned, everyone had drawn their chairs closer to Egolf to hear Von Ryan's report.

"Approaching the Edmund Challenger . . ."

Tension in the room mounted as the roar of the Talon's General Electric J85 turbojet engines quieted when Von Ryan leveled off at a thousand feet, reduced airspeed, and began the approach over the bow of the ship.

The vantage point would allow her to assess the situation and still preserve airspace to bug out if necessary.

As an extra precaution, Von Ryan reached over and switched on the jet's early warning system.

That decision would end up saving her life.

Bashir relieved one of Qasem's Quds commandos on the bridge wing to stand watch on forward lookout.

To keep everyone sharp, Qasem had shortened the watch cycle from hour-long intervals to just thirty minutes.

Sometimes it was the small things that made the difference between success and failure—a fraction of an inch, a minute this way or that way . . . pure luck. Bashir had no way of knowing how true that was about to become, or whether the dice had just landed snake eyes.

The skies were clear. If anything moved through the air, Bashir could spot it easily with the powerful binoculars pressed to his face. But after scanning an empty horizon for most of the half-hour, he allowed his mind to drift on to other thoughts. He reflected on one of Qasem's earlier speeches pertaining to a time just ahead him now, and how the cell's actions would help usher in a new day for mankind, and then their arrival in paradise to enjoy endless carnal pleasures with lovely young virgins.

It was a subject he'd heard many times since childhood, and one very enticing to young male minds. Visions of beautiful maidens had warmed his blood during puberty. Though none of the boys in his madrassa thought to ask what they'd have to do to get their hands on one of those virgins, and what of there only being seventy-two women, and other questions on the matter.

There was movement.

At first, Bashir ignored the tiny dot in the sky approaching the Edmund Challenger, dismissing the object as a bird.

Then it grew into an airplane.

<==== PIPELINE ====>

Seconds later, the aft lookout confirmed the sighting, suggesting it was only a rich American business tycoon enjoying his wealth.

Bashir's mind didn't return to the seductive visions virgins.

Rather, he saw a giant fireball lighting up the night while he tended the family's goats some distance outside of the village. It was a missile shot from the skies. He'd hurried home only to find his entire family incinerated.

But today, those responsible would finally pay with their lives!

Suddenly, a roaring noise made it evident the aircraft was a jet, not a prop plane. And it was heading straight at the Edmund Challenger.

The dot grew in size, and the sound of its engines rose.

Then the craft flew over the Challenger.

It wasn't a tycoon—it was the U.S. Air Force!

Bashir's pulse accelerated.

This could be his chance.

"The Americans," he shouted over the radio. "They've found us!"

Bashir rushed onto the bridge and repeated his warning to Tariq, who sat at his station monitoring the mission's progress on a laptop computer.

But Tariq paid no attention to the overflight.

Egolf removed the radio headset from the portable communications gear and called out, "Admiral . . . Major Von Ryan's back on."

Dodd ended his contact with Washington and went to Egolf's side. The rest of the team did likewise.

Egolf said into the radio, "The Admiral is present, please continue."

"Roger that. I can confirm the ship is the Edmund Challenger. But . . ."

Dodd stepped closer. "But what, Major?"

"I thought you said the freighter was a cement hauler."

Dodd said, "I did and it is."

". . . then why is the deck covered with LP tanks? There must be a thousand of them ringing the ship."

Dodd cast a look at Billy Ray. They knew the significance of propane gas added to fertilizer and nitromethane.

The gas vastly increased the explosiveness of the ANNM mixture.

And it meant that if the ship was fired upon, the bad guys wouldn't need to trigger the bomb—

The good guys would do it for them!

It also meant they were probably too late.

Only one way to find out, Dodd thought.

"What about human activity?" he asked.

"Quiet as church on a Saturday night," Von Ryan said.

Dodd was about to order another pass over the ship when Billy Ray shook his head. "Let's be sure about this."

Lam objected, "But we're losing time, Jenkins. We need to call in help."

"Not yet, though I get your point," Billy Ray said. "The ship's far enough from land that if it blows, there'd be no immediate loss of life. But let's not overlook that the radioactive material would cause an environmental disaster of unimaginable scope, in the water and the air."

Tafoya spoke up, "I agree with Jenkins. Let's not call in help just yet."

"This flyover is for confirmation only," Dodd gave a half lie.

Rebecca reported, "I don't expect a rash response from their leader."

Lam countered, "But every minute brings the ship closer to Chicago."

Dodd considered their options.

What he wasn't telling anyone was they weren't just racing against terrorists and a ticking doomsday clock, they were also contending with their own government, now gathering at the Whitehouse—a leadership that hadn't made many good choices of late.

Yet he believed it was best to rattle the terrorists now, try to get them to expose their weaknesses, if any.

He wanted to shake up their comfort zone, and hopefully they'd make mistakes. Then he and his team could develop a battle plan, one he would be confident enough with to run it up the flagpole with the little time he had left as an admiral.

His hunch rested on Rebecca's profile, that the enemy wasn't the type to have an itchy finger on the trigger.

But if they were a twitchy bunch, then Jenkins could be correct.

At last he made his decision and nodded for Egolf to toggle the radio.

Then he took a deep breath and said, "Major Von Ryan, let's ring those church bells."

Indeed, Dodd thought. *It was time to call all to mass.*

Bashir ran onto the bridge sounding the alarm.

Tariq looked up from his computer. "Settle down, my brother."

"But that was a military jet!" Bashir argued.

"Yes, it was. But it can do us no harm. Act natural and trust in Allah."

"But it carried a bomb, I tell you!"

The debate was interrupted by Qasem calling up to the bridge on the ship's phone. Tariq took the call.

"Report," Qasem said from down in the ship's holds where he was prepping the volunteer commandos for breaching the containment casks.

<==== PIPELINE ====>

"A flyover by an Air Force jet," Tariq said. "But no worries, the craft was just a trainer. Likely a new pilot."

Bashir shouted, "A military craft nonetheless, we've been spotted!"

Qasem caught the forceful outburst. "Send Bashir below decks after his watch period is through."

The line went dead.

Tariq put the phone back on its cradle and faced Bashir. "Get back on watch. And try not to imagine boogiemen lurking around every corner."

"I know what I saw," Bashir argued. "That jet was armed!"

"No it wasn't. It was just a curious pilot. Now go." Tariq dismissed him with a rude wave of his hand.

Bashir stormed off the bridge, displaying anger at yet another rebuff by Tariq who was acting far too cavalier.

With every inch closer they got to the target, the danger of them being stopped by an incoming missile short of their goal vastly increased.

Bashir decided to take precautions should the jet return. Actually, he hoped it would return.

At each watch station there were five-foot-long metal cases containing shoulder-fired surface-to-air Stinger Missiles, made in America.

What irony. Bashir thought.

He opened the Stinger case.

During Von Ryan's first pass over the Edmund Challenger there'd been several crewmen nonchalantly attending to their business. They'd even paused to wave up at her. She'd half expected the sailors to form a heart like the family back at the Muskegon beach.

But if Dodd was correct about the ship having been converted into a floating bomb and, worse still, carried tons of radioactive material, then *nonchalant* was the wrong attitude.

And The XXPRESS knew just how to change that.

Von Ryan took the T-38C Talon to near its service ceiling of fifty-five thousand feet and put herself between the bright sun and the ship below.

If she was being watched, as she fully expected, then the jet's forty-six-foot length and slim profile would be nearly impossible to spot dropping out of the sky. Reminiscent of gunfighters in the old west who made sure their adversary had the sun in their eyes before drawing.

Her plan was to feign a bombing run on the Edmund Challenger by crossing the freighter at midship. She would buzz the crew mere feet off the deck traveling close to the maximum speed allowed while still carrying the travel pod attached to the belly of the fuselage.

If not for that pod, she would love to punch it up to Mach speed and treat the bad guys to a sonic boom real close and personal.

Regardless, the aggressive maneuver and the roar of the Talon's turbojet engines would still send a mighty loud message.

Von Ryan radioed Dodd, "Beginning my run now."

She dove for the deck, gaining speed with the help of gravity while saving fuel in the bargain. At best, she had two more passes at the ship before needing to beeline it for home.

She monitored the UFCP instruments on the glass cockpit while the blue waters of Lake Michigan rushed up to meet her.

At approaching one thousand feet, or *one angel* in pilot-speak, she pulled up and vectored toward the freighter.

To the distant observer on the port bridge wing of the Edmund Challenger, her sleek jet may have looked like a hungry hawk swooping toward a mouse. Then Von Ryan noted the "mouse" pointing something her way, and not a middle finger hoisted in a last act of defiance.

It was a rocket launcher!

A half-second later, the cockpit's electronic threat indicator went nuts.

Von Ryan's immediate reaction was to jettison the storage pod and gain airspeed. Her next move was to initiate countermeasures, which normally would entail dispensing chaff and flares and electronic jamming.

Unfortunately, the T-38 trainer was presently fitted for airshows, and had none of those. It had red, white, and blue smoke makers.

She actuated them anyway and tipped her wings a full eighty degrees, then punched the afterburners for maximum G's to make herself a difficult target for the inbound missile.

Instantly, three thousand four hundred pounds of thrust from the Talon's power plant ignited a flood of jet fuel, and gave Von Ryan all she could handle.

Blood moved instantly away from her brain, threatening a blackout. To combat the extreme force of gravity on her body, she implemented the anti-G straining maneuver taught to all flyers of high-performance aircraft. If she lost consciousness, she was dead. Simple as that.

Only seven seconds had elapsed since the sounding of the threat indicator, an eternity in aerial combat. She craned her head around to get a visual on the missile but saw nothing. Surely the weapon was a Stinger, and likely gaining on her six.

Regardless, there was no time to waste debating make and model, nor would it matter. Lacking countermeasures, and unable to trick the missile back to its barn for fear of blowing up the Edmund Challenger, Von Ryan's only defense was to outrun and outmaneuver the damn thing.

<=== PIPELINE ===>

And for that, she needed height or distance—twelve thousand feet or five miles.

She chose the former and pointed the Talon toward heaven, then pumped another load of fuel through the afterburners.

Higher and higher she rocketed, seeking a dozen friendly angels before the devil came knocking on her door.

The T-38's climb rate was thirty-four thousand feet per minute . . . the Stinger's speed twice that.

It would be close, maybe too close.

She'd underestimated the enemy, and he'd pulled the trigger first.

But if she could just manage to climb above the Stinger's eleven-thousand-foot ceiling—

It wasn't to be.

Fourteen seconds into basic fighter maneuvers, Major Von Ryan saw the missile coming in hot.

The race was lost.

Had the bandit been another aircraft, she could've nosedived for the deck in a spiral maneuver.

But what then?

She had no weapons, and the bandit chasing her wasn't a pilot but a heat-seeking missile with one nasty warhead!

Von Ryan reached for the ejection lever.

"Mayday! Mayday! Mayday!" she called into her mic.

Six-point-six pounds of high explosives slammed into the Talon's port wing at the same moment Von Ryan ejected from the doomed aircraft.

As she jettisoned into open air, a tiny voice played in her mind, it was lecturing daddy about the dangers of flying.

Mama was right.

21

Static hissed and crackled over the radio.

"Oh my God, they shot her down!" Tafoya exclaimed.

Rebecca looked at Dodd. "I'm so sorry, Admiral. I didn't anticipate that reaction from the terrorist leader. His haste makes no sense."

Lam sneered. "Maybe there's a hothead onboard wanting first crack at those seventy-two virgins."

"Our mission just got dicier," Egolf added and turned off the radio.

The group hesitated, or maybe it was the shock of Von Ryan getting blown out of the air.

Either way he had his answer, Dodd thought. *And the ship still intact.*

"There's no mistaking it now," Lam said flatly and stepped away to dial his superiors in Washington.

Chief Petty Officer Miller dashed off to the comms room to organize a search and rescue of the downed pilot.

Then Admiral Dodd took control. He faced Tafoya. "Have your pilot ready the helo. I want us in the air ASAP."

In usual Tafoya form, hands on hips, defiant, she said, "And just who might 'us' be?"

Dodd the warrior not the scientist said, "The men."

Tafoya wasn't buying it. "You got something against women?"

"Stow the war-on-women crap, lady. If you were the right person for the job, you'd be going, you'd be fighting, and you'd be dying if that's what it took to win. We're one team and *WE* have to stop that ship. Because if we don't others will. And that would come at the cost of thousands of lives lost and millions more sickened."

Realizing their ominous situation, Rebecca gasped. "Tami said it before, the whole city of Chicago is gathered on the waterfront to hail that ship. They have to be warned!"

Dodd didn't answer.

Billy Ray knew the reason for Dodd's silence—the people would get no advance warning.

Governments could often be more terrified of pandemonium and unmanaged chaos than of a Black Swan event itself. They also feared the media crucifixion if the threat ended up false.

Chaos implied an administration's impotence.

Better a black eye than to show lack of balls.

The political spin doctors could later blame the bad guys afterward for the carnage, laud the victims as heroes, and rebuke the opposition party for blocking funding that would've kept people "safe."

<=== PIPELINE ===>

It was a scenario that dates back to the rulers of the Roman Empire up to its fall. But never had America known a potential for such disaster as it did now.

There had been no warning for the dead American servicemen during the Japanese attack on Pearl Harbor.

Nor did the two thousand nine hundred and seventy-seven souls murdered by Islamic terrorists on 9/11 receive text messages to vacate their World Trade Center offices prior to the first plane hitting its mark.

In both cases the matter of forewarning was still hotly debated: was the intelligence community caught asleep at the switch? Or did the nation's leaders possess actionable intelligence and then chose to ignore the threat?

Regardless, that wasn't the case this time.

They knew.

He—they—couldn't let history repeat. Each hit to the homeland had grown in magnitude. If the enemy succeeded this time, it could rock the nation to its knees.

Because all around Lake Michigan, from its east coast to its west coast, from its northernmost reaches to its southern shores, everyday common people were gathered for festivals and fairs, shop picnics and family reunions, marrying and giving in marriage, or simply flocking on the sandy beaches under the summer sun—

While death crept toward them.

Billy Ray's thoughts were interrupted by Tafoya not giving in to Dodd.

"So what are you going to do, just land my TV station helicopter on the deck of a terrorist ship filled with enough explosives to make one ugly bang, even out in the middle of the lake?"

Dodd hesitated, so Billy Ray stepped in.

"No. We're going to land it on a World War-II submarine."

"You sent for me?" Bashir asked Qasem with a little nervous wobble in his voice.

Qasem stood outside of the thick hydraulic bulkhead door of the middlemost hold that accommodated the nuclear containment casks.

With their presence now fully known to the Americans, he was forced to advance their preparations for arrival in Chicago.

His first thought had been to cut Bashir's head off for shooting down the jet. But instead, he would kill him with kindness.

"I must commend you, Bashir. Your mastery with Stinger missile was impressive." Flattery was like a siren song to the brash *shahid.*

Bashir beamed proudly. "The American was about to attack. We can't let them stop us now."

"That is the reason I called for you. You have a new assignment, one sure to enhance your position in paradise."

Qasem handed Bashir a respirator then nodded at the Quds members lining the passageway. Each man in the group wore yellow firemen turnout gear and rubber boots. There was an extra outfit for Bashir.

"You will be the leader of these men by completing the final phase of our bomb," Qasem said. "It shall be you, a Sunni, leading these Shia to glory."

Bashir looked none too thrilled, comprehending the type of death that awaited him beyond that door. But neither did the young terrorist voice any displeasure.

Qasem left Bashir and the Quds to their duty and went topside to join Tariq on the bridge. It was time to implement an impenetrable defense against the Americans. He'd earlier had the engine room and boiler spaces sealed off from the LP gas. The smoking lamp was out, and the crew had received gas masks and a very stern warning against flames and sparks.

Now it was time to prime the ship.

Qasem picked up the ship's phone and pressed the button for the main public address circuit, the 1MC as it was known internationally.

He again warned about flames and sparks and then ordered the crew to don their gas masks. Then came the opening of the propane tanks ringing the main deck. Within minutes, fumes enveloped the Edmund Challenger and forming an explosive bubble.

Qasem heard his own breathing inside of the gas mask, a sure indication that he was ready, too.

Paradise could come at any moment now.

Thus far, the above-water phase of the shakedown cruise had gone smoothly. Now it was time for the Silversides to do what it was built to do, submerge, which was something the boat hadn't done in many decades.

Captain Rinard and Creed went below, closing and sealing the topside hatches behind them. Creed went aft to check on the engines while Rinard joined Torch Terrill at the helm in the conning tower.

"How's she running, Chief?"

"Like a two-peckered greyhound, Captain," Torch said out of the side of his mouth, the side without a lit stogie jammed in it.

"How about watertight, Chief?" Rinard asked.

<===== PIPELINE =====>

"Like a frog's ass!"

Rinard chuckled at Torch's animal metaphors. "Carry on, Chief of the Boat."

"Aye aye, sir."

Rinard picked up the 1MC and addressed the crew, "The time we've all been waiting for has come. But before commencing submerging operations, let us first take one moment to remember the countless mariners who put to sea and joined the eternal patrol. And let us pray for ourselves and our mission success."

Everyone bowed their heads and the boat went silent save for the engine noises.

Rinard had heard it said there were no atheists in a foxhole. That may go doubly true for anyone about to deliberately sink a boat.

"Yea, though I walk through the valley of the shadow of death, I will fear no evil—"

His reciting Psalm 23 was suddenly interrupted by the obtrusive blare of the boat's ship-to-shore phone.

"That better be God!" Torch bellowed.

Colon was the onboard Sonar Technician, but also doubled as the radioman. "It's for you, Captain."

"Who is it?"

"Muskegon Coast Guard station, an admiral. Says it's most urgent."

Rinard took the call and could hardly believe his ears.

"Yes, sir," he acknowledged while scribbling notes. "We'll be on station in thirty mikes."

Rinard hung up the receiver and handed his scribbled notes to Torch. Get us to these coordinates flank speed on the surface, Mr. Terrill."

"Sir...?" Torch said out of the side of his mouth.

"The Silversides has its first combat mission in seventy years." The COB almost lost the cigar out of his wide open mouth.

Egolf and Billy Ray finished loading the team's equipment in the helicopter under the supervision of the pilot. Weight matters greatly to flying craft, and the pilot just announced they'd exceeded the limit.

"No choice," Dodd replied. "We'll take our chances redlining it and your piloting skills."

Tafoya and Rebecca remained out of the way near the station doors watching the men pile into the helicopter. Neither wore a happy face. Aside from not wanting to be left behind, they knew the possibility that these men may not be coming back.

The helicopter doors slid shut and locked. The pilot increased the rpm's on the rotor blade and was about to lift off when Lam motioned for him to wait. He removed his headset, exited the copter, and trotted over to Tafoya.

Lam took the lovely Cubana in his arms and kissed her deeply. Then he released her and said, "Wait for me," and hustled back to the helo.

Tafoya was left shocked and speechless, but beaming nonetheless.

As Lam belted himself in and slipped on the communications gear, he heard Billy Ray's voice in the headphones.

"So that's how the Army does it!"

The chopper lifted into the air and zoomed away.

The women watched the helicopter become a small dot in the sky then disappear entirely.

Finally, Rebecca turned to Tafoya. "OK. Now what?"

A rejuvenated Tafoya said, "We chase after them, what else."

"But we won't catch them before they reach the Silversides."

"No, but we can be there to pull their cute little butts out of the drink. Follow me."

Tafoya led them back inside the Coast Guard Station where she asked Chief Miller for a favor.

"The Terminator III, you say?"

"Yes," Tafoya replied. "Rebecca and I will be waiting by the dock."

Twenty excruciating minutes later, a charter fishing boat pulled up to the dock. It was crewed by a father and son team out of Pentwater.

The elder man tossed a mooring line to the women. "Heave-ho me hearties!" he shouted in his best mock pirate voice.

The ladies pulled the Terminator tight against the rubber fenders and hopped aboard. The son immediately reversed the engines and put them back in the channel, then headed to the Big Lake.

After securing the mooring line, the father welcomed them aboard and Tafoya made formal introductions. "Rebecca, this is Lyle, a close friend of my grandfather. And the handsome man at the helm is his son, Skip. When you want to catch monster fish, these are your guys."

Lyle said, "You keep trying to sweet-talk me. But I've told you before, Tami, I'm not leaving my wife of fifty-six years for the likes of you."

"Me neither," Skip called out. "You don't have what men want."

Rebecca couldn't help herself and laughed out loud.

Tafoya crossed her arms and acted hurt. "Now you know why I have such a complex around guys."

<===== PIPELINE =====>

Lyle first shook Rebecca's hand then gave Tafoya a big grandfatherly hug. "So what's the big rush, chica? What kind of fish are we after?"

"The invasive kind," Tafoya said. "I'll tell you more once we're clear of the channel."

"Fair enough," Lyle agreed.

As the Channel 13 News helicopter redlined it to the Silversides, both Lam and Dodd placed phone calls to their contacts in Washington.

Lam's call was brief, though it was obvious that the information he got was displeasing.

When Dodd ended his call he showed the same look.

Billy Ray and Egolf glanced over at one another, the meaning clear—
They were in for the battle of their lives.

The Silversides came into view.

The pilot approached the stationary boat, timed the rise and fall of the lake swell, and lowered to the deck with a little bump.

A few of the boat's crew rushed up to help unload the team's gear, cautious of the turning rotor blades and static electricity they generated.

All of the gear but Egolf's silver cases was quickly removed and sent below.

Finally, Dodd waved to the newsroom pilot and the helo lifted and flew off. Then he joined the lone man on the bridge.

"Captain Rinard, I presume."

Rinard saluted. "Welcome aboard, Admiral."

Dodd looked around. "I feel as though I stepped back in time."

Rinard smiled. "A good many people have worked to restore the boat to her former glory."

"It shows," Dodd said. "Shall we go below, we have much to plan for."

"Yes, sir. Mind telling me the nature of the mission? If our having just received a soaking wet and really pissed off Air Force pilot is any indication, shall I assume we're heading into harm's way?"

"You shall," was all the answer Dodd provided.

Rinard nodded at the hatchway. "After you, Admiral."

Everyone crammed into the largest space on the Silversides, the crew's mess, an area about the size of a mobile home dining room. Most stood shoulder to shoulder, allowing the older sailors to sit.

As Dodd and Rinard approached, all came to attention.

Rinard waved them at-ease and introduced Admiral Dodd.

Dodd's first comments were directed at Millicent Von Ryan. "I'm sorry for the loss of your plane, Major. Thank God you survived."

Von Ryan wore a pink sweat suit provided by the lone female crewmember, while her ginger hair was still wet from the dunking.

"Just give me one chance to get back at those bastards."

"You'll get that chance, Major, we all will. And God help us."

For the next ten minutes, Dodd briefed everyone. The information went into some detail about the enemy, as well as stressing the magnitude of the dirty bomb. Lam filled in a few points, while Egolf supplied technical data from his laptop computer.

Dodd described the horrors awaiting them aboard the Edmund Challenger: extremely radioactive material, a ship crawling with foreign soldiers heavily armed and eager to see paradise, and every inch enveloped in a cloud of LP gas.

After a moment of sobering silence, Rinard stated, "You do realize this is a World War II boat and that we have no weapons. Hell, we haven't even submerged yet to test our underwater integrity. We could all end up on the bottom of the lake, for that matter."

Billy Ray spoke for the first time, "Hold that thought, Captain. This may well be a one-way mission. But I assure you, we're also the only hope for millions of our countrymen."

With that grim revelation, the only man to have served aboard the Silversides when all of its combat missions were deemed its last, rose up on aged legs. "Please explain yourself, sailor," Creed demanded.

Billy Ray said "Roger That, Sir" and then did so. "POTUS won't allow that freighter to reach its target."

"Good," a crewman said.

"Not good," he countered. "Any attempt to fire on that ship will trigger the bomb as surely as if the terrorists pressed the switch themselves."

"I see your point, Mr. Jenkins," Creed conceded. "If the President orders the ship sunk in order to save lives on land, then Lake Michigan becomes a nuclear waste dump."

Billy Ray nodded. "And people will still die from the toxic airborne and water contamination."

"Holy shit!" Torch exclaimed. "We're screwed fore and aft."

Captain Rinard offered a more refined interpretation. "So you're saying we must somehow stop well-armed suicidal terrorists aboard a massive freighter filled with explosives and radioactive material that's primed to blow us all to kingdom come at the strike of a match—"

Torch removed his cigar for the first time since shoving off.

Rinard continued, "And you're saying our government is preparing to attack the ship while it's still in open waters, which will actually end up accomplishing the terrorist's goals for them."

"You are correct, sir," Billy Ray answered.

228

<===== PIPELINE =====>

"Well, unless you have a better idea than the President, then I'm siding with Mr. Terrill's colorful assessment. What the hell can we possibly do?"

Billy Ray looked around the tightly packed space, everyone strangers but for a common good—saving the nation.

"We beat POTUS to it. WE sink the Edmund Challenger."

There were baffled looks

A hand shot up for questions.

"Here me out," Billy Ray said. "If my team can get aboard the freighter, then we can open the seacocks and scuttle the ship. The flood waters will foul the fertilizer and nitromethane. And furthermore, the Challenger is a cement hauler, she's presently carrying hydraulic cement in its holds for a harbor project. Meaning, once mixed with lake water, the cement will harden around the nuclear containment casks."

Lam said, "Like Operation CHASE in the 1960's. The Army sank ships filled with chemical weapons encased in concrete."

"A concrete tomb . . . friggin' brilliant!" Torch stuck the soggy pacifier back in his mouth.

"That may solve the contamination problem," Von Ryan agreed. "But how do you get aboard a moving freighter crawling with heavily armed terrorists?"

Dodd took the question. "We have a rough plan for that, Major. But I'll let Jenkins explain it while I go hold off the cavalry."

"And then what?" a crew member asked Dodd.

"Then it'll be all hands on deck if we're going to save Chicago and most everyone else in the four state region within the blast contamination zones."

Knowing their risk of dying, Rinard announced, "If anyone wants off this boat, now's the time to speak up."

No one did.

"All right then, Jenkins has the floor," Dodd said and left the mess deck with his "special" phone in hand.

Billy Ray knew exactly what Dodd was about to do—get the generals to not sacrifice the privates.

He turned to Rinard. "What do we have in the way of torpedoes?"

"One dummy fish. But nothing's been fired from the tubes in seventy years."

The blonde sailor's hand shot up. Her nametag read, *Tina*. "That's my department, sir. I'm a Machinist's Mate by training, but torpedo systems are my passion. It took me scrounging for parts and workable batteries for our Mark 18 fish, then lots of weekends repairing the forward tubes. But I'm confident the system's operational. Although what kind of damage could a dummy warhead possibly do?"

Billy Ray was impressed. He'd come aboard the Silversides assuming they would have to ram the enemy ship. "Since the bad guys are using LP gas for a failsafe, explosives would do us no good," he answered then turned to Rinard. "How about we stick a torpedo up that ship's tailpipe and foul its propellers? Then my team can board when it has to stop."

There was no stopping the eruption of voices now. Several hands shot up. And many of the crew began chatting excitedly with each other.

Billy Ray let them run. These folks knew more about the vintage submarine's capabilities than anyone. Plus his words had embodied the objective, not a blueprint. Only Dodd knew what he had in mind, and there were still holes in his plan and a need for contingencies. He was betting on the Silversides crew to fill those holes.

But having a torpedo available solved one crucial problem already. Dodd no longer needed to order the ramming of the Edmund Challenger.

Had it come to that, there was a high probability the Silversides would be sent to the bottom alongside the enemy.

Furthermore, the escape hatch was limited to a few crew members per attempt, and consumed precious time decompressing the chamber, filling it with water, releasing, and then resealing the hatch. Because the escape process would need to repeat many times, from hundreds of feet down, while the darkened Silversides filled with icy water and ran out of breathable air, most if not all hands would perish in the cold depths of Lake Michigan.

In World War two, over a thousand submarines went to the bottom. Yet only a tiny handful of sailors attempted escape, many unsuccessfully. Sailors would choose death inside their sunken coffins over the crushing pressures of the deep.

But even with an alternative to ramming the enemy ship, Billy Ray knew there were no guarantees any of them would see home port again.

Especially if they failed to stop the Edmund Challenger.

<===== PIPELINE =====>

22

Many Americans will never forget seeing their President and members of his national security team huddled around a conference room video monitor in the Situation Room of the White House in May of 2011, all watching intently as the Navy's SEAL Team Six raided Osama bin Laden's compound in Pakistan during operation Neptune Star.

Dodd hoped that same kind of Hollywooding to the voters wasn't happening this time. Because he was about to phone the White House and rattle some cages, the one really big cage in fact.

And then what he had planned after that could get him hogtied, hauled off to federal prison in Leavenworth, and tossed in a cage of his own.

Or shot.

The last of the President's national security team arrived, comprising the top military and political leaders.

And then the critical meeting to save the nation from disaster began.

The National Security Advisor briefed the group on the present crises facing the nation, of which there were two: one external, one internal.

The matter developing overseas pertained to Iran having just apprised the world that it planned to conduct its first-ever nuclear weapon test in two hours—midnight in Tehran, late afternoon in America's heartland.

The situation was escalating by the minute, with the nation of Israel promising to shoot Iran's missile out of the sky. While Iran threatened retaliation should they do so.

The second problem for the President involved an imminent terror plot unfolding on Lake Michigan.

Thus far, no news of the threat had leaked to the press, and the President's team wished to keep it that way.

The matter involved a lake freighter that had been converted into an extremely large and deadly 'dirty' bomb, and was assumed to arrive at its target in Chicago simultaneous with the Iranian missile test...unless the threat could be neutralized sooner.

Complicating matters, and possibly serving as a catalyst for another war in the Middle East, a conflict POTUS had striven diligently to prevent, was the identity of the mastermind behind the al-Qaeda terrorists.

The man leading these bad actors, and now guiding the converted freighter to its target, was the former commander of Iran's secret Quds Force—General Qasem Khatami.

Furthermore, whether Iran could be trusted was still hotly debated.

Iran had come clean about Khatami's desertion and betrayal of Shia Islam. But they were also requesting America's help eliminating him before any more embarrassment happened to their nation and faith.

Not known for being an introvert, the Vice President pounded the table. "I knew those bastards were lying about their nuclear program! And now a dirty bomb is about to devastate our shores, and all they can worry about is being embarrassed!"

The CIA Director said, "They presume our porous borders are our problem, not theirs." Then he turned to the Vice President. "And to your point, sir, Iran mastered the art of deception back in the 7th Century and they've only gotten better at it since then. They might just be lying about a nuclear test, since my agency has no verifiable intelligence to support them having the bomb yet."

The general heading the Joint Chiefs of Staff as Chairman, or CJCS, responded, "And because they could be deceiving us about the missile being only a test, I ordered our military readiness elevated to DEFCON 3. With your permission, Mr. President, I shall proceed to DEFCON 2."

"I advise against elevating our war readiness, Mr. President," said the Secretary of State. "Iran showed good will coming to us about Khatami."

POTUS' Senior Advisor leaned close. "Table the Iran nuclear test."

The Joint Chiefs Chairman objected, "Wether it's a Ttest or not, the Israelis will not sit idly by while we pontificate. They will take action. We can't afford to start from behind if there's to be a war involving ballistic missile exchange."

The CIA Director was more subtle. "Mr. President, my esteemed colleagues, perhaps the two matters are related."

After shooting the DCI a cutting look, the Senior Advisor repeated herself more forcefully, "Focus on Chicago, Mr. President."

Few inside the President's inner circle were allowed such directness. But the Senior Advisor had never been wrong with her advice, yet.

POTUS nodded, and the topic switched to terror in the Midwest.

The Attorney General went first. "According to my FBI Director, the threat is not only real but poses an imminent danger to the country."

"Proceed," the President said.

Paired with input from Air Force Chief of Staff Chad Tatam, the AG informed the Security Council of the clear and present danger about to befall millions of citizens in Chicago and the surrounding region.

The report wasn't long, but it was terrifying.

Then as if on cue, the red phone next to the President rang, causing all around the Sit-Room table to go silent.

The name *John Dodd* flashed across the wall monitor.

POTUS frowned, then pressed the talk button.

<===== PIPELINE =====>

Dodd heard POTUS loud and clear through the satphone. This call could be the end of his long career, if not his freedom, or even his life.

Despite being piped over the Sit Room speakers, he figured what the hell, and went for bluntness. "Mr. President, do not attempt lethal force on the Edmund Challenger." It was not a request or a suggestion. It bordered on a directive.

"I thought I fired you, Mr. Dodd."

"If you recall, I resigned effective tomorrow."

"How about we make it effective today?" POTUS retorted snidely.

Dodd ignored the jab. "I can stop the terrorists before they blow up that ship—or before you do. Whether it's by your hand or theirs, millions of our people will die a horrific death. The Great Lakes will be made uninhabitable for millennia, should you so much as toss a firecracker aboard that ship. In case you're unaware, the Challenger is encased in a cloud of propane gas. You must give me a chance to sink it without incident."

"Hold—" said the President.

Dodd was put on mute.

He imagined talking heads advising POTUS. He could also imagine the leader of the free world seething with anger at being put on the spot in front of his subordinates.

After two full agonizing minutes, POTUS was back.

"Negative, Admiral. You are to stand down. Thanks for your offer, but I still expect your resignation on my desk first thing tomorrow."

"And you shall have it . . . if I'm still alive"

"You heard me, mister, STAND DOWN!" the President exploded.

"I shall not, sir. I'm presently aboard a submarine pursuing the baddest damned IED the world has ever seen. Unlike your response, my plan WILL save lives and spare the environment."

Dodd heard voices erupt in the background before getting shushed.

Then barely controlling his rage, POTUS said, "You're committing treason. I'll have you arrested—"

Dodd lowered the boom. "These terrorists have gotten this far due to your soft policies and your vanity pursuing a legacy. I shall not stand down while a politician puts himself ahead of the people. In case you forgot, you are serving at the will of the people whom you're willing to let die. If you do that, then think of where the history books will place your legacy— At the bottom of the toilet."

"How dare you speak to me in that manner!"

Dodd wasn't done. "If not me then who, the men around your table, the woman at your side? You are not a king. You're just a man to whom a majority of the nation entrusted their vote, myself included."

POTUS' Ivy League patina abandoned him.

"I'm the goddamn Commander in Chief. You will do what I say, mister!"

"As the Commander in Chief of these United States of America, I advise you to make the correct decision. I shall wait only five minutes for your answer . . . I have a national disaster to prevent."

Then Dodd hung up on the most powerful man in the world and waited.

This time, he imagined what was being voiced around the President's table were the collective shouts for his head lopped off on an old fashioned guillotine.

At the five minute mark, Dodd exited the diminutive Silversides stateroom to go give his life for his country.

At the five minute and three second mark, his phone rang.

It was the President. "We have no submarines in the Great Lakes."

"But indeed we do, sir, the USS Silversides and I'm underway on her."

Dodd had to pull the phone away from his ear to prevent it getting scorched.

After he explained in finer detail about using a World War II submarine to sink the Edmund Challenger, he got a partial peace offering.

It came in the form of GPS coordinates that corresponded to a spot on the water where five United States Air Force jets would unleash their missiles on the enemy ship.

But it would have to do.

Dodd also received another critical piece of the puzzle, the identity of the terrorist leader—Qasem Khatami.

No wonder! Dodd thought.

He'd suspected a high-ranking operative, but had lost contact with his deep cover asset after the gas hauler hijacking.

What the hell kind of game could a disgraced Iranian military general be playing, and then joining the company Sunni terrorists?

Then it hit Dodd. Not just Khatami . . . but Iran! They were making their move on the West!

Before rejoining the crew, Dodd tallied the time bought for his team and discovered he'd been shortchanged by the President—

It didn't account for any escape!

In real time and distance, and allowing for pursuit by the Silversides and disabling the Challenger, then getting his team aboard and scuttling the ship, they had two hours tops.

He may not be signing his resignation after all.

Dead men don't write.

<===== PIPELINE =====>

As the Terminator III sped along the vast expanse of Lake Michigan, Tafoya gave Lyle the short version of the invasive fish they were hunting.

Winks and nods substituted for details where confidentiality demanded. After all, she didn't want Dodd making good on his threat of banishment to a secluded island in the Indian Ocean.

Well, maybe if Lam would play Adam and Eve with her, she mused.

Nevertheless, Dodd had opened her eyes to the challenges of policing America's streets on one level while protecting the nation on another. And then the reason both institutions were bleeding into one—criminal gangs had merged with foreign actors resolved on destroying America and all she stood for.

As much as Tafoya hated to admit it, or worse, accept it, or worse still, participate in an alliance between law enforcement and the military, the die was cast. The Constitutional lines between what keeps individuals safe, *themselves,* and what makes the country secure, *the military,* had faded, leaving the torch of freedom to flicker in the crosswinds.

In the present crisis, Founding Father Patrick Henry's choice between "Liberty or Death" had been predetermined by a new evil stalking the land, allowing but one fate for infidels—death.

She loved being an investigative reporter and exposing truth. Above all, she valued a press free from government interference and unfettered by its newsroom editors.

Indeed, her industry was the fiery furnace through which the nation's leaders were made to tread. It was the very freedom that ensured America's leaders were forever accountable to the people. And sadly, it was a freedom that too many of her colleagues in the Fourth Estate had sold out on objective reporting for activist journalism. It was like eating the seed corn, soon they would starve.

Yet she saw no choice but to operate on behalf of the K-KEY Group, a fact that could get her branded a sellout too by her peers in the press.

Though in reality, freedom wasn't really *free.* Too many citizens had closed their eyes to that fact. Freedom was fought for, acquired by toil and blood, and then bound by personal responsibility.

Or it was lost.

Racing toward an enemy who'd declared death to liberty and freedom anathema, Tami Tafoya resolved greater circumspection in the future when applying her craft.

She, more than most, knew how dangerous truth could be, how hotly the media furnace glowed—

And how innocent people could get burned.

Billy Ray ended the strategy meeting and watched Admiral Dodd approach the mess deck.

Though he rarely, if ever, took the skipper's money playing Liar's Poker, he also rarely misread his commander's face when mission time came—they were in over their heads.

Beside Lam and Egolf, twelve other faces weren't hiding much either. From Captain Rinard, Chief of the Boat Terrill, Colon, Creed, Von Ryan, Tina, and all the others, it was evident they understood the risks as well. Everyone could soon be joining the eternal patrol.

Yet not a single one of them wanted out. Each person accepted the fact that there existed no other options . . . the enemy had to be stopped.

Dodd held up an index and middle finger to signify they had two hours.

Billy Ray did some quick math of his own. The magic beans Dodd got for trading the cow came up short by at least an hour, if not more.

During Dodd's absence, the Silversides crew helped Billy Ray solidify a plan to "delay" the Edmund Challenger rather than disabling the ship. He was going with the notion that if the terrorists figured their gig was up, they'd pull the det-cord and blow everything sky high.

The trick would be making the enemy think the damage was quickly repairable, then return merrily on their way to their date with oblivion and paradise. That's when he, Dodd, Lam, and Egolf would strike.

Billy Ray was pleased with the crew's swift thinking. Thanks to them, he had the missing pieces to his plan; the getting aboard part, anyway.

Before following the others to the torpedo room to ready themselves for battle, Billy Ray personally thanked this collection of heroes—dads, grandpas, engineers, lawyers, computer programmers, grade school teachers, a mailman, a CNC operator, the three active military members, and all the old sailors from a bygone era in naval history. Each had stepped away from their workaday lives to pursue a passion.

Now, assuredly beyond their wildest dreams, they stepped unto the breach to stop a diabolical enemy bent on stabbing the nation in its heart.

Billy Ray had heard it said back in Texas that big boots and a shiny buckle didn't make you a cowboy, steppin' into the saddle did.

Time to saddle up Cowboy!

They stood off to one side in the torpedo room cramming into their wetsuits, while Tina led several crewmembers in loading the Mark 18.

Winches, chains, pulleys, muscle, and a well-greased rail were a must for lifting the three thousand pound fish, and then sliding its twenty-foot length into place. Then the hatch was shut and the tube charged to the proper air pressure.

<===== PIPELINE =====>

"Tube one ready. One dummy torpedo standing by," Tina reported.

"You sure that thing is going to work?" asked Billy Ray.

Proud and confident, Tina said, "I'll bet my chevron on it. But the real trick will be if Captain Rinard can get us in tight, because this thing has a short range."

Lam said, "I've heard these old torpedoes can boomerang."

Tina nodded. "I can't guarantee against a circle run, but getting up close to the target will help."

Rinard entered the torpedo room. "It'll be a tricky shot, done at periscope depth rather than down deep. We'll be exposed to the enemy."

Dodd chose then to reveal who they were matching wits against.

Lam said, "Let's hope General Khatami doesn't have any surprises waiting for us like he did with Von Ryan."

"I would if I were him," Billy Ray remarked.

"We'll have to be on our toes," Rinard said then went back to the bridge to fine tune the firing solution so he could engage the enemy. Lacking the sophisticated and modern targeting equipment of a boomer, this would be a pencil to paper shot solution.

Billy Ray zipped up his wetsuit and then inventoried the equipment brought aboard by Dodd and Egolf.

The most critical item was the dive gear: Draeger rebreathers, fins, and masks. But unlike in Texas, however, these dive masks appeared run-of-the-mill, except for the strange tint to the lenses. Also, with LP gas clouding the Edmund Challenger, he was never so thankful to have his non-magnetic MPK dive knife with him.

Egolf opened up one of his silver suitcases and began handing out toy guns like if it was Christmas in July. Actually, they were Co2 dart guns. Then the wiry agent explained their function before pulling more lethal goodies from Santa's bag, such as non-metallic munitions and non-flammable grenades developed by DARPA for military missions when sparks or heat could set the world on fire.

When Egolf opened the other metal case, and it contained various equipment for assaulting ships at sea, that's when Billy Ray got real suspicious.

How could Dodd have known the mission parameters?

'One if by land, two if by sea,' he remembered Egolf saying.

So did Dodd flip a coin before rejoining the team? Or did he have inside information, like somebody on the ship perhaps?

Billy Ray stared at the equipment and wondered what else he wasn't being told. The last thing he needed was to be kept in the dark and fed a bunch of shit like a mushroom.

His look must've given him away, because his friend and fellow warrior stopped what he was doing and faced him.

They knew each other too well.

"I can neither confirm nor deny your thoughts," Dodd said. "You'll just have to trust me one more time, Wolverine."

Billy Ray offered no remarks, they were in too deep now. And quite possibly, their tickets would all be punched soon anyway.

He nodded and resumed equipping himself for battle.

Captain Rinard returned to the Control Room, then paused before ordering the boat to periscope depth.

He scanned the many faces of his crew. Each was busy at their duty stations, and guided over by Torch Terrill acting as Officer of the Deck, or the OOD. Everyone was pulling double duty. Even Air Force major Von Ryan was chipping in beside Colon helping with radio communications.

Never had Rinard commanded a crew like this, on a mission like this, and for a cause like this.

Nor had he ever dreamed he would.

The fate of the nation was riding on the shoulders of these twenty-nine retired submariners and weekend enthusiasts inside of a seventy-five year old boat with no armament aboard. Floating a museum exhibit atop the water was one thing. While cycling an ancient submarine through the rigors of underwater combat was something else . . . it was bat shit crazy!

Furthermore, they were being asked to attack a massive lake freighter converted into a city-killer and crawling with terrorists, then disgorge their mysterious riders, and get away cleanly.

And yet the fact remained, here they were plowing through the waves at max speed of twenty-one knots with life and death teetering in the balance on how well both performed over the next few hours.

May God help them all, Rinard thought. Because just the act of submerging the Silversides for the first time in seven decades to periscope depth could ruin their day.

If they only they could have completed sea trials before getting the Admiral's call, then maybe—

Rinard stowed the doubt.

If America was to be saved, they had no choice.

Plus they needed to get off the surface before the terrorists shot at them with another of their Stinger missiles.

"Chief of the Boat Terrill—"

"Yes, Captain?"

<== PIPELINE ==>

"Let's test your theory."

Torch removed his chew toy. "Theory, sir?"

"The one about a frog's ass. Take us down to periscope depth. Dive the boat."

Torch straightened. "Periscope depth aye, sir! All hands . . . rig for dive! Rig for dive!" the COB shouted. "Helm make your depth five-eight feet."

The helmsman repeated the command, "Making my depth five-eight feet, aye."

Rinard stepped up to the periscope.

There was no turning back now.

The soldier operating the Edmund Challenger's navigation system motioned Qasem over.

He pointed at the display. "We have company."

Qasem straightened and scanned the horizon.

The soldier looked at Qasem, his eyes large behind the acrylic glass shield, like someone who'd just seen a ghost. Though his men's mounting tension as they neared their objective could cause that, too.

Soon they would all be communing with spirits.

Then Qasem dismissed the notion, as his navigator had been a naval officer and an expert in such matters.

"The lookouts have reported no ships."

"Not above the water, General. Beneath it!"

"A school of fish?"

"No, sir. I've checked and rechecked the image."

"A sunken wreck or submerged logs perhaps," Qasem suggested, then leaned closer to see the image reappear on the screen.

The man tapped the display.

"That's a submarine, and it's trailing us."

Qasem's own eyes got big behind the mask.

Submarine . . . but that was impossible!

The Americans had no such assets patrolling the Great Lakes.

Worse still, the Edmund Challenger was fixed to thwart attacks from surface craft and planes, not from hunters beneath the waves!

Qasem hurried from the bridge.

So far so good, Rinard thought after diving the boat to periscope depth without mishap. It appeared that the frog's ass was puckered up tight.

Prior to submerging, he'd ordered up max surface speed of twenty-one knots and set an intercept coarse for the Edmund Challenger. Upon nearing within ten miles of the freighter, he cut the boat's speed and submerged to avoid the same fate as Major Von Ryan's downed plane.

Even with the underwater speed half that of the Silverside's surface speed, Rinard still managed to eke an extra knot from the old girl due to her weight being lighter without full crew, consumables, and armament.

No one spoke as they gained on the Edmund Challenger, masking their presence by staying inside of the ship's prop wash.

Rinard pressed his face to the periscope eyecups and gripped the left and right training handles. As he'd stated to the Admiral, their one and only torpedo shot would be tricky, if not near impossible.

It would take a miracle.

"Flood forward number one torpedo tube," Rinard ordered.

Tina repeated the instructions and executed the command. "One flooded and pressurized."

"Open outer door," Rinard commanded and adjusted the periscope magnification until the enemy ship appeared nearly dead center in the azimuth circle.

Then he ordered another course correction to the helm and reduced the boat's depth.

Just a few more feet . . .

Finally, the stern portion of the Edmund Challenger came dead center in the crosshairs.

"Mark! Fire torpedo one!"

The COB pressed the fire button and said, "One away!"

Crewman Tina announced, "Confirmed, number one torpedo away!"

Rinard kept his eyes fixed firmly on the target and watched for a circular run by the Mark 18 torpedo, notorious for such failures.

While standing inside of the forward torpedo room, Billy Ray felt a jolt then heard a *swoosh* as the three thousand pound fish shot from the tube aided by an immense charge of compressed air.

Crewman Tina announced, "Number one torpedo away—"

But just then, a mighty explosion rocked the Silversides!

Then more booms came in quick succession that rocked the boat.

"AHHH!" Colon yelled and ripped off the sonar headphones.

"Right full rudder, all ahead flank! Take her deep, emergency!" Rinard shouted a string of commands over the din, blood dripping from a gash above one eye.

There were more explosions, but less severe, as the Silversides increased its speed and distance from the Edmund Challenger.

<====== PIPELINE ======>

"COB Stand Fast. Helm maintain course, depth and speed. Get us ta hell outa here."

"Standing fast, aye, sir!"

"Maintaining course, depth, and speed, aye, sir!"

Rinard lowered the periscope. Then he plucked a handkerchief from his pocket, pressed it against his bleeding brow, and descended back down to the bridge with the others.

"Action report," he ordered.

Damage reports began trickling in. Many of the crew had been tossed against the bulkheads, against machinery, or onto the deck with the first blasts. There was one potential broken arm. But thankfully, nothing more than cuts and bruises.

Those forward, had taken the worst of it, the Admiral and his team. One of the crewmembers was a doctor in his "normal" life and already attending the injured. Major Von Ryan hustled forward to lend the doc a hand.

The last to report was Creed, who'd led a damage control party to inspect the boat. "A few leaks here and there, particularly in the forward torpedo room. But the old gal held up pretty well."

Rinard heard a "but" in Creed's voice.

"What else, Mr. Creed?"

"That number one torpedo tube leak could be real trouble. I suggest we surface ASAP."

Billy Ray entered the bridge rubbing his shoulder, and just in time to hear Creed's report. "Negative, Captain. We're still in range of the Stinger missiles."

"Then we need to close it off or risk sinking," Creed replied.

Torch joined the group. "What the hell was that?" he asked, spraying bits of tobacco from a cigar mashed against the side of his face.

"Depth charges," Billy Ray said.

One of the modern-navy crew spoke up, "None like I've ever heard."

Creed took that one. "Of course not, sonny. Or we'd be on the bottom of the lake already."

"Mr. Creed's right," Dodd said, appearing from the forward torpedo room. "Those were the homemade kind. And you're right about tube one."

There was quiet on the bridge while everyone processed the new reality.

For Billy Ray's part, he was gaining vast respect for the enemy.

Lam was first to state the obvious.

"I think Khatami knows we're here."

Qasem had had to order the LP gas shut off while the depth charges were being deployed.

He was about to order the tanks reopened when the ship's navigator announced, "The Americans are pulling back, General. But we also seem to be drifting off course as well."

"Helmsman, report," Qasem ordered.

"The rudder isn't responding properly. It began a short time after the depth charges."

Qasem went to the secondary steering stand and tried the wheel. Indeed, the ship didn't respond to his command.

"Maybe the explosions damaged our rudder," the helmsman offered.

Qasem didn't think their improvised depth charges were responsible, but was stopped from saying so when the navigator waved him over.

"General, I may have the answer. After scrubbing out the sound signatures of our prop wash and other noises, I'm left with this. I swear to Allah that's the sound of a torpedo being fired."

The navigator handed Qasem a set of headphones.

Sure enough, Qasem heard mechanical sounds followed by a loud *swoosh* and sustained *whirring*. Then the sound was lost in the explosions.

He removed the headphones. "If that was a torpedo, then why are we not in paradise by now?"

The answer came from Tariq, "Because it was a dummy. Come look."

Qasem stared in disbelief at Tariq's computer screen.

"A World War II diesel-electric sub, nonetheless!" exclaimed Tariq.

"It's nothing more than a museum exhibit?" Qasem thought aloud.

He was torn between laughing or blowing up the Edmund Challenger out of disdain for the dumb Americans.

He did neither.

Instead, he ordered his chief engineer to the bridge.

After a short conference, it was decided the rudder was probably only jammed and could be fixed fairly rapidly.

Qasem blessed Allah for the good news.

Exploding the bomb now would do little to accomplish his nation's goals, and might even appear as failure in the eyes of the world.

He ordered the ship to full stop and sent a damage control team over the side.

Qasem cursed. *More minutes lost!*

But only minutes.

Allah was the keeper of time.

<=== PIPELINE ===>

"Divers in the water," Colon reported, using his good ear. "Three total."

"Oh shit!" Torch shouted loud enough for all to hear. He was standing by the escape trunk, from which the Admiral's team was to exit the boat. "Damn thing's stuck, Captain. Musta' been from those explosions."

Dodd and Billy Ray shot each other a glance. It was a look most warriors recognize when Plan A gets flushed down the toilet.

Lam the pessimist said, "Leaky boat, ruined escape hatch, now what?"

Billy Ray stated, "We improvise, adapt and overcome this obstacle."

Then he observed Lam straddling half in and half out of the forward torpedo room, one foot dry, the other shin deep in water. And his mind changed about pessimists.

Pessimists actually did perform a valuable role in society. Beyond brutal honesty and voicing what others lacked the balls to say, they kept the wheels of progress rolling. In plain view behind Lam were six torpedo tubes. And his contingency plan finally presented itself.

Losing no time, Billy Ray turned to the expert on torpedoes. "Tina, can you shoot us out of those tubes?"

Tina's face lost its color. "I—" she stuttered, "That'd be risky."

Egolf piped up, "More risky than if we didn't?"

"Well, I can't shoot you out using compressed air, the pressure would kill you for sure. You'll need to swim out."

Tina sized up Egolf, then she cast rapid glances at Dodd and Lam. Everyone knew why. Earlier, she'd given them the specs on the Mark 18 torpedo: weight, length, and the fish's twenty-one inch diameter.

She nodded at Lam and Egolf. "You two should squeeze out okay. You as well, Admiral." Then the group cast their collective eyes on Billy Ray. "But I'm not so sure about you Mr. Jenkins."

Lam came to Billy Ray's defense, sort of. "He's big boned."

Tina ignored the jibe. "And we have another problem. Only three of the six tubes were operational, and number one is out for sure now. So getting all four of you and your equipment outside of the boat using just two torpedo tubes could take longer than if we'd used the escape trunk."

Billy Ray thought fast. First off, he was definitely pushing the *width* limit, maybe an inch under, no more. Dodd was the next largest, but longer framed. Whereas, Lam was lean and Egolf was wiry. Neither of them would have trouble wriggling out of the tube, especially if they were assisted by an inflatable buoy and tether line.

"We'll double up," he announced.

"What do you have in mind?" Egolf asked.

"A squib load . . ." Billy Ray explained his idea to the group.

23

"Huh?" Lam said.

"Come on, Army. You know what a squib shot is, two in the chamber."

"Sure I know, Jenkins . . . all pop and no kick. I also know it never ends well when the trigger's pulled."

Dodd came to Billy Ray's defense. "He may have something there."

"Yeah, a death wish."

Dodd overlooked Lam's sarcasm.

"We can put two men in each tube. The first guy out will pull the second guy out with a tether and a marker buoy to offset the weight in the tube, and so on."

Lam sized up Billy Ray like Tina had done.

"I Told you to lay off those Meauwataka crackers, Navy boy. You're more like a cannonball than a bullet. What if you get stuck?"

Billy Ray acted offended. "I'll grease up for you, if that makes you feel better, Army."

Dodd put an end to the Army–Navy stuff.

"I say we go for it." Then he turned to Tina. "What say you, miss?"

Tina smiled. "Well, sir, I say we stuff them damn tubes."

After no small amount of wriggling and grunting and cussing, the tubes were "stuffed," to borrow Machinist's Mate Tina's words.

Or as Lam put it more crudely, after the crew jammed Billy Ray into the rear of the number four tube, "The meatballs are in the bun!"

Because of the tight confines, fins and rebreathers were left off and placed in front of each diver, except for the mouthpieces to provide oxygen and comms.

The rest of their gear was secured to the tether line in front, so that when the outer muzzle door opened, and the buoy inflated, the men and equipment would be pulled out of the submarine.

"Like a party popper, only in reverse," Lam declared still not sold.

Creed, Torch, and Tina assisted the Admiral's team with loading the equipment and stuffing the human torpedoes into the tubes.

With growing alarm, they did so while sloshing through cold Lake Michigan water pouring in from the damaged breach door of the number one tube.

Creed spotted the water cresting at the lip of the hatchway. Soon it would spill into the rest of the boat. Then a water leak normally posing minimal danger, would go critical.

If only they could surface, Creed thought.

<==== PIPELINE ====>

But they couldn't surface for fear of Stinger missiles.

Worse yet, the Silversides was at full stop while discharging its riders.

Just as the inner breech doors came shut, locking the Admiral and his men in the tubes, Creed saw the flood waters top the hatchway door.

And yet, there still remained the chore of operating the tubes and getting their occupants and gear outside of the boat.

Creed knew what he had to do, or else risk the boat and everyone sinking into the abyss. He'd known brave men during the war with Japan and Germany who made similar sacrifices to save their comrades. Perhaps he was spared then for this time now.

The end came to all men at some point.

"Get out, you two," Creed ordered.

Torch began a Torch-like objection to the boat's honorary X.O.

Creed cut him off. "Get out now! You, too, young lady."

"But the controls—" Tina began.

"I know how to work the controls."

Creed drove Torch and Tina out of the torpedo room and then dogged the hatch behind them. He didn't see all the grim faces turned his way. A reinforced steel door blocked the view.

Then he got busy pressurizing the torpedo tubes until they equalized with the outside water pressure at a seventy-foot depth.

And still the waters rose inside of the torpedo room, up to his waist now. But it was all up to him if the mission was to be a success.

And if not . . .

Creed didn't finish the thought.

"How much longer?" Qasem demanded to know.

His agitation was growing because this wasn't a part of his meticulous planning. The Edmund Challenger had its date with the city of Chicago.

The chief engineer radioed back saying that the divers were nearly finished dislodging the twenty-foot long dummy warhead wedged in the space between the rudder and hull.

"In fact," the chief engineer sneered, "the sub commander is the worst torpedo shot in the world. He missed the propeller entirely!"

For that, Qasem was grateful.

A broken propeller would have ended their journey many miles short of their objective. Then again, what should he expect from a seventy-five year old submarine?

"Allah be praised," Qasem replied to his chief engineer.

"So this is how a bullet feels," Lam said over the comms.

"No, a meatball," Billy Ray corrected.

Dodd cut in, "Save your breath, you two. Sound travels a long way underwater."

The chatter stopped.

The pressure equalized to the outside depth. Then both tubes filled with water and the outer breach doors opened.

Egolf and Lam let go of the inflated buoys, which shot immediately toward the surface, spooling the tether lines behind them.

Although they were only seventy feet down, each man knew to take precautions toward proper decompression. One didn't just rush up and down under water without paying a heavy price from nitrogen narcosis. Though with two Navy SEALs, an experienced former Green Beret, and whatever Egolf was, there should be no rookie mistakes like getting the bends.

Egolf was the first out of his torpedo tube, and wasted no time getting his dive gear on and then hauling out Dodd and the team's equipment.

Lam was slower for some reason, but finally made the break and got into his equipment. Then he pulled on the tether linked to Billy Ray and the gear. The line wouldn't budge and inch.

Lam pulled harder. Still no dice. "I think my meatball's stuck!"

Billy Ray could've smacked the Army guy. "Pull harder!"

Egolf and Dodd swam over to help. Each diver grabbed the tether line, braced their fins against the outer shell of the Silversides, and pulled on the count of three!

Billy Ray popped out of the torpedo tube, like a kid's jack-in-the-box, minus the music.

"How's that?" Lam slurred through the mouthpiece.

Billy Ray didn't reply. He was tempted to tell them all to get back in the boat and he'd go it alone.

Instead, he waved them off and began the long swim to the Edmund Challenger.

And a date with some very evil men.

The aft lookout radioed Qasem. "Two emergency buoys," he shouted into the radio. "Approximately six thousand yards at one-six-seven relative bearing. It appears we sunk the submarine."

"Any signs of its crew or debris?" Qasem asked.

"No, General."

<== **PIPELINE** ==>

Qasem knew about submarine rescues.

A human body could only take so much. The lake bottom here was nearly three hundred feet, far and away enough pressure to crush a person caught outside the boat. Better to let help arrive with submersible recovery equipment.

He was pleased to be surrounded by expert soldiers and sailors from the Quds. Every man was worth their weight in gold.

"Very good. Carry on," he ordered the lookout.

The next call came from Bashir over closed circuit TV inside of the central hold.

Bashir's face came into view on the tiny TV screen, obscured behind the mask protecting him from cement powder and radioactive contamination.

"General, I wish to report the nuclear casks have been breached," said Bashir, his voice muffled. "All is ready for detonation."

As proof, Bashir held up a radiation dosimeter badge. It was already turning red, indicating the brave *shahid's* level of exposure to gamma rays. If not for everyone's soon-coming death when the ship exploded, these men would not see another sunrise.

The camera wasn't aimed toward the casks, but it showed Qasem's group of martyrs prostrated on their rugs devoutly praying to Allah.

Qasem was pleased.

The brash young man turned out not to be a problem after all. Bashir had even been the one to suggest the LP gas failsafe.

"I shall see you in paradise, my young lion."

"That you shall, General."

Bashir turned away and went to his prayer rug.

Twenty minutes later, Qasem's chief engineer radioed to report the rudder fixed and the divers being retrieved.

Even before leaving the Silversides, Billy Ray had balked at the time and energy needed to swim three nautical miles under water, then be fresh enough to battle scores of scores of proficient Quds Force commandos.

But Dodd said not to worry, that he had it covered.

Billy Ray now knew what Dodd meant that day he walked out of the flying saucer in Muskegon then proceeded to show off his prosthetics. He'd said the legs allowed him to run faster than Usain Bolt.

Amazingly, that land speed transferred equally under water.

The man was a human torpedo!

With the use of special fins and helmet, and trailing a tow rope, he pulled the whole team in tight formation at an astonishing eleven miles per hour, twice the speed of the fastest human swimmer on record timed in a fifty meter pool, and then doing so for a thousand times that length while pulling three men. Moreover, Dodd's mechanical legs pumped out most of the work, leaving him barely winded.

Billy Ray decided against challenging Dodd to a game of basketball.

Dodd stopped the team a hundred yards from the Edmund Challenger.

Then Egolf let go of the tether and rose slowly to the surface. He popped just the top of his head above water and pressed waterproof 10 X 50 binoculars with an infrared range finder to his face and began radioing his observations to the team.

Billy Ray and Dodd used the information to finalize the plan of attack.

The first big problem would be surprising enemy divers making their repairs in shallow water in broad daylight, especially in the clear waters of Lake Michigan.

So Dodd towed the team in a wide circle to the bow of the Edmund Challenger.

At that point, Lam and Egolf held up, while Billy Ray and Dodd continued swimming aft along the ship's keel. Dodd cautioned Lam and Egolf that if the ship started to move to get out of the way or they'd be crushed in its bow wake.

Colon had verified a trio of enemy divers.

Sure enough, there were three men focusing their undivided attention on Captain Rinard's damage to their ship's rudder, but taking no measure to post a lookout.

The Draeger rebreathers gave off no indication of Billy Ray and Dodd's presence—no bubbles, no noise.

Because the enemy likely employed comms in their dive equipment also, it was vital to prevent them from alerting others on the deck during the attack.

So they waited until the enemy divers finished their repairs then began reboarding the ship via a long accommodation ladder.

After his two comrades left the water, the third enemy diver made one last inspection of their work. Then he, too, headed for the ladder.

That's when they struck!

Dodd pumped his robotic legs and shot from their hiding place like an underwater high-speed torpedo.

The enemy diver never knew what hit him.

Before he could so much as yelp, Dodd yanked away the man's mouthpiece and slashed his throat with a dive knife.

<===== PIPELINE =====>

A red cloud spread rapidly in the cold waters. Thank heaven there were no sharks in Lake Michigan.

Billy Ray arrived a moment later and secured the man's oxygen tank from spewing bubbles. Then he pulled the diver deeper until his struggle for life ended and he sank into the depths.

"Not bad for an old guy," Billy Ray said upon his return.

"Old man, new legs," Dodd said, his brow furrowed behind the mask.

The plan now was for one of them to scale the ladder and eliminate the other two divers, and anyone else assisting the dive team.

Dodd volunteered for that chore as well.

"Again, Dolittle? You'll need to tear up your AARP card."

"Once a SEAL always a SEAL," Dodd said. "Besides, I'm testing these new prosthetics for our wounded warriors."

"Usain Bolt. Michael Phelps. Who next, Tarzan?"

"No, Cheetah!" Dodd said and rocketed away.

Billy Ray concluded Dodd was having way too much fun!

Qasem had nearly worn a path in the vinyl decking on the bridge.

The chief engineer was off on his estimate of the repair time for the rudder.

Already fifteen minutes more were gone, and causing another delay with Tehran's missile launch timetable.

Though strangely, there'd been no sign of the Americans. It had been over two hours since Bashir shot down the Air Force jet.

Surely U.S. forces weren't asleep at the switch.

Someone must be coming.

The bridge phone rang. It was the chief engineer again.

"Report!" Qasem snapped a bit too quickly.

"They're done, General. Start the engines."

Qasem replaced the bridge phone and then gave a nod to the engine order telegraph operator. A moment later, the ship powered up, and the old steamer got underway.

Even from his place on the forward bridge, the Edmund Challenger's fixed pitch propeller caused noticeable thrust and deck vibrations.

Qasem walked out onto the bridge wing to fill his lungs with fresh air before reordering the LP tanks opened and donning his gas mask.

He tasted the air's freshness, knowing it would be for the last time.

Their target lay just a few miles ahead—

And paradise a blink of an eye beyond that.

Billy Ray was awed by the way Dodd monkeyed up the long flight of stairs, and quietly, too.

Cheetah could take some lessons from the Admiral.

Dodd stopped just shy of the main deck, reached in his equipment bag, and retrieved what looked like a yellow boomerang.

Or a banana, Billy Ray allowed.

Dodd twisted the device and flung it over the gunnel. The weapon arced in midair and then landed among the enemy.

Curiously, there was no sound of any type, only a rapid spinning light inside a sickly purple vapor cloud, like a killer disco ball and fog machine from a Travolta movie.

Another of Dolittle's creepy inventions, Billy Ray concluded. James Bond's Q had nothing on Dolittle.

In either case, the dance was over for two more bad guys, he noted stepping over their still bodies and joining Dodd.

Why he wasn't dead too was probably owed to the dive mask.

But then what about the poison? It was obviously more permeating than LP gas.

Dodd caught Billy Ray's concern.

"Light-activated poison. Once the tiny gas molecules enter the lungs, it travels to the autonomic center of the brain. Upon activation by a specific wavelength of light penetrating the eyes . . ."

Dodd saw the usual bored-to-tears look on Wolverine's face and cut the science lesson short.

"It stops their breathing. Our dive masks are coated with a special UV film to protect us."

"Like sunscreen for the eyeballs," Billy Ray said.

"Only in the blast zone, Jenkins. Now let's get to work."

Dodd called for Lam and Egolf to join the party.

The team crouched partially hidden at the top of the accommodation ladder. The free moments for staging their attack would be over the second the dead divers failed radio contact.

Fortunately, much of their plan had already been mapped out on the Silversides, complete with blueprints of the Edmund Challenger loaded on their wrist dive computers.

It was to be a two-pronged attack: capture or render useless the detonator, then scuttle the ship before it could explode by any other means, particularly blue on blue.

Egolf and Lam were tasked with seizing the forward bridge to terminate General Qasem Khatami and secure the trigger mechanism.

Of course, nobody was naive enough to think that the Iranian general would be caught resting a sweaty thumb on a red plastic button like they do in the movies. They were dealing with a diabolical genius and experienced military leader of a nation-state. The detonator would incorporate high-tech devices and redundancies.

The area of operations, or AO, for Dodd and Billy Ray would be below decks, since there was the matter of first burying the nuclear containment casks in the hydraulic cement before scuttling the ship.

That was the foiling the dirty bomb part of the plan, anyway.

But dropping their odds of success considerably, was Billy Ray not knowing which of the Challenger's holds contained what materials.

He couldn't just go throwing open the doors hoping to get lucky, he might find himself buried under a slurry of skin-dissolving ANNM, or even spark an earth-shattering explosion. According to Lam he could stand to lose a few pounds, but that option was a tad extreme. Furthermore, a burst of radioactivity would definitely spoil his plans for a long life with Rebecca.

Yet, none of that really mattered now, since Dodd had failed to win time for escaping the ship before it sank to the bottom of Lake Michigan.

Only one thing truly mattered.

Saving Chicago.

Captain Rinard got the *all-clear* from the Admiral. The dive team had successfully extracted themselves from the submarine.

Plus, by Sonar Tech Colon's reckoning, they were now two nautical miles Southwest of the Silversides traveling inhumanly fast.

How Dodd and his men accomplished that, Rinard had no idea. Unless they were being pulled by a ski boat.

Regardless, it was time to get the hell out of the area.

So without further delay, he ordered all ahead flank toward shore to gain shallow water. If the flooding worsened while staying submerged getting beyond the range of enemy missiles, then at least he could set the boat on the bottom where they would all have a better chance at getting rescued.

A better hope, however, was that they could surface into the loving arms of the Coast Guard.

It would be close.

But the fact there were any options at all left for the Silversides and its crew was made possible by a very brave World War II veteran. Once again, Creed was an American hero.

Per Dodd's instruction, they wore dive masks on and breathed through the Draegers, allegedly for the LP gas saturating the atmosphere. Not to mention that choking on cement dust would be a very bad idea.

But after witnessing Dodd's badass banana boomerangs, Billy Ray wasn't about to argue. But still, how could Dodd have predicted a water interdiction, the boarding equipment necessary for the job, or the omission of heat and spark-producing armament?

Just then, the Challenger's big fixed pitch propeller came alive and the team elevated each of their pneumatic dart guns.

The sight of the specialized weapons, the strange poison gas grenades, as well as the rest of the sci-fi gear in Egolf's suitcases prior to the team knowing about the enemy ship, down to how they overtook the freighter, confirmed Billy Ray's suspicion—

Admiral Dodd had an agent aboard the ship!

As the Edmund Challenger got back underway, Qasem couldn't help feeling a sense of relief. No military general enjoyed a stationary posture in war over that of forward movement.

His relief was exceptionally short lived.

Prior to commencing combat operations, the team was forced to make a few assumptions. The first item being that disabling the freighter before sinking it was a no-go.

The bad guys would just trigger the bomb then and there.

Secondly, it was determined that the Edmund Challenger was riding too high in the water for the amount of weight in its cargo holds. She was a shallow draft cargo ship. That could only mean downtown Chicago was General Khatami's end target. And given that, then navigating the freighter up the Chicago River would be critical to his plan.

So it made perfect sense to Billy Ray why the Challenger's ballast tanks had been pumped dry. Although ship handling would suffer to a degree, it was clear Khatami's intention was to avoid grounding the Jinx Ship short of the desired kill zone.

But one man's problem could be another man's solution.

Those same empty ballast tanks would provide *safe* transit to the forward bridge, as well as additional breach points for the flood waters.

However, there had also been a second choice debated by the team for avoiding the enemy and main passageways.

<===== PIPELINE =====>

Being a bulk carrier, the Edmund Challenger employed a self-unloading system that used a ship-long conveyor belt and tunnel to discharge its cargo.

But Billy Ray won that argument, claiming the conveyor system machinery would alert the bad guys.

Not to mention that if one of their team failed to get off the moving belt in time, they'd be spit overboard.

So the plan was to breach the ballast tanks and move to the length of the ship to the forward wheel house before engaging Allah's faithful. Then Lam and Egolf would battle their way topside, while Billy Ray and Dodd worked as a two-man SEAL team exposing each of the cargo holds and opening the sea valves.

If the plan worked, the Edmund Challenger would flood in minutes and sink like a bag of wet cement before the bad guys could trigger the bomb.

The final warning from Dodd was for each man to break free of the sinking ship as quickly as possible, or face getting sucked to the bottom of Lake Michigan.

Then Dodd said, "We have less than an hour before the Air Force launches their missiles. Good luck and Godspeed."

Billy Ray nodded. "Let's roll."

The team left the O-1 level and arrived at the ballast tanks without incident, then went their separate ways.

Billy Ray took point, Dodd their six.

The hatch to the port side ballast tank was carelessly unguarded.

They entered the cavernous space and switched on their head lamps. The light penetrated a short distance before getting swallowed by the darkness. Then they began sloshing forward in ankle-deep water.

After only a few feet, Billy Ray stopped. A voice in his head reminded him of one of Murphy's laws of combat—*the easy way is always mined.*

"What is it, Wolverine?" asked Dodd, stopped several steps behind.

"Too painless— Team Two, hold up."

"Holding," Egolf replied. "What's on your mind, Jenkins?"

"There's four hundred feet of darkness ahead. A few bad guys can't secure a ship this large. If it was me, I'd set traps to cover my six."

"But wouldn't an explosion set off the bomb?" Lam cut in.

Dodd was also trained in *guerrilla* warfare. "Consider all options. But keep in mind we have less than sixty minutes before the Air Force blows us all up, less if POTUS changes his mind."

It happened fifty feet later.

Billy Ray spotted a suspicious line of new eyebolts fixed to the bulkheads, then a thin wire circling through the dark water and up to a cotter pin. The eyebolts had no rust on them.

He and Dodd shined their head lamps upward. The light exposed a heavy steel plate ready to crush unwanted intruders.

"Tripwires!" Billy Ray declared over the comms.

"Got it!" Egolf reported a moment later.

Lam said, "Good thing, too. I left my aspirin in my other pants."

Both teams minded their steps but only encountered one more set of booby traps, twin head-knockers to the others.

They'd each memorized the ship's blue prints, their rendezvous points, and the route of attack. So when the moment came to exit the ballast tanks, they were prepared for trouble.

They didn't have long to wait.

Egolf and Lam got the first challenge, though the speedy marksman had poison darts in the necks of two terrorists before Lam even got his weapon up. Then a heartbeat later, while approaching the team's rendezvous point at the ladder leading to the pilothouse, where Khatami was directing his evil plot, Billy Ray and Dodd were treated to the same experience, as a muscular terrorist with a machete strapped to his back and trousers half undone burst from a stateroom and nearly collided with Billy Ray.

The terrorist didn't hesitate.

The machete was out in an instant, and arcing toward Billy Ray's head, when a feathery dart suddenly appeared poking out of the man's Adam's apple, or *laryngeal prominence,* as Dodd would probably describe it in his usual scientific detail.

"Damn, Dolittle. Where'd you learn to shoot like that?"

"The practice range, Wolverine. You really oughta try it some time."

Touché! Billy Ray thought as he lowered the bulky terrorist to the deck, gratified he didn't have to 'rastle the dude.

Billy Ray leaned the dead guy against the ladderway and noted how the man wasn't wearing a gas mask. That had to mean General Khatami was either keeping the interior spaces airtight or that the LP gas hadn't yet permeated the lower levels.

Dodd's order was for the team to keep their masks on. And after seeing what happens during the magic banana light show, there was no argument from Billy Ray.

However, trying to battle villains while sucking air through the Draeger rebreathers put him at a terrible disadvantage, rather like duking it out in a bar fight with a bread bag pulled over your head.

<===== PIPELINE =====>

Without waiting to discuss the matter, Billy Ray pointed at the terrorist and pulled off his mask.

Dodd nodded and removed his mask, too. Egolf and Lam arrived just then and did the same.

Egolf shot a look at their motionless guest, then down the passageway at the closed doors of several staterooms.

"No time to recon them," Dodd said, knowing what his number two man was considering.

Billy Ray took quick stock of the shipboard phase of their mission.

So far so good, he thought, counting five dead terrorists thus far. Plus the team had managed to travel the length of the ship without detection or mishap.

How many more bad guys there were aboard the Edmund Challenger, and where they all were, had come down to guestimation. Before leaving the Silversides, they'd used intel from Von Ryan's flyover to estimate the number of jihadis, what they needed to execute their dastardly plan, as well as for crewing the big freighter.

Best guess . . . fifty combatants, minus five now, unless Khatami was using hostages to operate the ship. Though knowing the insular nature of terrorists, that seemed vastly unlikely.

Just then, Billy Ray's thoughts were interrupted by a clanging noise of something bouncing down the metal stairs.

He knew instantly what made that kind of sound—

A grenade!

24

The bridge phone was keeping Qasem busy.

"We have a problem," the chief engineer said. "Our damage control team was just found dead."

Qasem struggled to hear the man's voice because of the gas mask.

"Two divers, no sign of struggle . . . checking their air tanks for contamination. The third diver is missing."

What could that mean? Qasem wondered, dread rising in his mind.

The captain of the guard entered onto the bridge. "Sir, two of my men are failing to respond to radio calls. We may have boarded by intruders."

All at once, a loud cry of Allahu Akbar came from the deck below!

Qasem recognized the voice as the lone guard stationed outside of the staterooms guarding the female hostages.

Then the soldier's battle cry cut off mid-throat—

"We're under attack!" the captain of the guard shouted. Then with lightning reflexes, unclipped a grenade and tossed it down the ladderway.

But how . . . Who—? Qasem wondered as the bridge door was slammed shut to protect against flying shrapnel and igniting LP gas.

Then he knew.

That damn submarine!

A Russian RGO-78 frag grenade landed on the deck in the middle of the team.

Time could seem to stand still in a man's mind—fractions of seconds stretching into eternity.

But not for Billy Ray. He grabbed the dead terrorist and plopped them both on top of the grenade, as though it were a fumbled football and the team's only hope to see another Sunday was gaining its possession.

The blast heaved four hundred-plus pounds of human weight skyward.

Billy Ray was slammed against the overhead then crashed back to the deck atop the eviscerated terrorist.

But for the bruises to come, he was unscathed.

Better yet, the team was alive!

"Mr. President, the freighter is approaching the target area," the SecDef announced, pointing at the real-time satellite feed on the monitor.

The Chairman of the Joint Chiefs added, "I advise we wait no longer."

"Hold steady," the Senior Advisor stated emphatically.

<==== PIPELINE ====>

POTUS eyeballed each member as they spoke. Usually, his poker face hid the value of his cards.

But not today. Not with his decision boiling down between losing a great city or poisoning the fifth largest fresh water lake on the planet for a thousand generations to come.

What if Dodd was right—both doomsday scenarios could be avoided?

"Mr. President? Our jets are standing by," the CJCS repeated.

"Not yet, General. Admiral Dodd gets his way . . . for now."

POTUS could hear doubt rising in his own voice, and the people surrounding him could also hear it.

"It's on," Egolf said.

Lam crossed himself, and Billy Ray knew why.

Inside of the hard-boiled agent's vest was a photo showing a little girl with big brown eyes and a pink Rainbow Brite shirt.

"Let's do this," Billy Ray said, offering no well-wishes or bear hugs, all stuff for later over beers . . . if they survived.

Everyone nodded. And the teams went to war with a vengeance.

Egolf and Lam prepared to attack the pilot house, while Billy Ray and Dodd disappeared for the ship's holds.

Mostly from habit, Billy Ray took point. But Dodd stopped him and came around front.

They proceeded quickly past the crews quarters, conducting proper two-man room-clearing maneuvers past each door, until arriving at the ship's small mess.

Dodd held up, raising his balled fist in the air.

Billy Ray heard it, too. A muted sound came from the galley.

With his poison dart gun at the ready, Billy Ray proceeded, placing his steps carefully, quietly. He peeked around the bulkhead.

There trussed up like a holiday turkey, and lashed to the legs of a deep sink, was the ship's cook straining to free himself, but to no avail.

Billy Ray signaled to Dodd and then entered the kitchen.

Upon seeing Billy Ray's menacing black dry suit, rebreather, and other combat equipment, the man's almond-shaped eyes got immense. But it was the dart gun that made him scream behind the silver duct tape covering his mouth.

Billy Ray touched a finger to his lips and made the sign of the cross, then cut the man free.

The man tore the tape off his face, exposing Asian features. "Thank God!" Then he looked around. "My shipmates—?"

Dodd appeared, also dressed to kill. "There are more of you?"

The man nodded. "And from another ship, too. The terrorists tied me up last after forcing me to feed them." They said they'd behead a woman hostage in front of me if I didn't.

Billy Ray and Lam looked at each other, their thoughts the same.

Hostages!

"What's your name?" Billy Ray asked.

"Nguyen," the man said taking his feet. "Are you guys the police?"

"Something like that," Dodd said.

Billy Ray got down to business. "Hostages—how many and where?"

"My crew, plus the others . . . seventy men and four women. All in the first hold . . . the men, anyway." Nguyen lowered his eyes.

Seventy-four hostages, and women too!

The number shocked Billy Ray. How could they stop the terrorists in time and still save all those people?

Dodd showed more confidence. "We're headed there now. Follow us."

Several quick moments later, they stood in front of the sliding doors to the number one hold, thankful they hadn't run into any terrorists, but knowing it wouldn't be long. Whether General Khatami believed the hostages were loose, or whether a military team was aboard, Billy Ray had no clue. Either way, the response would be just as deadly.

"Hurry," Billy Ray said.

He and Dodd posted to the sides weapons at the combat ready stance, while Nguyen actuated the controls.

The large doors slid open and a group of pissed off crewmen rushed out wielding an assortment of tools, looking for terrorist heads to thump!

They nearly trampled Nguyen, and would've if their leader hadn't eventually recognized the ship's cook.

He was a man about Billy Ray's age with massive freckled arms wielding a two-foot long spanner wrench. And standing behind these were dozens more men prepared to brawl.

Fortunately, Nguyen had the presence of mind to jump in front of Dodd and Billy Ray to prevent any misunderstanding. Or put another way, the worst mismatch ever!

"No, Tony." Nguyen raised his hands. "They're here to save us!"

Billy Ray said, "We're all about to be blown out of the water."

Tony stepped forward, the wrench still at the ready. "But this ship's loaded with some really bad shit, man."

Billy Ray nodded at Dodd. "We're here to put a stop to that."

"Just the two of you?" the big guy asked.

"No. Three more," Dodd replied.

<===== PIPELINE =====>

Billy Ray shot Dodd a fast, hard look.

So the Admiral DID have someone aboard the Challenger!

"How can we help?" Tony asked, others nodding at the question.

Dodd took over.

"You civilians will give the terrorists false hope so that my team can get a jump on the bastards."

Dodd gave the men a quick rundown on the terrorists' plan, and how the freighter was indeed rigged for "some really bad shit." Then he pulled an extra set of comms from his waterproof tac bag and handed it to Nguyen.

"Form a team. Then go topside and shut off the LP gas. After that, get the hell off this ship."

Nguyen pointed to the seventy-plus men in the hold. "Everyone? How are we going to do that?"

Billy Ray thought fast.

He'd been racking his brain about how to escape the Edmund Challenger as it sank. A ship this size would pull everyone and everything near it to the bottom, like a giant bathtub whirlpool going down the drain, sucking everything and everyone with it.

Their battle plan had Lam and Egolf operating topside. If they lived through that, they'd possible get over the side in time.

Dodd would be midship opening the holds to the floodwaters. So the Admiral, too, should be able to escape.

But for Billy Ray, in the bowels of the freighter tending the seacocks, survival hadn't yet presented itself.

Until now.

Looking into the hold, normally filled with cement powder, human cargo filled the space instead. And the way to lasting life came to him.

"Here's what we'll do . . ."

Qasem stood close to Tariq, observing the young genius transfer the detonation codes onto a handheld device.

If indeed American Special Forces had managed to board the mother of all bombs, then it was time to send them to the depths of hell!

He ordered the engine room to redline the boilers and squeeze every bit of speed from the old ship, to get the bomb closer to landfall. Until then, his brave soldiers would safeguard him and the detonator until the last possible second.

Already, the Ferris wheel at the Navy Pier grew inside his binoculars. Every inch closer increased the impending death toll.

A part of him wished to remain behind to witness the new world order. Though such temptation was only human, he acknowledged.

No man naturally wished to die.

But with the alluring promise of paradise—

"General," the navigator called out. "The indicator light for the number one hold just flashed ON."

Qasem hurried across the bridge to the operations panel. Of the eight holds, all status lights showed red but one. "The hostages," he said. "*They* killed our divers and now the others?"

"One of the crew must've been overlooked," the navigator replied.

Nevertheless, the dread of defending against trained military intruders waned. While further lessening Qasem's concern was how none of his agents ashore had warned of hostile aircraft heading to attack the Edmund Challenger. Nothing. Not even a flyover.

It had been nearly two hours since Bashir shot down the Air Force jet.

The Americans were timid overseas, but on their homeland—?

The aft lookout crackled over the ships radio, "Hostages loose on the main deck . . . they're rushing for the LP tanks!"

The last of Qasem's dread turned to contempt—ragtag Americans were no match for his Quds, especially without firearms.

"Units One and Two, get topside. Destroy those infidels!"

The aft lookout kept up the live-action report, "Whoa! Two of our Quds down, smashed over the head with iron tools . . . their gas masks taken."

From their stations below, seven Iranian commandos took the fastest routes topside. Then in moments, the after lookout began describing what sounded like tribal warfare between men with clubs and machetes.

Qasem went to the back porthole on the bridge, and viewed aft at the long low-profile of the ship's midsection, with its many hatch covers atop the eight holds, and the long discharging boom at the stern.

Then he imagined the death below decks, and how in just minutes it would be too late for the Americans to launch any response at all.

Already he could detonate the ship and cause the worst ecological disaster since Noah's Flood.

But his heart told him to wait for more.

Qasem observed the skirmish raging on the deck.

At least three dozen more hostages arrived from various doors and hatchways. A few hostages joined their shipmates with pipes and other tools and battled three of Qasem's soldiers, while the rest went straight for the LP tanks, turning them off or pushing them overboard. Then they jumped ship like scared rats. A couple of the American cowards even ran toward the rear of the ship to get away.

<====== PIPELINE ======>

Finally, the two Quds units appeared and joined the battle.

They came in swinging their machetes, chopping down two of the hostages before severing the head of the man with large freckled arms and blood-soaked wrench . . . Persian blood!

On seeing the heads of their friends roll across the deck, the remaining hostages fled the fight and dove over the side to save themselves.

Qasem turned from the porthole, disgusted by the weak Americans and immensely proud of his Quds Force teams.

Then he noticed the air clearing as the wind dissipated the propane gas. So he tore off the restrictive mask.

His crew did the same even though the gas lingering inside the bridge would take a bit longer to clear. But no worry, the rotten egg smell was trumped by the sweet taste of victory.

"Switch to firearms," Qasem announced to the bridge crew and over the 1MC.

But before he or anyone could retrieve their guns, the bridge door exploded with a mighty roar.

The captain of the guard and others near the door were killed instantly.

While others, such as the navigator and helmsman seated in front of their instruments, were slammed violently into machinery, and now lay unconscious or bleeding profusely twisting in pain.

Qasem was spared from the force of the blast by having been near the back porthole. However, he'd also been partially buried under one of his dead Quds soldiers. He fought to clear his senses. His ears were bleeding and he was somewhat deaf from the overpressure of the confined blast. Men moaned from injuries or coughed from the thick acrid smoke clouding the bridge.

Someone called out his name. Tariq perhaps?

Qasem glanced toward Tariq's chair near the portside bridge wing, but failed to penetrate the smoke.

Where was his second detonator, or even Tariq's computer with the trigger codes and all of their mission's intel?

Then two ghostly figures in black dive gear and pointing strange guns charged onto the bridge!

Being a bulk carrier, the Edmund Challenger employed a self-unloading conveyor system that ran the length of the ship in the 'tunnel' space beneath the holds. Cargo would drop through a hopper and ride the conveyor to a discharge boom that jettisoned the raw materials hundreds of feet onto the pier or barge.

Billy Ray and Dodd left the captives with hope, then hurried off.

Behind them, a deck cover was removed, exposing a large conical hopper and conveyor belt. Man after man after man dropped onto the moving belt until all the remaining hostages rode to the stern, then lifted to deck level, and deposited two hundred feet off the ship through the discharge boom. They were now far enough away to avoid the big suck when the ship sank.

Yet, the great escape would've ended in disaster if not for two very brave volunteers who made it to the discharge boom to work the controls.

Egolf and Lam's attack on the bridge added further cover and chaos.

The volunteers reached the boom in time to save their mates.

Of course, courageous men died that others might live.

The blood of true martyrs, Billy Ray thought.

Tony and the others hadn't baulked, only resigned themselves to the fact they were dead already, and so why not take a few of the sons of bitches with them!

Billy Ray couldn't blame them for their sense of vengeance. He'd been guilty of taking lives in the same manner—sometimes depressing the trigger on full auto a bit longer than necessary.

A bad omen for warriors, Billy Ray thought.

Killing another human being wasn't always murder, but it was no less a bloody stain on one's soul.

He and Dodd approached the second hold on the run.

But surprisingly, Dodd passed him to take point, and kept on going.

With the threat of propane gas negligible below decks, they'd switched armament from Dodd's Martian play toys to their more normal tricked out SOCOM pistols for close quarters work.

A good thing, too, because only a few feet later, two very bad dudes came out of the athwartship passage between holds #2 and #3 and turned their way.

Everyone lifted their weapons.

The bad guys laid down cover fire and ducked back into the port-starboard passageway.

Inside of the metal walls on a ship, ricocheting bullets could be equally dangerous, with little need for cautious aim.

Lead pinged off the walls and deck and overhead.

Billy Ray felt two rounds clip him, one across his forearm, and one lodging somewhere in his dive equipment.

Dodd, however, took a direct hit to his left leg. But that too made a pinging sound as it ricocheted off the titanium prosthetic.

"Okay, now what?"

"Masks on," Dodd ordered and then pulled out one of his yellow Cheetah snacks.

Billy Ray hoped like hell the last ricochet hadn't punctured his mask or rebreather, or else he'd soon be a dead disco duck, too.

Dodd twisted the curved yellow laser-activated gas grenade and chucked it forward. With deadly accuracy, the device boomeranged around the corner and exploded near the two terrorists.

After another wicked light show, Dodd gave the GO signal. As they trotted past the passageway, Billy Ray saw two very deceased enemy soldiers.

A moment later, Dodd lifted a clenched fist and brought them to halt in front of the third hold. A plaque on the heavy door read *3-E.*

Dodd wrapped on the door using a code of three slow taps, then five rapid ones, and stepped back.

Billy Ray had his gun at the ready as the hold doors slid open.

Standing in the opening with his hands at his sides, a gas mask concealing his face, and dressed in firemen turnout gear, was a terrorist.

Dodd didn't react, Billy Ray noticed. So he lowered his gun too.

"Let me guess . . . Panther?"

Dodd made no introductions, neither did the tall stranger.

"Way above my paygrade, I take it," Billy Ray said sarcastically.

Dodd finally spoke. "Correct."

Panther thumbed over his shoulder at two rows of terrorists bent face down on their prayer rugs. "Dead . . . and the casks are safe, just as you ordered, Admiral."

Ten dead Iranian commandos . . .? How'd the guy manage that?

Billy Ray felt demoted to third string quarterback.

"Sorry, Wolverine. We finish the job, then you forget you ever met this man. Do I make myself crystal clear?"

"Clear as mud, Dolittle."

"Good. Now don't you have a ship to sink, sailor?"

"Aye aye, sir."

"And Jenkins—" Dodd stopped him with a hand on Billy Ray's arm. "Sir?"

"May God be with you, my friend."

Then surprisingly, the Middle Eastern man offered a Christian sendoff, but in *Pashto,* the language of Afghanistan.

Billy Ray two-finger saluted and ran off.

He had a job to do, and so did John Dodd and the mysterious Panther. *Sink the Edmund Challenger.*

Lam heard moaning as he entered the ruined bridge.

Bodies stirred.

Then a man lifted to his knees, drew a weapon, and took aim.

Egolf put a poison dart in the guy's right eye.

An eye blink later, Lam stuck a poison prick in the neck of another terrorist, and then scanned the foggy room for more trouble.

The air began clearing rapidly from the blown out windshields, so he and Egolf switched to their Beretta 9mm hand guns.

At least eight more combatants materialized.

They regained their senses and grabbed for weapons while jostling for cover.

He and Egolf unloosed lead hell, and downed most of them.

Then a flash of sunlight off metal caught Lam's eye—out on the port bridge wing.

He spun around to meet the dark, foreboding eyes of a terrorist.

Strangely, the guy wore chinos and a college varsity jacket, rather than the stolen blue Coast Guard Operational Dress Uniforms like all the other terrorists.

The man looked away and swiftly stuffed a laptop computer into an aluminum case. Then he pitched a palm-sized device back onto the bridge and completed his escape.

Lam ducked as a dark rectangular object sailed over his head and landed at the rear of the bridge.

A grenade?

Egolf saw it too. "Down!"

But nothing happened.

Egolf made a scramble for the mystery device just as gunfire erupted on the enclosed bridge.

A bullet whizzed past by Lam's ear from a terrorist lying prone near the helm.

He shot the man, hitting him in the throat, then turned back in time to see the college guy disappear down a vertical ladder with the metal case under his arm.

"Lam, get that computer!" Egolf shouted. "I got this. Now go!"

Lam bolted from the gun battle on the bridge, just as more shots rang out, one of them spinning Egolf around.

The last thing he saw of Egolf before he descended down the ladder, was the brave sniper holding a rectangular object in a bloody hand . . . as well as two more dead assholes!.

<===== PIPELINE =====>

Billy Ray sprinted the football field-long passageway of the Edmund Challenger, passing by staterooms and equipment spaces, ducking through hatch after hatch, on his way to the stern and the sea valves below. He swept the menacing Mark 23 Special Operations Command pistol from side to side. If a bad guy showed himself now, they'd get a .45 slug in the forehead.

What Billy Ray didn't count on, and should have, was someone with similar training to his own, waiting in ambush. Fortunately, his ducking while going through another hatch saved his life. But it didn't save him from an enemy bullet passing clean through his black neoprene diving hood and creasing the top of his scalp. It gave him a new part in his hair to comb.

Though stunned, he rolled and came up squeezing the trigger.

An enemy soldier receded behind a bulkhead to reload.

But when the source of Billy Ray's splitting headache peeked around the corner for another shot, he got a .45 caliber beaning. Billy Ray proceeded on, careful to avoid the blood and brains spreading on the non-skid deck.

Admiral Dodd finished inspecting the massive nuclear containment casks, and felt a sense of relief.

But they weren't out of the woods yet!

He turned and faced the deepest, darkest, secret operative he'd ever recruited to the K-KEY Group, if "recruited" was a word at all applicable to Ter Meer Khan.

Some men and women were imbued with immeasurable drive that powered their pursuits.

Some men and women owned an unshakable sense of justice.

And still others possessed vast talent and ingenuity.

Ter Meer Khan, aka Panther, had all of those and more.

"Comms?" asked Khan after shedding the firemen gear.

"Sorry, Panther, it went to a hostage. But I do have this for you."

Dodd handed Khan a suppressed pistol and ammunition.

Khan took the weapon. "It's as we thought, Admiral."

"Iran?" Dodd asked.

"Yes. And unless we stop them, the world will be cast into a thousand years of darkness."

"I have a team topside working to recover the detonator."

Khan inserted a magazine into the SOCOM pistol and racked a round into the chamber.

"Then I will help. These are special Quds Force soldiers. Furthermore, General Khatami is one of the best military strategic and tactical minds in the world."

"I'll radio my team, then. I don't want you mistaken for the enemy."

"No. If the hostage you mentioned was caught, Tariq may already have compromised the comms. Besides, it's better if everyone thinks I am Bashir."

"Do be careful, Panther. I promised your uncle—"

Khan cut Dodd off.

"We shall meet in his tents when this is over and discuss how we might stop World War III."

Khan ran off, leaving Dodd with ten dead terrorists and enough nuclear material to destroy the Midwest.

<=== PIPELINE ===>

25

Billy Ray slowed his progress. If he were the one posting sentries on the immense freighter, he would've chosen the most vulnerable spots.

Obviously, Khatami thought the same way he did. Because two armed Iranian Quds now impeded his advancement. One soldier guarded the engine room hatchway. While the other terrorist stood forty feet further on to prevent access to the ship's propeller shaft.

Billy Ray's course to the Kingston valves fitted on the bottom of the ship was blocked. If he failed to open the seacocks to scuttle the ship, then the mission was done for.

He checked his dive watch.

At present speed, they had fifteen minutes before crossing POTUS' "red line" on the water, and death to them all. Lake Michigan would become the second Dead Sea only this one would be manmade.

Billy Ray decided to warn Dodd. "Admiral. I need to report a challenge."

"Make it snappy. I'm kinda' busy here getting a leg up."

"My way to the hull isn't looking so good."

"And . . .?" Dodd was in warrior mode.

"If I fail—"

Dodd stopped huffing and puffing, jimmying the hold doors.

"Listen here, sailor, failure is not an option! If war was easy everyone would do it. It only pays the winner. Now get the job done."

Billy Ray was about to respond when a man with a Vietnamese accent said over the team's closed comms, "Can I help?"

"Nguyen! You're still here," Billy Ray said, recalling the cook's role was to lead the hostages off the ship on the conveyor system.

"I'm in the stern portion of the tunnel," Nguyen replied.

That put him below the second sentry!

"Check that, Dolittle," Billy Ray radioed back. "I got it covered."

Dodd double-clicked.

Had Billy Ray been keeping track, *that* would mark Dodd's shortest answer to date.

"Nguyen, here's what I want you to do—"

Lam skipped the last ladder rungs and silently dropped to the deck.

He looked both ways, but failed to see in which direction around the curved superstructure that the Computer Kid had gone.

Crossing himself, he chose the starboard side.

He chose correctly, because a varsity jacket disappeared through a door leading to the crew quarters.

Lam gave chase but drew gunfire from the top of the pilot house. He dove behind a loading hatch just as bullets sparked around him—

Sparks— But no gas explosion!

Lam owed his life to the brave civilians who'd taken the scrap to the enemy, some foiling the propane gas failsafe before escaping over the side . . . some still lying where they fell.

What to do?

Lam peeked over the hatch and was rewarded with the spark of a ricocheting bullet. He was thankful the enemy wasn't a true sniper or else he'd be dead already. But he had spotted his way out.

The Challenger crew had foiled the propane tanks ringing the lifelines, but not the few positioned atop the pilot house near the shooter.

Lam removed his dive hood and placed it on the barrel of the empty dart gun. Then he estimated the distance and angle to the target—not the man, the tank. Next he radioed Egolf and told him to prepare for another rearrangement of the deck chairs on the bridge.

The Admiral's mysterious assistant didn't answer at first, although Lam could hear heavy breathing over the comms, like that usually done while engaged in close quarters battle.

Finally, a reply came that was so soft and weak, Lam nearly missed it.

But it was the reply he was waiting for.

Lam lifted the dive hood to offer a tempting target for the shooter, and then leaned around the hatch and rapid-fired his pistol.

It may not have been the first, or even the second bullet to hit its mark.

But who was counting!

The LP tank detonated with a mighty roar.

Egolf had long wondered what life would've been like had he stayed short and become a professional jockey for his father's prized horses, or grew large enough to be a gridiron athlete like others in his family.

But those things weren't part of the grand design.

Rather, he possessed more peculiar talents.

He'd loved growing up on his family's Wyoming ranch, commanding majestic animals, and ordering their stables. Furthermore, life in the wild country taught boys and girls to buck up or suffer nature's wrath.

He shot his first coyote at age five, got him right between the eyes, while he was running. On his tenth birthday, he hunted down a full-grown cougar that was stalking the area ranches, again needing only one bullet.

<=== PIPELINE ===>

Then the weekend before attending his high school prom with the lovely Shelly Michaels, his little sister's quarter-horse pony and several of the family cattle were discovered mutilated and partially buried on the back section of the ranch.

That demon grizzly again!

Egolf's dad had passed away the previous winter, so it was up to him to defend the homestead. So he grabbed his father's Marine sniper rifle from the gun safe and trekked into the Shoshone National Forest.

Six days later, he came down from the mountains. The bear did not.

Sadly, though, the charming Ms. Michaels caught a head cold the day of the dance and canceled on him.

Those were the things passing through Egolf's mind as he bled out grappling with the most dangerous creature to ever walk the earth—*man.*

And he was failing.

Maybe when native warriors on the Great Plains shouted *hoka hey! It's a good day to die!* and blew eagle bone whistles rushing into battle that their lives transcended in the moment. Such that all a man does in his lifetime—every experience, every gain, every loss—brings him not just to the close of one journey but to the doorway of the next.

Amazingly, Egolf felt a power well up from someplace his soul. It was sublime, like nothing he'd felt before—warm, inviting . . . translucent.

Voices called out to him: some came from ancestors, some from love lost, still others from vanquished foes, like the bear.

He heard Agent Lam's voice, too. A warning? Or was it a promise, one barely deserved, if at all, for hunters of men?

Egolf summoned the last of his strength to end the battle with General Khatami, and rolled the despicable terrorist on top of him, pinning the small detonator between them.

Raspy words left his dry throat. "Take the shot, Lam—"

Then his voice joined the ghostly chorus of all the others.

H O K A H E Y . . .

And Egolf heard the roar of the Grizzly.

The eyes of every man and woman present in the situation room were riveted to the wall monitor as the top-down satellite perspective switched to close-in views from an armed Air Force MQ-1 Predator UAV approaching the target.

"*Eyes-on* coming up now, Mr. President," General Tatam announced.

People's nerves twisted tighter as the Edmund Challenger grew on the television screen.

Then suddenly, the ship's pilot house exploded in a massive fire ball.

There were gasps from everyone, including POTUS.

Some leaned away from the monitor.

"Mr. President, it's happening." the CJCS bellowed.

"I can see for myself, General." The President didn't appreciate the hawks in the room treating him as if he were a spineless simpleton.

The drone provided a chilling view of the Edmond Challenger, with the iconic Navy Pier closing in on the horizon.

"We should open fire now before the terrorists get any closer to land."

The President's eyes darted from the CJCS to the live television screen, and then to the mission clock and back again.

He could feel his blood pressure rising with each digital number ticking toward launch time. Dodd and his team still had fifteen minutes promised to them.

And yet, as Commander-in-Chief . . .

Dodd concluded that whoever masterminded the conversion of the Edmund Challenger into a shipborne bomb, had known exactly what they were doing. Yes, he'd been privy to some of what Iran had in store for the Western World, beginning with the United States.

But *knowing* was academic, *seeing* was believing!

A person wishing to spy on their own country could do so easily, if not comically, before getting busted by the best police force in the world, the U.S. Federal Bureau of Investigation.

Whereas a person recruited, trained, and placed overseas to gather intel on the nation's enemies, was a rare and safeguarded asset.

And then there was the rarest of dark operatives, his double-agent, Ter Meer Khan, who'd penetrated a transnational Jihadist terror organization, which in turn was being manipulated by a secret cabal in Tehran.

Circles turning inside of circles.

Yet Khan had come to the K-KEY Group, and not the other way around, sent by an uncle who was a powerful Afghan tribal leader.

In short, he didn't recruit Khan . . . Khan recruited *him!*

But how? Knowledge of the K-KEY Group had been restricted to just a few extreme-vetted individuals.

Now the Group's existence was being splashed all over the airwaves. The cat was out of the bag. The K-KEY Group was disbanded. And his resignation was expected on the President's desk in the morning.

Dodd wasn't so sure he'd be able to keep that appointment.

<== PIPELINE ==>

Still, who let out the existence of his group he'd worked so hard to form and protect?

Had it been loose lips, a lapse in internal security? Or worst of all, a triple-agent . . . *Khan, perhaps?*

Dodd dismissed the problem for now. There was no doubt in his mind that Khan was saving America from a horrendous event.

He just didn't know why.

Yet, if not for Khan risking his life under the nose of General Khatami, playing the role of the suave but hotheaded Bashir, Chicago and most of the Midwest would already be smoldering radioactive ruins.

After using Egolf's computer to tap into the Challenger's cargo loading controls, Dodd got busy prepping for the Jenkin's flood.

He donned his dive mask and rebreather, then actuated the ship's internal pumping system and transferred the powdered cement from the other holds on top of the containment casks.

Lastly, Dodd programmed a ten minute delay for opening the holds containing the fertilizer and racing fuel mixture. As for the plastic explosive attached to LP tanks inside with the ANNM, there was nothing he could do but pray that his team captured all of the detonators.

Highly radioactive materials, thousands of tons of explosive ANNM, wired industrial-size propane tanks, and choking cement dust—a deadly mixture in anyone's book—and Dodd stood in the center of it all!

He hoped like hell that Lam and Egolf got to Khatami first.

Then again, death would come in an instant if they didn't.

Just then the deck of the Edmund Challenger quaked from a large explosion somewhere topside.

Dodd braced himself. But death didn't come.

And then the chatter in his earbuds made sense. He'd missed most of Lam's previous words, but did catch Egolf's weak reply. Then Lam blew up the propane tanks above the bridge, which meant the civilians had been successful.

Things were looking up . . . until Dodd had a frightening revelation—

POTUS and the generals saw the explosion too!

Dodd knew the President—what kind of man he was, what lurked in his heart, and what good his promises were if feeling desperate. He also knew the people surrounding the President in the Situation Room, and what they would be recommending, even demanding.

The clock just went to zero hour!

"Hurry, everyone!" Dodd shouted. "We're out of time!"

Lam didn't need Dodd to repeat the order. It could only mean one thing, that the President just moved the goal line on them.

He quickened his pace, gun at the ready, listening for the Computer Kid's footfalls.

He didn't hear running, but he did catch slamming doors and hatches, then shouts and gunfire echo off the metal walls from an indeterminate location.

It felt to him like being a lab rat inside of a tin can maze, with life or death the final prizes.

Lam arrived at a passageway and stopped to listen for movement.

From his days leading an Army Ranger unit in South America, he knew an ambush could be lurking around every corner.

He stepped slowly into the passageway and saw three of General Khatami's soldiers lying dead, bullet holes giving all three of them a third eye, and their throats cut as well.

Who would do such a thing?

A well-placed bullet in the forehead was plenty dead enough. But to then cut a corpse's throat was mutilation. Surely Jenkins wouldn't do something like that, and the Admiral wouldn't waste his time.

The Computer Kid? One of the hostages taking revenge, maybe?

Lam got his answer. It came when passing by a stateroom. The noise inside sounded like arguing.

He stopped, motionless, and listened.

There was an argument taking place behind the closed door, and it was in Arabic!

Very carefully, he tried the doorknob. It was unlocked.

Then the *argument* pitched decibels louder.

Lam decided it was then or never and rushed into the room ready to shoot it out. The first thing he noticed was another dead terrorist staring at the ceiling with a powder-burned forehead and sliced throat.

But standing at the far end of the cabin by a video camera, attempting to film his martyrdom video, was the Computer Kid. But he was being prevented from doing so by one of Qasem's men, objecting in a language Lam didn't understand.

Lam wasn't the only one witnessing the event.

He noted the camera's *record* light was on, and a cord led to a satellite phone, indicating the scene was being transmitted live to others. The main prop in the Armageddon flick was the silver case and laptop computer on a nearby coffee table.

Frighteningly, the computer was cycling through a long string of computer code!

<===== PIPELINE =====>

Lam had been ready to pull the trigger upon entry. However, the enemy was quick as a cat, and used the Computer Kid as a shield.

A stare-down ensued, the silence seemed to last a month. Strangely, the soldier didn't put a round hole in Lam's forehead. Instead, the man put the gun to the temple of the Computer Kid and said in perfect English, "Hurry, Agent Lam. Stop that detonation code!"

"Dodd!" Lam announced, astonishment coloring the word.

He ran to the computer, then turned to Dodd's spy.

"What's the deactivation password?"

The kid hadn't spoken until then, and also used American English, a Minnesota accent, actually. "I told you, Bashir. It's not mine to give."

Lam had no idea what game was being played out here, only that there couldn't be much time left.

"And I told you how we've been used, Tariq, by the ones on the other end of your phone call." Bashir pressed the gun harder against Tariq's temple, forcing the kid to look at the video camera. "Is this what you intended for your personal jihad, to be a stooge for our sworn enemy?"

"But America is our enemy!" Tariq shouted out.

"For another day. Right now a worse enemy seeks our destruction, my brother. And they wish to control Islam for the rest of time. If they are so intent on martyrdom, then why aren't they here joining in with us? When your family sees this recording, and learns it was you who made it possible to destroy millions, they will be grievously ashamed. Is that what you want? Or would you rather be the hero who stopped this disaster?"

Lam couldn't believe what he was witnessing, two terrorists arguing over who got to kill who.

"Uh, guys . . . the code please?"

Slowly, Tariq swiveled his head toward Lam.

"iz8B47 . . ." Tariq began slowly, forlornly, until Lam had typed a long string of letters and numbers.

Finally, Lam hit the *Enter* button and the computer powered off.

Bashir, or whatever his name was, said, "Take the computer and go. I'm sure your FBI will relish what they find."

Lam didn't wait for seconds on pie. He put the laptop in the watertight case and got the hell out of there, closing the door behind him.

The last thing he heard as he hurried away was the start of another argument. Then a single gunshot.

Lam radioed Dodd as he headed topside, "Admiral, I have the primary detonator . . . it's a laptop computer."

"Protect that damn thing with your life, Agent Lam. Now get the hell off this ship. That's an order!"

"What about the backup device with Egolf?"

"I'll get that. Now go."

"Yes, sir."

Lam hated leaving without his team.

The Quds soldier guarding the way to the propeller room and bottom-most spaces, heard a knock on the hatch behind him.

Even from forty feet away, and on the tiny mirror Billy Ray used to see around the corner, the surprise on the man's face was unmistakable.

The soldier opened the hatch and got 15 grams of .45 caliber lead added to his head from Nguyen.

At the same moment, Billy Ray dropped the soldier guarding the engine room, and then sprinted to the brave little cook.

Together, they made their way forward along the bottom of the ship opening every Kingston valve and seacock they could find. In a couple of instances, it was the smaller Vietnamese cook who squeezed into tight spots to do the scuttling.

They finally reached the end and began the climb upward, Nguyen going first. Then suddenly, he halted.

"Hurry your ass, Nguyen. We have to get off this ship."

Nguyen stopped midway on the ladder, blocking their progress.

"What is it?" Billy Ray demanded.

"The women . . . my sister. I must find them first."

Billy Ray assumed the others had saved the female crewmembers. And now to learn one of them was Nguyen's sister—

"Why didn't you get them earlier?"

"I didn't know where to look. So I helped the others first."

"So that's why you stayed aboard."

Billy Ray had great respect for the Vietnamese people. And Nguyen just proved why. "Keep climbing. I think I know where they are."

Hearing that, Nguyen's climbing speed would've given Dodd a run for his money. Already, Billy Ray could sense the angle of the ladder changing as the Edmund Challenger filled with water.

Dodd's business with the holds was done. Now it was time to beat feet off the ship.

As he trotted down the main passage, free of enemy interference, he marveled at how far the team had come, and against such a highly trained and determined force.

<===== PIPELINE =====>

Lam was gone, heading to safety with one detonator, plus a treasure chest filled with intel on Khatami's computer.

Egolf was on the ship's bridge with the second detonator, or so Lam had said. But his assistant hadn't answered any radio calls in a while.

Dodd feared the worst.

He'd tried hailing Jenkins earlier to get a sitrep, but was unsuccessful. He tried again. "Wolverine . . ."

"Well hi there, Admiral. You back at the officer's club yet?"

"Hardly, smartass. State your progress."

"I'd say it's time for Noah to get off the Ark."

"I suggest you do the same, Wolverine. I'd bet my left nut that POTUS is about to order in the flyboys to bring down a world of hurt."

"My thought exactly, Dolittle. But there's something I must do first."

Dodd felt the ship leaning bow down. The sinking had begun.

"Like what?" he asked Jenkins but didn't receive a reply.

It was clear by the UAV's multiple-angle cameras that the Edmund Challenger was taking on water, and that its bow pushed deeper and deeper in the water.

"Look! It's going down!" the National Security Advisor exclaimed.

"But it hasn't stopped it's progress," the CJCS countered. "Do I fire the missiles, Mr. President?"

"There are hostages in the water," the Senior Advisor stated.

"It's them or Chicago," the CJCS replied.

POTUS stared at the Chairman of the Joint Chiefs of Staff. The four-star general had been relentless. Then again, that's what he expected from his warfighters—

Too slow to act could end as badly as too quick to act.

"Maybe Dodd's team was successful," the President posited.

"Or just nearly successful," said the CJCS.

The conversation had boiled down to just the President and the head of his military—life or death. Advice from any of the other members of his security team would be irrelevant now.

The choice was his and his alone.

POTUS straightened in his chair. It was important to show confidence in his forthcoming decision.

"Not this time, General. We've pulled the rug from under our warriors too many times. Dodd's team gets its chance to complete the mission. We shall see it to the end."

The President raised his hand to cut off any further discussion.

Dodd arrived at the destroyed pilot house.

Bodies lay scattered everywhere: on the bridge, in passageways, and on the loading decks below. Good guys and bad guys . . . the ravages of war—*death*.

Dodd searched for one body in particular among the carnage, that of his loyal assistant. Pound for pound, there was no greater man with a gun or knife who he'd ever commanded than Egolf.

Moving aside an overhead panel, caved in from the exploding gas tanks, Dodd spotted his friend.

He quickly swept aside the remaining debris and found the second detonator. It was clutched stubbornly in Egolf's hands.

Dodd pried away the trigger device and then searched the bridge for Khatami. None of the bodies proved to be the Iranian general.

The team had recovered both detonators, as well as a computer filled with valuable intel.

And though there still remained the chance that Khatami or another of the Barbary bastards could manually detonate one of the rigged LP tanks in the holds, Dodd was putting his faith in the flood waters and Wolverine to prevent a catastrophe.

It was time to go.

Dodd returned to Egolf—he was dead.

He gathered his friend's body, and swiftly left the Edmund Challenger.

His final thought before swimming to the rendezvous point with V, was for his other best friend still aboard the foundering ship.

He hoped Billy Ray Jenkins survived America's greatest battle yet against the enemies within the gates.

Billy Ray guided Nguyen to where he figured the women would be.

And indeed they were . . . three of them, anyway.

They sat motionless, bound and gagged, and tied to a stanchion at the back of the stateroom.

Nguyen's heart sank—his sister wasn't one of them.

Billy Ray recalled the machete-wielding Iranian, and how just before the brute took one for the home team, he'd been exiting from the next stateroom with his stolen Coast Guard ODU's disheveled and trousers zipper undone.

Billy Ray dreaded what he might find in the next room. So he offered a half-lie to Nguyen, having the cook guard the hostages while he checked all the rest of the crew's quarters.

<==== PIPELINE ====>

As he suspected, Nguyen's sister was in the next room, naked and restrained in a messed up bunk.

Billy Ray grabbed a blanket and covered the young lady.

Her eyes snapped open in stark terror!

Thank God she was alive.

Before removing the gag and bindings, he gently said, "I'm here to help. Nguyen is in the next room with the other hostages."

At the mention of her brother, tears formed in her beautiful brown eyes.

Billy Ray cut her bindings. While the woman righted herself, he spotted a shirt and pair of dungarees on a hook. They were way too big, so he cut the pant legs and fashioned a belt. As for the oversized shirt, that could be knotted in front.

But they'd have to do.

He handed her the clothes and turned his back.

As she swiftly dressed, he told her what they'd need to do to get off the ship and as far away as possible before it sank.

"Are you game?"

"Yes," she spoke for the first time. "Please take me to my brother."

Billy Ray took down two life vests next to the stateroom door and led the young lady to her brother.

Nguyen nearly launched himself through the roof at seeing is sister walk into the room.

They hugged tightly.

"Okay folks, you know the plan. Let's roll."

26

Rebeca's worry for Billy Ray grew with each passing mile, as the Terminator III sped along the great liquid expanse of Lake Michigan, far beyond the sight of shore or the Edmund Challenger.

What might they find when they finally overtook the pirate ship? Would they encounter only death and destruction, their own even?

Was she too late?

Rebecca's hands trembled as she passed the binoculars to Tafoya. Then she noticed how the beautiful Latina also suffered the shakes while holding the glasses and scanning the horizon. Both of their nerves were right on the edge... was it anticipation or dread for the unknown?

Rebecca could not imagine a life without Billy Ray. It was obvious Tafoya felt the same about Lam.

Even knowing the full nature of the emergency, Lyle and his son had remained stalwart.

Tafoya had tried apologizing for putting them in danger. But the Berry men were hearing none of it. Young and old, both waived off the attempt.

"If not us, then who?" Lyle had told her, Skip agreeing fully.

After that, Lyle spent the trip reassuring and lifting the women's hearts.

Rebecca was thankful for his presence, and grabbed him for balance as the boat crashed through waves and swells at full-throttle.

"Young lady," Lyle shouted over the headwind, "We'll win this fight, and your men will survive."

"But some won't," Rebecca responded, feeling less confident.

"That's how it goes in life." Lyle's words reflected a finite reality. And though not gleeful, they gave substance to faith.

Like a rock to cling to in a flood of despair, Rebecca reflected.

She squeezed his arm.

Just then, Tafoya pointed southwest. ""There! Smoke on the water!"

She handed the binoculars to Lyle, who took them and climbed atop the cabin for a better view.

"It's a freighter all right!" he yelled down to the ladies.

Lam made about a thousand yards away from the ship before stopping for a look back.

Having left the ship opposite of the hostages, he was all alone . . . just a lone head bobbing on the big lake swells.

He felt no fear of drowning, thanks to the dive gear. Rather, his biggest concern was for which direction he should swim to make landfall.

<==== PIPELINE ====>

From his perspective at water level, he couldn't spot land. But he could still see the rapidly sinking Edmund Challenger, and fire in the sky.

He hoped like hell that Jenkins and Dodd had made it off the ship in time. Egolf, he suspected, would not.

But for him, the mission had changed to that of getting Khatami's computer to the lab, *asap.*

So he looked up at the blue sky, as much for inspiration as direction, and made his choice, get as far away from Chicago and the Edmund Challenger as he could.

Then he began the hours-long swim to shore.

Lyle climbed down from the helm and rejoined the women.

Tafoya asked for the binoculars, mainly to give her something to do.

She scanned the waters, sweeping side to side, and not just focusing on the Edmund Challenger slipping beneath the waves in front of them.

She almost missed it, a dark object progressing slowly in the water toward the Indiana shoreline, like a beaver or deer or something.

Her brain wanted to avoid a debate for once about such matters as size, color, proximity to land, and keep on searching.

But her heart did not.

Wrong color for a deer, way too large for a beaver, and too far out on the lake for either.

She pointed. "Skip, there. Over there!"

Skip veered the Terminator III toward the object. A few feet closer and then Tafoya knew exactly what the creature was—or who.

"JOHNNY!"

Billy Ray was thankful that the conveyor belt controls were in the stern portion of the ship, which would be the last section to go under the waves.

But that would end the moment the bow tipped downward and the propeller drove the Edmund Challenger into the deep.

He and Nguyen had already given the ladies a crash course on how to ride the conveyor and then rise up and out through the discharge boom to open water. He handed the life vests to the first two hostages. They would be responsible for receiving the others and keeping the group afloat until help arrived.

The women dropped through the hopper of hold #1 and onto the moving conveyor. There was a look of sheer terror on each of their faces.

Now it was Nguyen's turn.

Billy Ray shook the man's hand then watched him dropped onto the belt and be whisked from sight.

A moment later, the flood waters covered the belt and began bubbling up through the hopper into the hold.

The pace of death for the storied freighter quickened with each passing second. In just minutes, the Edmund Challenger would go hurtling to the bottom of Lake Michigan, along with anyone else still onboard.

And that meant him!

The flood quickly reached Billy Ray's waist.

He inserted the rebreather mouth piece and pulled on the dive mask.

But just as he ducked beneath the water to take his turn on the still-moving conveyor, a strong brown hand grabbed his leg and yanked it out from under him.

The unexpected jolt caused him to smash the dive mask against the hopper, and then twisting it and blocking his sight.

He kicked out to break the grip on his leg.

It worked! But then something sharp pierced his side.

The pain was immediately excruciating!

The human body gave a person precious seconds to react to insult before debilitating pain or shock set in.

Billy Ray didn't waste that time. He thrashed about, and managed to right the mask, then vaulted out of the water and struck his opponent.

It was General Khatami!

His face was battered and bruised from the battle with Egolf, and one arm hung useless at his side. But the bastard's good hand was gripping Billy Ray's own MPK dive knife, ripped from its sheath a second ago.

Khatami wielded the knife with expert CQB technique.

Billy Ray backpedaled through waist deep water, dodging each swipe of the razor sharp blade.

But not all.

Now pinned against the bulkhead, he watched his captured knife plunge toward his body. Then he twisted, narrowly escaping the death blow within an inch. But by the grace of God, the titanium point pierced the rebreather and stuck fast. A tour bus floor came to mind. Regardless, his MPK was out of the fight now.

Failing to retrieve the blade, Khatami drew a deep breath and dove beneath the waters into the hopper.

The asshole was escaping!

Billy Ray ignored the pain in his side and the blood soaking his wetsuit. He jammed the rebreather mouth piece in and gave chase.

<═══ PIPELINE ═══>

He joined the submerged conveyor.

The floodwaters resisted him on the moving belt, pushing at him as he scrabbled foot by foot, yard by yard, until he finally caught Khatami just before they broke free into breathable air.

Billy Ray wrapped Khatami in a bear hug and rolled them off the conveyor belt.

They sank to the bottom of the tunnel.

Khatami twisted violently, desperate to free himself, desperate to fill his lungs with fresh oxygen.

But Billy Ray squeezed the Iranian general even tighter, with his formidable arms and legs, like an anaconda crushing its prey.

A moment later, Khatami's strength finally ebbed. Then his efforts slowed as the oxygen in his lungs ran out, draining him of hope . . . of life.

With the last of his malevolent breath, the fearsome General Qasem Khatami attempted to shout *Allahu Akbar* but managed only a garbled syllable and some bubbles as he sucked water nonstop into his lungs.

Billy Ray left the unrepentant man floating in the belly of the whale. What was to be the death of millions by evil incarnate became Qasem's own tomb in the end.

Billy Ray swam back to the moving conveyor, hoping it wasn't too late, praying he didn't share the same fate as the dead terrorist leader.

Just then the lights went out.

It could only be seconds before the belt quit, too—no longer taking him off the ship and into the arms of the woman he cherished, but down to Davy Jones' Locker.

At last, he felt the conveyor turn sharply upwards, taking him to light and air and freedom once inside the discharge boom.

Nguyen had done his job!

After getting the women off the Edmund Challenger, Nguyen was to change the boom's parallel position to more like the angle of a fireman's ladder. Then that courageous cook was to dive overboard and swim like hell itself was chasing him.

Billy Ray had anticipated that his escape from the sinking ship would be a wet one. He was glad to be leaving the dark, flooded spaces below decks, and soon reach the boom and open air. Two hundred feet later, escaping the clutches of the massive steel coffin, he would be free.

That hope was tested a second later when the conveyor belt stopped. He had reached the halfway point along the discharge boom, and was ready to breathe regularly again, to enjoy sunshine and dry clothes, to make fervent love to Rebecca.

Life was only feet away—

The freighter tipped headlong.

The big propeller rose above the surface of the lake, beating ferociously at the air, trying to find water. It finally bit and drove the ship toward the bottom three hundred feet down.

Billy Ray hugged the belt inside the boom with all his might. He'd witnessed sinking ships before—his underwater demolition skills the main cause—but never as a doomed passenger.

Ask mariners experienced with battles at sea and they might describe the sounds of a dying vessel as the shrieks and moans of demons.

Billy Ray prepared to die.

The White House Situation Room erupted in applause!

The Chairman of the Joint Chiefs of Staff stood, then nodded at the President and took his leave.

POTUS knew what the general was thinking—he had been accused of it before—weakness. But the man was terribly mistaken. It was not weakness he or others observed, but rather, steadiness. Though at this point, it hardly mattered.

America had been spared!

Perhaps first thing Monday morning, he would enter the Oval Office, walk straight to the *Resolute* Desk, and tear up the Admiral's resignation.

The pull downwards was immense.

Billy Ray thought fast.

He had but one option, and one option only—get away from the discharge boom, before it and the Edmund Challenger collided on the bottom of the lake.

And if not, expect to become a small red spot among a hundred thousand tons of twisted steel and debris.

So with every ounce of energy Billy Ray could muster, he moved from the stalled conveyor to the lattice bracing of the boom, and shoved free.

As with rip tides, he endeavored to swim perpendicular to the force, rather than against it toward the false promise of light and oxygen above.

But then his chance of survival diminished immediately in a massive clouds of bubbles brought with the sinking vessel. It felt like falling down a hole in the water, as much as from the suction by its displacement.

Billy Ray somehow dodged the jetsam plunging after the wreck of the Edmund Challenger. He was almost decapitated by a thick steel cable whipping past him like the tail of a great leviathan.

Still the ship pulled him down deeper into the black abyss.

The deeper he sank, the more that water pressure piled like bricks, layer after layer, on top of his body. If he didn't escape the water's relentless grip, it would mash his flesh and bones like putty.

Agony mounted.

Was his judgement to die a hideous death?

He ordered his muscles to fight on, and kicked violently at death's grip, stealing each handful of water in his liquid grave, and pulling it past him.

Inch by hard-earned inch, he progressed against death's pull.

His prayer was answered a second later when the cold waters of Lake Michigan invaded the ship's engine room and contacted with the hot steam boilers.

The boiler explosion blew apart the ship's stern, speeding the descent to the bottom.

The shock wave from the explosion punched him like a heavyweight boxer's blow to the midsection, knocking him unconscious, tumbling him head over heels through the deep—but pushing him well out of the dying ship's vortex!

God's answer to his question was, *"not this day."*

Billy Ray came to, sensing his body floating toward the surface.

He shook off the cobwebs, righted himself, and heeded his ascent rate. He ignored the whiny voice in his head pleading for him to get out of the water—*now!* Because the last thing he wanted, after surviving all the hell that man and Mother Nature put him through, was to die from the bends.

Billy Ray worked out the math on his wrist computer—

Four stops 'til freedom.

He only made three when the Draeger gave out.

Whether from Khatami stabbing it with the knife, or from absorbing an earlier bullet, the rebreather stopped working.

He still had one more decompression stop before racing for the surface, but with only a half breath in his lungs to do so. Furthermore, he was already light-headed and nearing absolute exhaustion.

Now would come the most valuable training of all learned at the Naval Special Warfare Training Center in Coronado for times like this—drown proofing—specifically the mental part.

Because he was about to order his brain to ignore the need to panic, then surrender the last of his breath uttering *ho-ho-ho* while rising slowly to the surface. Had he the luxury of escaping a submarine, he'd be employing a Steinke Hood and using the same procedure as now, with likely the same odds of success—near zero.

Almost to a man, submariners the world over, selected death inside their boats over submitting themselves to the merciless sea.

Billy Ray chose otherwise. He chose to earn his Trident again this day, and every day to follow.

He recalled part of the SEAL Oath: "I will never quit. I persevere and thrive on adversity. My Nation expects me to be physically harder and mentally stronger than my enemies. If knocked down, I will get back up, every time. I will draw on every remaining ounce of strength to protect my teammates and to accomplish our mission. I am never out of the fight."

Better to die trying!

It would be close, and his rational mind knew it. But his ever-present voice repeated his oath again, and then again.

He lost track of how many *ho's* he uttered, only that he was oxygen starved and going black. In moments, the need to take in air would overwhelm the concern of swallowing water.

He saw brightness, beams of light, and felt warmth.

He thought he heard his mother Lila's far-off gentle voice . . . and the cry of seagulls.

BIRDS!

Billy Ray came back.

He jerked sharply out of the dead man's float, immediately emptying the contents of his stomach, and hacking water from his lungs.

But he was alive!

Blurry-eyed, he rolled on his back and looked up into blue skies—overjoyed . . . blessed. As his senses cleared, he noted dozens of boats, large and small, converging on the area from every direction.

A military jet flew over just then, too, and tipped its wings. Then a large ski boat cut from the pack and headed his way.

Rebecca!

The boat cut its engines and drifted slowly toward him.

It wasn't Rebecca.

Shockingly, a tall individual dressed from head to toe in a black burqa stared down at Billy Ray through the webbing on the hood piece.

There was silence for a long moment.

Finally, the stranger said in a mechanical voice, "Next time." And then the ski boat gunned its motor and sped off.

Billy Ray didn't have time to consider if he'd seen a ghost or whether he was still suffering the effects of his partial drowning. Because just then he heard a chorus of shouts.

"Over there!"

"That's him!"

<====== PIPELINE ======>

These voices Billy Ray did recognize and they were real!

Another boat sped toward him. His friends were on this one, jumping around and making all kinds of racket. Even Lam looked like a high school cheerleader, though one who'd been in a wet T-shirt contest.

"Billy Ray!" It was the voice of his lover.

Rebecca jumped from the boat and swam to Billy Ray.

They hugged and kissed.

Then finally, Rebecca assisted him back to the boat, damned certain she wasn't going to let him slip away this time.

As Billy Ray followed Rebecca up the boat ladder, something far out on the lake caught his attention.

He paused to see.

It was a silver disc dropping down out of the sky. The craft made a gravity-defying stop mere inches off the surface of the calm water, and then extended a platform to receive two people. One of them was laid across the shoulders of the other.

Then the platform withdrew and the strange craft shot toward the east. It was gone in the blink of an eye.

When Monday morning came to Chicago and the Midwest region, ordinary men and women went about their normal business, clocking in at factories, offices, and stores, or tending to their livestock and fields.

Many of them missed a news flash of a puzzling incident the day previous involving a century-old steam ship sinking in Lake Michigan just short of its final voyage up the Chicago River.

But not everyone was bewildered, however. Downtown Chicagoans knew exactly why the Edmund Challenger sank—

Because it was a Jinx Ship, for cripes sake!

They'd gathered at the banks of the river to celebrate never having to be inconvenienced by the old steam ship ever again, and good riddance.

But most talk among Chicagoans had already moved on to another century-long jinx needing ending.

That of their beloved baseball team winning the World Series.

A mature couple wearing Muslim garb entered their "nephew's" Dearborn, Michigan, hospital room carrying a fresh bundle of clothing.

The previous set were incinerated due to radioactive contamination.

The couple handed over the clothes, then sat down to watch a breaking news feed on the hospital room television.

As the boy slipped a fresh set of underwear over his freshly scrubbed body, his attention was also drawn to TV.

American funerals had that kind of pull on him.

In this case, a memorial service was taking place on the deck of a World War II submarine over in Muskegon.

He watched the ceremony as he dressed.

. . . after a few short condolences by public officials, a Naval Officer in Captain's bars stepped to the lectern. The man announced his rank and service, and then his name—Mike Rinard.

Rinard first acknowledged four middle-aged women seated in folding chairs directly in front of him.

Then he went on to speak about heroism and sacrifice—how so often in America, dire circumstances required ordinary, everyday people to rise up for the benefit of others.

And how one man in particular chose to give his life to save the crew and the USS Silversides from disaster.

There had been an accident aboard the boat while on final sea trials that led to intense flooding in the forward compartment; and would have resulted in a total loss if not for the selfless actions of Executive Officer Burl Creed, former World War II operator in our nation's Silent Service.

Creed considered himself to be a common man, just an ordinary person with ordinary joys and concerns. However, we standing before you today—the captain spread his arms to the twenty-nine volunteers of the Silversides—are thankful that a common man rose up to perform an uncommon act of valor. And thus his burden now falls to us, that when chosen by the Hand of Fate, we do the same.

Please let us pray for Mr. Creed as he joins The Eternal Patrol . . .

As the boy slipped into his sandals and covered his head with a colorful knitted skullcap, he listened to the Christian prayer.

Soon it would be him calling to converts everywhere: on television, over radio, and from every rooftop and steeple.

Those words would go out to true believers—calling them to join Allah.

The last image the boy saw on the TV screen before departing was a large man with a wet cigar in his mouth. He was pasting a black pirate flag to the Silverside's sail amidst twenty-three Japanese flags.

One hour later, an FBI agent identifying himself as Thompkins was led into the room by a nurse and two armed hospital security guards.

The patient named Rasul was gone.

<===== PIPELINE =====>

EPILOGUE

November 2 – *Día de Muertos*
Michoacán, Mexico

High in the Sierra Nevada mountains of central Mexico, Mother Nature kept a secret hidden from the world until the late 20th century. In 1975, mankind finally discovered where monarch butterflies are born. Or more specifically, where the monarchs start a multi-generational migration, traveling thousands of miles from Mexico to Canada and back each year.

For millennia, indigenous peoples in the area came to anxiously await the annual arrival of millions, even billions, of the colorful broad-winged insects, believing them to be the souls of their dead ancestors.

The mystery for them was two-fold: why the spirits returned the same days each fall, and where they went after ending their rest in spring?

This miracle of nature was not lost on Tami Tafoya or the richness of the Day of the Dead celebration taking place all around her and Special Agent Johnny Lam in the tiny mining town of Angangueo.

They stood inside the cemetery of the Our Lady of Angels Church, surrounded by a sea of vibrant yellow marigolds, favorite foods, family photos, personal mementos, and colorful paper decorations adorning the graves. Beyond the high stone walls of the courtyard, townspeople and tourists paraded in bright clothing and skull masks, feasted, made music, and danced.

As she and Lam waited, Tafoya nervously stroked a small *angelito* doll she'd purchased from a street vendor selling offerings to the dead. In many cultures, a child's skeleton adorned in festive wear would not feel so adorable. But to these hardy people, death was not to be feared, and the return of their loved ones was treated as a joyous reunion.

It was for that reason Tafoya received permission from the head of a murderous drug cartel to enter his territory . . . and also because Mariposa was the man's daughter.

She'd purposely withheld from Lam how she managed the favor, only for him to accept the truce and show utmost respect for a grieving father.

Because sometimes things weren't business—they were personal.

There came the sound of pounding boots from a group of armed men rushing into the cemetery and posting themselves along the walls.

They were followed seconds later by a procession of cloistered nuns, who took up position across the open grave from Tafoya and Lam.

Finally, a man entered the courtyard carrying a body wrapped in white linen. He wasn't much older than Hector Gallina. With tear-filled eyes, he lowered the bundle into the grave, crossed himself, and walked away.

So it was, as it had always been, that a butterfly came home to rest.

AFTERWORD

"The price of freedom is eternal vigilance."
Thomas Jefferson (1743 – 1826)

The words of our third president should not abandon any of us today. We live in a world of varied emotions. There is faith, kindness and goodwill that permeates throughout this blue planet, and particularly in America. That is our creed. There is also pure evil, hatred, and intolerance that devours the very core of what it means to be a human.

Vigilance is defined as, *"the action or state of keeping careful watch for possible danger or difficulties". Oxford Dictionary.*

In military and security circles it is called "situational awareness." However you may define it, Americans have enjoyed their freedoms and protected environment since 1776 and are just now learning the habit of being aware of their surroundings. We have been a nation sheltered by being surrounded by two oceans and nations with similar values to the north and south. The world collapsed in around our lives on 9/11, the Boston Marathon Bombings, Columbine, Virginia Tech, Sandy Hook Elementary, and the list grows daily. Time allowed us the ability to forget Pearl Harbor. Soon these, too, could become a distant memory.

People tend to ignore the many warning signs in our youth, in our co-workers, neighbors and even family. No one will ever advocate for a society that continuously spies and informs on those around us like the days of the Nazi's or the *stukachi* of Soviet Russia and other regimes. Nonetheless when we see something we should say something. We should keep saying something until the authorities take note and do something. Or we should replace them at the ballot box. All the citizens of this world should have the right to a safe and secure life. But we don't control their governments, we only control ours. Defend your right! Keep your family and friends safe from the perils that we are facing in this world by being vigilant at home.

The events in PIPELINE are fiction but could they happen? Yes, without a doubt. The means are available and they are certainly possible. The intent and desire of bad actors to cause us harm are probable. I don't advocate going out and buying guns in a panic and hunkering down in a bunker. Our most powerful weapons are our eyes, ears and especially our voices.

Please help America remain the home of the free and the brave. Indifference is the opposite of vigilance—it creates a void—a vacuum, where evil thrives. Indifference has led to more death than all wars combined ever have. Be true to our creed, be vigilant, and make peace happen. Our safety depends on it.

William L. Deetz
Colonel (Ret) MP US Army

ILLUSTRATIONS

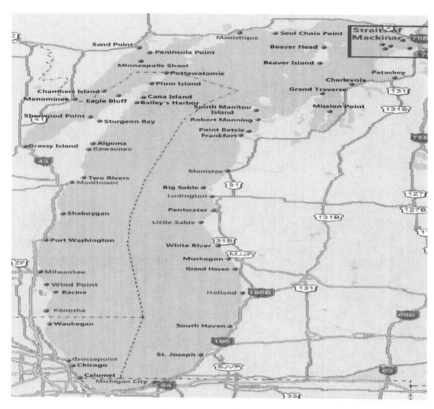

Self Unloading Bulk Carrier with an aft pilot house and discharge boom.

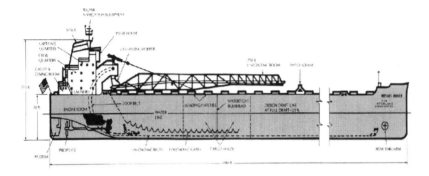

The St. Mary's Challenger — a.k.a. Edmund Challenger

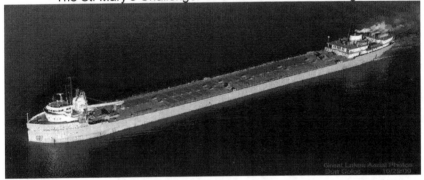

Chicago Loop Bridges

Map of Monarch Butterfly Sanctuaries in Mexico
Location of the 12 major overwintering sites

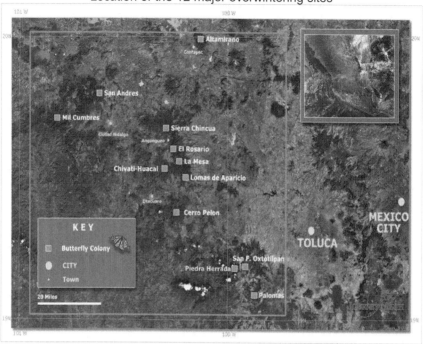

Angangueo, MX — "Where butterflies are born"

AUTHOR'S NOTE

It has been asked of me why I choose to have book characters who are military Special Forces, Federal and State Law Enforcement, and folks from the Intelligence Community, when I have never served our country in those capacities.

My short answer is that I admire the men and women who strap it on day in and day out protecting our nation and its vital interests.

The longer answer is that the mottos of these institutions embolden me, and their creed informs me. I do not pretend for a second that I could fill these warrior's shoes. But what I *can do* is take their advice and examples, try to live by them, and pass them on to others.

Going further, it is my opinion that every American should live by a motto. Hell, why not nine or ten mottos for that matter. After all, "it pays to be a winner." (SEALs) Let us study the mottos of our nation's military, police, and intelligence services, then adapt and implement them into our personal lives and businesses.

Moreover, I encourage my readers to visit the websites for the different branches of our security forces: the military, intelligence services, and law enforcement. From there, study their creed and codes of conduct. Also search out the mottos of successful companies, like Microsoft's "Empowering Us All" and Chevrolet's "Find New Roads". Or better yet, write your own motto and post it in plain sight, then put into action daily. Don't let mottos become hollow slogans, however.

Here are just a few mottos to get us started—

FBI . . . "Fidelity, Bravery, Integrity"
Army . . . "This we'll defend"
Navy . . . "Not for self but for country"
Marines . . . "Always faithful"
Air Force . . . "Above all"
Coast Guard . . . "Always ready"
Green Beret . . . "Free the Oppressed"
SEAL . . . "The only easy day was yesterday"
New Hampshire . . . "Live Free or Die"
Medical Providers . . . "Do No Harm"

So why do I invent characters who are SpecOps, FBI, IC, and others in my books? To honor them.

Thank You For Your Service!

--Steve Elam

About the Author:

STEVE ELAM hails from the suburbs of Grand Rapids, MI, graduating from Godwin Heights High School, home of the Fighting Wolverines. Elam served in the U.S. Navy as a technician specializing in anti-submarine warfare and a member of a nuclear weapons handling team. After his enlistment, he settled in Olympia, WA, where he worked more than twenty-five years for the Washington State Legislature and lobbying firm of Chiechi & Associates. Elam earned college degrees in both Texas and Washington. Elam splits time conducting research and writing between residences in Ventura, CA, Seattle, WA, and in West Michigan. Whether it's growing oysters in the Puget Sound, bodyboarding and fish tacos in Ventura and Malibu, or enjoying the fabulous sugar-sand beaches of Lake Michigan, you won't find Elam very far from water.

PIPELINE is Elam's second book in the Enemies Within the Gates series, which continues the thrilling exploits of ex-Navy SEAL Billy Ray Jenkins in his battle against evil forces destroying America from within.

His cause began in the first book, Backslide, with the murder of his brother by an ex-KGB agent with a diabolical plan to flood the United States with a deadly designer drug, called Rapture, a chemical so horrific it turns its users into rabid zombie killing machines.

Teamed with a hard-nosed FBI agent, a sexy redhead, an intrepid news reporter, and a mysterious government operative, Billy Ray Jenkins fights to save the nation from impending doom. But is it already too late?

Purchase signed copies of BACKSLIDE & PIPELINE at:

www.ElamBooks.com

Elam Books also available at Amazon, Barnes & Noble Nook Books, and iTunes.

Made in the USA
San Bernardino, CA
27 December 2016